Cindy

"WHY ARE YOU DOING THIS? WHY DO YOU INSIST ON HAVING ME?"

The fine-spun robe seemed to shiver against her breasts as they rose and fell with her great agitation.

Ravenspur pulled his attention from them and looked into her eyes. "We are pledged. 'Tis as simple as that."

As she looked at him she knew him for a man who made his own rules. He wouldn't keep a pledge unless it suited his own purposes. "There must be other reasons. Tell me!"

As he looked at her, he thought her beauty magnificent. He wanted to rip the filmy gown from her body and lay her back upon the bed. Her eyes blazed their defiance. She wanted none of him and made no bones about it. The challenge she offered was impossible for Ravenspur to resist!

His smile traveled from his sensual mouth to his night-dark eyes. "We are two of a kind, Roseanna. You will make me happy."

"I will make you wretched!" she vowed.

THE RAVEN
AND
THE ROSE

Virginia Henley

A DELL BOOK

Published by
Dell Publishing Co., Inc.
1 Dag Hammarskjold Plaza
New York, New York 10017

Dell ® TM 681510, Dell Publishing Co., Inc.

ISBN: 0-440-17161-X

Printed in the United States of America

July 1987

10   9   8   7   6   5   4   3   2   1

WFH

For Kathryn Falk . . . to whom we
all owe a debt of gratitude
and
special thanks to St. Jude for
answered prayers

1

"The King is coming!" cried Roseanna breathlessly as she ran into the great hall of Castlemaine Manor. In her excitement she failed to notice either the gasp of pleasure that escaped her mother's lips or the sigh of resignation that escaped her father's. A flush of excitement enhanced her face, and as her father watched her, he realized that her exquisite beauty outshone her mother's by a hundred-fold.

"His Majesty sent a messenger ahead; he'll be here in time for supper." She picked up her gown from around her ankles and flew up the stairs.

"Roseanna, where are you going?" her mother asked sharply.

She paused on the step. "To change so I can ride out to meet him."

"You will not! I know it's been over a year since we've seen him, but Roseanna, you are sixteen, almost seventeen—no longer a child. I will not have you tearing across the countryside on that wild animal you insist on riding!"

Roseanna lifted her chin willfully. "Try and stop me!"

"Roseanna, you must remember that Edward is the King of England and that you, I hope, are a lady. I forbid you!"

Roseanna, now very still, drew herself up to her full height and said quietly, "Forbid? I think not."

"Ah, if you would only use some of that cool disdain in the King's presence, it would be becoming. If you continue to fling yourself upon him, he will think of you as a nuisance."

She gave her mother a seething look, ran back down the stairs and outside, and slammed the door to the hall so angrily that it shook the armored shields upon the walls.

Sir Neville Castlemaine made no remark about his daughter's behavior but said quietly, "I'll go see how many we can expect in the King's party."

Joanna's eyes followed her husband as he left the hall. She briefly wondered what he was thinking, then swiftly dismissed thoughts of him as she realized that hundreds of things would need to be done before Edward's arrival.

Instead of going directly in search of the messenger, Sir Neville slipped around to the walled garden, where he found Roseanna angrily throwing pebbles into the lily pond. He smiled at the sight of her. Her dark hair fell like a cloud of smoke, reaching almost to her knees in its unbound disarray. Not even the plainest yellow linen gown could hide the lovely curves of her breasts. "The King could not possibly think of you as a pest, sweetheart."

"Oh, Father, why is it that every time Mother and I speak to each other, we fight?"

He smiled. Neville Castlemaine was a quiet man yet a wise one. "When you were a child and never questioned your mother's authority, your relationship was a loving one. Now that you are both women, you rub against each other's nerves. You resent authority; she fears losing control. You are natural rivals."

Roseanna's eyes widened at her father's insight. They were pale gray; the edges of the irises were ringed with purple. Her eyes were pools in which a man could drown himself.

Briefly, he wondered if they had been wrong to allow her so much freedom while she was growing up. She had had the freedom of a boy, really. She rode, swam, hunted, and yes, even cursed and gambled with his more youthful men-at-arms on occasion. No, he didn't believe it had harmed her in the least to let her run wild, but clearly it was now time to train her in the gentler arts of being a woman. Past time, according to Joanna. "Why don't you ride into the wind for an hour to sweeten your disposition?" he suggested. "But don't be too late coming back, Roseanna. Your poor servingwomen will be frantic if they don't have time to ready you for the royal visit."

Impulsively she kissed him, then lifted her skirts and sped toward the stables.

Castlemaine Manor was famous for its horses. They were Sir Neville's one passion in life. Roseanna had learned everything about their breeding that her father could teach her. It was as if she had a natural talent for horses; it took her away from the monotonous but serious business of being brought up to be a great lady of the manor.

Sir Neville was an advocate of selective crossbreeding.

Ever since he had begun to listen to Roseanna—and he now took her suggestions seriously—they had bred some of the finest stock in England. As a consequence, the fame of Castlemaine's horses was now surpassed only by the prices they brought.

Joanna disapproved totally. It was the bone of contention that could always be counted on to cause argument between husband and wife and between mother and daughter. Joanna was horrified that Roseanna—whose delicate beauty resembled that of a fragile flower—should sprinkle her conversation with phrases about mares in heat, stallions in rut, animals in danger of abortion, and foals to be gelded.

An aging man with a shaggy, gray countenance smiled his welcome as Roseanna stretched up to saddle Zeus. He reached under the stallion's great girth to fasten the strap, then rubbed his shoulder joint where the rheumatism plagued him.

"Dobbin, why don't you ask Mother for some of her herbal rub for your aching joints?" asked Roseanna.

Dobbin, so named for his lifetime association with horses, shook his head and replied, "Nay, my lady, the horse liniment I mixes will do me better than all your mother's potions and pastes." He helped her up into the saddle and murmured, "Careful as ye go." It was the closest he dared come to advising her that the brute was dangerous and would perhaps one day prove to be too much for her to handle.

After she departed, Dobbin gave the nod to a young groom, signaling him to follow the mistress at a discreet distance to make sure no harm befell her. Roseanna, aware that he would do so, dug in her heels and let Zeus have his head until Castlemaine Manor was out of sight.

The wind whipped her hair about like a sable mantle as she sped toward the fringes of great Ettrick Forest. With each mile the stallion's hooves covered, her spirits lifted higher.

The King was coming! Edward was her godfather. He had never made a secret of the fact that she was a favorite with him. They only got to see him when he came to his hunting lodge deep within the vast forests of Ettrick and Sherwood, which lay in Nottingham. Tonight the rafters would ring with merriment, despite her parents' efforts at formality, for the King was not one to stand on ceremony when he was with old friends.

Roseanna's sweetness of temper was fully restored by the time she returned home. The late afternoon sun had just begun its descent, throwing its golden glory across the skies. She lifted her eyes up and laughed, for it seemed that the heavens were heralding the King's arrival: Edward IV's device was the Sun in Splendor.

Roseanna hummed a merry tune as she bathed, while her young tiring woman, Alice, brushed the tangles from her dark hair, which hung to the floor over the edge of the bathtub. Alice was a soft-spoken girl with chestnut hair and blue eyes who admired her mistress's daring ways.

Roseanna was ready to capitulate to her mother's wishes. She would act the demure maiden tonight. Her mother would find no fault with her. As she and Alice examined the lovely garments in her wardrobe, trying to decide on just the right gown, Kate Kendall came bustling in with her usual air of command. Kate, the plain-faced, North-country woman who was Joanna's right hand and most trusted servingwoman, carried one of the

new gowns that had been sewn for Roseanna over her
arm. "Your mother says you will wear this."

Roseanna forced a faint smile and bit back the quick
retort that sprang to her lips at the gimlet-eyed Kendall's
tone of authority. Alice took the exquisite gown and posy
cap with its delicate hair veil from Kate, who delivered
another salvo before she departed: "I am to remind you
to keep your tongue from the subject of horseflesh, lest
the King and his gentlemen mistake you for a stable-
hand."

"Damn you both!" Roseanna's eyes kindled with the
light of battle, and Alice shrank back in anticipation of
the heated exchange that was inevitable between these
two. "How is it that no one ever finds fault with my
mother's hobby? She doesn't sit idle, plying her needle
like a gentlewoman. She works endless hours at designing
and fashioning jewelry, then sells it at exorbitant prices
like a good businesswoman. But because I do the same
with my horses, it's all wrong!"

"Your mother is an artist," said Kate Kendall in a
reverent voice that could have been used to describe the
Holy Mother of God.

Roseanna lowered her eyes and breathed deeply to
regain a measure of control. In a quieter voice she replied, "You are right, of course. Thank you for bringing
the gown, Kate."

The older woman cast her a long, penetrating look, as
if to discern what trick the girl would be up to next. Then
she left without a word, her composure unruffled. Kate
contended that Roseanna had been born with an oversup-
ply of "wicked juices" that bubbled over every once in a
while, and that she needed a firm hand.

After the thick oaken door was firmly closed, Rose-

anna cried, "The bitches!" She walked to the bed and
looked at her new garments with distaste. Only last week,
when she had stood for the final fitting, the delicate white
underdress with its trailing sleeves had brought her pleasure. Even now, Alice caressed the red velvet tunic and
murmured, "It's lovely. The red and white make a beautiful contrast."

Roseanna tossed her head. "I'll not wear it!"

Alice protested softly, "But you must, my lady."

"Ah yes, a command performance. Well, so be it!" said
Roseanna, stubbornness firming her soft pink mouth. In a
deceptively sweet tone, she bade Alice hang the white
underdress in the wardrobe. She slipped the crimson velvet tunic over her head and smoothed its slimness down
over her hips until it fell to her ankles. The overdress left
her neck and arms completely uncovered.

"You cannot go down like that!" gasped Alice, scan-
dalized.

"Why not?" demanded Roseanna.

"It—it is so bare!"

"My mother bids me to stop acting like a child, so
tonight I'll dress like a woman. Fetch me the coffer with
my gold jewelry, Alice." She chose eight golden bracelets
—two for each of her wrists and two to clasp about each
of her upper arms. She fastened a golden girdle about her
hips and surveyed the effect in the polished silver mirror.

As Alice came up behind her to cover her hair with the
veil, Roseanna shook her head firmly. "I shall wear my
hair uncovered. Hand me the brush while I try to tame it
a little." Her eyes fell upon a dog collar of garnets that
her mother had designed for her. Each stone had been
chosen for its depth of color, and when she clasped it
about her slender throat, they looked exactly like rubies.

"Mm, Mother is an artist, you know. I must be a sore trial to her sometimes."

Alice said low, "Oh, dear. I feel quite sick."

Roseanna put her arm around the girl and hugged her warmly. "Do stop worrying, Alice. It's me they'll punish, not you."

"But you look like a pagan, my lady!" whispered the girl.

Roseanna smiled radiantly. "I think perhaps I am a pagan, Alice!"

The good-natured laughter of the King reached Roseanna's ears even before she entered the great hall. As she stepped through the archway, she easily glimpsed Edward's golden-red hair; he stood head and shoulders over any assembly—six feet six inches when wearing his crown, it was rumored. Her father's knights and the King's gentlemen stepped aside to clear a path for her to the King. No man hid his admiration for her incomparable beauty.

When Edward spied her, he almost snatched her up to the rafters as he always did, reveling in his great strength. But now, when she demurely went down before him murmuring, "Your Grace," he raised her and kissed her hands. "My Rosebud. I see you have begun to bloom!"

She expressed her pleasure with a smile and took up the wine goblet her father offered her. As she turned toward Neville, her eyes widened in surprise. "Jeffrey! I did not know you had returned."

"*Sir* Jeffrey," the King emphasized. "Your brother was knighted by my brother during his service in Ireland."

Sir Jeffrey bowed to the King. "His Majesty graciously allowed me to travel from London in his party."

Roseanna smiled happily at Edward. "You have brought my mother the one gift in all the world that will please her most."

Jeffrey was one year younger than Roseanna, but now that he had finished his service with the Duke of Clarence and had fought in Ireland, he looked the elder. Jeffrey had his mother's blue-black hair and his father's handsomely shaped head. Roseanna knew without a doubt that he would set the heart of every one of her mother's ladies aflutter.

Edward winked at Roseanna. "I've a present for you, you saucy baggage."

She looked in wonder from the King to her father, who was fairly bursting to tell her the news. "A horse?" she ventured hopefully.

Edward's good-natured grin spread across his handsome Plantagenet features. "A pure-blooded Arabian. I can't wait to see what you breed from him."

The musicians arrived with their fiddles, flutes, harps, and dulcimers. Close on their heels, Joanna made her entrance. She was as slim as a reed, with high, upthrusting breasts that belied her thirty-odd years. No posy cap and veil for Joanna, but a jewel-encrusted device of her own design that lifted her blue-black hair high from her temples before it fell in a smooth waterfall to her shoulder blades. To honor the King, she wore the York colors of murrey and blue. Her underdress of pale blue was complemented by a velvet tunic of purplish murrey, its borders gilded by real thread of gold.

Joanna did not so much as glance at Roseanna, having eyes only for her men, but her daughter smiled inwardly and reminded herself not to think her mother hadn't noticed every last detail of her pagan attire. There would be a reckoning, but not now, not tonight. So Roseanna vowed to enjoy the royal visit to the fullest!

The hall was crowded tonight. All the Castlemaine men-at-arms had come for a glimpse of their King; they lined the walls, and young pages and squires sat high on the ledges of the casements. As the food was being brought in, Roseanna made her way toward the head table. Her brother Jeffrey touched her shoulder. Whirling toward him, she looked into a face that had a strong impact upon her senses. She heard Jeffrey's voice as if from a great distance: "Roseanna, I would present my great good friend, Sir Bryan Fitzhugh. We were knighted together."

The knight who stood before her was her own age, perhaps a year older. *He's beautiful,* she thought as her eyes lowered demurely; her cheeks flushed at his nearness. Through her lashes she saw him place his hand over his heart, and he bowed gravely. She saw his lips say, "I am honored, my lady," but there was such a roaring in her ears, she heard nothing but the thunderbeat of her own heart. He had a golden beard and a smiling mouth, and by a trick of the torch behind his head that bathed him in its golden light, he looked like the shining knight of her dreams.

Her mind went blank. No clever phrase flew to her lips, and her voice almost deserted her along with her wits. "Sir Bryan," she managed to whisper at last; then she fled to the safety of the King and her father.

She knew not what she ate; swan or boar—it was all the same to her. When her dinner companions spoke to her, she did not hear them, and they had to repeat everything. She answered with sighs. Her eyes ever traveled in one direction, slipping along the diners to the young man seated next to her brother. Finally, she had to turn her head away, for her eyes would not leave him of their own accord. Suddenly she wished she had worn the delicate white underdress with its pretty trailing sleeves and matching hair scarf. Sir Bryan would think her nothing but a bold piece dressed as she was, with her hair uncovered and falling to the backs of her knees.

She panicked when she saw the servants stack the trestle tables to make room for the dancing. What if he asked her to dance? Or worse, what if he did not? She sat rigid, unable to move; then with vast relief she saw Sir Bryan take leave of her mother to retire early. Suddenly she relaxed, found that her saucy wit hadn't deserted her after all, and rose to dance the first measure with the handsomest of the King's gentlemen.

The torches had burned low in their cressets and the hour was well advanced before the last servant at Castlemaine Manor laid down his weary head that night. Roseanna dismissed Alice to her bed quickly, for she wanted to be alone to savor the memory of Sir Bryan's handsome image. She shivered as her body touched the cool sheets; then she let her mind wander dreamily to the man with the golden beard and the smiling mouth.

But thoughts of her mother began to intrude. She tried to push them away as she concentrated on the young knight, but try as she might, the image of Joanna came stronger and stronger. Roseanna sighed. The trouble was, her conscience was bothering her. She had spoken disrespectfully to her mother and had added insult to injury by behaving overboldly. She knew her mother loved her and wanted only what was best for her. This was the lady who had dismissed the servants to tend her herself when-

ever Roseanna was sick with a childhood illness. She
turned restlessly in the bed, wishing sleep would claim
her.

Coincidentally, Joanna's mind was centered on her
daughter at that moment. In her cozy bedchamber in the
west wing of the manor, she lay curled in the King's lap
before the warm fire. She raised her head at last from his
massive chest as he murmured, "She is wondrously fair,
Joanna."

"The young baggage is monstrously conceited. She
knows she is beautiful," said her mother.

"How could she not know? When men see her for the
first time, their mouths fall open."

"She is willful and spoiled," insisted Joanna, "and she
has a fiery temper to boot."

Edward's lips twitched as he gently mocked, "Traits
that run in the blood of her mother and father."

"Your Plantagenet blood perhaps, not mine," she
teased. "Ned, promise me you will speak to her about
riding that wild uncut animal."

He stroked her blue-black hair, which reflected the
flames of the fire; his fingers sought to unfasten her bedgown.

Joanna stayed his hands. "Ned, my love, I know that
our precious time together is short, but I must speak of
this. Roseanna's betrothal to Ravenspur has stood for six
years, and he has never come forward to claim her. I
have no quarrel with the match; she could do no better
than your close friend, Roger Montford. But if he cannot
be brought to the altar, perhaps we should look elsewhere."

Edward shifted uncomfortably, and Joanna slipped
from his lap to stand her ground on this most pressing

matter. "Joanna, I'm sorry, but we were not completely honest with you at the time of the betrothal." He shrugged helplessly, knowing that the truth must now be faced. "At the time I was thinking only of what was expedient for Roger. You know he had two disastrous marriages, and he swore he'd never enter the state of wedlock again. To remove him from pressure applied by his family and matchmakers, I suggested a betrothal to Roseanna, who was only eleven at the time."

"Damn men! Women are only pawns to be used in your interests!" she said, clenching her fists.

To placate her and restore her loving mood, Edward poured them a goblet of malmsey and held it out to her as a peace offering. "My love, I promise you I will broach the subject to him. He's just back from a hellish campaign in Wales. You know what it's like to subdue those wild Welshmen. I've loaned him the hunting lodge for next month. God knows, he's earned a little sport and relaxation. I'll urge him to either claim her or withdraw."

"But it's a legal contract," she said stubbornly, hating to give up the prize.

He moved toward her purposefully, taking her slim shoulders in his strong hands. "You will be compensated if it comes to naught, and I'll find her a match with the highest in the land." He took the goblet from her fingers and drained it. "Enough of my daughter; it is you I need."

She laughed up at him, "You have a greater capacity for wine than any man in England."

"Not true. Ravenspur once drank me under the table! However, my capacity for making love is another matter entirely."

2

After a sleepless hour of tossing in her bed, Roseanna arose and slipped on her bedgown. She couldn't rest until she had apologized to her mother. The passageways that led to the west wing were cold and only dimly lit at this hour, so she hurried along, hoping her mother's fire would soon warm her hands and feet.

She passed quietly by Kate Kendall's adjoining chamber, hoping she would not come face to face with the watchful servant. Quietly she turned the iron ring that lifted the bar on the door to her mother's room. The dark oaken door swung back to reveal a pair of lovers. The King's massive torso was bare. The fire's glow highlighted his muscular shoulders as he lifted the naked Joanna high above him. She laughed down at him like a young girl with her first great love.

Roseanna's eyes widened in shock. Her hand flew to her throat as she gasped her disbelief. On legs that threatened to collapse, she fled the chamber.

"Roseanna!" her mother called her back in vain.

Edward lowered her feet to the rich oriental rug, and

she reached for her bedgown and whispered, "I must go
to her."

"Nay, Joanna. At this moment she hates you. I will go
to her." He pulled on hose and soft boots and reached for
his purple velvet bedgown. He had no trouble finding her
chamber, as her door stood ajar and the sound of choking
sobs reached his ears, mixed with the soft voice of her
maid, pleading to know what was amiss.

The King spoke softly to Alice: "Leave us."

Roseanna was huddled miserably on her bed. But Edward's voice made her fly from her haven and face him
like a vixen in her lair. "You have no right!" she hissed.
"You may be the King of England, but you have no right
to be here."

There was pain in his eyes as he said with quiet authority, "I have a right. Not because I am King, but because I
am your father."

Her eyes widened in disbelief. The truth of his words
had not yet reached her heart; she flung at him the accusation, "You are lovers!"

He winced at the ugly implication she attached to the
word. "Sweethearts, Roseanna. Since we were fourteen."

She stared at him as the thought formed slowly; *I am a
royal bastard!* The revelation took her by surprise, yet it
explained many things she had questioned in her childhood. Now the answers all fell neatly into place. " 'Tis
shameful to have carnal knowledge at fourteen and indulge until you got her with child," she whispered accusingly.

"We were in love, Roseanna," he explained.

"Then why did you not marry?" she demanded indignantly.

"Roseanna, but think for a moment," he asked patiently. "I was fourteen. I was only the Earl of March. My father had just been named temporary protector of the realm because Henry of Lancaster had gone mad. Suddenly my father and his brother, the Earl of Warwick, had ambitions for the crown. I was in service to Warwick. He gave the orders, and I obeyed him implicitly. Warwick said marriage to Joanna was out of the question, and Warwick's word was law!"

"Warwick," she reflected, "the one they call the kingmaker?"

"He earned the title. I was King at eighteen!"

She reflected for a moment on the events of the past few years, on gossip she had heard. "If I remember aright, Warwick forbade your marriage to Elizabeth Woodville also, but you made her your Queen!"

He laughed shortly at the memory of it all. "Aye, I was twenty-two years old and had ruled England for four years. Yet still I feared Warwick so much, I had to keep the marriage secret."

As she gazed at him, she could not imagine that he had ever been afraid of anything. Enclosed in a room with him, she could feel his strength.

He put a finger beneath her chin, and she did not shake him off. "My Rosebud, you were my firstborn, and ever have you held the softest place in my heart. Can you forgive me for not making you a royal princess?"

"I care nothing for that!" she flared, her pride stung. "Who knows of this?" she asked.

"None save your mother and of course Sir Neville. Roseanna, no one must know. For your own safety you must guard the secret. There are evil men who would eliminate all who have a blood tie to the throne."

"The Woodvilles?" she asked bluntly.

He searched her face with his eyes, wondering how much he could entrust to such a young girl. "The Queen's family is a large one—six sisters and five brothers, not to mention her mother and stepfather, Lord Rivers. They are the most ambitious family I have ever encountered, barring us Plantagenets, of course." He laughed. "My own brothers and Warwick, who loves me little now that I am no longer his puppet, would stop at nothing to further their positions."

"I understand, Your Grace," she said quietly. She did not want him to have to malign those he loved for her protection, for he was the best-natured man under the sun, bar none.

He gathered her to him and kissed her brow, then held back the covers while she slipped into the bed. "Will you be all right?" he asked.

She nodded, not daring to trust her voice further.

As she lay sleepless, her thoughts chased each other until she was exhausted. How did she feel? The same, yet different. Saddened, yet glad she knew the truth at last. Wiser, yet ignorant of the world and its ways. At last she admitted to herself that she understood his position and felt empathy for him. It was her mother's role in this deceit that she could not tolerate!

Ordinarily, Roseanna would have arisen before dawn to examine the Arabian stallion awaiting her in the stables, but today she was filled with lethargy. The aroma of food reached her nostrils, and she wondered what Alice had been about, to fetch her breakfast in bed. As she sat up slowly, she saw that it was her mother who was bringing her the tray. She wished Joanna a thousand miles away. Roseanna's dark lashes swept down to her cheeks;

she could hardly bear to look at her mother. Joanna was thirty-two years old, and she looked every minute of it this morning. She set the tray down onto a leather-topped side table and gently sat down on the bed. She offered neither excuse nor explanation, and as Roseanna slowly raised her eyes to meet her mother's, the image of the previous night's laughing wanton dissolved, and Roseanna saw in its place the image of a fourteen-year-old girl, heavy with child. How she must have suffered! Punished by accusations, threats, whispers. Facing the shame and the burden alone. Suddenly she reached out to touch her mother's hand. "I'm sorry. Do you love him very much?"

Joanna smiled. "No, I'm not in love with Ned. But oh, Roseanna, I was, I was!"

"I know the pain you must have suffered when they would not allow you to marry," she said quietly.

"Nay, you do not. You will never know unless you are forced to give up your first love."

A tear slipped down Roseanna's cheek, and her mother stood up briskly. "However, I soon discovered that women are very resilient and can face anything that must be faced. Eat your breakfast. I've a hundred tasks to see to. We'll talk again, Roseanna."

When Alice came in to help her braid and bind her hair, Roseanna could see that she was filled with curiosity about last night's tears and the King's nocturnal visit. So improvising quickly, she said, "You were right, Alice. I should have worn the underdress. I received a terrible scolding from Mother, and if it hadn't been for the King's intervention, the rift between us would have been irreparable."

Alice said with awe, "The King is reputed to be the

best-natured man in England, yet his very presence terrifies me."

Roseanna fastened her hose and pulled on soft riding boots. " 'Tis the office of Kingship that is awesome. But rest assured, beneath that Kingship breathes a man made of flesh and blood."

As Roseanna walked to the stables, the only man she dreaded to encounter was Neville Castlemaine, her father yet not her father. She did not know how she could ever face him again. Her delicate cheeks were pink at the thought.

The stables were alive with King's men and their servants saddling for departure to Belvoir, the King's hunting lodge. Edward was pointing out the unmistakable characteristics of the Arabian stallion to Dobbin.

"Oh, Your Grace," Roseanna said in deep appreciation, "he's white!" Quickly she spat upon the ground, and the King threw back his head and roared. "You are superstitious." He laughed. "By God's blood, 'tis years since I spat at the sight of a white horse."

Roseanna laughed back. "I still bow three times to the raven and never, ever look at the new moon through glass."

"And wish upon a star, and carry a rabbit's foot," said Edward with nostalgia for youthful days long past. He watched Dobbin lead the Arabian to a rear box stall. "See if you can breed me some war horses from that one."

Sadly she said, "The life of a war horse is short, and consequently the demand for them is great." They walked together to Zeus's stall, and the animal nickered a greeting to Roseanna.

Edward spoke after only a slight hesitation. "I prom-

ised your mother that I would speak to you about riding
this uncut horse. Why don't you choose a gelding, Roseanna? She would rest easier."

Her eyes darkened as she spoke with passion. "You
answer me a question first. Why do you ride an uncut
stallion into battle? There is no logic to it. A gelding
would be easier to control and wouldn't give your position away to the enemy by screaming wildly."

Edward grinned. "Damned pride! Stubborn Plantagenet pride!"

"Did you think I had none?"

The King looked at her with admiration in his eyes.
"Then all I can do is bid you to take care. Ride over and
join our hunting. We'll be there until the end of the
month, then I've promised the lodge to Ravenspur." He
strode off. For a moment it seemed the light was dimmer
after his departure. Deep in thought, Roseanna leaned
against Zeus's stall. A beautiful voice behind her startled
her from her reverie.

"Don't stand too close, Mistress Castlemaine. The
beast could harm you."

She raised her eyes to his, then lowered her dark lashes
quickly. "Thank you, Sir Bryan," she whispered demurely, and allowed him to place himself protectively
between herself and the black stallion. Anyone else would
have received a setdown for their presumption! With all
the emotional turmoil she had just been through, she had
forgotten all about Sir Bryan. Now she wished fervently
that she hadn't braided her tresses so severely nor worn
the plain blue riding dress. She forced herself to raise her
lashes and speak to him lest he think his friend had an
imbecile for a sister. "I pray you, call me Roseanna, sir."

He bowed; his manners were flawless. "It will be my honor, Lady Roseanna."

She sighed with relief when she heard her brother Jeffrey's voice hail them, for indeed she had exhausted her store of conversation with the young knight.

"There you are, brat! Father's been asking for you. I think he went into the garden to look for you."

Her color became high when she realized that Jeffrey was only her half brother. Then that thought led to another—that she had three little half sisters at Westminster, all royal princesses. To her dismay, she found herself curtseying to Sir Bryan as she excused herself. Then she murmured under her breath, "Silly girl, he's addled your brains!"

Her feet dragged as she walked toward the walled garden and entered through the little ornamental gate. He stood by a rosebush, and she searched desperately for words. But he spoke first.

"Joanna has told me that you know all."

"Joanna?" she echoed. "How can you bear to utter her name?" she asked in an agonized voice.

"My dear one, Joanna never deceived me in any way. I knew she carried you when we wed. She has been a good wife to me all these years, and the year after you were born, she gave me my son. No man could ask for more." He said it honestly, and she knew his words were sincere. At last she dared to raise her eyes to his, and she saw love there, clearly written. "You have been a good father to me. I shall always think of you as my father."

"And you will always be my daughter," he said simply. He held his arms wide, and she went into them, not caring that tears slipped down her cheeks. She whispered,

"I was afraid to face you, but you are such a good man. You have eased my way, as always."

Slightly embarrassed, he quickly changed the subject. "Come, I must bid Edward godspeed. Then we'll have a closer look at that Arabian. Have you a name in mind?"

"How about Mecca?" she smiled.

"Well, it's certainly a name to live up to."

Alice handed Roseanna a small parchment. "My lady, a certain knight bade me give you this."

Roseanna took it curiously, asking, "Which knight?" But as her eyes fell upon the lines, she knew it was from Sir Bryan.

> *Moon, moon shining bright*
> *White and silvered over,*
> *All night long you shed your light*
> *Upon her sleeping bower.*
>
> *Oh, that my lady dreams of me*
> *Would be my desire,*
> *Though I know well this cannot be*
> *Yet still my heart's afire.*

Her pulse quickened. "Very pretty," she told Alice, trying not to let her excitement show too obviously. *So,* she thought privately, *he feels as I do.* The thought pleased her inordinately. What a lovely day this was! Only yesterday everything had seemed clouded, and now

this day seemed shining; it felt as if it were a new beginning. And perhaps it was.

Everyone noticed that Roseanna was preoccupied. Her
thoughts had carried her off to some secret place; she
answered with sighs when she was spoken to.

When she took her place for the evening meal in the
great hall, which seemed empty after the crowds of yesterday, she found a white rose lying beside her plate. She
took it up, cupped its delicate beauty, and buried her
nose in its heady perfume. She smiled and felt positively
light-headed from its fragrance.

She raised her eyes to search the hall and like a magnet
found the face she sought. She smiled brilliantly; then,
overcome with sudden shyness, which was most unlike
her, she lowered her eyes to her plate. When the meal
was over, from the corner of her eye she saw Sir Bryan
leave the hall. She felt a small pang of disappointment
that he had not waited until she rose so they could have
the excuse of leaving together. However, as she walked
from the dining hall through the archway that led to the
courtyard, she saw that he awaited her, and her heart
lifted dizzily. Her footsteps slowed, and he fell in beside
her. They strolled across the courtyard, sending the pigeons and doves flying up to the eaves.

"Did you mind my sending you a verse?" he asked
tentatively.

"I thought it very pretty," she began. Then she asked,
"Do you have more?"

He laughed happily. "I'll send one each day, now that
I know you won't scorn me." He hesitated, "Lady Roseanna, you are so beautiful. You must have scores of
knights pouring their hearts out to you." It sounded like
a question.

"No, none," she answered simply, knowing it was the answer he sought. She was suddenly glad that it was the truth.

"Do you think that someday you could ride out with me and show me your beautiful countryside?"

She smiled at him. "Are you busy tomorrow?" she asked daringly, holding her breath until his answer came.

"I had not dared hope so soon."

"I think I shall go hawking tomorrow at dawn. If you care to join me, Sir Bryan, it would be my pleasure." It was the longest sentence she had uttered in his presence, and it left her attractively breathless. His eyes, which had lingered on her mouth, now fell to the rose in her fingers. Gently he plucked it from her hand and tucked it inside his doublet above his heart.

Castlemaine Manor had only one turret, and Roseanna had claimed it for her chamber long ago. Slightly removed from the rest of the household, it gave her the amount of privacy she needed to be happy.

The sky was still dark the next morning when she awoke and lit up the turret room with a dozen candles. Alice, used to Roseanna's arising early but not at this ungodly hour, shivered. "I'll send for a page to light a fire."

"No time for that, Alice. Help me with my hair. We'll braid and loop it and fasten it with ribbons. I need it very secure so it won't come tumbling down, for I'm hawking this morning."

Alice shivered again just at the thought of riding in the wind at dawn. Later, the summer day would be lovely and warm, but at this hour the outdoor world was decidedly chilly.

Roseanna chose a linen underdress and long tabard in matching forest green. Her riding boots were soft red Spanish leather, and her cloak was scarlet. She was well aware that scarlet was one of the colors that showed off her dark hair to perfection. She pulled on her leather gloves, then took a bright green apple from a bowl of fruit and bit into it lustily.

Alice shuddered. "Ugh, isn't that sour?"

Roseanna's tongue shot out to catch the juices, and she laughed. "It's so tart it sets my teeth on edge, but it's delicious!"

The two girls made a startling contrast: one very alive, the color high in her cheeks for what adventure the day might bring; the other pale and thin and shivering.

"Go back to bed, Alice. Here, put on my velvet bed-gown. If I'm hawking, I have to be up with the lark, but you most certainly do not. I'll tell you all the juicy details when I get back." She winked suggestively and whirled from the turret room, raced down the long flight of stone steps that led to the second story of the manor, then went quietly along to the backstairs, which led to the ground floor and out into the courtyard.

In the stables not even old Dobbin was astir yet, but Roseanna noted with pleasure that Sir Bryan was already there—as if he were impatient for the very sight of her!

He drew in his breath at the lovely vision in the scarlet mantle. She smiled up at him, not even trying to hide the pleasure in her eyes. "Come and select a hawk for yourself," she bade as she led the way through the stables into an annexed building and then up into the loft.

The birds, now disturbed, set up a screeching cacophony that was almost deafening. The light in the loft was very dim, and the musty smell of straw and bird droppings made Roseanna wrinkle her nose in protest. Then she unlatched the shutters and threw them back to let in the first light of day.

The birds were on wooden perches in long rows. Some were privately owned; the names of their owners were carved into the perches. One or two wore hoods with ornately fancy crests, but there were many varieties of hunting birds that were for general use by any of Castlemaine's inhabitants.

Sir Bryan chose a fine falcon with a massive wingspread and claws that could tear a man apart, let alone a bird. Roseanna almost chose a small sparrow hawk so that her companion would show to advantage in the hunting, but she changed her mind. She must not be too obvious, or he would know what she was about. She passed over the harriers, for she had been out with them before, and she knew that they did not always make a clean kill on the first try. She chose a female kite because of its smooth gliding motion and its forked tail and long pointed wings. Also, it went immediately from a view to a death.

Sir Bryan attached his falcon's jess to a leash, and Roseanna did the same. "Perhaps we'd better take a lure. I don't know how well trained your bird is," she admitted. Downstairs, she fastened the birds' leashes to a stall while Sir Bryan saddled his horse. She admired his deep-chested stallion and knew immediately that although it was a fine mount, it was not as many hands tall as Zeus. She moved along the stalls and selected a young mare for herself. A little voice inside Roseanna mocked her for playing devious, womanish tricks to make the man look and feel superior to her, but she ignored the little voice. As they rode out of the stables, Dobbin, who was now about, scratched his head in mystification at why the young mistress was not mounted on her favorite wild animal.

The sun was up now, and the dew sparkled before them like a carpet of green and silver. Roseanna had taken in every detail of Sir Bryan's appearance without seeming to do so. He wore deep blue hose, a doublet of the same color, and soft leather boots that reached to his thighs. Perhaps it was the deep color that made his eyes such an intense shade of blue. She found herself wondering whether, if he wore green, the shade of his eyes would change to match. The sun turned his hair and beard to spun gold. Roseanna found him most pleasant to look upon. On his shoulder was the Duke of Clarence's badge, a black bull.

"Is the Duke of Clarence very like his brother, the King? I have never seen him. I've seen Richard when he was a boy, but never George."

"The King's brother George is very like him in appearance. Tall, red-gold Plantagenet hair, handsome—perhaps more handsome than the King. He has natural grace and beautiful manners. He has a regal bearing. In fact, if you saw Edward and George side by side, you could easily mistake George for the King." He hesitated. "King Edward—or Ned, as he is called—is so informal, so heartily friendly."

She looked at him and wondered if by chance he was criticizing the King. Then she remembered how fiercely loyal knights were to the lord they served.

They raced across the meadow, and as a covey of birds flew up into the sky, they let their falcons off their leashes and slowed to a canter to watch their performance.

"Where is your home, Sir Bryan?"

"On Marston Moor, near York. My father was in service to the Duke of York, George's father."

Roseanna laughed. "I always think of the Duke of York as the King's father, but because of your service to the Duke of Clarence, you think of him as George's father."

"What odds does it make? My father lost his life in York's service."

Roseanna did not know if he meant York the man or York the faction that opposed Lancaster in the dispute that had resulted in the thirty-year War of the Roses—so named for the Red Rose of the Lancastrians and the White Rose of the Yorkists. "I am sorry, Sir Bryan," she began softly.

"It happened long ago, when I was only four or five. Richard, Duke of York, gave up trying to rule through a mad puppet king and claimed the throne as his legal birthright. There was a Christmas truce in effect, and the Duke of York, his son Edmund, and a small Yorkist force including my father were out foraging. They were ambushed and annihilated by a force of Lancastrians led by Lord Clifford. They fashioned a paper crown for the battered head of Richard and mocked him as a king without a kingdom."

Roseanna felt pity rise up within her. He spoke of her grandfather!

"My mother had the grisly details from my father's squire. The tale goes that my father begged Clifford to spare Edmund's life, but he coldly answered, 'By God's blood, his father slew mine, and so will I do him and all his kin!' After thirty years of battles, vengeance was the order of the day." His eyes focused on Roseanna as if he had only just realized where he was. "Forgive me, my lady. I shouldn't speak of such things to one gently born."

"I hope you feel you may tell me anything. I am your friend, Sir Bryan."

"I hope for more than friendship," he said boldly.

Roseanna's heart fluttered as she realized how he felt about her. She was attracted to the young knight and more than ready for her first romance.

He stroked his falcon when it brought back a pigeon and praised it lavishly. Then he took a piece of meat from his doublet pocket and fed the bird.

"Why, you're bribing her!" Roseanna laughed.

"I believe in the reward system. What act is ever undertaken without hope of gain?" he asked.

She raised her eyebrows, considered giving argument, then thought better of it. Their time together could be spent in more pleasant ways than arguing. The kite brought back its kill and presented it to Roseanna. They both laughed heartily when they saw it was a mouse. "Your pigeons can go into the stewing pot, but what on earth am I to do with this?"

"Try the reward system. Give it to her, then she will bring you something larger."

When their saddlebags were filled with grouse and pigeons, they returned home. "Will you come again tomorrow?" he asked fervently.

"Yes, I'll ride with you tomorrow. But I don't think we need the pretense of the hawks, do you?"

After her brother Jeffrey handed her the second missive, he spent the rest of the day teasing her unmercifully about Sir Bryan. Roseanna didn't care. The only thing that mattered to her was that he had written her another verse.

All I ask of thee, oh lady dear,
Is but what purest love may hope to find;
And if thine eyes, whose crystal light so clear
Reflect thy thoughts, be not to me unkind.
To thee my heart, my wishes I resign,
I am thine own, oh lady dear, be mine.

Her heart sang with the innocent melody of first love. But the change that had come over her caused her mother concern. Suddenly, Roseanna was amenable and biddable, and Joanna wondered if it was because she had learned that royal blood flowed in her veins. Roseanna did not seem to be brooding; rather, she smiled a lot, and her secret thoughts seemed miles away. These days she rode a mare more often than not, and after the evening meal she seemed enraptured by the ballads that the minstrels offered. Joanna put it all down to Ned's talk with his daughter. Indeed, she herself had had to curb a tendency in herself to daydream and sigh after the King's rare visit.

Joanna invited her daughter into her workshop, where she designed her jewelry. It was a small room that had been added onto the west wing to catch the afternoon light. Roseanna admired the sketches her mother was working on. They were for a clasp to fasten the neck of a cloak. The clasp was in the shape of a large letter E and was set with purple amethysts on a spiked background of diamonds, representing the Sun in Splendor.

"Oh, it's truly lovely, Mother," said Roseanna with admiration.

"I'm not sure I'll actually make it, though," replied Joanna.

"Why ever not?"

"Because though 'tis designed for the King, *she* could wear it."

Roseanna asked, "Do you mean Elizabeth, the Queen?"

"Yes, the Woodville woman!"

There was such a depth of feeling in Joanna's voice that Roseanna asked, "You hate her?"

"It is not just I who hate her. All England hates her! The Woodville tribe will suck Edward's generosity until it dries up. They are swollen with gain like fungus on a tree!"

Roseanna knew her mother was a strong-minded woman who had strong opinions that she was never loath to express, but she had never heard her speak with such undisguised hatred before. "She hadn't a farthing to her name before the King set eyes on her. She was a widow with two small sons and a tribe of brothers and sisters. She's five years older than Edward, you know," said Joanna with satisfaction.

"Why did he marry her?" asked Roseanna, perplexed.

"She's a witch who led him by his prick! Oh, I'm sorry Roseanna. Now I've shocked you."

Roseanna's lips twitched into a smile. "No more than you did the other night!"

The two women looked at each other and dissolved into laughter.

"This isn't just jealousy. Her father is Lord Rivers, and there is a spate of jokes up and down England about how 'Rivers' are multiplying and overflowing the land, and about how all 'Rivers' stink! No one speaks well of them.

There are too many of them, and they have too much wealth and power. I'm afraid Edward will have grave cause to regret allowing them to rise so high."

Roseanna suddenly realized how sheltered her life was at Castlemaine Manor, far from the intrigue of the Royal Court, and she was glad of it.

Later, Roseanna sought out Jeffrey in his chamber. She was not the least surprised, after she knocked, to see a disheveled serving maid slip past her as she entered. "I've come to seek a favor," she said solemnly, but her eyes were alight with amusement.

He teased back, "Are you sure you have the right chamber? Sir Bryan is down the corridor from me."

She ignored his words. "I want to take the new Arabian out for a run, but Zeus needs exercise. If you would ride out with me, we can do both."

Jeffrey grinned, "Ah, now I know why you have chosen me over Sir Bryan. You don't want to show him that you can ride the pants off him, while you don't mind for one moment humiliating me. Brat!"

"You think the Arabian's faster than Zeus?" she questioned.

"With a lightweight like you on him, I wouldn't be surprised."

"They are famous for being swift and graceful. I'd like to cross him with a garron—they're broad-hooved and sturdy but not fast."

"Take some advice from a brother. Don't speak of breeding horses this afternoon at the rendezvous."

"What rendezvous?" she gasped.

"The one I've promised to arrange between you and Sir Bryan. And for heaven's sake, Roseanna, don't go about this liaison so openly if you don't want mother to put a stop to it."

"Why would she do that?" questioned Roseanna.

"God, girl, you are thick-witted. I can think of a dozen reasons, aside from your being spoken for."

"Oh, that," said Roseanna, dismissing the long-standing betrothal with the contempt it deserved.

"Here's the plan. You and Alice take cushions and your lute and stroll down through the orchard toward the river. The banks of the Trent can be very romantic, take my word for it." He winked. "Bryan and I will bring food and wine. Then Alice and I will disappear."

Her eyes widened, and she said in mock surprise, "I didn't know you were pursuing Alice."

"Brat!" he said, pulling a tress of her long, dark hair. She gave him a hefty push that sent him sprawling, then dashed off to the stables with Jeffrey in full pursuit.

Roseanna had chosen her gown with infinite care. It was a delicate shell pink that gave her a fragile air yet made her lips look like rose velvet. The four young people laughed the afternoon away beneath the willows that dipped their branches to the water. They had enjoyed the first plums from the orchard, and they had drunk both wine and cider. Eventually, Roseanna found herself alone with Sir Bryan.

She sat on a cushion and strummed her lute while he translated romantic verses written by a German poet. All at once, they looked up into each other's eyes, and a moment later the book lay forgotten; Bryan closed the distance which separated them. He set her lute aside and slipped his arms around her. "Roseanna," his lips murmured as she breathlessly received her first kiss. It was so exciting, she trembled against him. "I did not mean to frighten you," he said low.

"You . . . did not," she answered shyly. He was emboldened to repeat the kiss. She lay against his arm, enthralled at the love words he whispered.

"You are the loveliest maiden I have ever seen. I lost my heart the first moment I laid eyes on you."

"I felt that way, too," she admitted.

"Don't toy with me, Roseanna. It will break my heart!" he said passionately.

Her eyes widened, "I'm not toying with you," she said seriously. "I . . . love you." She was flushed and breathless; her love was in her eyes, plain for him to see.

Then he threw himself upon the grass beside her, dejectedly. "It can never be!" he said miserably.

"Why not?" she asked, a crease furrowing her lovely brow.

"Your parents would never give such a prize to a landless knight," he told her.

"But I have land in my dowry," she pointed out.

"A woman's attractiveness increases with the size of her fortune. You must be spoken for," he insisted.

She put her hand out to him to reassure him. "When I was eleven I was betrothed, but he doesn't want me. He has never come forward to claim me. He should have done so when I was fifteen. Now I am seventeen—at least a year older than most girls when they wed—so you see, the betrothal is just a formality that will be dissolved."

Sir Bryan looked happier. "Perhaps there is hope, if all these years he has never claimed you. Who is he?"

"Montford, Baron of Ravenspur," said Roseanna.

"Ravenspur!" He recoiled at the name. "He stands high in the King's favor."

Watching his face carefully, Roseanna asked, "Why do you look horrified?"

Sir Bryan hesitated, then blurted, "His reputation with women stinks to high heaven. He's already had two wives; both are in their graves!"

"His wife died in childbed," said Roseanna thoughtfully.

"The first one did, perhaps. The second one died under very suspicious circumstances. 'Tis rumored she was murdered—or worse!"

"Bryan, please, don't be upset over this. My parents would never force me to wed a man I didn't love." She smiled into his eyes. "They have always given me my heart's desire."

He took her into his arms again and held her fiercely. "I'll not let you go to him," he swore.

She reached up a finger to smooth the frown from his brow; he took it and kissed it. "Pledge me your love, and I'll be satisfied. For now," he added.

"I pledge you my love with all my heart," whispered Roseanna.

Jeffrey and Alice rode up, and their privacy was at an end. But before they parted, they pledged their love again, silently, with their eyes.

4

Roseanna was spending less time in the stables and more time indoors these days, her mother noticed with satisfaction. Her daughter actually asked Kate Kendall's advice about housekeeping duties and was seen in the kitchens writing down some menus. When Joanna remarked on her new interest in womanly occupations, Roseanna said sweetly, "I will need to know these things when I become a wife."

Joanna drew in her breath. "Darling, you won't be devastated if the betrothal with Ravenspur comes to naught and is dissolved, will you?"

"Oh, Mother, of course not. I know it can come to nothing. I'm not naïve enough to think he will ever claim me."

"Then you will be happy if we look about and consider another husband for you?"

Roseanna smiled. "It is what I desire most." She almost said more but caught the words and smiled her secret smile instead. Silently she added, "You won't have to seek far, Mother."

In the stables, she helped her father dose a mare who had delivered a foal easily enough but whose afterbirth was proving troublesome. He appreciated Roseanna's gentle hands. As he held the mare's head at a good height, Roseanna poured warm gruel laced with black treacle into the mare's mouth. She did it very slowly so that it wouldn't go into the windpipe.

"Ah, Roseanna. What would I do without you?" he asked with admiration.

She teased, "You'll have to train someone before I get married—unless of course I marry one of your knights and live at Castlemaine."

"That would please me." He smiled fondly. "But what of your mother?"

She ignored his question and asked one of her own. "Father, if I did fall in love with someone and wished to marry, would there be any difficulty with Ravenspur?"

He shook his head. "I think not. You'd be honor bound to beg off, but I think the vow was forgotten years ago."

Whenever they were in the great hall together, Roseanna's and Bryan's eyes followed each other's every move. Roseanna was blooming. She wanted to shout her love from the rooftops! Everyone must be blind. Couldn't they see she was walking around in a love trance? Whenever the two young people managed to steal a few moments alone, the scenario was always the same: bliss while a few breathless kisses were exchanged, followed by Bryan's misery because she was pledged to another. She could not convince him that everything would work out for them if only he were patient.

Roseanna had a plan. It was simple, really, and it

would solve everything! Ravenspur was now at Belvoir, the King's hunting lodge, not six miles distant. She would simply go and ask him to release her from the old betrothal because she loved another. She would go tomorrow. She blew out her candles, and having made her decision, she was asleep almost as soon as her head touched her pillow.

The morning was hot and unbelievably oppressive for such an early hour. Roseanna decided to tell no one of her plan so it could not be thwarted. She was a girl who was used to making her own decisions and acting upon them. She seldom needed anyone to aid and abet her. In fact, she rather despised women who could not do things alone and forever went about in twosomes, propping each other up.

On a fancy, because she would be going through the forest, she chose a pale green dress of lightweight material and a matching scarf to cover her long tresses. She wished to appear properly demure when she appealed to the baron. She wore her new green leather riding boots embossed with winged horses. How clever the workmanship on them was! Her father had known she would love them on sight.

She took her breakfast late so that her father and most of his knights and men-at-arms would be long gone from the great hall. This was one morning she did not wish to tarry with Sir Bryan.

She gave Zeus an early apple and rubbed the black velvet of his muzzle; then she thought better about riding him. Perhaps it would be more seemly to ride a palfrey. So she picked out a young filly and saddled it quickly. As old Dobbin ambled up, she smiled at him and said, "As you see, I've chosen a gentle mount today, so there will be no need to send a groom to follow me to pick up the pieces."

He grinned up at her, exposing the gaps in his teeth. "What's the use? You usually manage to give him the slip anyway."

As she rode, the sun beat down unmercifully upon her shoulders, and she felt her neck becoming damp beneath her hair and the head covering. She noticed, however, that a few sultry, bruise-colored clouds were gathering ahead of her; briefly, she hoped the storm would not come until night.

A fat partridge flew out of the gorse, and the young filly reared up in fright. The horse was still skittish after she brought it under control; it danced aside at every shadow. She slowed her pace and patted the animal's neck and soothed it with calming words, but its nervousness increased. Then Roseanna heard the far-off rumble of thunder, and she realized the horse's keen hearing had picked it up long before she herself heard it.

"Damn," she swore, and dug her heels in, hoping to reach the shelter of the forest before the drenching began. She almost made it. She was within two hundred yards of the trees when the deluge came. Animal and rider entered the woods at full gallop, curving around the trunks of trees and jumping over fallen branches. Then the rain, coming in sheets, began to penetrate the foliage above, and the forest floor became slippery with mud and weeds.

Roseanna dismounted and led the nervous young animal by the bridle deeper into the forest, where the oaks were so large, their trunks were six feet in girth. She tied the filly's reins to a branch where it was quite dry and sheltered and sat down close by on a fallen log to wait out the thunderstorm. She was aware that her appearance had been ruined by the rain; reluctantly she pulled off the pretty head veil that had been so becoming this morning but that now resembled a sodden rag. She ran her fingers through her wet hair in an effort to spread it across her shoulders so that it would begin to dry.

After about an hour the thunder and lightning began to abate, and she knew the storm was moving off. With a sigh of relief, she arose to untie the horse's reins. At that precise moment, the shrill blast of a hunting horn carried through the trees. The young animal panicked instantly: it screamed, showed the whites of its eyes, and bolted.

She cursed the horse's cowardice and thought, *Zeus is a thousand times safer than this untrained filly.* Roseanna ran through the trees in the direction the horse had taken and began what she thought might be a fruitless search. She had almost given up when she heard an unmistakable cry for help. She followed the horse's pitiful cries until she came to a wide stream. The horse's back quarters had gone down into the water, and though the river didn't appear deep enough for real danger, she realized that the animal's fright alone made it necessary for her to go in after it.

She sat down and removed her new green boots carefully, calling out soothing words that she was far from feeling at the moment. She pulled her gown up above her knees although it was already quite wet from the rain. "Hold on, girl. I'll help you," she called softly, wading out into the middle of the stream.

Just as she reached for the trailing reins, the frightened young filly lunged forward, thrashed her back haunches free of the stream bed, and took off as if the devil himself were prodding her tail with his pitchfork. Roseanna was splattered from head to foot, and she was very angry. She staggered from the water up onto the bank, and for a moment she was disoriented. She didn't see which way the horse had gone; she didn't even know which side of the stream she had entered. It was unbelievable the way the day had turned out after such a promising beginning. Even her lovely gown with its subtle shade of green was now a colorless, sodden rag. She had no horse, no boots, and she harbored a suspicion that she just might be lost.

After almost two hours of wandering around, her anger melted away and was gradually replaced by apprehension, approaching fear. These great forests of Sherwood were alive with wild beasts, and although she was fairly safe during daylight hours when on a good mount, such was not the case when she was alone, on foot, as the evening shadows approached. Firmly she put the picture of wolves, boars, and wild bulls from her mind and cupped her hands on either side of her mouth. She called, "Hello? Hello?"

To her amazement she heard a horse approach through the trees. A male voice, filled with amusement, said, "Well, what quarry do I have here?"

She saw a handsome young lord whose white teeth flashed in his dark face and whose eyes fairly danced with mischief under heavy black brows. He was leading a second horse that carried a very bloody wild boar across its saddlebow.

"I'm lost," she blurted.

"Not anymore, sweetheart." He grinned with a leer.

Roseanna was instantly wary and drew her dignity about her. "I am the Lady Roseanna Castlemaine. I—"

He threw back his head and laughed with glee, "You're a liar, little wench!"

She said stiffly, "I beg your pardon?"

"Pardon freely given, sweetheart. Do you often suffer from delusions of grandeur?" He grinned.

By God, the laughing, gaping oaf didn't believe her! She almost threw at him that she was the daughter of the King, so stung was she by his laughter. She caught sight of the hunting horn slung at his side, and anger gripped her. "Your stupid screeching through that horn is what frightened off my horse! Who are you?" she demanded.

He bowed gravely from the saddle. "Tristan Montford, and you are? Oh yes, I forgot, you are the Queen of Sheba."

She was so angry, she trembled. He mistook it for a chill. For a peasant girl she was exquisite beneath the grime. His eyes traveled from her bare feet up her body and rested on her stubborn, tempting mouth.

"Where are you bound, my queen?"

She didn't answer him. Then she realized he was her only means of deliverance. "I am on my way to Belvoir."

His eyes began to dance again. "No doubt by special invitation from Baron Ravenspur."

"Yes. No—I mean, yes, that is who I wish to see."

He dismounted. "Come, I'll take you up before me. He will be delighted with you."

Her cheeks flamed with embarrassment now that he had drawn close, for the thin material of her gown clung wetly across her breasts. Though she tried to stand with her chest in as concave a manner as possible, her breasts thrust up impudently between them, causing his devil's grin to widen.

"I'll not ride with you," she said, lifting her head high.

He mockingly indicated the packhorse with its bloody burden. "Take your choice."

"I prefer *this* boor," she said acidly.

One heavy eyebrow slanted with appreciation at her stinging wit.

She mounted behind the carcass and glared daggers as Tristan looked his fill at her shapely legs. Soon she was chagrined to find out that she had been very close to Belvoir. She could have gotten there without this imp of Satan if she had only known.

Tristan turned the horses over to a groom and led her through an archway into the rambling lodge. She resolutely ignored the stares of two young squires and followed Tristan up a winding stairway to a chamber on the upper level. Thankfully, there was a fire, and Roseanna stepped toward it gratefully.

"I'll find you something dry to wear," said Tristan, going to another chamber door and calling, "Cassandra, come and see what I've found."

Knowing the young knave was referring to her, she whirled toward him with a mouthful of invective, but the words dissolved as she stared at the most vividly flamboyant creature she'd ever seen. She wore a low-cut gown of shining gold material that revealed rather than concealed her breasts. Her hair also was a most unreal shade of blond; it looked as if it had been sprinkled with gold dust. To top it off, she wore face paint—her lips were brightly crimson, her eyelids gilt.

The woman appraised Roseanna carefully as Tristan approached them. "I thought she'd make a unique present for Roger."

Roseanna had had enough. She sprang at him. "You bastard!" she cried, punching him until he grabbed her by the arms.

"Before you give her to Roger, best draw her sting, darling," Cassandra whispered. She passed Tristan a tiny vial of sleeping drops distilled from the poppy, then left him to it.

"For God's sake, settle down," Tristan said. "No harm will come to you." He moved a huge armchair before the fire and poured her a goblet of wine. Then he pulled off the voluminous silken tapestry that served as a bedcover and handed it to her. "Take off that wet rag, and I'll go find you a gown. Then I'll take you to Ravenspur, if that's what you want."

"It is, you grinning goat!" Roseanna glared at him.

He closed the door behind him, and she stood immobile, determined not to remove one stitch. Then she caught sight of herself in the mirror and gasped in horror. Her appearance was a thousand times worse than she had imagined. She was in rags, she was dirty, and her hair was in such wild disarray, it fell down her back in a tangled mass of curls that looked as if a brush and comb hadn't touched it since birth.

Quickly she washed her hands and face, then her feet and legs. She stripped off what used to be her gown and wrapped herself in the silken tapestry. There was no hairbrush in the room, but if he could produce a gown, a hairbrush should be possible, too, she mused. She sat down before the fire to wait and drained the goblet of wine.

When Tristan returned with a couple of items of female attire draped over his arm, he found her asleep before the fire. The empty goblet was on the rug, where it had rolled from her hand. Christ! The sleeping potion had worked faster than he thought. He hoped he hadn't given her too much. He took Roseanna's chin in his hand and lifted it. God, she was lovely! It had been so long since he'd seen a woman without face paint, he was enthralled. The natural texture of her skin seemed as luminous as a pearl, and her lips were like soft pink velvet. The tapestry fell away to reveal a luscious pink-tipped breast. She was a prize indeed, and by God, he knew exactly how he was going to present her to Roger.

The feast below in the dining hall of the King's hunting lodge was sumptuous. All the game that had been bagged the day before had been roasted for tonight's banquet. Roger Montford, Baron of Ravenspur, sat on the small raised dais with Cassandra at his side. He was as dark as his name implied, an older, broader version of Tristan. But instead of open humor, his dark eyes held cynicism. Where Tristan's mouth lifted in laughter, Roger's was hard and masculine. In fact, everything about Roger was more vivid, more pronounced, more striking than his younger brother.

Forty of his favored knights who had served him well in Wales sat along two rows of trestle tables facing each other. The tables groaned beneath the platters of game and venison and the flagons of wine and ale.

Between every pair of men sat a young woman; there were twenty in all for their enjoyment. As the evening progressed, the drinking was deep and the atmosphere grew louder and more bawdy with each drained goblet. The women also were well-flown with wine; one stood on a table and performed an erotic version of the dance of the seven veils to enthusiastic shouts from the men.

When this performance finished, there was a natural lull in the proceedings. Tristan chose his moment well. He strode into the hall with the silk tapestry rolled up and draped over his arms. He stopped before Roger and bowed. "We have a special prize for the man who bagged the most game on this hunt." All eyes went to Ravenspur, since everyone present knew their lord always took the most game. Roger looked on, amused and curious as to what the young devil was up to now.

Tristan went down on one knee and gently rolled out the silken tapestry. Whistles and shouts broke out as the naked maid was revealed. Only her dark mane of hair provided cover from the men's avid eyes.

The smile was instantly wiped from Roger's face. "Who is she?" he demanded.

"A peasant girl," said Tristan, feeling the back of his neck prickle because his brother was not pleased.

Roger stood up and swore. "Jesus Christ, you'll get us all hanged before you're finished! These peasants are not ours, Tristan. They belong to the King. You young fool— sometimes I think your brains must be in your arse! Is it not enough for you that I brought along Madame Cassandra and these young ladies from her riding academy?" he asked with cutting sarcasm.

It always annoyed Roger that although Tristan had a lovely young wife and child, that didn't keep him from whoring. He took up his cloak and stepped down from the dais. He bent and wrapped the maid in his mantle, picked up her limp form, and handed her back to Tristan. His dark eyes bored into his brother's and he said firmly, "Put her in my chamber until she recovers. Lock it!" Tristan left without a word, but he wondered what the hell was up with Roger that he spoiled all the fun. He must be getting old, Tristan decided.

Cassandra soon coaxed Roger's sense of humor to return by regaling him with the details of an evening's entertainment in honor of the Archbishop of York that she and her girls had attended. She had dressed her girls as nuns, and the romp that ensued had almost caused a

scandal when the Archbishop's brother, the great Warwick, heard of it.

Roger laughed. "No wonder the King took away the
Archbishop's office of Lord Chancellor and gave it to
young Richard."

Cassandra wrinkled her nose at the mention of the
King's youngest brother, Richard. She was about to re-
late an eyebrow-raising tale about him, but Roger
touched her nose with his finger. "Don't gossip about
young Richard to me. I know he isn't popular, but Ned
gives him all his dirty work to attend to. At least he's
loyal, and that's more than can be said for the King's
other brother, George."

"Brothers can be a sore trial, can they not, my darling?" she purred, and she ran her hand along his thigh,
which was as hard as steel. "Come, your men can manage without you, but I cannot."

They went up to her chamber, taking with them a full
flagon of malmsey. He had indulged her by allowing her
to pick the most lavish chamber for herself, and now he
noted with a jaded eye that the room was already in wild
disarray. When she stripped off her gown, he saw that her
nipples were gilded to match her eyelids and that her
pubic hair was dusted with gold powder. He cocked an
eyebrow. "The latest fashion?"

"Not really," she drawled, touching herself suggestively with long, slim fingers. "The very latest fad is to
shave off the hair completely, but I didn't think that
would please you, somehow."

"Damned right," Ravenspur grinned. He picked her
up and deposited her onto the bed to complete the act
they both desired. Between bouts, sated for the moment,
he lay on his back and half listened to Cassandra's con-

versation. With one finger she traced his lips; then she
tried to insert it into his mouth so that he would suck on
it. Instead, he bit her, and she quickly withdrew it and
traced the deep cleft in his chin. Then with the same
scarlet-tipped finger, she traced the black line of hair that
ran from his chest, directly over his navel, and down into
the heavy black mat of hair that covered his groin.

By the time she had reached her goal, he was rigid
again, and she licked her lips in anticipation. Cassandra
wished she had more power over him. By this time she
would have had the King mindless and young Tristan
positively groveling, but not Ravenspur. She thrilled to
the stories that were whispered about him, about the
things he'd done to his wife because of her infidelity. Cassandra knew that if a man was dangerous, he was attractive—and by God, this man was dangerous!

She shut her eyes as her hot mouth closed over him,
unable to wait a moment longer. He lay back and allowed
her to have her fill, thinking cynically that at least it kept
her quiet for a while. He held back a long time to prolong
his pleasure as well as the silence. She doubled her efforts,
flicking and swirling her tongue, wanting to hear him
moan, to watch his head arch back and the tendons stand
out on his strong neck. At last he came, with such force
that he was only dimly aware of Cassandra.

The moment she got her breath back, she was talking
again. "Next week, my lord, why don't I arrange for you
to have two girls?"

A corner of his mouth lifted in amusement. "Both
making love to me at the same time?"

"No. The idea is that you make love to them at the
same time. They say that if a man can bring two women
to climax simultaneously, one with his shaft, the other

with his tongue, it gives him a surge of power such as he has never experienced before."

He drew away from her. "Cassandra, excess sickens me," he said flatly.

"Nonsense," she whispered.

"It's titillating to speak of, perhaps, but in reality it's disgusting."

She laughed. "How old-fashioned you are!"

"I have nothing against more than one woman," he said smoothly. "It is just that I prefer that the first one leave before the second arrives." He threw back the covers and removed his long legs from the bed.

"Where are you going?" she asked, alarmed.

"I think I'll sleep better in my own chamber." He said it with such finality that she dared not protest.

He cursed at his locked chamber door, then sorted through the bundle of clothes he carried under his arm until he found the keys. He threw his clothes onto a leather-topped coffer and lit the candles that stood about the room. His eye caught sight of the young girl asleep in his bed. "Hellfire, I forgot about you," he muttered. He picked up the candelabra and strode naked to the bed. As the candle glow fell on her delicate features, his eyes dilated with pleasure. Carefully, he drew back the coverlet and let his eyes play up and down her exquisite body. He drew in his breath at the loveliness laid out before him. Her breasts swelled up temptingly—soft, white, round globes, gleaming like satin, tipped with pink rosebuds. They seemed to beckon him to touch them, to kiss them as they rose and fell with her gentle breathing. He resisted for a moment, savoring the opportunity to explore her with his eyes before she awoke. Her luxurious mane of glossy black hair reached all the way to her knees like a sable cloak, its rich darkness contrasting with her pale, smooth skin.

He knew he had never before beheld such a magnificent crown of glory. Unbidden, his fingers lifted a silken tress where it fell across one thigh. His physical response to touching her was immediate and pronounced.

"Splendor of God," he muttered thickly, licking lips gone suddenly dry. He observed things about her that he had never noticed on women before. Her hands were small, as pale as new ivory freshly carved; her nails were a delicate pink. His eyes traveled over her breasts again, up the delicate column of her neck, and lingered on her full, soft mouth. He longed to taste that mouth—and in a moment he would! Her long lashes made dark crescent shadows upon her cheeks; her eyelids were so delicate, he could discern tiny blue veins.

Roger Montford had only one use for women; he had a theory that only whores and prostitutes were beautiful. Apparently he was wrong; peasant women could also be beautiful. At this moment common sense and caution— two qualities he usually had in abundance—deserted him. He had never quite felt like this before. A heady intoxication made him oblivious to everything but his need for her. Her body's scent reached his nostrils, making them flare with lust.

He slipped into the bed and reached for her. The moment his hands came in contact with her velvet skin, his shaft lengthened another inch, so intense was his response. He cupped her delicate cheeks and lifted her mouth to his, but she slept on, unaware of his touch. Her limp helplessness excited him further. By all heavenly delight, he would be able to do anything to her, and she would not protest!

He dipped his head to her delicious breasts and touched the tip of his tongue to her nipples. They did not bud in response to him; a frown creased his brow. He took her mouth in a demanding kiss and was sorely disappointed when she did not open to him to allow his tongue entrance. No answering pressure met his lips; no arms entwined lovingly about his neck; no gasps or moans of pleasure met his ears. She was rapidly becoming a grave disappointment.

He took her firmly but gently by her shoulders and shook her.

"Wake up, my beauty."

She remained limp, totally unconscious of his urgent voice and hands. Stubbornly he kept trying. He must have her or go mad. The friction of his hardened member against her smooth, supple thigh increased his desire, while her total lack of response to him almost crazed him with frustration.

He increased his efforts, covering her with his body, determined to kiss awake this earthly sleeping beauty. Gem upon gem of his kisses encircled her face, her brow; he kissed one cheek and then the other and then the tip of her nose and eyelids until her face was covered with his offerings, but nothing he did would awaken her. She seemed a beautiful ivory figurine with closed eyes and carved ebony hair.

"Peste!" he swore in fury at himself and at his limp bedmate. He flung himself to his own side of the bed and lay struggling with his desire. Slowly, slowly the red mist of passion cleared from his brain, and he began to see how utterly ridiculous his behavior was. There was no pleasure to be gained in taking advantage of an uncon-

scious female. Love play must be shared to be enjoyed. Like it or not, he had to wait until morning, when they could both enjoy it. He grinned into the darkness. Pleasure for both or neither; it was only fair!

5

Roger awoke to the fragrance of roses. A rush of memories from the previous night made him turn his head upon the pillow to gaze at the exquisite creature beside him. His physical reaction was instant and powerful. He was fiercely aroused and his loins were aching because she had been with him in his dreams. She had been gowned in scarlet, a color he believed suited her nature exactly. Now she was scantily covered with only her raven hair, and her heavy round breasts were thrust out at him, tempting him to touch them, to kiss them. Slowly he eased up on his elbow and bent toward her. He found himself longing to know the color of her eyes and longing also to awaken her with his kiss, as if they were in some fanciful tale. As his head dipped to hers, her eyes flew open and widened in disbelief, and he saw with delight that her eyes were clear gray pools rimmed with lavender. He saw them sparkle with anger, and suddenly, with the clarity of morning light, Roger realized that this was no peasant girl.

Startled and angry to awaken to find herself in bed

with a man, Roseanna screamed and gathered the bed-clothes around her. This action uncovered the man's na-kedness, and her eyes flew down his long, hard body, which was insolent in its masculine splendor. She raised her eyes shamefully to his and saw a face so darkly strong, so fierce and primitive that she thought she was looking at an all-powerful god. His pent-up energy trans-mitted itself to her like a threat. She felt endangered, weak, and wholly at his mercy.

"You beast! What have you done to me?" she cried. His eyes were so dark that night seemed forever locked in them, yet laughter threatened at their brink.

"I have done nothing—yet," he said, smiling. "But I must admit I find you very desirable." He reached out to touch her, but she recoiled as if his hand were a hot iron.

She tried to scramble from the bed; unfortunately, her long hair was caught beneath his body, and she couldn't untangle it without touching his naked flesh.

"Let go of me!" she cried.

He laughed, the rich dark sound sending shivers up her spine. "Not until I've made love to you, my beauty."

She gasped and instantly tore at his face with her nails. In a flash he gripped her wrists and crushed her mouth beneath his. She struggled fiercely but found there was no way she could release herself from his grasp. He impris-oned her in an embrace; she felt small and frail beside his powerful chest and steely muscles. The scent of his body and the pressure of his hard mouth upon hers were aphrodisiacs that ravaged her senses, and she struggled to keep herself from melting into his embrace. What saved her was his rigid hardness thrusting into her thigh. With an age-old instinct of knowing what happens between a man and a woman, she knew he would have her on her

back in another moment, thrusting that rigid hardness
deep within her. Her sharp white teeth closed upon his
bottom lip until she drew blood. He withdrew his mouth
sharply, freeing hers momentarily, and she panted, "I
demand to speak to Baron Ravenspur!"

"Who are you?" he asked, wiping the blood from his
lip.

She lifted her chin and said coolly, "I am Lady Roseanna Castlemaine."

"Who?" he thundered.

"Rose—Roseanna Castlemaine," she repeated, frightened at his tone.

He was on his feet instantly. He pulled on hose, boots,
and doublet and strode to the chamber door. He flung it
open and bellowed, "Tristan!"

The young squire who had been asleep outside the
door clapped his hands over his ears as if he'd been deaf-
ened. Roger cuffed him and said, "Get my brother.
Now!"

He must have graphically communicated Roger's
mood, for Tristan appeared quickly. Roger almost hauled
him through the door. "This is a plot the two of you
cooked up to put my betrothed in my bed so I'll have to
marry her!" he roared.

"Your betrothed?" gasped Tristan.

"Marry me?" shouted Roseanna, who was in a high
rage now that she realized she'd slept with Ravenspur. "I
wouldn't marry you if you were the last man on earth! I
came here yesterday to dissolve this distasteful betrothal
that hangs around my neck like a millstone!"

Roger's eyes narrowed warningly.

"Honestly, Roger, I mistook her for a peasant girl,"
Tristan said.

Roseanna's eyes clouded in anger. "Strange," she said in a menacing tone, "since I told you the moment we met that I was Lady Castlemaine!"

Roger swung around to his brother, who had the decency to look shamefaced. "She speaks the truth."

Hoisting the slipping sheets around her, she said regally, "I always speak the truth. You are two depraved monsters of lechery! Do you not realize the misery your childish little joke has caused? I have been away from home all night. My family will be frantic. When my father learns of my treatment at the hands of you Montfords, he will issue a challenge!"

Roger, ignoring her impassioned words, said to Tristan, "Keep those whores behind locked doors."

Roseanna looked startled. That was why the woman she'd seen yesterday had looked so strange and fascinating—she was a prostitute! My God, men were vile. Is this what they did under the guise of hunting? She was overcome by hatred for them. She wanted to shriek her rage and rake their handsome faces to ribbons, but the elder one would likely fell her with the back of his hand.

"I'll need at least two servingwomen," said Roger.

Tristan shrugged, "There are only—the young ladies from the riding academy," he finished lamely.

Roger gave him such a scorching look, the younger man stepped back.

"I'm going to the kitchen," Ravenspur announced, and then threw over his shoulder, "Stay!" as if they were two dogs.

As soon as Roger left the room, amusement danced into Tristan's eyes. "By God's bones, this is rich! Do you really wish to get out of your betrothal?"

"With all my heart!" she spat.

He grinned wickedly. "Then you'd best not tell your parents you spent the night in his bed."

Roseanna's mouth fell open as she realized she couldn't use that weapon against him.

Roger returned with two women from the kitchens. "This lady needs a maid and a chaperone," he explained to them.

"But yer lordship, I only knows kitchen work," the first woman protested.

Roger said smoothly, "My good woman, I have just promoted you. Find this lady some modest attire. If none can be found, then you will have to stitch something." He turned to the other woman, whose eyes were like saucers at the exalted company. "You will stay with this lady at all times as her chaperone. Under no circumstances is she to be alone for one moment."

Roseanna opened her mouth to protest, but Roger ordered, "Silence!" He turned to Tristan, "I want ten knights for her escort, and by Christ they'd better be sober. See to it!" He issued one last order before he departed. "Be ready to leave by the time I've finished breakfast."

Roseanna gasped at the sheer arrogance of the man. She said to Tristan, "I shall get down on my knees every night and thank God for delivering me from such a union!"

Tristan thought to himself, "Roger will do as he pleases as usual, but if I had any sort of claim on you, I'd never let you slip away."

Roseanna turned to the women and decided to take charge. To the first she said, "I'm cold. Please get one of the squires to light this fire." She turned to the second woman. "While the baron is at breakfast, I too shall dine."

The servants were in a bit of a quandary. They had received orders from Ravenspur to find her clothing and also to chaperone her.

Tristan looked more amused than ever. "It seems two servants aren't enough for you, my lady."

"It seems not," she said coldly.

"Then allow me to be of service. I shall go in search of a gown and shoes. My brother doesn't like to be kept waiting."

"In that case you'd best carry out the orders he gave you to get the escort readied. I assure you, you can be of no service to me, sir."

He bowed mockingly, "Well, that's put me in my place. But somehow I don't think you'll manage Roger quite so easily."

When Ravenspur returned, he found Roseanna curled before the fire, finishing her breakfast. His heavy eyebrows rose in surprise. "Why aren't you dressed?" he demanded.

The serving woman hurried into the chamber with a pair of dainty boots in her hand and a silk dress over her arm. "One of the ladies was kind enough to let me have this, yer lordship," she said breathlessly.

He lifted the low-cut gown disdainfully. "I said *modest* attire!" He threw the dress to the back of the fire. The old woman gasped in horror. "Get some table linen and fashion a gown. I want it to cover her from her chin to her toes. Do I make myself clear, madame?"

Roseanna was bubbling into a froth of fury, and it took all her willpower to stop herself from flinging herself upon him. She had an overwhelming desire to strike him,

and she was teetering dizzily on the edge of attack when
a little voice told her that her best weapon against him
would be feigned indifference. Still, she was determined
to address him in an insolent voice. "Are you finished
giving your orders?"

His dark, assessing eyes swept over her. "I haven't begun. Shall I give you your orders now?" he asked in a
deceptively pleasant voice.

"No one gives me orders, my lord," she informed him.

"That is quite obvious. You are an undisciplined child
who has been allowed to run wild. If your family thinks it
can palm you off onto me, they are sadly mistaken." He
swept her with his dark eyes. "I find most high-born ladies to be shrews and harpies."

"Is that why you consort with prostitutes?" she
shouted.

The servingwomen gasped. His dark eyes looked
deeply into hers for a moment. "It is," he said evenly. He
did not allow himself to smile until he had turned his
back on her. He took one of his cloaks from the wardrobe
and turned to the gaping servants. "I set you both a task;
I want her dressed." Then his gaze settled on Roseanna
once more. "You will need this. Yesterday's storm ended
the summer weather. There is a distinct autumn chill in
the air." He bowed. "I shall await you in the courtyard."

Roseanna surveyed herself with dismay. Never in her
life had she been dressed in such a plain, modest, un-
becoming garment! She pulled off the headcovering as the
servingwomen looked on with pursed lips. Briskly she
braided and looped her long dark hair and bound it back
in a style every bit as plain as the gown. She had been
utterly determined not to wear the cloak he had given

her, but the thought of facing ten knights dressed as she was made her change her mind. She wrapped the cloak around herself and lifted its great length from about her ankles so that she would not trip. Emerging from the hunting lodge, she walked with her head held high past the ten mounted knights who would act as her escort. Ravenspur led out two horses, his eyes glinting with amusement. "If you are afraid of horses, my lady, I will take you up before me."

"Afraid?" she choked, and words failed her. He had offered her the final insult! She mounted with the sleek, supple movements of a panther, wheeled the animal about, and took off at such a reckless speed that the men had difficulty keeping up. Roger enjoyed himself. Everything about her delighted him.

It soon dawned on Roseanna that she did not know the way home, so she had to swallow her pride and allow Ravenspur to take the lead. They did not exchange one word or one look on that long ride home, yet no man or woman had ever been more acutely aware of each other. Her thoughts were wild and disordered. He was a barbarian, a devil! She had conceived an instant disgust for the man. He was too arrogant, too virile, too—male!

She shuddered at the narrow escape she had had, not only from this morning, but from a lifetime tied to him by a Gordian knot. Sensations teemed through her body —indignation, smoldering anger, and relief, as well as strange blossoming sensations that darted through her body in the most extraordinary fashion. Imagine! Marriage with Ravenspur would submerge a woman's very soul, so dominant would he be. Her spirit would be vanquished. Whenever he willed it, she would be in the bondage of his arms! He was obviously a much-practiced womanizer, used to having his way. Well, she was the exception to the rule. She was one woman who would never give him the chance to have his way. Although some women might find him attractive, she did not!

Roger's thoughts chased each other about, preventing him from thinking logically. He was cynical enough to suspect a trick and angry that she and his brother had tried to use him, but he was also deeply relieved that he had not ravaged her. Although he was outraged that she was running around the countryside unchaperoned, he was nevertheless bemused by her saucy allure. All in all she was a magnificent, though unusual, piece of baggage!

When they came in sight of Castlemaine, they were met by a posse consisting of her father and his men-at-arms. Neville looked haggard.

"Thank God you are safe. I've had men out all night."

"I'm sorry, Father," Roseanna said. "I went to Belvoir to see Baron Ravenspur. I should have told you where I was going." She seethed as Neville thanked Roger for returning his daughter safely. She wanted to scream aloud that he had bedded her so that her father would draw his sword and run the bastard through. But she clamped her teeth down hard on her tongue to ward off the specter of marriage.

Neville thought of Joanna. She would be annoyed to be caught unprepared for a visit from Ravenspur. Neville knew what high hopes she had for this union, and he also knew how slender was the thread that bound the great baron to Roseanna. "Allow me to offer the hospitality of Castlemaine to you and your men, my lord."

Roger held up his hand. "I will not stay. Today I merely act as escort. But I shall accept your hospitality and return at the end of the week to discuss the betrothal."

Neville nodded his head. As usual, Roseanna had taken matters into her own hands. There would be no peace for him at Castlemaine tonight. Joanna would run mad when she learned what Roseanna had been up to.

In Castlemaine's hall, Joanna was taken completely off guard when Roseanna flew past her to her turret room and she found herself curtsying low to Roger Montford. They had known each other years ago; Roger and King Edward had been companions since they were twelve and had trained together under Warwick. Joanna's thoughts flew back to those days. How they had swaggered in their scarlet livery with its golden bear and ragged staff! Warwick trained his men to be a breed apart. They knew at least half a dozen more ways of killing a man in close combat than any other fighting men did. Warwick instilled in them the confidence that grew with the development of their own capabilities. With his motto, *"Seulement Un,"* he taught men absolute reliance upon themselves.

Roger's stance before her now was wary but regal. He looked like a conqueror—darkly primitive and savage— and he was as proud as Lucifer. *No wonder the women run after him,* she thought with awe. She firmly smothered her own physical response to him because she knew she was playing for high stakes. She wanted him for her daughter. "Welcome, my lord. We are honored by your visit."

"Perhaps you will not think me welcome when I have had my say." He fixed her with his dark eyes. "I am shocked at the amount of freedom Lady Roseanna is allowed. While our betrothal stands, I wish a closer guard of her person. I shall return at week's end to discuss dissolving it."

Joanna looked affronted. "On what possible grounds could you dissolve it, my lord?"

"Many! For one thing, is she still a maid? At seventeen most girls are not." He looked her directly in the eyes, and she knew he was referring to the fact that she had not been a virgin at seventeen. Beneath his knowing gaze, she swallowed the scathing retort that jumped to her lips. He continued. "And quite apart from my feelings in the matter, Lady Roseanna herself wishes it dissolved. It is the reason she sought me out."

Joanna's mouth fell open.

Ravenspur bowed low, turned on his heel, and departed. The ring of his golden spurs upon the stone steps shattered the hush that had fallen. The moment he stepped out through the portal, Joanna gave vent to a high rage.

Neville cautioned, "Don't go to her now. Allow your temper to cool, I beg you, Joanna." She swept past him, but he noted with relief that she went in the direction of her work studio. He sighed heavily. He must get word of Roseanna's return to Jeffrey, who had taken out another search party.

6

Roseanna sat in a soft ivory underdress as Alice brushed the tangles from her long hair. Joanna burst into the chamber without ceremony, with Kate Kendall at her heels.

"Mother, before you say anything, let me explain a few things," began Roseanna.

"No, let me explain a few things. I am replacing Alice with Kate Kendall. Since you need a keeper, I've chosen one you won't be able to twist around your little finger. You will wear this, and Kate will have charge of the key."

Roseanna looked with disbelief at the object her mother held out to her. "A maidenbelt? Mother, you cannot be serious?"

"I've never been more serious in my life. Ravenspur questioned your virginity!"

"He what?" hissed Roseanna as white-hot hatred seared through her. "That whoremaster dared question my virginity? In the name of Christ, what has it to do with him?"

" 'Tis his way of slipping out of the betrothal. An excuse you've handed him on a golden platter by running about the countryside like a wild thing!"

"He needs no excuse. *I* demand that the betrothal be dissolved!"

"You, little madame, will stop demanding and start obeying. You will wear this maidenbelt to ensure your purity. You cannot deny you have been making calf's eyes at Sir Bryan."

"Why would I deny it?" she cried. "I am in love with him. I want to marry him!"

"My God, you are afflicted with temporary insanity. Let's hope it runs its course by the time Ravenspur returns. At which time I will do my utmost to mend this breach."

"It can never be mended!" cried Roseanna passionately. "We already detest each other!"

"There is a very fine line between love and hate. As long as he is not indifferent to you, all can yet be saved. Put that on."

"I will not!" hissed Roseanna.

"Kendall, take her legs," directed Joanna. Although Roseanna kicked and scratched and swore and cried, in the end she was locked into the maidenbelt.

"Cry all you want. Roseanna, as your mother, I must take this action to protect you from your own foolishness. Damn it, do you think you invented infatuation? It has followed the same pattern for centuries. When a young boy and girl become infatuated, they hold hands and sigh. Then they kiss, and next comes a French kiss. If you return that kiss, you are saying, 'I like it—carry on.' You give him permission to develop twelve pairs of hands, which he will instantly use to undress you and take possession of your body."

Roseanna was white-lipped with shock. "You are the slut, Mother, not I! Leave my chamber! I will never forgive you," she whispered.

"I think you'd best dine up here tonight. You are not fit company for the hall," declared Joanna.

"I will not leave this chamber until this *thing* is removed from my body. I will not eat one mouthful of food until this *thing* is removed from my body. I will not speak ever again until this *thing* is removed from my body!"

Her mother ignored her and pushed the two servants ahead of her out of the room. The moment the door was closed, Roseanna turned the key in the lock with an ominous click, and heavy silence enfolded her.

Roseanna lay on her bed and stared at the ceiling, but her mind was busy with a hundred little details. Her mother had designed this ridiculous maidenbelt in her workshop. It was made of two heavy silver chains that went around the waist and a flat piece of silver mesh, very like chain mail, that went between her legs. It had a small lock at the waist. She suddenly remembered a small lock and key that her mother had given her to secure her jewel casket. When she tried the key on the maidenbelt and it unlocked the contraption, she sighed with great relief.

Next she gathered together a store of food. She had a bowl of apples; in one of her coffers she found a bag of walnuts and hazelnuts; and on her bedside table she had a large box of sweetmeats made from marzipan. She also had a jug of water, and a flask of wine; she could go for two or three days at least. She would make them all sorry!

Her eyes fell on the cloak Ravenspur had given her. She snatched it up with the intention of rending it to shreds, but with the first tear came a subtle scent. She rubbed the cloth between her fingers reflectively and lifted it to her nose, wondering what its fragrance was. She picked up a little volume that always gave her pleasure on the language of flowers. Balsam was for impatience. As she read it, she could smell the balsam. She smiled as she read that broom was for neatness; how apt. The white lily stood for purity. Her mind wandered briefly to the maidenbelt. Dead leaves represented sadness, which was sensible when you thought about it. Jasmine . . . jasmine! That's what his cloak smelled of. Quickly she ran her finger across the page to see what it meant. Sensuality! She shut the book with a little snap. She visualized his dark eyes and the thick black lashes and brows that intensified his gaze. She closed her eyes to dispel the image, but it only became sharper. His jaw was so aggressive, his mouth so frankly sensual, that she blushed at the memory. His naked body rose up before her, so real that she could almost reach out and touch him. Lord, why ever was she having such wicked thoughts? She could see him and smell him—aye, she could even taste his kiss upon her mouth. His rich, dark laughter came back to her, making her spine tingle; the very danger of the man filled the room, so tangible was her memory of him. Again she tasted his blood on her lips when she had bitten him, and she shivered with excitement. *Damn Ravenspur to hell,* she thought savagely. He was the root of all her misery!

When Kate Kendall knocked on the door, she ignored it. The woman called through it, "I've brought your supper." Roseanna didn't respond. "Don't be a silly lass. Ye must eat." Again receiving no response, the sensible north-country woman decided to leave the tray outside the door. No doubt as soon as she left, Roseanna would eat.

Her face was grim two hours later when she returned to find the tray untouched. She bent close to the door and called, "Roseanna!" There was no response. She put her ear to the door and listened for a few minutes, but there was only silence. She did not report this to Lady Joanna. No doubt by the time breakfast arrived Roseanna would be ravenous.

Very early the next morning, Roseanna's attention was caught by a piercing whistle from outside. She went to the window and saw her brother Jeffrey below, accompanied by Sir Bryan. Quickly she picked up a piece of paper and wrote,

Please don't worry about me. Ravenspur will give us no trouble. We hated each other on sight! I've locked myself in because of a disagreement with my mother. I beg you not to worry about me. Roseanna.

She folded the note tightly, wrote "Sir Bryan" on the outside, and threw it from the high turret down to the young men below. Jeffrey stooped to retrieve it and handed it to Sir Bryan. Then he winked at her and waved his hand in approval.

When Kate Kendall found Roseanna's breakfast tray undisturbed outside her chamber door where she had left it, she knew she must inform Lady Joanna. But Joanna was still annoyed at her daughter's behavior the day before; this only fanned the flames of her grievance. She came to the turret and rattled the doorknob, ordering, "Open this door at once!" There was no reply. "Roseanna, I have had enough theatrics! Open the door." Still Roseanna didn't respond. "Very well, madame, two can play this game! Kate, you are not to bring any more food up here today. By tomorrow there will undoubtedly be an improvement in her appetite."

Joanna did not discuss her daughter's behavior with her husband. He had a knack for making her feel as if she were in the wrong, and in this instance she knew she was not. She had plenty to keep her busy. Ravenspur would return the day after tomorrow, and everything must be perfect for his visit. She had the maids clean and plenish the best bedchamber, overlooking no detail. Even the candles were scented with pine, and the bed linen was embroidered with the initial R.

The next day when Joanna ascended to the turret, she was ready to make some concessions if Roseanna was. "Roseanna, open the door, and we will discuss our differences like civilized human beings." Roseanna kept silent. "Kate Kendall is here with the key to the chastity belt," she tempted. Silence. Her anger rose again. If there was one thing this mother and daughter shared, it was stubborn pride. "If you are willing to harm yourself by starving just to punish me, then so be it!" she said with suppressed fury. As Joanna walked away, Roseanna pressed her ear to the door and heard her mother say to Kendall, "What am I to do? Ravenspur comes tomorrow!"

Roseanna smiled. She had been on the verge of opening the door, for she was truly longing for a substantial meal. But now she realized that if she held out until tomorrow, the showdown would be postponed until Ravenspur arrived.

* * *

Roger dressed with great care for his visit to Castle-maine. He rejected the clothes he wore at Court; they were too flamboyant for his taste. The tight silk hose had to be lined with heavy satin, which molded and exaggerated his manhood to the point of indecency. The doublets that were being worn were shorter and shorter to display to advantage everything a man possessed. He passed over these peacock-colored garments and chose sober black hose and boots and a wide-shouldered wine velvet doublet. His fine lawn shirt boasted lace at the neck and cuffs, but then, he would have been hard pressed to find a plain shirt in his entire wardrobe. He wore a large ruby on one hand and a heavy gold seal ring with a cruel-looking spurred raven on the other.

Ever since he'd returned her to Castlemaine, Roseanna had been with him constantly, almost as if she were haunting him, he thought grimly. The images his mind conjured of her were so vivid, he could almost reach out and touch her cream velvet skin, and when he was abed, he could swear he actually felt her long tresses trailing across his nakedness to inflame his desires. He should have made love to her while he had her in his bed and gotten her out of his system! Then he blanched at the thought of being charged with rape. Again.

He had forced himself to relive the nightmare of his first two marriages so that he would run like a scalded cock from even the hint of a third wife.

Now, fortified with the company of ten knights, he rode forth to Castlemaine, secure in the knowledge that by this time tomorrow he would be free of her.

Sir Neville met his visitors at the stables, where Raven-spur and his men were attending their own horses. A knight worthy of the name usually did this rather than leave it to others, since so many times his life depended upon his mount. Neville, noting that Ravenspur's black stallion was almost identical to Zeus, showed off the animal to his guest. Roger was so impressed with the sleek, wild creature that he offered to buy it.

Neville shook his head and laughed. "Nay, my lord, he is my daughter's favorite. However, I'm sure we have other animals here that meet your high standards. My daughter is an expert when it comes to horse breeding."

Although keenly interested in learning of Roseanna's expertise with horses, Ravenspur was nevertheless alarmed. "You don't allow her to ride this wild animal?"

"My lord, I cannot stop her," said Neville mildly.

Ravenspur's dark eyes searched the other man's face. Then he said quietly, "I see."

"Lady Joanna eagerly awaits you in the hall. I'm sure she is better prepared for your visit today. I'll show your men to their quarters."

"Thank you, Castlemaine. I'll visit your stables again before I leave."

Joanna greeted Roger effusively. She was regally gowned in a deep royal blue tunic and underdress that attractively showed off her blue-black hair. She wore a jeweled posy cap, but no veil was in sight. Like Roseanna, she was inordinately proud of her hair and covered as little of it as possible.

Ravenspur bowed formally and without hesitation said, "Lady Joanna, before we discuss the betrothal, I wish to speak privately with Lady Roseanna."

"Certainly, my lord." She smiled brilliantly, wondering wildly whatever she was going to do. "Kate," she called brightly, "inform Roseanna that Baron Ravenspur has arrived. Come, my lord. I will show you to your chamber. You know how long it takes young girls to complete their toilet these days."

He knew immediately that something was wrong. It was unlike Joanna to be so fluttery. And the look she had exchanged with her servingwoman spoke volumes.

He was pleased with the richly appointed chamber she had plenished for him. Joanna immediately poured them two goblets of her best Chablis. As he sipped the wine, he was alert to the signs of her agitation as she made animated small talk. Finally, Kate Kendall arrived. Her plain features were set in grim lines. She parroted the words she had been rehearsing ever since she had been met with silence at the turret-room door. She was worried to death, in actuality; the child's safety meant more to her than Joanna's desire to save face in front of the baron. "Lady Roseanna begs to be excused today. Perhaps tomorrow," she said vaguely.

Joanna's lips tightened. "Go back and tell her she will not be excused, Kate. I insist that she come down."

Ravenspur added, "Explain that I wish to have a word with her in private and that it won't take more than a moment."

The servant bobbed a brief curtsey and went on her hopeless mission. As soon as Roseanna learned that Ravenspur had returned and wished to see her, she hurriedly put on the maidenbelt. Her mischievous heart leaped, and her wicked juices bubbled with anticipation as she slipped into a fawn-colored underdress, exquisitely embroidered with stalks of wheat, that she'd purposely chosen because it emphasized the pallor of her skin. Satisfied with her ethereal appearance, Roseanna was ready to indulge in the very theatrics her mother had accused her of.

When Kate returned to her mistress, she said plainly and simply, "I can get no response."

Joanna set her empty goblet down with a bang. "I'll handle her," she said with determination. Indeed, if Roseanna refused to open the door this time, she would send for Neville and have the door forced open. How dare her daughter show her up before the baron?

As soon as Joanna had left, Ravenspur turned to Kate Kendall. "What is upsetting you so much, ma'am?"

Flattered to be so addressed by such an exalted personage, she expelled her breath and proved the old adage that when under stress, women confess. "Oh, my lord, Lady Roseanna has been locked in her room all week without food."

"Good God!" he exclaimed, and strode out of the room and up the staircase that led to the turret. Taking Joanna firmly by the shoulders, he removed her from the doorway. "I had no idea you would punish her, madame," he said coldly.

Joanna's eyes widened in disbelief. "She is punishing me, sir, I would have you know!"

He pitted his great strength against the door by wedging his foot firmly beside the lock and kicking with all his might. At the first loud thud Roseanna fell to the floor in a very appealing faint. At the third kick the lock gave, and the door swung in to reveal the small, limp figure. Roger was on his knees instantly, his hands upon her body searching for signs of warmth and life. His fingers encountered the metal chastity belt. He raised condemning eyes to Joanna and said, "I would never have believed a mother could be this cruel!" He lifted the delicate girl and strode from the turret room down to his own chamber; Joanna followed him.

With eyes tightly closed and heart hammering wildly, Roseanna knew she had aroused his vow of knighthood to protect with his life a maiden in distress. Good God, she'd gone too far, as usual. Somehow she had to find a way to make herself unattractive to him.

Gently, he laid her upon his bed and chaffed her hands. He poured her a little Chablis and lifted it to her pale lips.

She opened her eyes slowly and said weakly, "Where . . . am I?"

"You wicked girl! Stop this play-acting at once!" demanded Joanna.

Ravenspur turned on her instantly. "Outside! I want to be alone with her." His eyes blazed with such dark fire, that she dared not goad him further. She swept past him, taking Kate with her. Very well, Joanna thought angrily, the little wildcat could face him alone. They deserved each other!

"Roseanna, are you feeling strong enough to talk to me?" he asked.

Instinct told her that she would get more from this man by appealing to his chivalrous heart than by making demands.

"Whatever have you done to provoke your mother to such extremes?" he asked gently.

She allowed one tear to slip down her cheek. "It's because we wish to dissolve the betrothal, and"—she spoke softly, but passionately—"because . . . I love—another."

A frown came between his heavy brows. "Who?" he demanded; some of the gentleness had left his voice.

She shook her head woefully. "Alas, I cannot tell his name. He would suffer greater punishment than I."

"Is this why she's forced you into the maidenbelt?" he asked, his eyes holding hers.

He was no longer carrying her, but the closeness of his body to hers reminded her of his great strength. She lowered her eyes. She knew the question that hovered in his mind as if he had spoken it aloud, and she also knew that her fate rested on the answer she gave to that question. Suddenly, brilliantly, she knew how to free herself from this man, knew how to devalue herself in his eyes. "The maidenbelt was in vain. I am no longer a virgin," she lied, and the intimate words stained her cheeks a delicate pink.

His eyes clouded with anger. He got up and took a turn around the room as if he were trapped in a place too small for his great vitality.

Holding her breath, she waited for him to repudiate her and hoped his anger would not explode into violence. Slowly, he turned to face her. "I have decided not to dissolve the betrothal. I have decided to take you for my wife."

"No!" she cried, aghast, springing up from the bed.

His dark eyes narrowed. "For one so close to starvation, you have amazing recuperative powers! Why do you prefer a union with the other man? Has he gotten you with child? Do you need an abortifacient?" he shouted.

"How dare you?" With all of her strength she slapped his cheek.

He grabbed her wrist and held it in a cruel, ironlike vise until she thought he would snap the fragile bones.

"I dare do anything, Roseanna Castlemaine—never doubt it! I dare strip you and verify your virginity or lack of it this very moment. Now you will apologize for slapping me." His dark eyes bored into hers as if he were reading her thoughts.

She pursed her lips stubbornly and kept silent.

"When you do that with your lips, I don't know if you want to kiss me or spit on me," he said with glittering eyes. Seeing her eyes darken with anger, he dipped his head to take possession of the lips that seemed to have been fashioned solely for his kisses. He held her mouth firmly with his, not wanting to give her the opportunity to bite him again.

She had the same inflaming effect on him that she'd had the night he'd found her in his bed: He was like iron, erect and ready. He pressed against her softness so she would have no doubts about his desires. His kiss took and took and took, plundering her mouth, deeper and deeper while one hand cupped her round, full breast, his thumb stroking her nipple until it hardened like a diamond. His scent of jasmine made her dizzy, and where their bodies touched, her nerve endings burned with a mixture of pain and pleasure that she'd never before felt. He let her go, and she backed away, rubbing her wrists to restore circulation.

"Why are you doing this? Why do you insist on having me?" The fine-spun robe seemed to shiver against her breasts as they rose and fell with her great agitation.

He pulled his gaze from her breasts and looked into her eyes. "We are pledged. 'Tis as simple as that."

As she looked at him, she knew him for a man who made his own rules. He wouldn't keep a pledge unless it suited his own purpose. "There must be other reasons. Tell me!"

As he looked at her, he thought her beauty magnificent. He wanted to rip the filmy gown from her body, lay her back upon the bed, and fuck with her all night. Her eyes blazed defiantly. She wanted none of him and made no bones about it. The challenge she offered was impossible for Ravenspur to resist!

He smiled, and it reached all the way from his sensual mouth to his night-dark eyes. "We are two of a kind, Roseanna. You will make me happy."

"I will make you wretched!" she vowed.

The evening went surprisingly well for a day that had
begun so disastrously. Kate Kendall's motherly qualities
came to the fore as she took charge of Roseanna. She
gave her the key to the maidenbelt, helped her bathe, put
her to bed, and brought her a tray that held broth, calf's-
foot jelly, and restorative egg custard. When Roseanna
wrinkled her nose and asked for roast boar, the good
woman was off to the kitchens at double speed.

In the hall, seated between his host and his hostess,
Roger Montford broached the subject of their daughter
before the first course was served.

"Sir Neville, I formally request your daughter's hand
in marriage."

Sir Neville, ignorant of the day's details and the week's
events, gave his wife a congratulatory look and wondered
how she had pulled it off.

Utterly surprised but nonetheless delighted with the
turn of events, Joanna picked up her goblet and raised it
to Ravenspur. "My lord, let me be the first to congratu-
late you. I offer a toast to Roger and Roseanna."

If Ravenspur noticed that two young knights sitting farther down the table did not respond to the toast, he gave no sign of it. Joanna rapidly calculated when the best time would be for the marriage to take place. Harvest was almost upon them; since Roseanna was stubbornly opposed to the match, she would need time to be brought around. Christmas was a festive time of the year when everyone was free to celebrate and indulge; if the wedding were then, the months between would give them time to sew Roseanna a spectacular trousseau.

"I think Christmastide is lovely for a wedding, my lord."

Ravenspur frowned. "The betrothal has already been overlong."

Joanna hastened to suggest November eleventh. "Martinmas, then?"

His frown deepened. "I thought next week, but perhaps I am precipitate. Let's say the first day of Autumn."

"But September twenty-first is less than a month away," she pointed out. When she saw his brow slant like the wing of a raven, however, she acquiesced. "We will be hard pressed, but I will see that all is ready."

"Sir Neville, Lady Joanna, please don't think I am being difficult, but it will be impossible to have the wedding here. The King wants me in the North, where there is unrest," he explained shortly.

Joanna's eyes went quickly to his. "There's trouble between Edward and Warwick, isn't there? Men's ambitions! I told Edward he would make a mortal enemy of Warwick if he offered Warwick's daughters husbands from the hated Woodville tribe."

Since Joanna seemed to know the King's business, Roger was free to speak of it. "I suppose that is at the bottom of it. Warwick wants no less than both the King's brothers to marry his daughters."

She replied, "It is a great wonder to me that Edward refused him; he is too easygoing."

"Easygoing, perhaps, but a fool he is not. If Warwick got George for his son-in-law, the kingmaker would be at it again."

Sir Neville was aghast. "You mean he would pull Edward from the throne and set up George as King?"

"Let us not even speak of treason," warned Ravenspur.

"Warwick holds the North in the palm of his hand," worried Joanna.

"That's why I go north, madame. I have three strongholds. Ravenglass in the west, Ravensworth in the center, and Ravenscar in the east."

"You wish the wedding that far north?" asked Joanna.

"Nay. The King goes to York shortly. I think York would be best," he decided.

Joanna smiled complacently. York, Edward, and the King's Court. How fitting!

Ravenspur turned to Sir Neville. "Allow yourself at least three days for the journey to York. I know you have ample men-at-arms, sir, but I will send thirty of my own men to assure safe escort."

Ravenspur departed at dawn, so when Roseanna came downstairs to break her fast, he and his men were long gone. She let her mother and her women, including Alice and Kate, chatter on incessantly about the wedding details. An air of such urgency had befallen the household that they even seemed to speak more rapidly; their brains were even ahead of their tongues as they planned for the wedding.

Roseanna was totally unconcerned with it all, for she had no intention of going through with these particular nuptials. She cast Sir Bryan a devastating smile and knew he would follow her out into the orchard.

"Sweetheart, I've been nearly mad. Jeffrey has kept me informed as best he could, but last night when I had to sit and listen to Ravenspur's wedding plans, I almost committed murder."

"Bryan, Ravenspur's wedding plans and mine have nothing in common," she assured him.

"You daydream, Roseanna. Your parents have agreed to it all," he said miserably.

"Bryan, do you wish to marry me or not?" she demanded.

"You know I do!" he swore with fervor.

"Then we'll elope!" she said, laughing.

"Run away?" he questioned. "Where? How?"

"We will make plans. What did you intend we should do?" she prompted.

"I—I didn't think. It seemed so hopeless."

"You mean you were going to let me go to him?" she asked incredulously.

"Of course not," he hastened.

"We could go to your home at Marston Moor. Oh, I know! We'll elope across the border. It's easier to get married under Scottish law."

"Yes, yes. Then I'll go back into service with the King's brother," he said, as if just coming to that decision.

"Jeffrey will help us. Don't trust a note with anyone else," she cautioned, "not even Alice."

"Roseanna—Ravenspur didn't touch you, did he?"

She wondered what he would do if he knew she had

shared a bed with Ravenspur. Instantly, blushes suffused her neck and cheeks. She shook her head, and he was satisfied. Later, the errant thought came to her that Ravenspur wanted her, virgin or not; she wondered if the same could be said for Sir Bryan. She dismissed the thought as unmaidenly and vowed to put all thoughts of Ravenspur out of her mind permanently. But it proved to be more difficult than she had imagined, for it seemed that each night when sleep claimed her, Ravenspur was there, beckoning her, luring her, tempting her, and in her dreams she did not resist him. Of course, she had no control over her dreams, she reminded herself.

As Roseanna made her secret plans, she knew that the first thing they would need was money. She selected certain pieces of her jewelry to take into Nottingham to sell. She mustn't go too soon or the goldsmith would recognize Joanna's work, and he would have time to inform her mother that he had bought the pieces from her daughter. She patiently stood for hours while new gowns, underdresses, tunics, and tabards were designed and fitted. She tried not to take pleasure in the pale peacock silk with gray fox fur edging the sleeves, or in the mauve velvet embroidered with silver thread, for she knew she would have room to pack only one change of clothes for her furtive journey north.

She went to her brother's chamber; she had a special request of him. "Jeffrey, I want some of your clothes."

He looked her up and down and grinned. "You forget, I've grown. My clothes would drown you."

"Dolt! I mean clothes my size from when you were twelve or thirteen."

"I'll see if I can find where Kate has them stored. Come back tomorrow night for a dress rehearsal."

As it turned out, the entire day was like a dress rehearsal for Roseanna. The material for the wedding gown had arrived, and even she had to admit that it was breathtaking. It was white satin with white roses embroidered overall. White on white. It was symbolic of the white rose of York.

Joanna designed the gown along traditional lines with a train and long-trailing sleeves. Roseanna stood for hours, turning this way and that as the gown was pinned, tucked, and sewn. When she finally removed it and handed it over to her mother's sewing women, she felt a pang of regret that she would not be able to wear it on her wedding day, for it was truly exquisite. Later, in Jeffrey's chamber she selected a linen shirt, a mulberry-colored doublet, and a pair of tight black hose. She quite looked forward to wearing the nonrestrictive hose for riding. She caught sight of Jeffrey's cheeky grin as he asked, "But brat, whatever will you do about your hair and your —er, other female accoutrements?"

She snatched a velvet cap from the trunk. "I'm not passing myself off as a man; it will just be easier to travel this way."

A low knock came on the door, and Jeffrey opened it for Sir Bryan. Roseanna turned to her brother. "Oh, bless you, Jeffrey. I'll never forget your support and kindness to me. Bryan, what do you think? Should we travel by night and rest by day?"

"Nay, night-riding is fine for a short run, but my home is nearly seventy miles from here. We'll rest easy there before we go to Scotland."

"I think we should stay overnight at the abbeys where they take in travelers."

"Well, it will be cheaper than inns. I haven't much money," he apologized.

"I have enough for the journey, Bryan. We'll be all right."

He took her hands and gazed at her with loving eyes. "You are a wonder. You risk everything for me."

"And you do the same for me, Bryan."

He enfolded her in his embrace. "How am I to wait until we are wed?" he whispered.

She lifted her half-parted mouth to his and wished he would not wait. She wished he were more reckless; then she realized that he put her first and that she must be grateful for it.

Jeffrey produced a ragged map, and the three of them pored over it for long minutes. Finally, after waiting for his decision, which didn't come, Roseanna said, "We'll stay at Welbeck Abbey the first night. That's only twenty miles from here. That way we won't have to go at first light. If we went very early, they would soon discover me gone and it would give them a full day to search for me. If we leave after the midday meal, they'll think I've gone riding. By the time I have not returned, darkness will be nigh, and they won't be able to search."

The two young men exchanged glances. "You are marvelously devious, Roseanna," said Jeffrey.

"Thank you," she said, inordinately pleased with the compliment.

"If we can get to Selby Abbey by the next night, that's only seventeen or eighteen miles from my home," said Sir Bryan.

Jeffrey wore the doublet with the Black Bull badge of the Duke of Clarence on the sleeve. "When you take service with George, I will join you," he reaffirmed to Bryan.

"Why don't you come with us?" asked Roseanna.

"Nay—whoever heard of three on an elopement?" he teased. "I'll help take suspicion off Bryan. I'll tell them he's gone to London; then they'll search south instead of north."

She looked up at Sir Bryan and thought for the hundredth time that he was almost beautiful. He looked so open and honest, so sweet and gentle. "I think we should go day after tomorrow, if we are all in agreement." The two knights once again exchanged significant looks as if congratulating each other; then all three offered their hands in a silent pledge.

Roseanna in doublet and hose rode Zeus north and met Sir Bryan at Newark, as previously arranged. She had not worried unduly that she could bid no one good-bye, for she knew that once she was wed to Sir Bryan and it was a fait accompli, her family would forgive her and welcome her back into its bosom. Then she would pick up Mecca, the Arabian that the King had given her, and a few of the others that she had specially bred. It would be added income to keep on with the horse breeding.

Their hearts high with their daring adventure, they smiled into each other's eyes every time they looked at each other. The pair of riders who looked like two youths from a distance caused no comment. They covered the twenty miles easily and arrived at Welbeck Abbey long before the gates were closed for the night. They saw to the feeding and watering of their own mounts and were given bread and cheese for their meal; then they were

assigned two cell-like rooms that were very small. Each
had whitewashed walls and an iron cot.

Roseanna knew Sir Bryan would not come to her. A
monastery filled with monks was not conducive to romance. She fell asleep anticipating the adventure that
would be theirs on the morrow. She could hardly wait!

As the steel-gray light of day dawned, her heart sank:
it was raining. When she looked outside, she realized that
raining was not the precise word for it. It was coming
down in bucketfuls and the air was icy, making her shiver
and shrink into her cloak.

Sir Bryan was hesitant. "Perhaps we shouldn't venture
out in such cursed weather."

"Don't say *cursed*. Keep thinking luck is with us.
Don't worry about me," she said on a cheerful note, "I'll
keep up."

The day was as dismal as it had promised to be, and
the whole of the landscape was the color of a drowned
rat. The rain kept on against a sky of lead. Sir Bryan's
horse seemed to flag in the afternoon. Roseanna knew
Zeus could stand a faster pace, but Bryan's horse did not
have the stamina, and she schooled Zeus to the slower
speed.

The rain had soaked entirely through their clothing
hours before and was now doing its damnedest to seep
into their bones. The horses and the riders were all
weary, hungry, and low in spirit when they finally rode
into the yard of Selby Abbey. There was such a crush of
men and horses there ahead of them that they were immediately alerted. They dismounted and sheltered their
horses for a few minutes and saw that the travelers were
mostly King's men on their way to York.

Roseanna pulled the velvet cap low and kept her head

down. Then she saw a badge with a raven on it and knew
some of the men must be Ravenspur's. "We cannot stay
here," she told Bryan desperately.

" 'Tis filled anyway. I doubt if we'll make it to York
tonight. The gates would be closed even if my mount
could make it."

"Here's money. You'll have to buy it some food and let
it rest a little. Then we'll press on until we come to an
inn. Zeus will have to wait. I don't want any of these men
to recognize me."

She leaned against one of the abbey's outbuildings,
knowing she had never been so cold and miserable in her
life. Was it only yesterday that running away had seemed
such a high adventure? In less than twenty-four hours it
had turned into a nightmare. The very elements were
against them. She shook herself mentally. Thinking that
way brought defeat. A thing could be savored all the
more if it was hard won.

When they led their mounts from the abbey courtyard,
the light that was left in the day was fading quickly.
Roseanna wondered if Sir Bryan was feeling as dispirited
as she herself was. They galloped the Great North Road
in silence and occasionally other riders passed them by at
a faster gallop. Just outside York was a large hostelry
known as The Fighting Cocks. They stabled their horses
and paid for feed, then gave them a good rubdown before
they even thought of themselves. The stables were filled
to capacity, and they knew the inn would be crowded.
The innkeeper shook his head at their request for rooms
but took pity on their drenched and sorry condition and
told them they could get warm in the common room and
probably get a bite to eat. The common room was busy
with men eating and drinking, dicing, and laughing. The

atmosphere was thick with smoke and cooking odors, but it was dry and warm.

"Are you all right, love?" asked Bryan, his face pale with dark circles beneath his eyes.

She nodded her head, too weary to speak.

"I'll go and get food for us. I'll try to push my way to the front of the crowd."

"I'll sit here in the corner," she murmured wearily, hoping no one would notice that she was a female. Her eyelids began to close in the smoky warmth. Suddenly an outside door was thrown open, and half a dozen fully armed men strode into the room. The tallest man swept off his cloak. The rain ran from it and pooled onto the floor. Roseanna shrank back in alarm. It was Ravenspur!

Six men-at-arms surrounded Sir Bryan as he approached her with a steaming dish of mutton stew.

"Sir Bryan," boomed Ravenspur, "I thank you for escorting Lady Roseanna to me. I see you have kept her safe."

Sir Bryan opened his mouth, saw the mailed fists of the men-at-arms poised over their sword hilts, and stammered, "Y-yes, my lord."

Roseanna, looking for all the world like a small drowned cat, took a defiant step forward. "He was not escorting me to you, Ravenspur!"

"Really?" he asked in a deceptively mild tone, his heavy brows slanting upward. "What other explanation could there be, pray? Think well on your answer, for his life may depend on it."

Her mind flew about for an answer that would absolve Bryan from Ravenspur's vengeance. "He was escorting me to the King at York. I am going to beg Edward to dissolve our betrothal," she said triumphantly, pleased at her own quick thinking.

He bowed so low, it was a mockery. "I shall escort you to Edward myself." He saw her fatigue. "I think tomorrow will be soon enough. We'll take rooms here."

"There are none left, my lord," ventured Sir Bryan, swallowing hard.

"Nonsense," said Roger affably. "Thank you again for escorting my bride. I will look after her now. Innkeeper, I'll need three of your better rooms." He turned to Sir Bryan. "You don't mind sharing with my men?"

The young knight swallowed hard again and murmured, "Thank you, my lord."

They were ushered upstairs by the innkeeper's wife. The men-at-arms went into one room, and Ravenspur entered Roseanna's room with her. He swept the room with a critical eye, then fished a gold coin from his belt and gave it to the woman.

"My lady will need a hot bath. Build up the fire, and I'd be obliged if you could find her a warm bedgown and a girl to help her dry her hair. When you bring supper, fetch us each a bottle of your best wine."

"Yes, my lord." She bobbed as if it were her great privilege to serve him.

Roseanna resented his high rank that made innkeepers fawn over him. Yet in truth she was grateful for the warmth. A burly servant entered and dragged a wooden tub into the room; then a serving maid brought a flannelette bedgown and a pile of towels. Roseanna stood silently while the tub was filled with buckets of hot water. She longed to sink down before the blazing fire, but her pride would not allow her to unbend before Ravenspur.

He glanced at her stiff figure and admonished, "Get out of those wet clothes."

Her eyes blazed. "I am not witless, Lord Ravenspur. When you have removed your unwanted presence, I shall do so."

He refused to be goaded by her tone and said pleasantly enough, "Remember, I am just next door if I can be of any service, my lady."

"Yes. You may serve me by seeing what is delaying my dinner." She paused for emphasis, then said, "Be sure to have them knock when they bring it, for I shall bar the door the moment you are through it!"

He bowed mockingly, his eyes dancing as if they held secret knowlege of which she was ignorant. He admired her defiant spirit, yet at the same time he was determined to give her a lesson this night that she would not soon forget. She flouted all the rules and dared much with him. Although this amused him, he decided to show her he was the master here.

A great sigh escaped her lips as she lowered the bar into place. For a weary moment she leaned against the heavy doorjamb with weak legs. Finally she rallied the last of her strength to move to the fire and strip off her wet clothes. Damn the man to hell for thwarting her and Bryan's plans! Ravenspur was the author of all her misery, she concluded as she peeled off her damp stockings and climbed into the wooden tub.

The water felt like heaven as it closed over her shivery, aching body. Roseanna unbraided her long hair and shook it out to hang over the side of the tub closest to the fire. She lay back, languorously allowing warmth to seep into her limbs. Her eyes closed, and she began to float in

that delicious limbo before sleep descended. A sudden
noise caused her eyes to fly open.

Ravenspur entered her room through an adjoining
door with a steaming platter of food in one hand and a
goblet of wine in the other.

"Mm, you must try a mouthful. It's not half bad," he
said with aplomb.

She gasped. "I thought that heavy curtain concealed a
window, not a door," she said with dismay as he approached the tub and held the plate beneath her nose. He
towered above her, clad only in a velvet robe.

I am naked, and so is he beneath the robe! she thought
wildly. He was the only man she had ever encountered
who made her afraid.

"You are a horrible man. Get out!" she cried.

He ignored her. Seating himself on the edge of the tub,
he selected a succulent piece of veal and lifted it to her
mouth. "Open wide," he tempted.

His nearness had an instant effect on her. Her pulse
raced and her heartbeat quickened with anger and, yes,
fear of his intentions. When she clamped her lips tightly,
he ordered, "Eat!" His command left no room for disobe-
dience, so she took the proffered food and almost melted
at the delicious taste of it. He put the plate and goblet on
a coffer beside the tub within easy reach. "I'd like to
bathe with you."

She gasped. His words sent a scalding sensation curling
inside her. Shocked, she read the wicked intention clearly
visible in his dark, savage face.

"Never!" she said with cold finality.

"Selfish little wench. By not sharing with me, you deprive me of a bath."

"Horse piss!" she said angrily. "All you need do is

order one, and the servants will grovel at your slightest desire."

His dark eyes flashed the reflection of the fire. "You are no lady to use such language. I think your arse needs a spanking."

"And you, sir, are no gentleman to suggest such a thing!"

He looked upon her with admiration. She was only one step from exhaustion, yet still she stood her ground with him and parried his every thrust. He plunged his hand into the water. She cried out with alarm, then put her hand to her mouth to stifle the sound, mindful that if Sir Bryan heard her cry, he might come to her rescue, and there could be murder done this night.

Roger's brown hand emerged from the water and held out a large sponge. Her breasts rose and fell with her labored breathing; her hands flew to them in an effort to conceal herself from his night-black eyes.

He laughed mockingly. "Don't bother to hide your charms from me, Roseanna. I am to be your husband, and you forget, I've already had you in my bed."

Feeling totally vulnerable, she knew her only weapon against him was her sharp tongue. "Then why are you staring at my breasts?" she demanded.

He leered wickedly. "I'm debating which one to wash first." His hand swooped down, and the sponge encircled first one breast, then the other. Threads of fire shot from her nipples to down between her legs. He was a beast! She was afraid to cry for help. He had her exactly where he wanted her, and they both knew it. He tossed the sponge aside, picked up the large towel, and reached toward her. For a moment she thought he was handing her the towel so she might at last conceal her body from his gaze, but

he deftly wrapped the towel around her and lifted her
from the tub.

"Put me down!" she hissed furiously. Obeying her
command, he laid her upon the bed and began to rub her
body with the soft towel. Her limbs were weak as he
awakened sensations in her that felt as delicious as sin. At
last she realized that, in his mind at least, she was his
bride-to-be and that he could do with her as he wished.

"Why are you compromising me like this? How can
you take advantage of my predicament?" she pleaded as
the last of her strength melted away.

"To teach you a lesson, my lady. If you had traveled
with your parents, properly chaperoned, this predicament would never have occurred. Instead, you chose to
run around the countryside like a wild thing. A young
woman can get into all kinds of trouble when she allows
herself to be alone with a man. What kind of trouble, you
ask?" he teased. "Well, he could do this to you, for instance." His hand cupped her breast, and he caressed its
silky fullness. As she opened her mouth to protest, his
head dipped down to take the kiss he lusted for. The
strong physical power he had over her awakened her
sleeping sensuality. As he plunged his tongue into her
sweetness, she found herself actually wanting him to do
forbidden things to her. As if reading her mind, he
obliged.

"Then, of course, he would be free to do this to you."
He ran his long fingers down her abdomen and caressed
her between her thighs, slowly tormenting her with exquisite, overpowering sensations. A moan escaped her
lips, "Please, please."

"Are you begging me to stop or to continue, Roseanna?" he asked. Looking at her beautiful body writhing on the bed, he began to caress her more forcefully.

Suddenly she knew she would let him do anything to her. Later, she would hate herself; later, she would hate him; later . . . later.

When he stood up and his expression changed to one of seriousness, she gasped and almost begged him to come back to her.

"Yesterday I dispatched men to escort your family to York. Your mother will be with you soon. I bid you sweet dreams, my lady."

Her eyes widened for a moment. My God, did he know she dreamed of him? Nay, she was exhausted and was not thinking straight. She lay weak with relief after he left. Her body still tingled where he had touched her; her hatred for him hardened. "Too much," she whispered. "Too big. Too strong. Too dark. Too many wives."

Her thoughts drifted to Bryan, and she worried for his welfare. If Ravenspur harmed one hair on his head, she would kill him. Then she laughed at herself. Surely Sir Bryan did not need a maid to defend him. He was a knight, wasn't he? What could he have done differently under the circumstances? she asked herself. He couldn't throw down the gauntlet and challenge Ravenspur. The chivalric law did not allow a man of noble blood to be challenged by a man below his rank. And yet . . . and yet. Roseanna was asleep before she finished the thought.

8

York was built on the site of an ancient Roman town. It sat in the vale of York; the dark hump of the North York Moors rose beyond it.

The landscape lifted its rainy veil and let the pale sun finger the light-colored Yorkshire limestone buildings and glint on all the church weathervanes in the crystal-clear air. York's walls stood strongly against any enemy. The spires of its magnificent cathedral soared high above the other buildings and could be seen from miles away.

The party of eight clattered through the gates onto the cobbled streets that led toward the Royal Palace. Roseanna wore the only dress she had brought with her. It was of rose-colored wool with a square neckline and long sleeves edged with soft gray squirrel. Her cloak was the color of deep wine, with a high collar of the same gray fur. Ravenspur also was cloaked in wine, which irritated Roseanna, for on his black stallion that so closely resembled Zeus, they looked like a matched pair.

King Edward was in the great dining hall for the midday meal. The room was filled with trestle tables to ac-

commodate his Court and the men-at-arms who traveled
with him. Edward knew everyone by name, down to the
lowest scullion, and it endeared people to him. Always
informal, anyone could approach him. He even allowed
children and dogs to take advantage of him, never fussing
over their messy pawing.

Roseanna stood coolly by the entrance, trying not to
let the large gathering of men and dogs intimidate her.
Ravenspur strode in without hesitation. When the King
saw him, his face lit up with a welcome grin and he cried,
"Roger!" and held out his arms. Roseanna watched in
amazement as Edward, grinning like a lunatic, picked up
Roger and lifted him rafter-high. Not to be outdone,
Roger then hauled the King up with arms so strong, she
couldn't believe the bulge of the muscles. Even from a
distance she could see that their right wrists were almost
twice as thick as their left wrists from practice with the
heavy sword.

"Plague take you, man, where have you been?" demanded Edward. "I've decided to hold a tourney in
honor of your wedding next week. When's the bride to
arrive?"

"She's here now, sire." Roger bent toward Ned's ear.
"She's come to beg off. I'd like a private word before you
give her an audience."

The King chuckled, "The young baggage is monstrously conceited. You'll have your work cut out for
you. Go up to my apartments—I'll see you now." Edward quit the great hall and took his daughter's hands
into his to prevent her from curtseying. "Welcome, my
Rosebud," he said low.

"Were you two conspiring against me?" she asked
hotly.

"Nay, you saucy wench, but 'tis an idea." He chuckled. "I want you to go with my chamberlain, who has set aside a suite of rooms for you. In a couple of hours, when you are rested, come along to my apartments, and we'll discuss whatever it is that has sent you hell-bent for leather up here ahead of your family."

"Yes, Your Grace," she answered with docility that he knew she did not mean.

"Plague take you, can't you call me Edward once in a while?"

"When we are alone I will call you many things, sire," she promised.

He grinned at her audacity, and she went off meekly with the chamberlain. She had things to do before seeing the King privately. One was to seek out Sir Bryan and make some fresh plans.

In the King's apartments it was quite a few minutes before he could dismiss all the servants and squires whose duty it was to attend his person at all times.

Roger poured ale into leather tankards and handed one to his friend and King. He waited until Edward sprawled into an easy chair, then he straddled a wooden chair and folded his arms along its high back.

"So," said Edward. "You no doubt guessed long ago that Roseanna is my love child."

Roger nodded silently.

"God knows who else has guessed. None, I hope! For her safety I want it kept secret."

"I agree, Your Grace," said Roger solemnly.

"Plague take you, call me Ned! So you've changed your mind about marriage. Are you sure, Roger?"

Roger was sure. She had been his from the moment he

set eyes on her. "Never have I done anything in my life with a thousandth part the joy which I do this."

The two men's relationship was close and easy. When they supped together, the tales went ringing around the hall; there had always been more laughter shared than curses. They had wrestled and fought since boyhood, had drank and whored together, and when alone they had shared inner thoughts on death and life that they could trust to no other ears.

"I entrust her to you without hesitation," said Edward.

"I'll cherish her always," pledged Roger. "But as I told you, she's come to beg you on her knees to get her out of this marriage."

"Has the chit set her sights on an earl? All Plantagenets are cursed with ambition."

"Nay, she is in love with her hatred for me. She has set her will against mine and is determined to have her own way at all costs."

Edward grimaced. "Poor Roger. Leave her to me. Women can be the very devil!"

Roger hesitated. His face softened as he thought of Roseanna. "She fancies she is in love with a young knight. Don't be too hard on her, Ned."

The King changed the subject. "I decided on a tournament as a show of strength here in the North. You know I refused Warwick when he asked for my brother to marry his daughter, and I expressly forbade George to marry the girl. But I have information that they are going ahead with secret plans, and the marriage is imminent. Warwick cannot pull my strings any longer. The moment he gets George for his son-in-law, I fear he will try to depose me and set George up as King."

"You should have clapped them in the Tower and had

their heads for treason long ago," said Roger flatly. Yet
he knew Edward was never the first to pick a fight.

"Warwick thinks he is still the kingmaker. His brother
Northumberland holds the North, and his youngest
brother, the Archbishop of York, holds Hertfordshire. It
runs alongside Warwick's holdings in Warwickshire and
Buckinghamshire."

"Which conveniently converges with your brother
George's estates," said Roger dryly. "Add to all this that
Warwick is still Lord Warden of the Cinque Ports with
the warship Trinity at his command, and I tell you he has
too much power!"

"He was my mentor for the first twenty years of my
life—yours also, Roger. It isn't easy to betray him.
Harder still to betray a brother."

"Yet they will betray you," said Roger flatly.

"Two wrongs never made a right. They must act first;
only then will I be truly convinced."

Roseanna went back down to the stables, ostensibly to
check on her horse but really to find Sir Bryan. It was not
many minutes before he was beside her. They slipped
down past a long line of animals and into an empty box
stall. The miasma of horses, leather, and oats tickled her
nostrils, and she suppressed the urge to sneeze.

"Bryan, are you all right? Ravenspur's men didn't
threaten or ill-treat you, did they?"

"No, no, we have become good companions. I don't
think the thought even entered Ravenspur's head that we
were running off to get married."

"Well, things have probably worked out for the best.
I'm going to see the King and tell him that I want to wed
you, not Ravenspur."

"My God, don't do that, Roseanna. I'll disappear off the face of the earth and never be heard from again!" he said, greatly alarmed.

"Don't be silly. My family will arrive in a few days, and we can be married properly with the King's blessing rather than run off to Scotland. Bryan, the King won't deny me my heart's desire."

"You must have great faith in him to risk my safety," he said quietly.

She reached up and kissed him on the mouth. "Of course I do," she promised. "In the meantime there is a whole wing set aside for my family, so you can stay there."

"I think I'll slip home for a fast visit to Marston Moor. I'll return tomorrow or the next day," he promised.

"Then take care, my love, and don't worry about me. Everything will be the way we want it," she assured him.

Before she kept her appointment with the King, she removed her cloak and brushed out her long dark hair. She had packed no veils or posy caps, so she fastened it back demurely with a pink ribbon unthreaded from her garter. As she was ushered into the King's presence, she made a low curtsey until the last of his attendants departed. It was a beautiful room filled with priceless tapestries, but Roseanna concentrated on what she had come to say. She sat upon the window seat, which was piled high with velvet cushions, and Edward joined her there.

"Father, I beg you to release me from the pledge to marry Ravenspur. Instead, I wish to marry the knight who gave me safe escort here, Sir Bryan Fitzhugh."

Everyone, including Roseanna, assumed Edward was good-humored to a fault. He was not.

"You are my ward, Roseanna. No better husband than

Roger Montford could be found for you in all of England."

She flared, "He's had much practice at being a husband, but his wives are in the grave and cannot recommend him to me!"

Edward was used to haughty, high-handed, spoiled women. He was married to a woman who acted as if she were Queen of Heaven rather than of England. "Roger suffered grave misfortunes in both his marriages. No doubt he will reveal all to you in his own good time, and it will put to rest whatever gossip you may have listened to."

"I thought you of all people would understand that I have a sweetheart and wish to marry him!" she cried piteously.

"A young knight is not what I would wish for you," he pointed out patiently. "Someday you will very likely need the protection of wealth and strength, which Ravenspur offers." He tried for a lighter tone. "If I refuse him, the damned fellow would think nothing of running me through!"

"Sir Bryan's father died trying to protect your father," she flung at him. Tears stung her eyes and rolled down her cheeks.

He knew that Sir Bryan's father was brother to Henry Fitzhugh, who in turn was brother-in-law to Warwick. "Sir Bryan's father was a loyal man," the King said enigmatically.

"What does that mean?" she demanded.

"Nothing, really. Just that Sir Bryan was in my brother's service and has yet to prove his loyalty."

"Must he die to prove that loyalty, as his father did?" she cried.

"Roseanna, twenty thousand men died at Towton to put me on the throne. You think I want more deaths on my conscience?" he asked quietly.

"I'm sorry, Father," she said, appalled at herself.

"My Rosebud, you are very hard to resist with the tears of a supplicant marring your beauty. But I do resist. You will marry Ravenspur to please me, and one day you will thank me for denying your request."

She couldn't believe that he would not let her have her own way! She wanted to fly at him and scratch his eyes out. Instead, she would withdraw her love and treat him coldly from this day forward. With pinched nostrils, firmly compressed lips, and narrowed eyes, she tossed her head and walked deliberately from his presence. She vented her temper on the door and crashed it closed with all her strength. She would flee from this place instantly! Then she remembered with sinking heart that Bryan had gone home.

In fact, Sir Bryan had not gone home. At the White Rose, York's largest inn, he met up with his friend, Sir Jeffrey Castlemaine. To a casual observer it seemed as if the two friends had met by chance, but such was not the case. Jeffrey had been following Roseanna and Bryan since they left Castlemaine. It had been he who had anonymously informed one of Ravenspur's men where his sister could be found. That is, his half sister, he thought bitterly.

The two young men quit the White Rose and rode as if the devil himself were at their horses' tails. Their destination was Middleham Castle, some thirty-odd miles from York. Warwick owned Middleham, which had such high walls about the round tower that it was a formidable

fortress. While the King held Court at York, a secret
gathering was taking place at Middleham. George, Duke
of Clarence, was in residence with his new father-in-law,
Warwick.

By the time the two knights reached Middleham they
were dressed in the Duke of Clarence's livery, which carried the unmistakable device of the Black Bull. The two
knights had been in service to George for many years,
which really meant they were in service to Warwick.

Warwick, who made it his business to know everything, had known for years that Jeffrey's sister was the
King's bastard. But only when he saw a close friendship
spring up between Jeffrey and blond, beautiful Bryan,
who was related to himself through marriage, did he clev-
erly let slip that Roseanna was only Jeffrey's half sister
and had royal blood in her veins. Then he nurtured the
boy's envy until it turned into jealousy and festered into
hatred.

The knights had been sent home to Castlemaine with
the express purpose of securing Roseanna in marriage to
Sir Bryan. A King's bastard would be a valuable weapon
to hold ready when blackmail seemed necessary. Now
that Ravenspur had come forward and agreed to marry
Roseanna, the plans had changed. Would she not be more
valuable married to Ravenspur than Sir Bryan? That way
they could not only blackmail the King but also render
his strongest ally useless.

When they rode over the drawbridge, they found that
Middleham was acting as host to a multitude. Warwick's
brother Northumberland was there, and so was Lord
Stanley, the greatest lord in Lancashire and Cheshire. He
had reason to hate the King, for half his holdings had
been repossessed and handed to the Yorkists when the

Lancastrian nobility fell. But they were surprised to learn
that the northern rebel Robin Mendell was also being
entertained at Middleham.

Though the young knights were not privy to the plots
that were being hatched inside this stronghold, their
common sense told them that it would not be long before
events would explode into action. They told Warwick
that Bryan's plans to secure Roseanna had been thwarted
by Ravenspur but that they believed she would be more
useful to them married to the baron. Warwick clearly
agreed and told Jeffrey to get back to his sister's wedding
with all possible speed. He advised Sir Bryan to seek service with Ravenspur so that he would be doubly valuable
as a spy, and to keep the King's daughter close to his
hand, should they need her.

Neville Castlemaine's abundant patience was put to
the test every mile of the journey to York. The baggage
train was considerable. Now that they had been assured
by letter from Ravenspur that Roseanna was safe at York
with the King and that wedding plans were going forward, Joanna had packed every article that Roseanna
possessed. There were also three wagonloads of furniture,
carpets, tapestries, and bed linen that Roseanna would
take to her new home. As well as this, there was the
baggage that the family would need for the journey to
York and back. Joanna in a generous moment had decided that Roseanna would have both Alice and Kate
Kendall to look after her. Neville himself added to the
procession by bringing Mecca and three other horses that
Roseanna had bred.

There had been a terrible flap at Castlemaine when
they had discovered Roseanna missing, but Jeffrey as-

sured his parents that he knew where the young couple
was headed and would catch up with them within hours.
It had been a great relief to them when Ravenspur's
knights had arrived to act as escort and had brought the
letter from Roger.

Neville brought along a dozen of his own men-at-arms
as well as a dozen household servants, and he made use
of every man there. The wagons bogged down in mud,
stuck in ruts, and lost wheels at the most inconvenient
times. The Great North Road itself was marvelous, built
by the Romans so that the rain drained off it well, but the
roads that led to and from it were nightmarish.

The women complained continually about the weather,
the delays, the food, and the sleeping accommodations at
the inns they used. Only their sense of humor prevented
Neville and Joanna from murdering each other. After
four long days they arrived at York, and it took a fifth
day to unload and settle into the apartments assigned to
them.

Roseanna was prepared for a battle with her mother,
but no words of censure came. Joanna merely gave her a
penetrating look that conveyed a wealth of meaning, then
proceeded to direct the serving maids in unpacking Roseanna's wedding gown and trousseau.

Joanna was happy that the Queen—or the Woodville
woman, as she called her—was not in York but had remained in London with the rest of her clan. But she had
no intention to dally with the King. Such behavior at her
daughter's wedding and under the eye of so many spectators would be inappropriate.

Roseanna haunted the stables, looking for signs of Sir
Bryan's return. She knew that Kate Kendall followed her
steps, that her mother had once again set her watchdog

upon her. But finally, Bryan was there, and nothing else mattered to her. She went into his arms as he emerged from the royal stables. "Oh, my love, never have two days gone by so slowly in my life."

Gently, he took her arms from around his neck and drew her into the stables, where he hoped they would be less conspicuous. "Sweetheart, we must be more discreet," he chided.

Tears flooded her eyes. "Love is not discreet—love is flamboyant!" she cried.

He took her hands into his and said low, "We both know that your marriage to Ravenspur is inevitable."

"How did you know that the King refused me?" she cried.

"Sweetheart, it was just wishful thinking that we could wed, but listen to me. It doesn't have to be the end of everything. Somehow I will take service with Ravenspur, and we will be together. I swear it to you!" he promised fervently.

"Can't we elope?" she begged.

"Be sensible. At this moment your woman servant is keeping watch on us. Think you she's the only one? The King has spies everywhere. Even Ravenspur may have you followed. Our staying together depends on our keeping his suspicions at bay. Don't try to see me anymore. I will write you some sweet poetry, and when he finally takes you to his castle, I will be in his service. Tell me you understand."

For a moment she thought she would die. Then she nodded slowly, knowing he had no idea how she felt. *Bryan, Bryan!* she wanted to scream. But she couldn't speak because she was crying so hard. Her heart felt as if it were bleeding.

9

Pavilions and tents had been erected for the great tournament that was to be held the day before the wedding. The tents where the nobility and royalty would don their armor were glorious, made from silk and velvet. Each flew pennants and banners emblazoned with colorful shields of arms.

The contestants haunted the pavilions. Each had his own squires, armor-bearers, and baggage men; the most important man in their employ was always the master armorer. Armor was designed to save a man's life, but unless it was fitted perfectly, so that he could move his arm easily to wield his sword in battle or his lance in a tournament, it was next to useless. Good steel and a good mount put the odds in his favor. If a horse carried itself true and straight and helped the rider keep his balance, it often saved that rider's life.

The joust today was for pleasure only, although it always carried inherent risks. The flower of England's nobility was out in full force—Pembroke, Hastings, Devonshire, Norfolk, and Percy—and the tents were filled with earls, dukes, barons, and lords, and the spectator stands overlooking the field of honor were filled with their ladies.

Lord Hastings, who was Chamberlain of the Royal Household, was acting as field marshal of the joust. He had placed the color standards along the east flank of the field to mark its length. The King's heralds sounded their trumpets, and the combatants rode out onto the field for a couple of rounds to learn the ground. Each horse wore armor, which was then caparisoned by silken trappings with each rider's arms emblazoned on the flank. Over their armor the men wore emblazoned tunics, and each carried a shield and a plumed and crested helmet.

The ladies were dressed in their very best, vying with each other for the most eye-catching head fashion. Some wore steeple hats with veils; others wore horned confections, not realizing that they left themselves wide open for catty comparisons to cows. Roseanna, seated in the high place of honor with Joanna beside her, wore a jeweled posy cap whose floating silver veil shimmered as mistily as a spider's web. These veils had detachable scarves to be given to their champions as favors. As the men rode to the field's edge to receive these favors, their identities were easily discerned.

The King was adorned in purple, with the Sun in Splendor superimposed upon the white rose of York. Roger Montford was in black silk surcoat with a black clawed raven on a scarlet background. The plume in his helmet was also scarlet. It was expected that the bride bestow her favor upon the groom; however, as he rode up to her, she ignored him. So Joanna, doing her best to cover her daughter's lapse, draped her own scarf on the tip of Ravenspur's lance. He affixed it to his scabbard-ring and wheeled away.

A hushed whisper went through the crowd of women. Perhaps the bride had reserved her favor for the King, as many ladies did. When Edward came in front of her, however, she turned her head away to show her displeasure with him. The crowd's murmur increased. A rumor was going the rounds that this was no love match. Who would the bride bestow her favor upon? Surely not some lover from her past—not openly here in front of the world?

As Jeffrey stopped in front of his ladies, Roseanna smiled upon her brother affectionately and took the silver veil from her head. He saluted her by placing his right hand over his heart. The crowd's relief was so great that a little burst of applause broke out.

As Roger and Edward rode from the field together, Roger said to him, "Ned, I want to exchange opponents with you." He grinned helplessly. "I've been challenged by Roseanna's swain, and she would never forgive me if I injured the young devil."

The King grinned back. "You're caught between the devil and the deep, for my challenger is her brother."

"Let's make short work of them, Ned. We've a dozen other challengers to face yet," Roger urged.

"Are you forgetting we are almost twice their age?" replied the King. Then as always, his vulgar humor came to the fore. "Mayhap their lances are stiffer than ours."

Roger winked. "I am hoping experience will win the day—and the night."

The King opened the ceremonies by riding in the first joust. The marshal looked to left and right to each man. When he saw they were ready, he lowered the mace. Sir

Bryan Fitzhugh lowered the visor of his helmet and began to sweat. He was in a no-win situation. One did not try to shine at his monarch's expense. Besides, to unhorse the giantlike King with his long reach would be no easy task. He knew a few underhanded tricks that he had been prepared to use against Ravenspur, but since the King had asked for him especially, he feared a test of his loyalty rather than of his jousting ability.

The drumming of the hooves was the only sound that could be heard until the two men clashed and the crowd roared with one voice the name of their champion: "Edward, Edward!"

The King, who seldom got angry, was close to that feeling at this moment. For when they had closed, the young knight had deliberately lowered his lance, which ripped the silk trappings of the King's horse. Edward's lance hit its intended mark with his full weight behind it, and Bryan Fitzhugh lay sprawled in the field.

Roseanna's breath caught in her throat, and she was on her feet before she realized it. The blood had left her face; she was white and shaking. Fortunately her agitation went unnoticed, for all the other spectators were on their feet, too—cheering. She wanted to rush to Sir Bryan's side, but she knew she could not. She had to sit on through one contest after another, for they went according to rank and the earls of the realm jousted before the barons.

By the time it was her brother's turn to challenge Ravenspur, some of the color had returned to her cheeks. She decided she did not enjoy these silly dangerous games that men seemed to take so seriously. Yet as she saw Ravenspur close his helmet and grip his horse with his thighs, she wished she were riding against him. She

would have gloried in a chance to oppose him and perhaps defeat him. Then she realized that she would get
that chance tomorrow and all the tomorrows to come.
Her weapons would be different, but the challenge was
almost identical.

The stallions were in their stride; the distance closed.
As Roger took the measure of Jeffrey Castlemaine, he
fancied that hatred glittered out at him from the slitted
visor. He knew he must unhorse his foe at the first
charge. Castlemaine feinted to the left to draw
Montford's shield, but Ravenspur was too old a dog to be
fooled. He veered in so close and hit Jeffrey with so solid
a blow that the young knight was on the ground before
he knew what hit him.

Roger wheeled his great mount with deceptive ease
and bent to retrieve the silver veil from his opponent.
Then he rode up to the edge of the field, where Roseanna
stood covered in shame for her brother. Ravenspur lifted
his visor. His night-black eyes burned into hers with sear-
ing intensity. Slowly, he brought her veil to his lips, then
fastened it to the tip of his lance, where it fluttered triumphantly.

My God, she thought with alarm, *he has won the first
bout!* She withdrew from the crowd. Her lips tightened
when she saw Kate Kendall detach herself from the other
servingwomen and follow her. There would be merry-
making in the great hall tonight, but Roseanna would
have no part of it. Tomorrow she faced the greatest challenge of her life. She would stay alone in her chamber to
gather her strength.

It was past midnight when the tears came, flooding her
pillow. The quiet night air was shattered with her sobbing. Suddenly, she felt comforting arms about her.

"There, there, my lamb. All will be well. I'll look after you, my little one."

For a breathless moment she fancied her mother had come to comfort her, but as she fell upon the comforting bosom, she saw that it was Kate. Had she been wrong? Had she judged the North-country woman too harshly? Roseanna did not know the answer; she only knew that she felt safe and comforted in the haven of Kate's compassionate arms.

Roseanna awoke with a start. For a moment she was slightly disoriented to awaken in the strange room; then as knowledge came flooding upon her, her heart fell. She realized that it was her wedding day. She lay staring at the ceiling for long minutes; then her resolve hardened. What a poor-spirited creature she was to lie there so woebegone! Today was a challenge, and she would rise to meet it. She would show them all that it mattered not a fig to her. She would meet fate head on and spit in its eye! Her voice raised in song, and she found that it helped considerably to keep the darklings at bay.

The reception room, which was part of the suite of rooms allocated to the Castlemaines, was filled with females. Weddings had such irresistible attraction and endless fascination for women that every lady of the Court had for one reason or another found her way to the bride. The dressers, the sewing women, and the ladies of the bedchamber were there to help, but others, such as the Countess of Pembroke and the Duchess of Norfolk, were there out of curiosity. Roseanna only had a passing acquaintance with most of them, but her mother seemed to know everyone.

Into the crush came the Countess of Devonshire with a

young lady in tow. The girl, Roseanna noticed, was very,
very pretty. She had hair that could be described as
strawberry blond; its attractive color could be seen
clearly through her transparent head veil. Her gown was
yellow and heavily embroidered with gold thread. Although it was an exquisite dress, it didn't do her justice.
She appeared to be quite shy, judging by the way the
countess was having to coax her along.

"Joanna, here she is at last. I've finally managed to
locate her."

Joanna looked puzzled for a moment, then her lovely
brow cleared. She grabbed Roseanna's arm before she
disappeared into the throng.

"Roseanna, here is your new sister-in-law. I'm sorry,
my dear. What's your first name?"

"Rebecca," said the girl. She was so soft-spoken that
they only just caught what she said. Roseanna looked
questioningly toward her mother, who launched into an
explanation. "Ravenspur is having his brother Tristan as
his groomsman, and this is his wife, who will stand up
with you as witness and be your matron of honor."

Roseanna took the girl's hands into hers. She found
them icy and clammy to the touch, as if the ordeal were
hers to face rather than Roseanna's. Suddenly, Roseanna
felt a great desire to protect this pretty child who was
married to that young devil, Tristan Montford. "Are you
all right?" asked Roseanna.

"Y-yes. It's just that I've not been very well, and—and
I don't like crowds."

Roseanna placed a firm hand in the small of her back
and propelled her through the door into the bedchamber,
where Alice and Kate were laying out Roseanna's wed-

ding gown. "There. It's not so crowded in here. Sit down, and I'll pour you some wine, Rebecca."

"Oh, no, no," protested Rebecca weakly. "I—I don't drink wine."

"Why ever not?" asked Roseanna.

"It—it's very fattening," said Rebecca on a whisper.

"Well, that's certainly something you don't have to worry about," said Roseanna in her forthright manner.

"Oh, I do." She blushed. "My husband is revolted by fat women," she offered, as if this explained everything.

"Did you say you'd been ill?" asked Roseanna.

"I—I don't enjoy good health. I thought I'd feel too poorly to attend the wedding, but of course it is expected of me. So Tristan insisted," she finished lamely.

Roseanna stared at her in fascination. The girl was a horrible example of what she must never let herself become. Marriage to Montford had crushed her spirit. Christ, she was as timid as a mouse! She wondered what had attracted Tristan to her in the first place. Rebecca was exquisitely pretty, of course, but she seemed to be the type who would acquiesce rather than risk her husband's displeasure.

Joanna stuck her head inside the room and said, "Roseanna, I think perhaps you'd better dress now. I have to go down to the audience chamber to see that the wedding gifts are displayed well. You'll be very pleased with them. There are some particularly fine pieces of silver and a pair of carpets that must have been brought back from one of the crusades to the Holy Land. My advice is to take all the best stuff to Ravenspur Castle. Don't leave any of it at the northern strongholds; I've heard they're no better than barren piles of stone."

Rebecca shuddered. "I don't like the North. I always feel unwell here."

Roseanna smiled at her. "Do you live at Ravenspur Castle?"

"Not in the castle itself. We have a manor house in Ravenspur Park. It's only about two miles from the castle."

"Good. We can ride over and visit each other." Roseanna wondered why the girl looked so doubtful. *God, don't tell me Tristan doesn't allow her to have friends and visitors,* Roseanna thought contemptuously. But she didn't know if her contempt was for Tristan or Rebecca.

Alice fluttered about holding a chemise that was so fine-spun, it looked as if it were made from fairy thread. But the dressing of the bride didn't begin until Kate Kendall put her stodgy hand upon Roseanna's shoulder and anchored her to the spot. Silken stockings and two pairs of garters adorned her legs; one pair could be stolen by any gentleman bold enough to dare. After the chemise, the wedding gown was lifted over her head. Alice knelt to attach the love knots to the skirt so that they could easily be pulled off for favors. If they were attached too firmly and the crowd of merrymakers became too enthusiastic, the bride ran the risk of being stripped naked.

Kate Kendall was doing her utmost to brush every last curly tangle from Roseanna's magnificent hair. It fell down her back like a shining dark waterfall, glorying in its freedom on this nuptial day. "Hold still, or I'll rattle yer teeth," threatened Kate. Roseanna giggled because she didn't know if Kate meant her or Alice.

Roseanna saw the full beauty of the gown with its white roses and rosebuds embroidered on shining white satin. Before, she had been blind to its beauty, never allowing herself to think of the ceremony with Ravenspur. Now she took pleasure in its beauty. Her fingers caressed the smooth material and traced the embroidery on the rose petals. The sleeves were long and wide, falling in points to her knees. Her mother had designed a tiny coronet of pearls that Alice now fixed in place. Then she pulled the frothy white veil down over her face.

Roseanna repeated instructions her mother had given her earlier. "I'm to go to the minster with Father in the coach."

"Right," said Kate, pursing her lips as she always did before delivering a piece of home truth. "Spare a few minutes for the poor man, Roseanna. He's losing his spoiled darling today. Though I'm sure he's very proud of you, he's covering up a great deal of sadness, too."

Roseanna squeezed the older woman's hand; she was just beginning to know Kate. Ready at last, Roseanna looked around the room to see if she had forgotten anything. She had not yet seen the sleeping chamber that had been set aside for the bride and groom on their first night, but she knew it was in the general direction of the King's apartments, well away from these rooms. Suddenly feeling nervous, she turned to Kate. "Be sure that my combs and brushes are taken along to the bridal chamber. You know how easily my hair tangles."

Kate nodded. The women from the outer room were now crowding in to get a last look at the bride. They gave her sly looks that clearly said, *We know what you're in for tonight.*

Not if I can help it, she vowed to herself. "Kate, don't forget a warm bedgown," she added, stalling for time.

"Lass, lass, I'll see to everything, from your favorite

scent to your velvet slippers. Now be off and go with God, Roseanna."

Impulsively, she hugged the older woman and kissed Alice; then she looked about for Rebecca. She sat wanly in a corner, her face the color of parchment. "Come on, Rebecca. You're supposed to help me lift my train so I can walk in this gown."

The girl seemed at a loss, so Roseanna flipped the excess material over her arm and offered her other hand to Rebecca.

The girl stood up willingly enough, but before they had gone through the arched doorway, she was in trouble with her own gown. Roseanna grinned ruefully as she bent to untangle Rebecca's hem from a footstool.

"I'm sorry," whispered Rebecca pitifully.

"Come on, girl. Buck up. I'm going to my wedding, not to my execution," said Roseanna, laughing.

"Aren't you afraid?" asked Rebecca in wonder.

Roseanna considered for a moment. Of course she was afraid, but she would die before she'd let anybody know it. Actually, she knew she would only get through the door if she thought of it as a challenge. "Afraid?" she asked Rebecca incredulously. "Ravenspur's the one who should be quaking in his boots!"

Her father awaited her beside an ornate royal coach. "Father, I think we'd better get Rebecca inside first. She doesn't seem very strong."

Neville lifted the young woman in yellow into the coach and tucked her golden embroidered skirts around her ankles so that he could close the door. Then they went around the coach, and both entered from the opposite door. He looked at his daughter anxiously. "Are you all right, sweetheart?"

"I'm in fighting fettle," she answered, trying to smile. "This is Rebecca Montford. She's married to Ravenspur's brother, God help her."

Neville cast a warning glance at his daughter to watch her tongue. "The cathedral has a very long aisle; you don't think you'll faint, do you?" he asked Rebecca worriedly.

"I might," she conceded with a whisper.

Roseanna rolled her eyes heavenward. The coach didn't have far to go because the minster was part of the Norman-built royal buildings of York.

The bride and groom were not supposed to see each other until they faced the altar, but Roger and Tristan Montford had just arrived when Roseanna's coach drew up. Neville reached across Rebecca to open the small door. She had a difficult time extracting herself from the ornate vehicle. Tristan stepped forward, his older brother hard upon his heels, and helped his wife to alight.

Roseanna looked down directly into Ravenspur's dark eyes and said deliberately, "I need no man's help!"

Roger bowed low. "You are flying your banners. I recognize your challenge." His eyes swept her from head to foot. He knew he had chosen well. She was the loveliest sight he had ever beheld, and he could not wait to claim her. She swept past him on her father's arm; Rebecca had to scurry to catch up with her.

One corner of Tristan's mouth went up as the pair walked toward the vestry door. He spoke the battle prayer that was used before going into combat: "May God grant you gain this day, my lord."

Roger gave the reply to the battle prayer: "This day is mine, for God defends my right." The two brothers subdued their grins before they approached the altar.

York Minster was the largest Gothic cathedral in all of England. As Roseanna looked up toward its vaulted ceilings outlined in gold, her breath almost left her, so magnificent and rich was the setting.

The voices of the choirboys raised on high were so sweet and so innocent that they brought a lump to Roseanna's throat. Though the cathedral was vast, the pews were filled to capacity. Roseanna had a difficult time picking out familiar faces in the large crowd.

King Edward and his attendants were seated in his private pew at the front of the cathedral. He drew everyone's eye. Still annoyed with him and not ready to forgive him, Roseanna was determined not to look in his direction once during the ceremony.

The singing voices died away, and the clear notes of the virginal rose and echoed throughout the church. Neville squeezed his daughter's hand, and they began their slow promenade.

Roseanna's eyes flew to the figure awaiting her at the altar. With his back toward her, she was free to indulge in bad manners. She stared her fill. He was dressed in black velvet. The shoulders of the padded doublet were so wide she could hardly believe it, yet she knew the garment exaggerated his width only slightly. He was so tall, he towered above his brother and even above the prelate, who stood on the altar's steps. His raven-black hair had been freshly trimmed, yet it curled against his white collar.

The Latin prayers seemed interminable, but finally the bishop stepped forward and in forbidding tones began the solemnization of matrimony. Roseanna clutched the arm of her father as the bishop intoned, "It is not by any to be enterprised, nor taken in hand, unadvisedly, lightly or wantonly, but reverently, discreetly, advisedly, soberly, and in the fear of God; duly considering the causes for which matrimony was ordained." He looked at Roseanna sternly and raised his voice as if he were passing a sentence upon her. She listened tensely.

"Marriage was ordained for the hallowing of the union betwixt man and woman; for the procreation of children" —Roseanna shuddered—"to be brought up in the fear and nurture of the Lord; and for the mutual society, help and comfort, that the one ought to have of the other, in both prosperity and adversity. Into which holy estate these two persons present come now to be joined. Therefore if any man can show any just cause, why they may not lawfully be joined together, let him now speak or else hereafter forever hold his peace."

Roseanna closed her eyes and envisioned a shining knight stepping forward. His face was beautiful, for it had God's light upon it. *"She is mine,"* he said simply. Another man stepped forward, dressed in black robes with a hood covering his head, looking like a judge who was about to pass sentence. *"Ravenspur is no fit husband. He murdered his last wife."*

Roseanna's eyes flew open as the bishop intoned, "Who giveth this woman to be married to this man?"

"I do," said Neville Castlemaine solemnly. Before he took a step forward, Roseanna stood on tiptoe and kissed her father's cheek. Such an unorthodox thing to do, yet so touching. A murmur of approval went through the congregation. Roseanna saw tears in Neville's eyes as she stepped forward and Ravenspur turned to receive her.

She did not lower her lashes, for she knew the veil concealed her features well. He was so close, she could

see the faint dark shadow upon his chin that remained no
matter how closely he shaved. She saw the diamond earring he was wearing, yet it glittered no brighter than his
eyes as their darkness reflected the flickering light of the
tapers on the altar.

All her senses were heightened. The acrid smell of candle wax, mixed with the cloying scent of incense, came to
her. Her ears picked up a jealous remark and also close
behind her the soft sound of Rebecca's weeping. She felt a
garter cutting into her thigh and the embroidered chemise rubbing against her nipples.

She wanted to cry out in protest, but when she opened
her mouth, the response, "I will," slipped out of its own
volition. Her eyes were drawn to her left hand, which
Ravenspur was holding so tightly, she thought the circulation of her blood had surely stopped. With hands at
least twice the size of hers, he was placing a band of gold
upon her third finger. Half an inch in width, it gleamed
dully as she felt its substantial weight. The bishop said
something about a kiss, and Ravenspur was lifting her
veil. She had time only for an indrawn breath before his
mouth came down firmly upon hers; then her thoughts
exploded. *You dare to assume you can seal this marriage
with a kiss! I'll show you otherwise if it kills me! You may
be my husband, but you will never own the smallest part of
me!*

After the kiss her mind seemed to go blank. Later, she
knew she had signed the register; she knew she had tra-
versed the long aisle held close against Ravenspur's side;
she knew she had run through clouds of rice and rose
petals to the din of deafening cheers; and she knew she
had ridden back to the banquet with Ravenspur anchored

to her side. Yet she did not emerge from her trancelike
state until she was seated on the dais with her husband on
her left and the King on her right.

Edward's eyes teased her. "So fair, yet so cruel," he
whispered. "You could not spare me one look."

"And what was your reply when I asked to be
spared?" she retaliated.

"Spared?" echoed Roger, hearing every word.

"From a fate worse than death!" she added with relish.

Ned and Roger exchanged grins.

The dishes served were culinary masterpieces: roasted
swans and cranes sat beside platters holding suckling pigs
and haunches of venison. The spits had been busy since
dawn roasting lambs and oxen; kitchen boys staggered
carrying roasted boars.

Acutely conscious of Roseanna, Ravenspur bent low
and murmured, "You'd better eat something before all
the toasts begin."

She bristled. "Are you afraid I will become flown with
wine and disgrace you, my lord?"

"You cannot disgrace another, only yourself," he said
with a twinkling eye.

The first toast was to the King; the second was from
the King to the bride; the third was from the groomsman
to the groom; and the fourth was from the bride to her
parents. The fifth was from the groom to his bride:

> *If all your beauties one by one*
> *I toast, then I am thinking*
> *Before the tale were well begun*
> *I would be dead of drinking.*

The onlookers banged their goblets on the trestle tables in appreciation of the groom's wit. Roseanna would not be outdone. She replied to her husband's toast,

> *Here's to you, as good as you are*
> *And here's to me, as bad as I am.*
> *As bad as I am, as good as you are,*
> *I'm as good as you are, bad as I am.*

Ned winked at Roger and raised his goblet. "She's right, you know!"

Roger and Roseanna shared one platter, as was custom. He took all the choicest pieces and placed them on her side. She knew it would be petty to refuse, but the next time a fresh dish was placed before her, she took a choice cut and placed it on his side of the platter. Nothing could show him more plainly that she meant to start out on an even footing. It did not annoy him; it amused him. He picked up the food she had selected for him and ate it with gusto.

Ale, mead, and malmsey were flowing; the crowd of guests lost all semblance of decorum as they indulged freely. Roseanna saw Rebecca arise from the table looking paler than death. Feeling protective of her, Roseanna arose and walked with her. "I'll come with you to the garderobe before the dancing begins."

Roseanna became very concerned when she heard Rebecca vomit down the jakes. "Oh, Rebecca love, you are ill. I'm afraid it's all been too much for you. You should have been allowed to stay home in bed today. I'll tell that husband of yours just that."

"Oh, please, no," begged Rebecca. "Don't spoil his pleasure, and please don't tell him that I was sick."

Roseanna made no reply but guided the girl back to
the table. She had just opened her mouth to speak to
Tristan when she caught Rebecca's imploring expression,
which seemed to clearly say, "Please don't anger him or I
shall suffer." So she said to Tristan, "I need Rebecca to
go upstairs for me to see that all is in readiness in the
bridal chamber. You don't mind if she goes up now, do
you?"

"I shall claim forfeit for your first dance," he bartered.

Roseanna turned to Rebecca and whispered, "Go up to
bed, love. I'll take care of Tristan."

The air was filled with the notes of fiddles and flutes as
the trestle tables were being stacked to make room for
dancing. When Tristan closed in the dance with Roseanna, he whispered, "I know your secret!"

She arched a brow at him.

"You have a soft heart."

"And how do you know that?" she challenged.

"You were being kind to Rebecca. What you don't
realize is that she makes herself sick on purpose."

"What an outrageous thing to say! You don't know
your wife very well."

"On the contrary, I've studied her behavior at my lei-
sure. When you went to the garderobe she vomited didn't
she?"

Roseanna nodded reluctantly.

"What she didn't let you know was that she stuck her
finger down her throat to get rid of the food."

"Why would she do a thing like that?"

Tristan shrugged, "She's obsessed that she will become
fat!"

Roseanna realized that he might be speaking the truth,

but she hotly defended Rebecca nonetheless. "Only because you are repulsed by fat women, you young lecher!"

"Be fair, sweet sister. Have I ever been lecherous with you, tempting morsel that you are?" As her mind flew back to that day in the woods when he took her to the hunting lodge, he grinned. "From the first moment I saw you, I meant you for Roger. I admit freely that you are the prettiest woman I've ever known."

How could she hate this young devil when he said such pleasing things? "Ah, Roseanna, I didn't know what happiness was until I married." She looked surprised. "Then it was too late," he whispered. She laughed in spite of herself.

No sooner did Tristan return her than she was claimed in the dance by the King, then by her father, then by her brother and every nobleman present. Roger lounged back in his chair, playing the indulgent bridegroom. He was relieved, mostly for Roseanna's sake, that her young swain was conspicuous by his absence.

Gradually, Roseanna became aware that her husband's eyes were following her wherever she went. Why did he watch her like a dog with a bone? Suddenly her wicked juices, as Kate Kendall called them, began to bubble, and she decided to do something to goad him and wipe the complacent look from his face. She was dancing with young John Stafford, an earl of the realm. He could hardly believe his luck that she had favored him with two dances.

Suddenly she leaned against him and whispered into his ear, "You dance divinely; my last partner had all the grace of a spavined cart horse." He threw back his head and laughed. Then she said, "Ravenspur is watching us with interest." Immediately young Stafford's eyes flew across the room to where the baron sat. She calculated that it would seem as if the two of them were sharing a secret joke at her husband's expense. The little ploy backfired as Stafford murmured, "I've just received a signal to return you to your bridegroom. He doesn't look amused."

"Oh, good," she said sweetly.

"In fact he looks vastly displeased."

"Better and better," said Roseanna, laughing.

Stafford returned her to Roger and bowed himself away. Ravenspur's dark eyes grew intense when he saw her flushed and lovely. "You enjoy dancing, Roseanna."

"You don't mind, do you?" she asked sweetly. "I know older men don't care to dance." She saw a muscle tighten in his jaw, and her wicked juices bubbled deliciously. He stood up to partner her, and suddenly he grinned. "Are you trying to provoke me to see if you can bring out the savage in me?" he asked low. Then his hands reached inside her wide sleeves and slipped up her bare arms. The gesture was so intimate, she gasped and then shivered. As he swept her into the dance, he laughed down at her. "You like to play teasing games. 'Tis a fine art, and a game two can play. I think I am going to be well pleased with you, Roseanna." By the time the dance was over, she was quite breathless. She sank into a little curtsey and went into the arms of her next partner, but she was careful to act with decorum this time.

It was inevitable that the jokes turned bawdy and then downright lewd. Ribald songs began; Roseanna tried to close her ears to the refrain, "I dipped my pole in Eve's deep hole." She turned from the singing man in disgust and advanced toward the King. Ned had his great arm about Roger's shoulders and was singing, "He worked hard all the night and fucked till it were light."

Ravenspur caught the look of panic on his bride's face and extricated himself from the King's embrace. "I think we'll go up now, Ned, and for God's sake, spare us a royal bedding."

Edward winked at Roseanna. "Have to obey the damned fellow. He'd think nothing of running me through."

Ravenspur swept his arm around her waist to help her through the throng. She clapped her hands over her ears as they sang, "Her font I longed to lick, to strengthen up my prick!"

10

They maneuvered the corridors and staircases rapidly, hoping no one would follow. She was relieved that Ravenspur knew his way around, for she would have become hopelessly lost if left to her own devices. He opened a door to a large and sumptuous chamber, where she found Alice and Kate Kendall awaiting her. They dropped into a deep curtsey and murmured, "Good evening, Baron Ravenspur. Good evening, baroness."

"Don't call me that! I hate it!" said Roseanna.

The room was oval-shaped, with a painted ceiling of shepherdesses, lambs, cherubs, and clouds. Pale blue curtains swept down from the clouds and were fastened to the four ornate gilt posts of the bed. A fire was banked in the white and gold fireplace, and blue brocade couches sat on either side of it. Tall gilded candlestands holding clusters of twenty candles each stood on each table, along with a liberal supply of wine and sweetmeats. One wall was covered by an immense tapestry that continued the pastoral scene of sweet shepherdesses; another wall displayed paintings in heavily gilded frames; and the third wall had two long windows with brocade curtains drawn over them. The floor was covered with a deep-piled rug that felt like blue velvet.

Roseanna had never seen anything so fine. Her mother loved beautiful things but could never afford this kind of luxury.

Ravenspur said behind her, "The King honors you. These rooms are usually reserved for the Queen."

Suddenly the chamber door burst open, and two dozen people spilled into the room. They were laughing and joking and were led by Tristan and the King; they were intent upon a bedding. The men grabbed Roger, tossed him into the air, and began divesting him of his garments with ribald suggestions. Luckily their noisy laughter prevented most of the lewd words from reaching Roseanna's delicate ears.

The women surrounded Roseanna and urged Joanna and her maids to strip her of her wedding finery. Roseanna looked accusingly at her mother. "How could you?" she cried.

"Darling, a wedding is for fun and games. They won't be denied. They demand proof that you go to your bridegroom unblemished, and I am proud to show them that it is so."

The color drained from Roseanna's face and she went rigid as Alice, Kate, and Joanna began to undress her. Alice was blushing furiously, while Kate's eyes held hers for a moment to convey a look of pity. Then she shrugged and with nimble fingers slipped the gown from her mistress's body, thinking the sooner they got this over with, the better it would be for Roseanna.

They didn't stop at her shift but stripped her of stockings, garters—everything. The noisy laughter hushed as she stood naked before the assembly, and she quickly turned her back upon them. Her dark hair fell to the backs of her knees and shielded her from everyone's eyes, but Joanna reached out and lifted the sable tresses to show her creamy back and long, slim legs. In an instant Kate slipped the white silken robe over her nakedness. Roseanna stood stiffly with downcast eyes, the material clinging to the outline of her upthrust breasts. The virgin was deemed ready to be taken by her bridegroom, the raven.

On the other side of the room there was a commotion. Roger was demanding his black velvet bedrobe and was told it was nowhere to be found. They made a pretense of hunting for it, but Roger knew that Tristan's fine hand was in on this plot and that the robe would not be forthcoming. He was being urged to "have at" his bride; the men began to jostle him toward Roseanna.

The women tried to lead her to the bed, but she stubbornly refused to move. "No, no!" she cried firmly. Then her eyes met his, and he was stabbed to the heart with her mute look of appeal.

Demands of "Bed her! Bed her!" assaulted their ears. Roger knew they would not leave without at least a token display on his part.

"Time you slid your great sword into her sheath!" cried one. "Put your yard up her!" bellowed another.

Roger turned to the King. "When I make my move, get them out of here!" Then, magnificently naked, he strode toward Roseanna. Her eyes traveled the length of him, lingered a moment on his sex, then blushingly lifted to his determined face. He embraced her with strong arms and dipped his dark head to find her soft mouth.

Her lips met his with a sob, and he whispered, "My sweetheart, it will be over in a minute."

Her legs went weak from the nightmare of it all, and she knew she would swoon. The moment he felt her sag against him, he bent and slipped his arm beneath her knees and lifted her against his muscular chest. Suddenly, in spite of the onlookers, he hardened. The great rigid length of him stood up until the tip touched the silken burden he carried. A great cheer rang around the room as he revived her with his kisses, and as he strode toward the bed, the King ushered the protesting merrymakers from the chamber.

Roger set her down gently onto the bed, then moved swiftly to the wardrobe. He donned his velvet robe and turned to the bed. "I'm sorry, my love. They were far gone in drink and couldn't be dissuaded."

She held up her hands as if to stop him from coming closer.

"Ravenspur, some things must be settled between us," she began nervously.

He cocked a lazy brow. "Really?"

"Yes, really. I wish to have my own bedchamber and my own suite of rooms after tonight. I would find it intolerable to have to share with a man I do not love, nor even like," she said. Risking a glance at his hard, lean face, she saw a mixture of lust and amusement. He was like a predatory animal; this close, she felt menace in his big, powerful body. Quickly, she moved across the bed and went on rapidly. "I want to make it plain that I married you because I had no choice, but I have no intention of becoming your wife in the true sense of the word."

"You mean willingly," Ravenspur amended silkily.

Her eyes widened in horror, "You wouldn't rape me?" she cried.

He almost reassured her that he would not, then caught himself in time. With Roseanna he must keep the upper hand, or she would bewitch him and wrap him around her little finger. Before he was finished with her, he would make her as hot to fuck as he was.

"Rape?" he repeated. "I'll have no need to resort to rape. Before we're done, you'll be begging me for more pleasure."

"Pleasure?" she scorned. " 'Tis all men think of! Well, you had better know from the beginning that I am no meek, amenable creature like Rebecca, to lie with supine acquiescence."

He threw back his head and laughed. She saw his white teeth flash and the cords stand out in his powerful neck.

"Supine acquiescence! Roseanna, your vocabulary lays me low."

"I was trying not to be vulgar!" she flared.

"Be vulgar, Roseanna," he whispered.

"All right. I won't lie on my back with my legs open!"

Her words conjured such a vivid picture for him that he knew he must touch her and taste her or go mad. He plucked a silken curl from her naked shoulder and wound it about his fingers possessively. "Now let me be vulgar. You will lie on your back with your legs open, you will lie on top of me with your legs open, and you will lie with your legs wrapped around my neck if I ask it of you—and I shall." His strong hand now cupped one of her breasts and lifted it from her nightgown. His shocking words had once again lit fiery sensations between her legs and spread burning flames along her veins.

She pulled away from him angrily. "Don't touch me!"

His eyes narrowed. Deliberately he unfastened his robe
and stood over her with naked menace. "Are you finished
laying down the law to me?" he asked silkily.

She licked her lips. She was afraid of him—and worse,
he knew of her fear and would take advantage of it. Still,
she had enough spirit to defy him. Or was she goading
him to his limit to see how far he would go so she could
experience the things he would do to her now that he was
her husband, her lord, and her master?

"Touch me," he ordered softly. Her eyes widened, for
she perceived instantly that he wanted her to touch him
there.

She sat frozen, so he took her hand gently and guided
her fingers to the long shaft that rose between them so
shamelessly. The instant her fingers came into contact
with him, he lengthened and hardened even further. She
snatched her fingers away as if they had been burned.
The mixture of lust and amusement came back into his
glittering dark eyes. He shook his head. "Roseanna, such
a to-do over nothing!"

"Nothing?" she flared.

He slipped from the robe slowly as if he were stalking
her. She turned to flee from the bed, but he took hold of
her silken nightgown, undid the buttons, and slid it off
her shoulders. When he let go, she moved backward
quickly. The nightgown fell in a circle around her waist.

"I only meant that you have already lost your virginity," he said smoothly. "That is what you told me, isn't
it?"

"You are no gentleman to throw that at me!" she retorted, covering her breasts with one of the bed sheets.

"And if it is true, you are no lady!" he mocked.

She sat uncertainly on the bed, yet she was determined

that this was as far as she was going to be undressed. As Roger looked at her, the firelight colored one side of her face, and the finespun sheet seemed to shiver against her breasts. He longed to take her in his arms, longed to kiss the insolence from her bold mouth. When she looked away from him, his eyes softened; she was young. "Lie down before you take cold," he said softly.

She slipped under the covers, keeping well to the edge of the bed. He extinguished the candles across the room but left burning the ones beside the bed. Then, naked, he got into bed. He lay on his side and propped himself up on his elbow so he could converse with her. She was prickly as a hedgehog. How to begin his wooing?

"Child, you need not fear me. I'll not hurt you," he murmured, reaching out strong arms and drawing her against him.

"I'm not a child, I'm a woman!" she said hotly. He took her mouth in a savage kiss. His heart was thudding, and she could feel the echoing beat inside her as his strong arms crushed her to his chest.

"Whose heart is beating so loudly?" she whispered.

"Ours," he murmured. "Roseanna," he whispered against her mouth, "I am going to show you what a woman gives to a man and what he gives her in return." His right hand slid between her legs, and his fingers unerringly found the sensitive jewel of her womanliness. Coaxingly, he whispered, "Marriage is a matter of give and take."

Her body jumped back from his touch, and she again took refuge in anger. "Ah, yes, Ravenspur. I give and you take!" she cried.

He raised his voice for the first time. "Be fair, Roseanna! I give you my name, my protection, all my worldly

goods, a position of honor in my castles, and more. I am
willing to give you freedom—the same freedom you've
always enjoyed, to come and go as you please, to consort
with whomever you wish, freedom to breed your horses
or whatever. What are you prepared to give me?"

There was a heavy silence in the room as she thought
desperately for long moments. Finally she said, "Nothing," and lapsed into silence.

"Let me love you, Roseanna," he said low.

"No! You won't turn me into a frightened little rabbit
to do your bidding!"

"I would not change you by one hairbreadth. I want
you exactly as you are!" His hands cupped her buttocks
and drew her against his hardness. She went stiff in his
arms and cried, "Don't touch me!" Her breath was cut
off as Roger kissed her thoroughly. The taste of her on
his tongue and the scent of her fired his fantasies until his
mind reeled with the delicious things he was going to do
with her.

Roseanna's body was awash with wicked sensations.
Any moment now she would arch against him wantonly
unless she fought it. His mouth left hers, and his lips
seared a fiery path down her throat to her breast. She
recoiled from him. "I love another. Don't touch me
again, or I shall retch!"

Angered at last, he flung himself from the bed with a
fertile oath.

"Leave me in peace. There are scores of other rooms."

"I'll not make us the laughingstock of the whole
damned Court," he said, and threw himself down onto
one of the couches. An ominous silence filled the room,
broken only by the crackling of the fire.

Roseanna's mind and body were filled with contradictory impulses. Her mind rejected Ravenspur and cried out for the sweet, safe love of Sir Bryan. But her body lusted for the primitive, wild experiences Ravenspur's very touch promised. She crushed down those wicked impulses, vowing that she would not be guilty of sins of the flesh as her mother had been. Then in a complete turnaround, she asked herself how it could be a sin when they were married in the eyes of God. As always after Roseanna had uttered something particularly cruel, her conscience began to bother her. A half hour of heavy silence passed; she hoped he had fallen asleep but knew in her heart that he had not. "Ravenspur?" she whispered. There was no reply. "I—I'm sorry if I was cruel. It's just that we are total strangers." Silence. "I would like to get to know you so we could become friends." Again silence. "Tell me of yourself. Talk to me."

Even the air was still. Then after a long time she heard a low laugh. It held no happiness, yet it was not bitter, just self-mocking. "Perhaps it is poetic justice," he murmured. She listened. After a pause he went on. "My first marriage was arranged by my parents to a widow ten years older than myself. I protested like hell, but I had no say in the matter. I was fifteen years old."

Roseanna drew in a startled breath.

"My mother was an avaricious bitch. The widow brought me land and a fleet of merchant ships, and that was all that mattered." He paused as the memories came flooding back. "She had bad teeth and foul breath and could not get me to bed fast enough." The mocking laughter came again. "I covered myself with shame on my wedding night. I could not complete my husbandly duties." He wondered why he was telling her all this.

What was the profit in giving a woman weapons she could use against him? Why expose his past weakness?

Roseanna imagined the fifteen-year-old in the bed, and she was filled with compassion for him. He went on quietly. "She died in childbed. Poor Lady Agnes. No matter what our differences, I would not have had that happen."

"I'm truly sorry, my lord," whispered Roseanna.

"It was long ago."

"What of your second wife?" she dared.

"We will not speak of it." His words were cold and final. He turned his back to her and seemingly went to sleep, but his mind was relentlessly dredging up his past. He'd been the greatest young fool in Christendom after that. He was so hell-bent on a wife of his own choice, he'd flown in the face of his parents' advice and had married a girl from the lower classes. He craved someone beautiful who would please him in bed, but unfortunately for him, Janet pleased other men in bed, too—half his knights, if the rumors were true. It had all ended in murder.

He deliberately stopped all further thoughts of his second wife. To allow his mind to dwell upon it, going over and over it, was a sickness. Roger questioned his own wisdom in marrying for a third time after he'd vowed never to remarry; then slowly a smile came to his lips, and he knew with a certainty that Roseanna had been made for him.

Roseanna lay awake for a long time. She did not feel sorry for herself, but her heart ached for Sir Bryan. This would be a night of a thousand hours for him, yet she felt proud that she had not betrayed him.

Roseanna drifted upward through a pleasant dream in which she lay in a sunbeam in a field of new-mown hay.

Then her eyes opened slowly and focused on the blue brocade couch. He was gone! She sprang up, suspecting that he had crawled into bed with her.

He chuckled. "Did you expect to find a viper in your bed?" He loomed over her. She had to tilt back her head to take in the great height of him. As she did so, she was struck by his dark, masculine splendor. This primitive, godlike creature was her husband. The thought sent shivers down her spine. He saw her shudder, and his pent-up frustration demanded that he touch her one way or another. "If you insist on acting like a spoiled child, then I shall have no alternative but to spank you."

"You wouldn't dare!" she challenged, sparks instantly flying between them. He sat down on the bed and dragged her across his lap. Exquisite sensations flooded his loins as her body lay across his thighs. His anger melted as he lifted her nightgown to reveal her deliciously round buttocks. The smell of new-mown hay again filled Roseanna's nostrils, and she realized that the attractive smell was woodruff, which Ravenspur must have used in completing his toilet. She tried to struggle out of the vulnerable, undignified position in which he held her but to no avail.

Kate Kendall was outside their chamber door listening. The moment she heard voices, she nodded to Alice. They entered, carrying a new riding outfit. They were rendered speechless when they saw their new master kissing Roseanna's bottom. Embarrassed herself, Roseanna felt pity for what she knew Alice must feel. She scrambled to a semidignified position, smiled at the girl, and murmured, "I'm so glad you picked that outfit." The tunic was of golden wool, edged in scarlet with a matching cloak and scarlet riding boots—the Plantagenet colors.

Ingenuous as always, Alice replied, "Oh, my lady, it was chosen by Baron Ravenspur." Kate sent Alice a look that could kill and only wished she'd been close enough to give the feckless girl a good pinch.

Roseanna's expression changed. "On second thought, I think I have a very pretty lavender outfit with matching riding gauntlets. I have a fancy for that one today."

"Miss Contrary," muttered Kate.

Roseanna threw a smug little smile at Ravenspur. "You don't mind how I dress, do you?"

Beneath the covers his hand swept up her bare thigh, and when it moved deliberately to the velvety inside, she gasped. "You do the dressing; I'll take care of the undressing," he taunted.

Alice blushed to the roots of her hair.

"Tit fer tat," nodded Kate with satisfaction.

Roger picked up his cloak and threw it negligently over his arm. He surveyed his wife, still sitting in bed. "If I ask you to hurry so we can reach Ravensworth before dark, I suppose you will purposely dawdle. Of course, if you don't mind sharing a bed at some cramped little inn, I certainly don't."

"I may have many faults, my lord, but tardiness is not one of them!" She flung back the bedcovers and swung her legs to the carpet.

"Delightful," he said, more to himself than to anyone in the room. She stifled the urge to throw a candelabrum at him.

Kate saw that she still wore her chemise and surreptitiously examined the bed sheets. When she found neither blood nor semen stains, she pressed her lips together.

This boded no good! If Roseanna was playing games, leading him all around the houses, she was playing with fire. It happened that she had caught his fancy and he was willing to indulge her a bit, but any fool could see that if he were pushed too far, he'd be dangerous. Aye, Roseanna had met her match—and more! She just hadn't realized it yet.

"I'll bring him low yet," vowed Roseanna a couple of moments after he had safely departed.

"There's many a slip 'twixt cup and lip," muttered Kate darkly.

"Oh, I wish we were going to London instead of farther north. I've heard so much about the Court at Westminster. I wish I could get a look at the Queen."

"If wishes were horses, beggars would ride," said Kate.

"Kate, if you utter one more of your damned sayings, I'll scream. From morning till night, all I hear is 'If you cry more, you'll piss less,' or 'Laugh before breakfast; cry before bedtime.' I'm fair toty with your sayings!"

Kate nodded. "Somebody's made you toty, and I don't need three guesses to name him."

"A truce, Kate. I must bid my family farewell; then I'll come and help pack. I want to be ready and waiting when His High and Mightiness returns. I won't give him the satisfaction of gloating over my tardiness."

Roseanna knew it was her duty to bid her mother farewell. She didn't think she could ever forgive Joanna for forcing this marriage on her, but the thing was done and nothing could change it. It had begun to dawn upon her that love and marriage were not the same thing and that she had been naïve and unworldly to expect to be allowed to marry for love. Joanna had not been allowed to do so, and when she thought over every marriage she had seen, she saw clearly that most men and women sought love elsewhere. She could see clearly the reasons why her parents had chosen Ravenspur, for the advantages to her were numerous. What puzzled her was why Ravenspur had been so determined to have her. She brought him nothing. The only explanation she could come up with was that he had been determined to have his way. He would not be thwarted, and when she had asked to be released, she became the one thing that he had to have at all costs. She shrugged, hurried along to her parents' room, and knocked politely.

Neville was dressed, but Joanna was still abed. "Darling, you're just in time to eat breakfast with us. Come, let's have a look at you. For all your pitiful tears and protestations, you don't look any worse for wear."

Roseanna didn't think she'd ever forgive her mother for this marriage, but she'd be damned if she'd let her wounds show. "Oh, I'm all right, but you should see Ravenspur. Poor devil!"

Her mother drawled, "Exhausted, is he?"

Roseanna caught her mother's eye and glared, "No, he's suffering from night starvation!"

Joanna said, "Neville, your daughter can be downright vulgar at times."

"Yes, she takes after you, my dear." He smiled and brushed his lips across Roseanna's brow. "I'll miss you sorely, you know."

"I'll miss you too, Father."

"Nonsense. You'll be so busy breeding, once you get your clutches on Ravenspur's stable, that you won't have time to miss us."

"She may be busy breeding more than horses," laughed Joanna, offering her daughter a plate of food.

Roseanna looked her in the eye again and said, "Don't hold your breath!"

Neville caught a signal from Joanna that she wished to speak privately with her daughter. He quickly kissed Roseanna's brow and withdrew tactfully.

Joanna put down the little silver dish of plums she was eating and took Roseanna's hand. "Oh, my darling, if only I could impart to you my knowledge of men. You are far lovelier than I ever was. If you are clever, you will soon have him eating out of your hand." Roseanna's stubborn chin went up.

"Roseanna, it is a man's world, never doubt it! The power is in their hands. Yet a clever woman, by choosing the most powerful man she knows and enslaving him, gains all his power for herself. Darling, you won't enslave him by denying him your body."

"I am Lady Ravenspur," shrugged Roseanna. "That's enough power for me."

"Simply being married isn't enough. He could take a mistress anytime, and she would have the real power," cautioned Joanna. "You have the man now—but can you hold him?" She hesitated, then admitted, "I couldn't."

Roseanna thought of Edward and the power the Queen had over him.

"The trick is to become a real woman. I can't tell you how to do that; some things can only be learned from a man. Other lessons can only be learned from life. But I urge you to take the cup of life in both hands and drink of it deeply. Ravenspur is a magnificent man! Deny him nothing, and I wager you'll never regret it. Roseanna, I envy you. Go quickly—you have your whole life before you, and you are the only one who can live it. Know that

I love you. If you truly cannot bear it, your home will
always be open to you."

Roseanna, who had entered the room intending to be
cool and unforgiving, threw her arms around her mother
and kissed her farewell.

Roseanna hadn't realized the unwieldy size of the
party that was to travel up to Ravensworth. They were
ready early because she had pushed Alice and overruled
Kate—a wondrous achievement—but Roseanna realized
that if she didn't have the upper hand or at least an equal
voice with Kate, she would be overruled for the rest of
her life. She had escaped her mother's authority and
looked forward to giving orders from now on instead of
taking them.

Kate would ride in the baggage coach, while Alice
would ride beside Roseanna on her gentle palfrey. The
wagons containing her household furnishings were ready
to roll, and her string of Thoroughbreds were being seen
to by Dobbin.

Yet that was only the smallest part of the cavalcade.
Ravenspur had thirty knights, half of whom had brought
their wives to York for the wedding. He also had eighty
men-at-arms, without whom he seldom traveled. Then
there was Tristan Montford, who had his own men, to
say nothing of Rebecca and her servingwomen and baggage. Tristan and his men would travel to Ravensworth
first, then go to Ravenscar toward the east coast.

At first light Sir Bryan Fitzhugh approached Roger.
"Baron Ravenspur, I seek service with you, sir."

Roger raised a brow and examined him closely. The
boy seemed open and honest enough, yet Roger could
hardly believe he would have the gall to follow Roseanna.

"You are the young knight from Castlemaine?" asked Roger, knowing full well his identity.

Sir Bryan looked shamefaced. "I was dismissed from Castlemaine, my lord, because I gave safe escort to Lady Roseanna when she—when she ran away," he finished lamely.

Ravenspur was about to shake his head when Sir Bryan pressed further. "It was I who gave the message to your men at Selby Abbey."

Ravenspur's eyes narrowed. What was his game? Perhaps it would be best if the young devil were where he could keep an eye on him.

"I can always use an extra sword. In the meantime you can keep an eye on the wagons and the people from Castlemaine. Don't let them hold us up on the journey to Ravensworth." Before the words were out of his mouth, Fitzhugh was off his horse and swearing fealty. Roger smiled to himself. God's feet, how fervent young knights were! Perhaps he'd misjudged the boy. Most likely Roseanna had been using him to get to the man she really loved—perhaps one of the King's gentlemen.

He made an effort to throw off the black mood that threatened. He'd never closed his eyes last night, but his blood had been too hot and demanding, enclosed in the same chamber as the object of his desire; he'd been unable to cool his thoughts. From the moment he'd discovered Roseanna was his betrothed, he'd been filled with pleasurable anticipation that flooded through him every time he thought of her. Then she had denied him childishly, and if he knew aught of her tricks, she would do so again tonight. Though he longed for it to happen, he knew she would not yield to him willingly. Well, two could play her game, he thought with amusement. He would have to seduce her, tease her, wear down her resistance until she begged him to make love to her. Roger was determined to win her body and soul, and as he rode along, planned his assault.

When Roseanna was urging Zeus back toward Kate's coach and the horses from Castlemaine, she caught sight of Bryan. Her heart leaped with joy. He had somehow managed to join her household! Their eyes caught and held, but they were both cautious enough to make no greeting. Surreptitiously he placed his hand across his heart, and before she turned Zeus, she did the same.

Tristan rode abreast of her and threw her an admiring glance. "Ravenspur doesn't know how lucky he is to have you. I'd give anything if my wife showed some of your spirit."

"What do you mean?" She smiled.

"You intend to ride part of the way," he explained.

"I intend to ride all the way," she asserted.

His eyes kindled, and he didn't try to hide the admiration he felt for her.

"Tris, don't hold Rebecca in contempt because she rides in the coach with her ladies. I don't think she's very strong."

"Her frailty is deliberate," he began; then he dismissed his wife with a shrug. "Here's Roger."

He rode up with another dark giant at his heels and bowed to Roseanna. "This is Kelly, captain of my men-at-arms. I've asked him to keep an eye on your safety, Roseanna. You may depend on him at all times."

She nodded formally to the man and looked away quickly. She didn't like the way he looked at her. His build was enough like Roger's and Tristan's that he could have been a brother to them; yet something in his dark face repelled her. That he was a hard-bitten soldier, with none of the courteous ways of a gentleman, was plain. Perhaps that was what caused her uneasiness with him.

As she surveyed her new husband, she had to admit that he was a splendid man. He sat on his black Thoroughbred with a regal air of command. His soft leather boots reached above his knees, where his heavily muscled thighs gripped the saddle and the flanks of the stallion. His dark purple mantle was closed by a magnificent clasp of diamonds set in the shape of his initial. She knew not whether it stood for Ravenspur or Roger.

Probably because of her royal blood, Roseanna had a great sense of show and ceremony. She realized instantly that this was her opportunity to display herself to advantage before her husband's people—her people now. Because two previous wives had held her position, she was determined to become *the* Baroness of Ravenspur: the most beauteous, the most gracious, the most beloved. She would not stoop to bicker with her lord before his men. She gave him a brilliant smile; she would keep her barbs for when they were alone.

For a moment Roger was dazzled. His eyes warmed to her beauty, and he said, "Will you do me the honor of riding beside me, Lady Roseanna?"

The breeze carried her voice to all those around them as she deepened her smile and replied, "The honor is mine, my lord husband." Her lavender riding mantle and his a few shades darker complemented each other. Her long black hair was held in a lavender-colored silk net set with amethysts, and amethysts were set among the embroidery of her riding gauntlets.

Roger thought her radiant, as if a light shone from her like a jewel. She was his jewel, and he knew a moment of pride such as he had never known before. His dark eyes roamed possessively over her, and Roseanna became aware of a peculiar sensation that she had never before experienced. It began in the pit of her belly and radiated upward to set her breasts tingling. More disturbing, it also traveled downward to between her legs. It was a wicked feeling; she was confused and alarmed. Bryan affected her heart, but this man who rode beside her with desire hot in his eyes affected her body. Her pulse began to race at a frantic pace; her breasts rose and fell with her rapid breathing. She stole a glance at him, and he winked suggestively as if he knew of the sensations felt inside her. She looked away quickly and fell back to ride beside Alice.

"Oh, my lady, you seem filled with energy. Didn't the last few days exhaust you?"

"To be truthful, Alice, I've never felt so exhilarated. Didn't you have the time of your life at the King's Court and the jousting?" asked Roseanna.

"I'm so unused to crowds. I—I find it all so unsettling."

Roseanna laughed, because at last she was tasting life. "I love new experiences. I thrive on them! Alice, just think of the castles we'll live in from now on. Tonight it will be Ravensworth, but soon we'll be moving to Castle Ravenspur, which overlooks the ocean. I can't wait!"

"Won't you be homesick, my lady?" asked Alice mournfully.

"Homesick? Why, I hadn't considered such a thing. I hope I'm too busy for any such nonsense, Alice. Do you realize that I shall be chatelaine of Ravenspur and that I don't know how to run a household?"

"You'll soon learn, Lady Roseanna. Nothing frightens you."

"I should hope not!" Roseanna looked at Alice and wondered if she was already homesick. "When we move to Ravenspur, it is close enough to Castlemaine that we shall be able to visit often."

"Would you like to ride in the coach with Kate and rest for a while, my lady?"

"Rest?" asked Roseanna, uncomprehending. "Alice, I don't want to miss one moment of this glorious ride! Look down there—it must be the River Ure. From this great height it looks like a silver ribbon. And look, Alice, over there—the woods are black and red and gold! And breathe deeply; this Yorkshire air is so crystal clear, it's like breathing French wine, and it's just as intoxicating."

Alice looked pinched and miserable. "Oh, love, why don't you go and ride with Kate in the coach?" urged Roseanna.

"Will you be able to manage?" Alice faltered.

Roseanna threw back her head and laughed deliciously. "Alice, if I cannot, I have a hundred men at my beck and call!"

Alice felt disloyal to think it, but there were times when Roseanna was like a pagan. That was the only word for it!

From time to time the large cavalcade passed other travelers on the Great North Road. If any were in trouble or needed help, Ravenspur always courteously bade his men attend to it in spite of the delay it caused. Their own party was prey to the usual problems of travelers, such as loose wheels and balky animals; the slow progress would have tried the patience of a saint.

Roseanna rode beside Rebecca's coach and talked with

her for the best part of an hour, learning all about the castle they were going to. Rebecca wasn't happy about going north and wished they were bound for Ravenspur, which was much more comfortably furnished than the northern strongholds in her opinion.

When late afternoon arrived and the slow pace of the long journey had begun to pall, Roseanna unconsciously sought the company of Ravenspur. She would sharpen her wits with a verbal duel, for one thing was certain—he never bored her. The two brothers were riding together and were deep in conversation. Whatever it was they discussed must have been serious, because both their faces were grim. But when Roseanna rode between them, they ceased the discussion instantly. She looked from one face to the other and asked lightly, "Must marriage be such a tragedy?"

They laughed heartily, glad of the diversion, and Tristan fell back so the newlyweds could have a moment of privacy. Ravenspur raked her with his eyes. "Am I under a spell, or do you grow more beautiful with each hour?" He maneuvered his horse close against hers, reached up, and unclasped the diamond R from his mantle and fastened it at her neck.

Her eyes blazed with anger. "Must you brand me with your initial?" she demanded.

"Is it not also yours, Roseanna?" He said her name caressingly.

Her eyes widened when she realized how quick she was to look for insult; she had been ungracious of his gift of diamonds.

"You are all the jewel I need," he said warmly, and she actually felt her knees grow weak. "What do you say to a gallop?" he asked, wondering if she was up to it after

traveling all day. Her eyes lit up, and when he saw her
eagerness, he explained, "We're only about ten miles
from Ravensworth. I could send riders ahead to let them
know of our impending arrival, or we could leave this lot
in our dust and be the first to ride in."

For her answer she spurred Zeus, and horse and rider
flew into the lead. He heard her challenging laughter float
back on the wind and was after her in a flash. She had
every intention of beating him, and she bent low over her
stallion's neck, knowing Zeus had the heart for it in spite
of the long journey. Her hair streamed loose from its
jeweled net, and she felt the silken snood slip down her
back inside her gown. As he came even with her, she
glanced across at him and caught a flash of white teeth in
his dark face. Then the wind whipped a long tress of her
hair across his face, and he exulted in the feel of it. His
black animal, as wild as Zeus, overtook her and threw up
big clods of soft earth as it dug in with its powerful
hooves.

When she clattered into the castle courtyard, his
mount stood still, its sides heaving. Roseanna was
piqued; she was so used to winning, she was a poor loser.
Surreptitiously she reached down and loosened the girth.
"My saddle came loose," she said, challenging him with a
haughty look.

Ravenspur's brow arched. He had just learned a valuable lesson about Roseanna. Rather than admit defeat by
him, she would cheat. Grooms ran from the stables to
tend the horses; they stared openmouthed at the beautiful
wild woman their lord had brought home.

Before she went into the castle to meet her household,
she wanted to put her disheveled hair in order. But try as

she might, she could not fish the amethyst net out from down her back.

Roger's tall shadow fell across her. "Do you need any help?" he asked in his deep voice.

She thought that if he touched her, she would scream. "Unfortunately, I do," she responded coolly. Like a child she put her back to him and bent her head down. He slipped his hand down her bodice. His long fingers caressed the satin skin of her back, then swiftly moved beneath her arm to capture a soft breast. He chuckled with delight as her nipple budded and hardened beneath his teasing fingers.

"That's not playing fair, Ravenspur," she said breathily, trying not to moan from the pleasure he was giving her.

"I'm going to play with you all night," he whispered in her ear, "once I get you to bed." His lips playfully nipped her earlobe. Finally, he pulled the jeweled net out from down her back. She gasped aloud.

"Did the stones scratch you?" he asked with concern.

She shook her head. It was the touch of his fingers that had burned her. She lifted her hands to her head, but he quickly gathered the silken waterfall of her hair into its pretty net. The touch of her hair had the usual effect upon him—it made him hard, erect, and ready for her. He put his great hands beneath her elbows, lifted her high against him, and took her mouth in a long, hard, demanding kiss. Lord, how he lusted for this woman! He gazed down at her from his great height and reached to tuck in an errant curl.

"I can manage," she said, doing her best to regain her composure as she pulled away. She changed the subject rapidly. "I'd like to attend Zeus myself after such a rigor-

ous journey." She said it as if she were challenging him
for the right to be in the stables.

"I approve of your tending to your own horse," he
said, "although you are the first woman I have ever
known who wanted to do such a thing. But just this once,
I think you can safely leave Zeus in the hands of my
grooms, as I will my horse today."

She acquiesced as graciously as she could and turned
to view the castle. It had been built by the Normans in
their solid square style from the pale limestone that
abounded in the area. There was only one barbican tower
over the entrance. A great wolfhound came loping up to
Roger, and he greeted the beast with familiar affection.

The first floor of the castle housed the armory and the
men's sleeping quarters; on the second floor was the vast
dining hall, and behind that the living quarters for the
household servants. Ravenspur's chambers were on the
third level of the castle. Uppermost in Roseanna's mind
was the fact that she intended to have her own rooms,
separate and at some distance from his. She knew it
would take a battle of wills to get her own way.

They began their tour of the castle in its vast kitchens,
to which the warmth and delicious smells had drawn
them. Two great hearths, so large a man could stand
upright in them, were filled with roaring fires. In one an
oxen was being roasted, and in the other fireplace were
spitted a sheep and two deer. Flitches of bacon and hams
hung from the rafters amid bunches of dried herbs and
strings of onions. Scrubbed wooden tables held cheeses,
tubs of butter, and freshly baked loaves. A plump woman
had just baked a dozen blackberry pies. Roseanna bent
over them and sniffed their ambrosial aroma with a heavenly look upon her face. The woman beamed and asked if

she would like to try some. "Yes, please," said Roseanna, stripping off the jeweled riding gloves so she could eat it with her fingers. The kitchen was a beehive of activity, filled with kitchen workers of every age, from the elderly pie maker to the young boys who turned the spits and kept the dogs from the kitchens.

As Roger led her up to the great hall on the second floor, they were met by the household chamberlain. He was a man of middle age, squarely built with a strong face and an air of authority.

"Mr. Burke, I want you to meet my wife, Lady Roseanna. We have been a household of men too long, but I think we will manage the transition smoothly if we all learn to compromise."

Mr. Burke bowed formally to his new mistress, but she smiled inwardly at her husband's attempt at diplomacy. She could tell that Mr. Burke was used to ruling the roost, and compromise was probably a thing he'd never done in his life. She smiled, imagining how the sparks would fly when Kate Kendall and Mr. Burke met head on. She glanced up at Roger and saw from the amusement in his eyes that he had read her thoughts. He took her upstairs to the watchtower; she knew it was his way of maneuvering her to his own chamber. As they looked out from the tower, they saw that the rest of the party were beginning to wend their way up the hill toward the castle.

She turned to him quickly. "I know you'll want to go down and direct things, so I'll just look around and choose a chamber of my own liking." It wasn't a question; it was a statement of her intention. He stood very close, looking down at her without speaking. Then he put his hand beneath her chin and raised her face so that he could look directly into her eyes. "So you still intend to deny me the rights and pleasures to which a husband is entitled?" he demanded.

Her eyes widened. "By God, Ravenspur, are you actually trying to appeal to my sense of fair play when you know damned well that you forced me into this marriage? When I appealed to you, it fell on deaf ears. Let me remind you, I made it plain right from the start that I would not yield to you."

His eyes licked over her like a candle flame; then his mouth was on hers in a kiss that showed how savage he could be. He pulled her body into his so that she was left with no doubt about his hardened condition. Only when he allowed her to was she able to tear her mouth from his. A small curl of fear gripped her. "I shall kiss the insolence from your overbold mouth every time you speak to me in such a manner," he warned her.

"So that's to be my punishment," she said with more daring than she felt.

His arms tightened, and her breasts were crushed against the hardened muscles of his broad chest. "If I wanted, I could take you right here on the floor."

She almost panicked but held her ground with shaking legs. "That would prove you the rutting animal I think you to be."

"You have only yourself to blame. You provoke me, you goad me, you turn me into a savage." He released her, and they stood glaring and panting, their blood high.

Roseanna would not back down, so Roger made up his mind to make her. Very deliberately, he hooked his hands into the neckline of her gown and tore the bodice to the waist. Her bare breasts sprung out at him.

"How dare you!" she cried.

But he ignored her. His head swooped down, and he took her pink nipple into his mouth and sucked hard. At the same time his right hand went up her skirt and his fingers played where they would until he felt her wet and soft. She writhed, trying to escape his grasp, but he was too strong for her. At last he let her go and ordered, "Be on your best behavior tonight when we dine in the hall before our people."

Stunned by his outrageous actions, she nonetheless knew he was at his limit and that pushed further he would indeed be bold enough to take her there on the floor. "Of course I shall be on my best behavior," she said, clutching the ripped bodice and trying unsuccessfully to cover her breasts. "These people are mine now as well as yours."

He allowed her to move past him to leave. When she had safely gained the door, she said, "You owe me a new gown, Ravenspur."

His dark eyes gazed at her breasts. "You're well worth the price of a dress, Roseanna."

11

Roseanna had felt his kiss all the way down to her legs; they had actually become wobbly. *Damn him,* she thought. Damn herself, while she was at it. Whenever he touched her, she was driven so wild that she wanted to scream. Yet she couldn't resist tempting him, so that she almost dared him to touch her.

As Roger went down to the courtyard, he thought, *Damn her! She lures me, then rebuffs me, daring my manhood.* He wasn't going to put up with it any longer. If force was necessary, then so be it!

Roseanna stepped inside his personal apartments and quickly repaired the top of her gown as best she could. Then she donned her cloak and looked around her. His chamber had every comfort imaginable. The blazing fire reflecting the paneled walls and deeply polished furniture was warm and welcoming. The bed was massive and curtained against the draughts. Fur rugs covered the floors, and a large wardrobe extended the length of one whole wall. By the slitted window sat a desk piled with books and papers that quickened her curiosity. But she did not tarry lest he return.

The rooms on the west side of the third level were all plainly yet adequately furnished, but Roseanna searched farther afield. In the northeast corner she came across an outer chamber that connected to an inner chamber through a little vaulted door. It was perfect for her needs, yet the rooms were empty and obviously hadn't been used in some time.

She left quickly to find Alice and Kate. It would take a good deal of work to plenish those chambers before nightfall, but she was determined to do it. "Kate, you know best which wagons hold our furnishings. See if you can get the servants or even some of Ravenspur's men to bring all our stuff up here, and I'll go and see about getting fires lit in these rooms. Alice, you are not to lift anything heavy. You can find out which chamber Rebecca uses while she is here."

Roseanna soon found a squire, who brought live coals from another fireplace; then she sent him off for some flagons of wine. When Kate hadn't returned in twenty minutes, Roseanna went down to find her. She stood in the entrance hall amid piles of bedding, tapestries, and carpets, hands on hips, engaging Mr. Burke in one of the fiercest battles Roseanna had ever heard.

"In a pig's arsehole!" shouted Kate, red in the face.

Roseanna gasped. She was aware that Kate Kendall was a formidable opponent in an argument, but she had never heard her use such vulgarities before.

Mr. Burke stood his ground. "You miserable woman. Get it through your thick skull that I am in charge around here. If I were daft enough not to take her things to the master's bedchamber, he'd cut my balls off!"

"Ha! Out of my way, you pisspot, or I'll pound your balls to powder—that is, if you have any," shouted Kate.

Roseanna choked back laughter. Whatever had gotten into Kate? Didn't she know that that wasn't the way to handle a man? "Mr. Burke, is there some problem?" she asked sweetly.

He turned to her, and his manner did an about-face. "No problem whatsoever, ma'am. You just let me know your wishes, and I'll move heaven and earth to see that they are carried out."

Kate muttered, "You can always tell an Irishman, but you can't tell him much!"

Roseanna quickly held up her hand to warn Kate. She smoothly put her other arm through Mr. Burke's. "Do come upstairs, Mr. Burke, and see the wonderful rooms I've chosen. You run such an efficient household, the squires have already lit fires for me." They entered the rooms. "Now, I thought I'd take the inner room for myself, and my two serving ladies can have the outer chamber. I have brought with me beds and linen, carpets and coffers, and dozens of beautiful tapestries to cover the walls. But alas, I fear it would take Kate weeks to furnish the rooms well, as it should be done."

"Tonight, ma'am." He nodded firmly.

"I beg your pardon, Mr. Burke?" She hung on his every word helplessly.

"While you are in the hall tonight for supper, I shall see that these rooms are made ready down to the last detail. By the time you are ready to retire, you will think you have lived here for years. Leave everything to me, my lady."

"Oh, I will, Mr. Burke. You have no idea what a relief it is to know I can place complete confidence in you."

Kate exploded the moment he was out of earshot. "The constipated cockatrice! I was ready to shove a red-hot poker up his arse!"

"Very pretty sight," said Roseanna, smiling.

"Oh, child, I'm sorry to use such language," she apologized.

Roseanna laughed. "I'm happy to know I'm not the only one with a ripe vocabulary, but thank heaven Mother couldn't hear you."

" 'Twas Lady Joanna taught me to curse"—Kate grinned shamefaced—"and 'twas the King taught her!"

"Oh, here are our trunks," said Roseanna, throwing one open and pulling out some gowns. "Find me something special to wear, and we'll go along to Rebecca's chamber to change for dinner while they plenish these rooms for us."

Rebecca was abed when they arrived at her room. Her servingwomen had already unpacked her clothes, along with Tristan's, and had hung them in the wardrobe.

"Aren't you going to dine in the hall tonight?" asked Roseanna, surprised to find her sister-in-law abed.

"I'm not hungry," she said, "and far too fatigued. Why don't you have a tray sent up, and we can have a visit?"

"If I know Ravenspur, he'll come and drag me by the hair if I didn't go down. This is my first night, and I've already been warned to be on my best behavior," Roseanna said with a grimace.

Rebecca shuddered. "They'll all want a good look at you, especially the women. They flirt openly with Tristan and Roger, you know. Every one of them is eager to lie with them."

Roseanna's eyebrows shot up. "Surely their husbands wouldn't permit such behavior!" she protested.

Rebecca shrugged. "Some of them are widows of knights or daughters not yet married. Many of the men are at Ravenspur's other strongholds. They are an uncouth lot, and I try not to mix with them."

Roseanna was determined to outshine all the other females tonight. She chose a gown of the palest green. The underdress had hundreds of little pleats; its sleeves were transparent and edged with silver ribbon. The velvet tunic was split all the way up each side and was tied by silver ribbons to show off the filmy underdress. She let Alice brush out her long black hair and decided to wear it loose down her back, caught at one temple with a silver butterfly that her mother had fashioned for her.

A sudden thought came to her. She picked up the cloak she had worn and removed the diamond clasp from it. Then she pinned the large R between her breasts because her wicked juices had begun to bubble and she wanted to see Ravenspur's eyes when they fell upon it. The corners of her mouth went up. The bauble was so glitteringly eye-catching, he wouldn't be able to keep his eyes from her breasts.

Roseanna insisted that Alice and Kate wear their most attractive gowns. She had decided they should sit at the head table in a place of honor because they were her special ladies. She made a point of arriving at the hall a few minutes late so that every eye would be upon her when she entered.

The head table was dominated by a large, ornately carved chair at the center. Beside it Ravenspur stood conversing with Tristan and Captain Kelly. As soon as she entered the hall, he raised his head and smiled his welcome to her. She wondered if the smile was for the benefit of those who watched them or for her alone. Before she reached the dais, two servants came staggering in under the weight of a second ornately carved chair, which they placed beside the first. Ravenspur came to the edge of the dais to assist her to her place.

Close up, she saw that he was dressed in dark green. They looked like players on a stage who had been costumed in the same color because they were lovers. He raised both her hands to his lips, and the diners in the hall began to shout and whistle and stamp their feet. The hall was crowded tonight; even the windowsills were occupied by the younger pages and squires. Roger grinned at his people and Roseanna gave them a dazzling smile. Finally, when they would not quiet, Roger held up his hands for silence.

"For those of you who have not yet met her, I would like to present Lady Roseanna Montford, Baroness of Ravenspur." They took up their cheering again, and Roseanna laughed happily. Every hand present raised a goblet to her. Again Roger held up his hands so they would listen. "This has been a bachelor's stronghold for many years. I once swore that nothing would ever again compel me to take a wife, and I have remained unmarried for eight long years. Yet here I stand, a married man." The laughter rolled around the hall. "How do I explain it?" he asked. "It was a *coup de foudre*—the stroke of lightning that changes everything. I saw her, and I was stunned as a bird that's flown into a wall!"

They cheered and stamped their feet. Roseanna was thrilled and strangely moved by his words. "I want you to take her to your hearts—as I have." His warm eyes caressed her; he raised his goblet to her, then drained it.

She held up her hand, and the crowd politely quieted for her. "I raise my goblet to you, the people of Ravensworth and Ravenspur." Her words were drowned by thunderous applause as one by one every man and woman stood to offer her tribute.

They sat down, and the meat was served. Roger gave her a warm look of approval. "That was prettily done. I'm very proud of you." His eyes lowered to his initial and lingered on her breasts. When he raised his eyes, he saw that she was blushing furiously and had to lower her lashes to her cheeks. He laughed deep in his throat. When she glanced up quickly, he let his eyes lick over her like hot flames.

Tristan leaned forward and said laughingly, "You look as if you want to eat her."

"I do," said Roger suggestively. Roseanna shivered.

Tristan grinned at her; the devil was glittering in his eyes. "Why don't I stand up and propose a bedding for the new bride and groom?"

"Tristan, don't do this to me," she hissed.

"There's something about newlyweds that turns us all into voyeurs." He laughed. "Everyone in this hall is dying to see you two in bed together."

"I'll kill you, Tris!" she threatened.

His merriment increased. "In two or three years I'll start to worry!"

Roger leaned forward and said, "Find your own woman. This one's mine."

Tristan grinned wickedly, "I was the one who laid her naked at your feet, brother. How soon you forget!"

Roseanna was utterly still for a moment. She looked from one dark face to the other, then said quietly, "What do you mean?"

"Nothing—just a jest," said Tristan. But he looked as guilty as sin, and Roger's lips tightened in a warning that

he had said too much. Roseanna searched her husband's
face. She'd get out of him what they had done to her, but
not here, not now in front of their people.

Roseanna finished her meal in silence without once
looking at her husband. But she was very much aware of
him sitting close beside her. The physical power of his
body could actually be felt when she was this close to
him; he silently overwhelmed her. When his thigh
brushed hers beneath the table, she drew in her breath as
if she'd been burned.

She forced her mind on to another subject. Her interest
fell on the other women in the hall as she watched them
covertly. She was relieved that none could compare to
her in beauty or dress, but there were many women with
voluptuous bodies who cast inviting glances to the men at
the head table. As the meal progressed and the goblets
were drained, the laughter and license increased apace.
She glanced at Tristan and said primly, "This looks like a
night for torn bodices or worse!"

He whispered, "Or better, depending on how you look
at it!"

She turned her back on him and said to Roger, "I've
had enough, my lord. May I retire?"

A heavy, sweet ache suddenly flooded his loins. His
dark eyes showed clearly the desire he felt. "We shall
retire together," he murmured.

Her eyes threw back her challenge: "We shall not."

"And if I order it, madame?"

"I am your wife, my lord, not your slave. I don't take
kindly to orders." They spoke as softly as they could, yet
still Tristan heard and was shocked to hear her speak so
to her husband.

"How dare you, madame?" Roger demanded. Tristan's

face mirrored the exact same phrase, as if he himself had spoken it aloud.

"I must dare or be crushed, married to Ravenspur." Her breasts heaved in her agitation, and Roger could see that in another moment she would throw away discretion and fly at him. The light of battle was in her eyes, and her blood was up. In a flash he pushed back his chair and swung her up into his arms. The hall went wild. Under the din they had made, Roger said, "If you put your arms around my neck, I will carry you to your bed. If you resist, I shall carry you to my bed and teach you to be an obedient wife!"

She gasped, then slowly slipped her arms around his neck. He carried her from the hall. She could feel the cords in his neck; the arms that held her so possessively were like iron. A weakness came over her that she could not control. She was utterly amazed at herself. *By God, he's so handsome he almost makes me swoon,* she thought. She did not yet realize that a strong-willed woman needed a man who would try to master her. That delicious lesson lay in her future—to be dreamed of, anticipated, and devoutly desired.

Suddenly, she stiffened in his arms. "Sir, this is not the way to my chamber."

"Of course not. It is the way to mine," he said easily, mounting the stairs without even breathing hard.

"But you promised! You promised that if I didn't make a scene, you would take me to *my* bed."

He grinned down at her. "Promises are made to be broken. You taught me that," he added with relish. He shouldered open his bedchamber door, then leaned back against it to close it firmly.

"I?" she faltered as the bed loomed large before her, seeming to fill the room.

"Roseanna, my love, you break promises and vows without even thinking about them."

"I've made you no promises save to make you wretched!" she said hotly.

He put her down before him and cupped her face with his hands so that she was forced to look up into his eyes. "What about your wedding vows, Roseanna? Did you not promise to love, honor, and obey me?" He emphasized each word slowly.

She blushed. "I cannot love you, my lord. Love is something that cannot be commanded. However, I am a woman of honor, and I shall honor you and your name and your position." She veiled her eyes with her lashes and said softly, "I will also obey your orders and try to be a dutiful wife."

The corners of his mouth twitched with amusement. "Meekness doesn't sit well with you Roseanna. You don't mean one word of that fine little speech."

She opened her eyes wide with innocence. "My lord, you are wrong! Only set me a task."

"Kiss me," he said simply.

Her heart skipped a beat. He had kissed her, but she had never kissed him, and she never intended to. Why, she would have to stretch up against him onto her very tip-toes and lift her mouth up to reach his. She knew he was waiting. She decided he could wait forever. Finally he said, "You see, you will not even comply with the smallest wifely duty."

The intimacy was overpowering and she knew she must get out of this room. Desperately, she resorted to bargaining with him. "I will comply with a wifely duty if you will show me you are a man of honor and let me go to *my* bed as you promised." She expected that he would again ask for the kiss and decided it was a small price to pay to get to the safety of her own chamber.

"Undress me," he commanded suggestively.

She was trapped. She would have to keep her promise to ensure that he kept his. She lifted shameful eyes to his, then swept her lashes down shyly. Slowly she reached up to unbutton his doublet. She was aware of him more than she had ever been before, and she knew his eyes were fastened on her mouth. He shrugged his shoulders from the garment and tossed it aside, then took her hand and drew her across the room to the great bed. She followed him reluctantly, having little choice in the matter.

He sat on the bed and awaited her next move. She reached out to unfasten the silk shirt he wore beneath his doublet, knowing that his chest would be entirely naked once it was removed. When her fingers came into contact with the crisp black curls at the neck of the shirt, they trembled slightly, and she heard him laugh softly.

Damn him, he was enjoying her discomfort to the full! When he raised his arms so that she could lift the shirt over his head, she saw the thick, black hair beneath his armpits and shuddered at the sight of his masculinity. She could hardly believe the width of his shoulders as he sat half naked before her. An image of her soft, white breasts being crushed against his heavily furred chest filled her head, and she turned to flee.

A strong hand shot out to anchor her before him. She took a deep, steadying breath and knelt to remove his boots. Watching her, he felt an aching tenderness in his heart that spread throughout his chest. He knew without a doubt that he loved her. This was his woman!

Only one article of clothing remained. Her lips trembled, but dutifully she reached out to his hips. His large hands covered hers as he lifted first one to his lips, then the other. She looked at him questioningly and saw his eyes had gone smoky with desire. Suddenly he swept her up into his arms, and she screamed with alarm.

"I believe I promised to carry you to your bed, my love," he whispered into her ear. Without speaking, they communicated. He raised an eyebrow, and she showed him the way to her chamber, where, half naked, he swept past the servingwomen in the outer room.

She couldn't believe her eyes. The rooms had been transformed. Everything was in readiness for her. Mr. Burke had even turned back the bedcovers so that the warmth from the fire would take the chill from her sheets.

"So this is where you've decided to hide yourself," mocked Roger.

"Put me down," said Roseanna; then she quickly added, "Please."

He set her down onto the window alcove and touched the velvet cushions piled there. Then he saw the fur coverlet on the bed and noted, "Mr. Burke has robbed my chamber to furnish you with every comfort." He glanced behind a leather screen in one corner and saw a slipper bath decorated with hand-painted roses.

"Yes. Everything will be perfect once you have removed yourself," she said sweetly.

Though he knew not how, he held on to his temper. "So you mean to banish me, to cast me out to my own devices?"

"I care not how you amuse yourself, Ravenspur, as long as you leave me in peace."

His eyes fell on the diamonds glittering between her breasts. "Can you not call me Roger?" he asked almost wistfully.

"Never!" she vowed.

He sighed and took a turn around the room, reluctant to leave. "Do you play chess or backgammon, Rose-anna?"

"Yes," she said shortly.

"Do you play well?" he asked, his dark eyes intent on her.

"Of course. I do everything well!" She tossed her head, and her long, dark hair shimmered in the firelight.

"I'll bet you do," he murmured, and a hot curl rose at the pit of her stomach because his words carried a double meaning. "Will you play with me, Roseanna?"

She blushed and could have screamed because he had the power to do this to her. "No! I will not come to your chamber to play games!"

"Then I challenge you to a match on neutral ground. Are you afraid?" he taunted.

"Afraid?" she scoffed. "Ravenspur, I am not afraid of losing at chess, and I am not afraid of you!"

His teeth gleamed in the firelight as he flashed his wolf's grin. "Then I shall look forward to a high-stakes game," he said before he turned and left the room.

Alice and Kate entered the moment he left. "Are you all right?" asked Kate like a mother hen to one of her chicks.

"Perfectly," said Roseanna, stretching her arms high above her head in a very feline gesture. She was weak with relief that he had allowed her one more night. She fully realized that Ravenspur was in command whenever they were alone together and that it was his decision to take her or leave her whenever he felt like it.

Now she put on a brave face before her women. "Mr. Burke has done a marvelous job. I can't believe the transformation!"

Kate Kendall snorted, "No better than I could have done if you'd left me to it."

"Dear Kate, you had much too fatiguing a day to haul beds around. Oh, Alice, don't bother unpacking those coffers tonight. Tomorrow will be soon enough to hang up all my dresses. Your chamber is as well furbished as mine, I hope?"

"Oh, yes," said Alice. "We have a pile of towels and lavender soap, and even the candles are scented."

"And so they should be, with all Ravenspur's wealth. We haven't married into a tinpot family, you know," said Kate.

Roseanna was thoughtful. She could detect a note of pride in Kate's voice whenever she said *Ravenspur*. As she prepared for bed, she mused on Ravenspur's tolerance. He let most of her barbs pass; then when she provoked him too far, he always kissed her. Of course he'd had a lifetime of experience with women—both ones he'd been married to and ones he hadn't.

Her thoughts drifted to his second wife. How curious that he would not speak of her! She wondered idly where she could glean some information. She was willing to bet Mr. Burke had been Ravenspur's household chamberlain for more than eight years. She fell asleep determined to learn all she could on the morrow and in the days to come.

* * *

Dressed in a pretty wool riding dress, Roseanna ran lightly along the corridor to Rebecca's chamber. "It's a glorious morning, Rebecca. I'm going for a ride to familiarize myself with the countryside. Would you care to join me?"

Rebecca, roused from sleep, sat up in bed and blinked. "What are you doing up in the middle of the night?"

Roseanna drew back the heavy curtains to let in the autumn sunshine. "It isn't the middle of the night. It's past eight in the morning. See, your husband's already up and about."

Rebecca made a face. "Tris doesn't bother to come to my bed most nights."

"Oh, I'm sorry, Rebecca," she said shyly. "I thought you were in love."

"I am—that's the trouble. But he doesn't care a fig for me."

"But he must have loved you, or why would he have chosen you for his wife?" pointed out Roseanna.

Rebecca looked woebegone. She whispered, "I was foolish enough to let him seduce me. He got me with child. Ravenspur was the one who insisted he marry me."

"You have a child?" asked Roseanna in amazement.

"A little girl. She's back at Ravenspur with her nurse."

"Don't you miss her?" asked Roseanna, trying to understand the girl's apathy.

She shrugged. "I'm usually not feeling well enough to look after the child. Her nurse does a much better job than I ever could."

"Oh, Rebecca, all your ideas are exactly the opposite of mine! I want to take hold of you and shake you! You say you are in love with Tristan, yet you're not willing to make any effort to secure his interest. You purge yourself of food so you won't become fat, but you don't realize that it makes you listless, apathetic—almost an invalid!"

"It's easy for you to talk," said Rebecca, showing a little spirit at last. "You're beautiful, slim, full of vitality, and your husband is besotted with you."

Roseanna ignored the last of her words and replied to the first. "You think I'm slim, yet my breasts are twice as full as yours."

Rebecca shook her head. "I'm fat and lumpy."

"My God, you exasperate me. I could rattle your teeth! You have a totally warped picture of yourself. You are emaciated, Rebecca! What can I do to drive home the fact that you are killing yourself?" Roseanna was suddenly struck with an idea and acted on impulse immediately. She took off her dress and her chemise, peeled off her stockings, and dragged Rebecca from her bed. Both naked, they stood in front of the mirror together. Rebecca was so white and thin, she looked no more than twelve years old. Her ribs were completely visible, her stomach was concave, and her breasts were little empty sacks. In contrast, Roseanna's flesh glowed with health. Her hips curved saucily, and her breasts thrust up firmly. Rebecca burst into tears.

Instantly filled with compassion, Roseanna said, "Oh, love, I didn't mean to make you cry. I only meant to show you that you are hurting yourself."

"How can I look like you?" whispered Rebecca.

Roseanna began to dress. "You must eat—and exercise a little. I don't mean go crazy all at once, but you must try to eat three small meals every day and be determined never, ever to make yourself vomit again."

"I'll try," promised Rebecca tearfully.

"Good! You will sit next to me in the hall, and we will be company for each other. After a few days when you get some strength back, we'll begin walking and riding. You'll see—energy begets energy! Once we restore your beauty, we'll begin working on Tristan. You have handed him over to other women on a silver platter. We will turn all that around and break *his* heart for a change."

"Do you mean I should try to make him jealous by flirting with other men?" asked Rebecca.

"If you want to flirt with someone, flirt with Tristan. He'll respond instantly. You've neglected him far too long. I'm off on my ride now, but I'll come for you tonight, and we'll go to the hall together. Wear something very pretty."

12

The King's youngest brother, Richard, Duke of Gloucester, had arrived at the first light of dawn. He had ridden
all night, since he did everything with great intensity.
Roger took him up to the barbican tower, where they
could consult maps and see if Richard was being followed, as he half suspected he was.

"Roger, I know in my heart that our brother George is
plotting treason, but Ned just won't listen to me. He
won't face facts. I've been patrolling the Scottish borders.
Warwick is inciting the rebels in the North, led by Robin
Mendell. My spies saw a meeting between them. Warwick
would not try to bring down the King unless he had
someone to replace him, someone standing by ready, willing, and eager to assume the kingship as his divine right.
George has secretly married Warwick's daughter! I'd
have to be a blind man not to see that they have formed
an unholy alliance—the kingmaker and the King's
brother. Why can Ned not see it?"

Roger shook his head. "In his heart he does not want
to believe such evil of the brother he grew up with. I

doubt if he will take precautions, because that would show he suspects them."

"Christ Almighty. Will they have to take arms against him before he'll do something?" demanded Richard.

Roger nodded slowly, "I think so, Richard. I've warned him; we all have. That's why I'm up garrisoning my northern castles. I know they're plotting. All I can do is try to find out when and where, then frustrate their plans."

"I suspect Warwick of plotting with the Scots. I think he's hand in glove with them. If he gave the nod, we'd have an invasion by the Scots. And on the pretext of safeguarding the nation, God alone knows what measures Warwick would take."

"Well, we both did our service with Warwick. I'd never make the mistake of underestimating him," said Roger.

"I also know what Warwick's capable of. When I was his squire, he knocked my tooth out for allowing a drop of wine to run down to the foot of his silver goblet! The only thing I don't understand is how a man with such rigid, high standards has thrown in his lot with a weakling like George."

"You have put your finger on it. He's not using him because he admires him; he's using him because he is weak and stupid and vain enough to be manipulated."

Richard's eyes scanned the purple hills in the distance. "George was a hateful youth. He was jealous because Ned had a fondness for me. I was much younger and smaller than the rest of them. Well, you know I was the runt of the litter. If I took pleasure in a toy or an animal, he wasn't satisfied until he'd destroyed it," said Richard bitterly.

"He was a disagreeable young man," Roger agreed.

"He hid his savagery from you and Ned because you were older. I recall the time after our father and our brother Edmund were killed. One day he was gloating over some prophecy about 'the first shall be last and the last shall be first.' I was only eight at the time, and I asked him to explain the words of the prophecy. He said it was his destiny to become King, and the proof of it was that one of the brothers who stood before him in line to the throne had already been removed. Like a schoolboy, I pointed out to him that if 'the last were to become first' then it was I, Richard, who would someday be King of England. He kicked me in the face and broke my nose. Though I was only eight, I learned my lesson with George."

"Ned offered Warwick the supreme insult when he offered one of the Queen's brothers for Warwick's daughter," said Roger.

"That's another blind spot Ned has. He will not see how venomously the Woodvilles are hated and detested. Westminster is home to all the worst whores, pimps, and thieves in London. If I were in Ned's shoes, I'd have George and Warwick in the Tower!"

"And half the Woodvilles, too, by the sound of it?" suggested Roger.

Richard laughingly agreed. Suddenly he stiffened. He gazed down into the courtyard. "By God, Roger, you've a spy in your midst! There—that fellow is one of George's men."

Roger looked down and saw Sir Bryan pass a note to Roseanna and move quickly away. "I have him under constant surveillance until I discern his mission here." Roger smiled.

"Who was that lovely creature with him?" asked Richard, his jaw hanging openmouthed.

"That was my wife," Roger said coldly.

Roseanna, her heart hammering, hid the note inside her glove and walked briskly to the stables. Old Dobbin saddled up Zeus for her. "Lady Roseanna, I'm in sort of a cleft stick." He looked at her helplessly, which appealed to her instantly. "I've orders not to let you go without a good groom. Usually that puts you in a tizzy, but to tell you the truth, I think it's a sound idea. Better to be safe than sorry, and this far north, you could run into some uncivilized barbarians."

She smiled at him. "What would you say if I told you my hoyden days are behind me? That now I'm a respectable married woman who acts with discretion on all occasions?"

"I'd say horseshit!" he said bluntly.

"And you'd be exactly right." She laughed. "Go on, I'll take a groom. I don't doubt you've already got one picked out."

He chuckled. "I'll be right back." He returned with a squarely built young man who was already booted and spurred. "This is Kenneth. He's a strong set of fighting muscles, and he's armed."

"Good morning, Kenneth." The young man eyed her warily and answered, "Morning, ma'am."

"Look, I'm afraid we're stuck with each other, so let's make the best of it. Give me a leg up." Kenneth cupped his hands to boost her into the saddle. She placed her hand on his shoulder to hoist herself up and grinned. "God, you're as square and solid as a mason's block!" He grinned up at her, his wariness gone.

In minutes they were out on the dales and fells. The green ferns were turning to bracken. This was the time of year when everything turned from lush green to russet and dun. The heather still bloomed, giving the distant fells a purple hue, but the heather's stems and leaves were turning to rough brown bracken, too. The fells were dotted with sheep and stone walls, and above them were scudding gray clouds and cries of the lapwing.

They galloped at a pace so fast, they surprised an occasional rabbit or moorhen. To the west in the distance rose the great Penine chain of mountains, linking the moors and the valleys like the backbone of some huge prehistoric monster. Roseanna curved in a wide circle and began to ride in the opposite direction. When at last she brought Zeus to a walk and let him nibble the turf, Kenneth said, "That's a fine horse. In our stable only Ravenspur's can compare with it."

"I bred him myself," she said proudly.

"So, the tales old Dobbin tells of ye are true then, my lady?"

Her eyes sparkled with amusement. "Well, I think it's safe to say he probably didn't exaggerate. I want to breed some fine horses and build up Ravenspur's stable."

"That's a beautiful white horse ye brought with ye," he said.

"That's an Arabian. I'm going to breed him right away, if I can."

"We don't have any mares fine enough for him to cover, ma'am. One or two of the knights have some Thoroughbred stallions, but most of the fighting men ride big geldings. We only have one or two mares."

"I'll have a look at them, Kenneth. If we don't have any, we'll have to buy some. Breeding your own is a long process. A mare takes a year to gestate, and I suppose most stables find it simpler to buy what they need. But my father taught me how, with selective crossbreeding, you can acquire the very best horseflesh for the very least expense. You'll see—in a few years Ravenspur's stables will be the envy of every landowner in the country." She heard her own words, heard the pride in her voice when she said the name *Ravenspur.* She was speaking of a long time into the future, but she wasn't even sure of tonight's events. She shook her head in perplexity.

The note inside her glove pricked her skin as well as her conscience. She dared not open it until she was alone in her chamber. After she returned to the castle, she passed through the main living quarters on the second floor and saw that her husband and Tristan were entertaining a guest.

"Roseanna, come and meet Richard, Duke of Gloucester," said Roger.

She moved forward with anticipation, her curiosity almost making her forget to curtsey. Then belatedly she sank down before him. "Sire," she breathed.

The boy before her blushed. "Nay—no formality, I beg you, Lady Roseanna. I am most sorry I was not able to be present at your wedding."

She couldn't believe her eyes. He was only about seventeen, slightly built, with dark auburn Plantagenet hair and the most serious air about him that she had ever encountered in a young man. "Welcome to our castle, Prince Richard, I know Ravenspur will show you every hospitality."

"Yes, he is a loyal friend to Ned and myself. I prize loyalty above all other qualities." His eyes bored into hers as if he were pressing home a point, and suddenly the note inside her glove began to burn a hole in her palm.

The contrast between the King and his young brother was startling. Here he stood without any trappings of office in a very worn leather jerkin, yet he held himself with such dignity that she knew there was intense force to be dealt with in the slight youth. As she studied his face, she saw its beauty and realized that she resembled him far more than she resembled the blond giant who was her father. So this was her uncle. She liked him, she decided. Gray eyes smiled into gray. "Will you sit with me in the hall tonight?" she asked.

"If Ravenspur will not look daggers at me." Richard smiled.

"No, no, that is his natural look," she teased, and sent her husband a challenging glance.

Tristan followed her upstairs. "Not quite the peacock you expected, is he?"

"No, but by God, I'll bet he's a man," she said thoughtfully.

"Don't tell me he has made a conquest of you. What will I do for amusement tonight if all your attention is reserved for Richard?" he complained.

"Oh, didn't you know? Rebecca is joining me for dinner." She slipped into the outer chamber and leaned back against the door to laugh. That would teach him not to be such a tease!

As Kate went to follow her into the inner chamber, she said, "Give me a few minutes alone, Kate. The King's brother Richard dines with us tonight, so I want us all to look our best." She closed the door, stripped off her glove, and unfolded the piece of paper.

I will keep close watch, and when it is safe, I will
come to you sometime between the hours of midnight and four.

Her breath caught sharply. God, he must not! Come to
her for what? To make love to her? To sleep with her?
This wasn't what she wanted at all. Why hadn't he sent
her a poem, something she could sit and dream over? She
realized that she did not want a flesh-and-blood lover.
She had one of those to fight off every night. She needed
Sir Bryan to be her gentle, perfect knight to love from
afar. She sat down at her dressing table and silently
thanked Mr. Burke for providing her paper and quills.

Do not come to me. I cannot receive you in my
chamber. We must only meet in such public places
as the hall or the stables.

There was a knock upon her door; she folded the message quickly and called, "Come in." It was Alice with her
gown. "Alice, I need you to find Sir Bryan and give him a
note. Don't let Kate know, or anyone else for that matter. Go quickly—I'll get Kate to help me dress."

Roseanna picked up the beautiful velvet gown after
Alice left and looked at it critically. It was the deep color
of rich burgundy wine, and it was lavishly decorated with
cream lace at the neck and sleeves. "Kate, come in here a
moment and give me your advice." She knew that that
was an irresistible invitation. "I want to get rid of all this
lace and leave the gown plain."

Kate frowned. "Cream and burgundy are a perfect
contrast for each other. With your black hair, you need
the cream color for a highlight."

"I agree about needing the cream color, but I was thinking of pearls. I have a six-strand choker with a ruby pendant attached, and I have strings of creamy pearls that we could thread through my hair. Yes, that's the answer. Help me unpick this lace. You do the neckline, and I'll do the sleeves. What gossip have you picked up about Ravenspur? Anything about his last wife?"

Kate was taken off guard. "Nay, nothing about his wives. I did learn that he has no special mistress tucked away. He consorted with whores when the need took him —oh, my lamb, have I shocked ye?"

"Not at all. I've seen Cassandra, the infamous courtesan, although I didn't realize her profession until the next day. God help my ignorance!"

" 'Twas not ignorance, 'twas innocence, and innocence is very becoming in a bride."

Roseanna snorted. "I want to get dressed early so I can go to Rebecca's chamber and bully her into dining with me. Tristan's another man with a taste for whores—or anything else in skirts—and Rebecca and I are going to wean him," said Roseanna firmly.

Kate Kendall shook her head and spoke into the air. "One Montford isn't enough for you. Oh no, you have to take on both. Roseanna, you are a glutton for punishment."

Roseanna laughed, eager for the challenge. "Kate, save your pity for the Montford brothers. They are going to need it."

When every last string of pearls she owned was threaded in intricate patterns through her tresses, Roseanna swept down the corridor to Rebecca's room. She found her on the verge of tears amid a pile of gowns.

"I cannot go down. I have nothing to wear!" wailed her sister-in-law.

Roseanna went to her wardrobe and subjected each gown to scrutiny. "This is perfect!" It was a deep rose pink with a quilted satin bodice and sleeves. "See, the quilting will fill out your figure deliciously, and think of how well our colors will look together when we sit next to each other."

"Oh, if only I had some pearls so I could thread them through my hair like yours," pined Rebecca.

"We can do the same thing with ribbon. In fact, it's much easier to thread ribbon through hair—you'll see."

"The hardest part for me is walking into the hall. I wish there were some way I could slip in unseen." Rebecca sighed.

"A fate worse than death! I love to be dramatic. We shall be purposely late, and that will assure that every eye is trained upon us. I learned long ago that you cannot control what people say about you. They can say kind, admiring, flattering things, or they can say cruel, jealous, catty things. I don't care which, as long as they don't pity me!"

The remark hit home. Rebecca thought that if she followed Roseanna's advice, perhaps they wouldn't pity her anymore.

Ravenspur's face glowed with pride as Roseanna walked to the dais. Men really did gaze openmouthed at her beauty. Tristan blinked rapidly when he saw how lovely his own wife looked for once, and it reminded him of the first time he'd seen her, five years before.

Richard had changed from his rough leathers into a black velvet doublet with wide padded shoulders and a most startling pair of white satin hose that clearly showed the bulge of his manhood. The device of the Duke of Gloucester, a white boar, was emblazoned on his shoulder. He had a grace about him that the Montford men did not possess. His manners were impeccable. First he kissed Roseanna's hand, made her a leg, and complimented her gown. Then he repeated the process with Rebecca, who blushed prettily.

Roseanna quickly rearranged the seating. She placed Richard as guest of honor between herself and Ravenspur, sat Rebecca on her other side, and invited Tristan to sit next to his wife. Then Roseanna proceeded to engage Richard in such an animated conversation, skillfully drawing in Rebecca, that the three of them laughed their way from the first course through the main course. She kept a strict eye on everything that went onto Rebecca's plate so that she would not be overfed while at the same time she plied Richard with many questions about London and the Court at Westminster and the latest fashions.

"I fear I've raised eyebrows here tonight with these white satin hose, but I swear they are conservative by Court standards. The latest fashion is particolored hose, and the clergy are denouncing fashions such as beribboned codpieces as licentious—which of course they are," said Richard, laughing. "Each season the doublets get shorter and the hose tighter, which is all very well for those of us in the prime of our youth. But it makes for some hilarious caricatures in older men."

"Like Ravenspur?" asked Roseanna with a twinkle in her eye.

Richard said, "What a wicked thing to say." But he couldn't help laughing.

Roger at one end and Tristan at the other were almost

ignored. Their eyes met, and they commiserated with each other.

"Can you stay with us awhile, Your Grace?" Roseanna asked.

"Alas, this has been a delightful respite for me, but I return to border patrol at dawn."

"Then we must have some music and dancing so you can drop your heavy responsibilities for a few hours." She turned to Rebecca and softly asked, "Are you feeling well?"

Rebecca smiled and nodded. "Promise me you'll stay long enough to dance with Richard," Roseanna whispered.

Rebecca whispered back, "I might even dance with Tris if he asks me nicely." She giggled. "He had to take my hand under the table to get my attention."

Good, thought Roseanna. *Now if I can only run my own life as easily as I run others'.* She gave Ravenspur a swift sideways glance and found his eyes upon her. Suddenly he gave her a very suggestive wink. Flustered, she turned to Richard and said, "I claim the first dance, Your Grace."

"Please call me Richard. I want us to be friends." As they danced, he said, "When you visit London, be sure to take a ride in the Royal Barge at night. It's most exhilarating. The Thames current runs very fast, especially under London Bridge, and at night the lit torches stream tails of sparks like comets. But be sure to take a perfumed pomander with you—the Thames stinks, I'm afraid."

She looked up at him. "From what I've heard, all Rivers stink!" He doubled over with laughter, for she referred to the Queen's father, Lord Rivers, who at sixty was still as randy as a goat.

"Though I'm loyal to Edward in all things, I must admit I quite detest Elizabeth and her whole tribe," he confided.

"Why?" asked Roseanna with simple curiosity.

He thought for a moment and then said, "I think it's because, as the King's brother, she insists I kneel before her and kiss her hand. Yet never must my lips actually touch her skin. She is absolutely inviolate!"

" 'Tis most curious, but I've yet to meet someone who likes her." Now that she thought of it, even King Edward, her father, had warned her of the Queen and her family. Hated by all, she would be a formidable enemy. Roseanna decided to ask Ravenspur his opinion of her.

The musicians played tirelessly. Roseanna was pleased to see Rebecca partner first Richard and then Tristan for the gay galliard, that deliciously decadent dance in which the male lifts his partner high enough in the air to show her ankles and petticoat.

Ravenspur took Roseanna's hand and led her to the dance. "I'd rather not, my lord," she protested.

"You have purposely ignored me all evening, Roseanna. You will learn that that is a dangerous thing to do," he whispered teasingly. The pressure of his hand on the small of her back forced her feet forward reluctantly. Then suddenly, breathlessly, he lifted her higher than any other woman in the room. The musicians quickened the tempo, and the dancers became more abandoned. On the second lift, he kept her in the air for thirty seconds. "Ravenspur, please!" she cried. All the dancers were kicking up their heels wildly now, and it became a contest to see who could hold their lady longest in the air. Everyone was laughing playfully, and even Roseanna began to enjoy the silliness. She couldn't help giggling when her husband held her in the air and his fingers curled into her ribcage and tickled her unmercifully.

"Put me down!" she cried, now almost helpless with laughter.

Roger's eyes glittered up into hers wickedly. "Cry mercy!" he told her, and he only allowed her feet to touch the floor for one second before he lifted her again.

"Ravenspur, please?" she begged.

"Say Roger," he laughed. She shook her head, and he held her on high until her skirt fell about her thighs and exposed her stockings.

"Roger, Roger!" she cried, and quickly he let her down and took her into his embrace. She looked up at him, and suddenly they both stopped laughing. He was aflame with desire, and his secret part grew hard against her soft body. Needing the taste of her, he bent his head to ravage her mouth. Her response was so instant, so hot, that it shamed her. She pulled away, horrified at the desire she felt for him. Her body's reaction mauled her pride.

"Are you mine, Roseanna?" he murmured softly.

"Never!" she hissed, and ran from the hall. Her heart was beating wildly. He always affected her that way. First she would feel so cool and calculating and think she could easily manipulate and handle him; then without warning her body would turn traitor on her, and she would no longer be in control of herself. She knew her time was growing short. He would not be put off much longer. He was far too virile to put up with this arrangement indefinitely.

When she reached Kate and Alice's chamber, she suddenly thought of Bryan. If Ravenspur ever found him there, he would kill him without hesitation. She prayed that Bryan would not come. "Oh, Alice, help me un-thread these pearls from my hair. I've danced too much; my poor head is spinning." Alice put her jewelry away in its coffers, and Kate helped her remove the burgundy gown.

She moved toward her own chamber, then stopped and took Kate's hand. "Kate," she said very seriously, "if ever I had a visitor—one who came very late—you wouldn't let him into my chamber, would you?" she pleaded.

"Need you ask such a thing? Off to bed with you, child!"

Roger lay in bed a long time, but sleep had seldom been as far away as it was this night. Why had he allowed this situation to develop? he asked himself over and over. He had made a very bad blunder on their wedding night when he left the nuptial bed to sleep on the couch. The marriage should have been consummated that night, even if force had been necessary. What bridegroom didn't have to use his superior strength to overcome a bride's reluctance? The trouble was, Roseanna was no ordinary woman. She was not only more beautiful than other women, she was finer in every way. She was accomplished and intelligent, and he did not need to remind himself that she was royal. Her bloodlines were evident. She was his heart's desire, and he wanted her for his soulmate. He longed for that transcendence, that sense of crossing each other's boundaries and becoming one.

He mocked himself for a fool. At this moment he was so frustrated, he would be willing to settle for a purely physical relationship. If she had haunted him before they were married, now she was like a fever in his blood. His need for her grew with every heartbeat. He was obsessed with her in body and mind. If he allowed it to go on much longer, there could be such a cataclysmic encounter that it would destroy them both.

He threw back the covers and reached for his robe. He would go to her and lay her on her bed and arouse her to the point where she would beg him to love her. His hands knew tricks that would make her mindless. Once he had made her his once, she would be his for a lifetime. After all, he was nearly thirty-two, with a man's experience. She was just seventeen and untouched, if he guessed right.

He made his way to the northeast corner of the castle and recalled that to get to Roseanna he would have to pass through the outer chamber. He muttered a fertile obscenity, hating the idea of knocking and asking for permission to visit his own wife. But he suppressed his anger and knocked on the chamber door. Kate Kendall opened it and held a candle high. "Is aught amiss, my lord?" she asked low.

He swallowed a savage retort and stated evenly, "I want to visit Roseanna."

"Oh, my lord, she is not expecting you. She went to bed unwell. Her head was spinning vilely." Kate was determined to thwart him. Hadn't she just given her word that she would not let him have entrance if he chose to visit her?

Roger looked toward the inner door and saw light shining from beneath it. He kept his temper but pressed the servingwoman. "If she is unwell, I think I should see to her."

Kate shook her head firmly, as if dealing with one of her young charges. "You wouldn't be kind if you disturbed her, my lord. She only needs rest, and she wouldn't get that if you visited her, would she?"

The old horror of being denied entry to his wife suddenly gripped him. What if she were entertaining her lover? He'd seen the young knight pass her a note this morning. No, the thought was too vile to contemplate! Yet it lingered so that he doubted the wisdom of forcing the issue. As he turned to leave, Kate said, "Good night, my lord."

Good night? Nay, one of the worst he'd endured. Christ, she had vowed to make him wretched, and she was succeeding. He slammed his chamber door and ground his teeth. Though the chamber was large, it caged him. It imprisoned the essence of him, the strength, the male recklessness. Suddenly he booted a stool across the room, then hurled an obscenity after it. He fought the urge to go and see if Fitzhugh was in the men's quarters. Nay, that way lay madness.

The old pain washed over him. Not again, Christ, not again! He breathed deeply and calmed himself. No, his last wife had been a whore, but Roseanna was as far removed from that as day from night. She was his rose without a thorn, and he would not profane her with vile thoughts or doubts that only sprang from his unsavory past. He schooled his thoughts and then his blood. He sipped a glass of wine and promised himself, tomorrow night!

The morning was taken up with Tristan's departure for Ravenscar, about forty miles distant on the east coast. The journey was being made to scout out the countryside, to watch for any movement of men or ships on the coast. It was a precautionary measure on behalf of King Edward, who was far too trusting. If Tristan found nothing untoward, Roger had given him orders to return within the week. It was to the west that they really looked for treachery; Roger would not rest secure until Tristan had returned and together they had journeyed to Ravenglass and back.

Rebecca was not accompanying her husband but would stay at Ravensworth with her ladies. Tristan was surprised and pleased when his young wife bade him a lingering farewell and whispered that she would miss him. "If Roseanna were your wife, she would ride with you and disregard the danger."

Tristan observed his wife closely and was pleased with the influence Roseanna was having on her. He bent down and whispered in her ear, "When you are stronger, you can ride with me. I'll look forward to it."

Rebecca blushed prettily. "Hurry back, Tris!"

He grinned wickedly. "I shall. But be warned, the separation will make me randy as hell."

Roseanna accompanied Rebecca to the stables to bid Tristan and his men godspeed; then Rebecca returned to the castle and Roseanna inspected the horses they owned.

Old Dobbin was at her elbow, holding each animal for her examination. "Ravenspur has a few good stallions and, of course, dozens of geldings. But his stables are sadly lacking in good mares to breed from," she told Dobbin.

"Aye, my lady. The mare you brought from home is better than any they have here."

Roseanna nodded. "I'm so thankful I brought one that's breeding. She was served by Zeus and no other that I know of. She'll produce something quite fine in the spring."

"I think this mare here is breeding. The head stableman told me she was covered by Ravenspur's stallion, but she has a history of abortion."

Roseanna frowned as she ran her hands along the sleek belly of the only mare Ravenspur owned besides the one she had brought with her. "Get the head stableman for me, Dobbin," she said with determination.

Dobbin left and returned in the company of a strapping young man who looked as if he could lift a horse if it were necessary.

"This is Tom. He's in charge of Ravenspur's stable."

Roseanna smiled warmly. "You do a fine job with Ravenspur's animals, Tom. It's quite a large stable."

He grinned. "There's over a hundred men-at-arms to

be mounted. 'Course, most knights take a personal interest in their animal. See that it's fed and groomed and exercised. But they know naught about doctoring a sick animal or binding up its wounds after a battle. I hear ye have a special interest in horses, my lady."

"Yes, we bred the best in England at Castlemaine, and I see no reason why we can't do some breeding here, Tom. Dobbin tells me this mare has a history of abortion?"

He answered her as if it were the most natural thing in the world to be discussing these matters with Ravenspur's new bride.

"I've had lots of experience with that problem, Tom, and I think we'll be able to save this one if you'll follow my advice. It's worth a try if she was covered by Ravenspur's black stallion; he's a beauty." She looked around the stables to find a quiet box stall removed from the heavy traffic of horses. "I want her checked every week. Keep her quiet and warm and comfortable. Wash her shapes down every few days with strong soap and water. Keep her meticulously cleansed, and at least one of her feedings every day should be oatmeal gruel."

"Does that prevent abortion?" asked Tom with deep concern.

"It certainly helps. Whenever a mare aborted, we always disinfected the stall immediately, gave the horse an enema to clean the bowels, and then rubbed it with olive oil. And of course, most important of all—always burn the fetus."

Tom nodded sagely as these new ideas were presented to him.

"I'm going to buy Ravenspur some new mares so we can breed the Arabian."

"They have horses something like that one over Middleham way. Some monks at an abbey breed white horses," said Tom.

"Really?" asked Roseanna with interest. "I'd love to see them." When she raised her head, she saw Sir Bryan saddling his horse, so she quietly excused herself and unhurriedly made her way in his direction. She must take the chance of being seen together, for at all costs she must warn him not to come to her chamber.

"Bryan, your note has distressed me," she said low.

"My sweet, I miss your company sorely. How have I distressed you?"

"You must not come to my chamber, especially after the hour of midnight. It would cover us with guilt. If any saw you, we would be charged with adultery!" she warned.

He stiffened. "What I feel for you, my lady, is love, not lust. It is a pure love, beyond the physical, on a higher plane," he insisted as if she had offered him grave insult.

She softened. "Oh, Bryan, I know, and that is why I love you. But we must keep it secret between us, or I shall not know a moment's peace. If our love were known, you would be in mortal danger."

"When Ravenspur travels to his castle at Ravenglass, I will endeavor to stay here. Then we may spend some time together." When they saw Captain Kelly headed their way, they quickly separated.

Roseanna discovered that Mr. Burke had been looking for her.

"The master asked me to prepare dinner for the two of you and serve it in the living quarters. He said you would choose what to serve and give me my orders, Lady Roseanna."

"How very thoughtful he is," said Roseanna sarcastically. "Mr. Burke, tell me, is he very accomplished at cards and chess and games of chance?"

"He's challenged you, has he?"

"He has, Mr. Burke, and I intend to beat him. I've diced with Castlemaine's men-at-arms since I was five. The King himself taught me to play chess and how to be devious. So if you will tell me which game Ravenspur does not excel at, it will give me the advantage."

He chuckled and stroked his chin. "Well, I've never seen any beat him at chess, but young Tristan always wins when they play backgammon."

She gave him a conspiratorial grin and said, "Set the backgammon board up before the fireplace, and we'll dine over there in that alcove beneath the pretty stained-glass aureole window."

"Very good choice, my lady." He nodded his approval. "What do you wish me to serve?"

"Let's see. We'll begin with smoked salmon or trout. Then I suppose we should have some sort of game bird because they are so plentiful now, but I hate grouse, and pheasant flesh sometimes has a strong taste."

"May I suggest partridge, my lady? There's nothing as sweet as a plump partridge."

"Perfect, Mr. Burke." She nodded her agreement. "Serve Ravenspur whatever wine he prefers, but I'd like mead, please."

"I'm pleased that you like the mead, my lady. 'Tis made with honey and gets its distinctive flavor from the heather. When we go back south to Ravenspur, I shall take some barrels of mead along for your enjoyment."

"Thank you, Mr. Burke. Tell me, what was Ravenspur's second wife like?" she asked disarmingly.

He looked taken off his guard for once; he measured his response carefully before giving it. "Well, I would say she was a man's woman, if you know what I mean."

Roseanna felt annoyed and her voice rose slightly. "No, I don't know, Mr. Burke. Whatever is a man's woman?" She almost felt jealous; what was the matter with her?

He looked most uncomfortable. "It's hard for me to explain, my lady. It's almost nine years since she died. What do you wish to know about her?"

"Was she beautiful?" she asked bluntly.

"Very beautiful, in a voluptuous sort of way."

Roseanna bristled. "How long were they married?"

"Ah, not long, not long at all. She died while still a bride, technically. Within two years, I mean."

"I see," she said. "I understand he was married for the first time at fifteen?"

"Yes, that is so, to a lady who was older than himself. That first marriage could not be called a love match, though they were wed over five years."

"That means his second marriage was a love match?" she queried.

Mr. Burke coughed to clear his throat and wished he were not being put on the spot. "He was certainly in love when he first met the lady. He was widowed at twenty and rushed headlong into a second marriage before his twenty-first birthday, disregarding a decent mourning period."

"Thank you, Mr. Burke. I know you feel you are breaching his confidence, but I have no one else to ask." She had a hundred questions about the "voluptuous" bride Ravenspur had loved so madly, but she bit her tongue. She would save them for another time, after she and Mr. Burke had become more comfortable with each other. "Mr. Burke, would you be good enough to have hot water sent to my chamber? I must bathe the traces of the stables from myself before I dine with Ravenspur."

Suddenly it was very important to her that she look beautiful tonight. She wished herself to be the loveliest woman he had ever dined with in his life. She would choose something revealing that his maleness would respond to and that would keep his mind from the game.

She stepped from the tub and allowed Kate to wrap her in a thick towel. She opened her wardrobe with Alice at her elbow and began to search through the great number of gowns. She stopped when she came to the red velvet that she had worn so long ago for King Edward's visit. Her mind flew back to that night and to the influence it had had on her life.

"Oh, you can't wear that red velvet tunic without the underdress again!" pleaded Alice in a frightened voice.

Roseanna gave her an amused look over her shoulder. "As if I would do such a thing. No, tonight I'm going to do it the other way around. I'm going to wear the diaphanous white underdress without the tunic."

Alice gasped. "But Lady Roseanna, it's so sheer you can see through it!"

"Yes," mused Roseanna with relish. "I know." She opened one of her coffers and selected a white shift delicately embroidered with silver thread, then donned the sheer underdress and stood before her mirror to gauge its effect. She lifted her arms high; the long filmy sleeves floated down until they touched the delicate folds of the skirt. If she stared very hard, she could just discern the deep rose-pink aureoles that circled her nipples. Kate stood behind her with pursed lips. "Kate, stop disapproving and fetch my jewel coffer."

Kate Kendall handed her mistress the heavy leather coffer that held the lovely jewelry her mother had designed for her.

"When Ravenspur came to your chamber last night, I sent him away on the thin excuse of your spinning head. If you dine with him dressed so, I doubt that even I will be able to fob him off tonight."

"Did he really come last night?" asked Roseanna, inordinately pleased with herself. "Thank you, Kate. You saved me, and you will do exactly the same tonight or I shall banish you back to Castlemaine!" Roseanna teased. "Alice, I want you to brush all my hair to one side, like so. Let some of it fall down my back and some fall down my front so that it almost but not quite covers my left cheek and shadows my eye. Brush the other side up and back completely so that my neck and ear are bared, and then put this lovely sapphire moon-and-stars clasp just to the side of my temple."

Kate scrutinized her as Alice brushed her hair. "Ravenspur will be able to see clear through to your titties!"

Roseanna blushed. "I don't care."

Kate shook her head. "I'll have to get you some hemlock to put in his wine."

"Good God, I don't want to kill him!" said Roseanna, shocked.

Kate was disgusted. "Brainless child. It's good against your husband's lechery—in small amounts, of course."

"A poisonous tongue is a better weapon than a poisonous cup of wine," said Roseanna firmly. "I must go down, for I don't wish to arrive late. He must find no fault with my behavior this evening."

Kate rolled her eyes. "That will last ten minutes, and that's stretching it. Roseanna's best behavior, forsooth!" she hooted.

Serenely Roseanna floated from the room and went down to the castle's private living quarters. Mr. Burke had set up a lovely table for two in the alcove and was just placing the goblets for the wine. Roseanna nodded to him politely but stayed across the room in case his sharp eyes saw through the material of her bodice.

One wall was covered by a large tapestry that must have taken years to complete. The workmanship was so fine, it actually looked like a painting. It showed some sort of banquet in which a man and woman were being served by many and were even being entertained by musicians. Ravenspur's voice, close behind her, momentarily startled her, but she did not jump.

"It is a banquet of the gods. The eagle and peacock mark the presence of Zeus, king of the gods, and his consort, Hera. The god Pan provides music, as does Apollo with his lyre. Ganymede is serving them nectar, and the bow, arrows, and wings denote the presence of Eros, god of love."

"I did not know you were a student of the classics." As she turned to face him, his dark eyes lingered a moment on her mouth, then lowered to her breasts, which thrust boldly above the neckline of the filmy underdress. "I am not a serious student, but I have a fondness for beauty," he said as he lifted his eyes to hers. "Thank you for joining me, Roseanna," he murmured.

She raised a delicate brow. "I wasn't aware that I had a choice."

A slight frown creased his brow. "You will always have a choice. You think me some monster who must be obeyed?"

"You forced me to wed you against my will. Where was my choice then, my lord?" Her eyes blazed their challenge. Her best behavior had lasted nowhere close to ten minutes.

"A fate worse than death," he murmured with a humorous glint in his eyes. He was determined that she would provoke no arguments tonight. He was dressed in a black padded doublet that emphasized his unbelievably wide shoulders. The only touch of color was a ruby in his ear. In their black and white they looked like bride and bridegroom. He bowed before her, took her hand, and led her to the table. He held her chair for her. His hands ached to caress her shoulders, but he restrained the impulse and took the chair opposite her. "Let us enjoy Burke's supper without being at each other's throats, my love."

"I quite like Mr. Burke. He's been with you for many years and must know where all your skeletons are buried."

He ignored the barb. "Yes, he came from our estate in Ireland over twenty years ago."

Her eyebrows went up. "You have a castle in Ireland?"

"Not exactly a castle. An estate of about fifty acres with a lovely manor house," he told her as he poured mead into her goblet.

"They say Ireland is ideal for breeding horses. Whereabout in Ireland is your land?" she asked with quick interest.

The corners of his mouth lifted in amusement as he saw the speculation in her eyes. "It's not far from Ravenglass Castle, on the west coast. It's just a short run across the Irish Sea to the Isle of Man, and then another short sail to Drogheda."

"Do you have ships?" she asked.

"Of course," he replied smoothly. "Do you enjoy sailing?"

"I've never been aboard a ship, but the thought of sailing across the sea is thrilling."

He smiled as he raised his goblet to her. "There are many thrilling things you haven't yet tried."

She looked him directly in the eye and answered boldly, "Perhaps I have tried more things than you give me credit for, Ravenspur."

He smiled at her. "You avoid my given name like the plague, Roseanna. Are you afraid to call me Roger?"

"Me? Afraid? Don't be ridiculous," she said, tossing her head. Her hair flew back over her shoulder, then fell to the carpet in a silken, rippling, dark waterfall. He vowed that he would wrap himself in that hair before long. It was the most sensuous hair he'd ever beheld, and he longed to play with it.

Mr. Burke removed the first course and returned with two heavy silver tureens. When the covers were removed, a delicious aroma arose with the steam from the partridges. One dish held four roasted birds; the other held partridges cooked in wine with mushrooms and chestnuts. There was a panaché of fresh greens to go with the game, but no other vegetables. The meal was simple yet elegant. They ate at a leisurely pace, yet each was filled with anticipation for the backgammon game that lay ahead. The air was charged with a subtle tension, for each was eager to challenge the other and emerge victorious. They were so alike in temperament that neither even considered the possibility of losing.

Roger threw scraps to the wolfhound, who had roused himself from before the fire to investigate the delicious smells coming from the table. Roseanna reached for a ripe pear at the same moment as Roger, and their hands touched for an instant. It was as if a flame ran up her arm from his touch. She couldn't keep a blush from staining her cheeks and was relieved when Mr. Burke created a diversion by bringing them rosewater bowls and towels to wash their hands. Roger nodded imperceptibly to Mr. Burke that he wished no further intrusions into the room; then he filled their goblets and took them over to the games table beside the fire.

Roger drew in his breath as Roseanna passed in front of the fire. Her body was clearly silhouetted through the filmy underdress. Again Roger held her chair, but this time as her hair brushed his hands, he stroked it. It crackled beneath his fingers.

"Beware, I give off sparks," she laughed tauntingly.

The black stones on the backgammon table were carved from ebony, and the whites from ivory. He waved his hand that she should make the first throw. She picked up the two dice and rolled them onto the board. She had rolled a double of four and four, so she moved four stones four points each. She played intently and was determined to get all fifteen stones into her inner table before Ravenspur managed to do the same with his stones. He was playing negligently, allowing his attention to focus on her, so she wasn't worried about losing. "You were so eager to begin. What stakes are we playing for?" he drawled.

"Money, of course," she said, laughing.

He smiled. "What do you need money for?"

"Horses. I'm going to buy some decent mares to breed."

"Then money it shall be. Five hundred pounds." He watched her carefully, then asked casually, "Do you have five hundred pounds?"

"Of course not," she said.

"Then how will you repay me?" he asked pleasantly.

"I'm going to win, not lose!" she pointed out.

"I see," he said calmly, not seeing her logic at all.

With each throw of the dice, she made her point. She combined moving with bearing off, and in a short time she was elated because she'd won.

"I am playing at a disadvantage, Roseanna."

Her eyebrows lifted. "How so?"

"Your beauty distracts me," he murmured.

"What a poor excuse. You must concentrate. What shall we play for next?" she asked.

He considered a moment, then suggested, "Jewels? My ruby earring against your sapphire hair ornament."

His lean brown fingers unfastened the earring, and he placed it before her on the board. She reached up for her moon and stars, and when she removed it, her hair tumbled down where it had been held back. He smiled into her eyes. "I suggested your sapphires only so that when you removed the clasp I would have the pleasure of seeing your hair fall around you in all its glory."

"Ravenspur," she said, beginning to feel a little uneasy, "pay attention to the game." She picked up the two dice to roll.

"How can I?" he whispered. "You have deliberately used a perfume that robs me of my senses."

"Fool!" She laughed nervously and challenged him to double.

"You have deliberately dressed to arouse me," he said low.

"Liar!" she threw back.

"And you have succeeded," he finished.

Toward the end of the game Roger had not borne off a single stone belonging to Roseanna, and she scored a gammon. She could not hide the triumph in her eyes. "Perhaps you will play a better game if we play for something closer to your heart," she suggested.

"Name it, love."

She ignored the endearment. "Your stallion has covered your only decent mare, and my Zeus has one of my mares in foal. I'll put my colt up against yours."

He watched her lovely lips as she concentrated on the play, doubling, and making point after point. He wanted the taste of her in his mouth; he wanted the feel of her beneath his body. He sipped his wine, knowing it did nothing to cool his hot blood. She was flushed with her victories and looked him directly in the eyes. "This time shall we play for the truth, my lord?"

"By that I suppose you mean the winner asks the loser a question and is entitled to the truth?"

"You take my meaning exactly, my lord." She drained her mead and recklessly asked for some of his wine. Roger once more allowed her to win the gammon. Her eyes sparkled. "Now you will tell me exactly what happened when I came to the hunting lodge," she said triumphantly.

He loved to watch her face; it was so expressive. She had a way of raising her delicate brows, and the light of challenge in her clear gray eyes pierced his, and he saw the color change from gray to amethyst. The fire reflected one side of her cheek and caught sable highlights in her magnificent hair. Best of all was her mouth. As her name implied, it was deep velvet rose. Full, as if it were swollen by too many passionate kisses. It was shaped to give a man pleasure, whether he was looking at it or tasting it.

"I asked you a question," she said, and he recalled what she had asked as he came out of his reverie. Of course he had no intention of telling her she had been rolled naked from a carpet in front of everyone present, so he passed over that bit and replied, "After Tristan gave you a sleeping draught, he put you in my bed as a delightful surprise for me. You know what a young devil he is," added Ravenspur.

"When you found me naked in your bed, what did you do to me? And remember, I want the truth!"

His eyes glowed with the remembrance. "Well first, naturally, I had a damned good look at you."

Her cheeks flamed their shame, and she choked angrily. "How could you be so disgusting?"

"Roseanna, there was nothing disgusting about it. You were the loveliest maid who had ever graced my bed. I would have had to be deranged not to look my fill."

"Then what did you do?" she demanded fiercely.

"I got into bed and took you in my arms."

She glared at him and waited for him to go on.

"I began to kiss you and caress you," he continued.

"How dared you!" she spat. "Tell me, did you take further advantage of me?"

"No, Roseanna, I did not. I found kissing your unresponsive mouth too frustrating and unsatisfying. I decided to wait until morning when you awoke. At which time I admit I had every intention of making love to you until I discovered you were my betrothed and a virgin."

"I'm no virgin! I've had at least three lovers—aye, and I wish it were a hundred and three!" she threw at him.

He reached his hand across the gameboard and put his finger beneath her chin. "Roseanna, when dealing with an adversary, never lose your temper or you lose the advantage," he advised.

"Are you my adversary?" she flared.

"I am not. However, you insist on casting me in that role." His gaze licked over her like the tongue of a flame; she lowered her eyes quickly lest he see her involuntary response to him.

He asked lazily, "Why don't we be reckless and play for something we really want?"

"What do I really want?" she challenged him.

"The manor and lands in Drogheda to raise your infernal horses."

She laughed because he knew her so well. She felt lucky and knew the desired prize was only a few throws of the dice away. He was a reckless man, indeed, to gamble such a prize.

"If you lose," he said, "I claim you spend one night with me."

"Only one?" she taunted. "I hope your skill in bed surpasses your skill at backgammon." He cocked his eyebrow, and she cried recklessly, "Done!"

She took the dice and rattled them hard, her head filled with visions of Ireland. For the first time he rolled a higher number, allowing himself the first turn. He rolled many doubles, while her dice came up unbelievably low. He made his points and moved his stones to his inner table so rapidly that she blinked in amazement. Raven-

spur was unperturbed and played so well that she began
to suspect he had purposely allowed her to win up to
now. He had deliberately tricked her into lowering her
guard so she would fall into his trap! Her cheeks flamed
with anger. She was determined that he would not beat
her. She concentrated hard, but the doubling cube was
already up to thirty-two in his favor, and she realized
wildly that there was no way for her to win the game.

"Oh!" she cried and stood up quickly, upsetting the
board and scattering the stones into the hearth. For a
moment he looked at her in disbelief. "The dog brushed
against my leg and startled me!" she exclaimed. The dog
had been lying at Roger's feet until the upset; then it
quickly departed the line of battle. She said breathlessly,
"Oh dear, now we shall never know who would have won
the game."

He towered over her, angry with himself for not realizing she would cheat to get her own way. He gripped her
by the shoulders and said, "Roseanna, we both know
who won the game."

She threw him a challenging look. "Surely as a gentleman you will allow me the benefit of the doubt?"

"I am not a gentleman, only a man, with a man's
desires!" he asserted. He saw a flicker of fear in her eyes
but was determined not to soften toward her. His fingers
dug cruelly into her creamy shoulders, and his eyes narrowed. "Do you know what I think? I think you enjoy
the stalking, the wooing, and my advances just so you
can retreat. We are fencing. You parry every time I
thrust."

"Wooing has a devious purpose—to get something!"
she accused.

"To give something as well as get something—pleasure in bed. I would like to do that with you," he said.

She tried to pull away from him. "You are hurting me!" she cried.

"Hurting you? By God, I haven't begun yet. What you need is a good beating, followed by a good fucking, and I'm going to give you both!"

She wrenched herself free of him and fled the room sobbing. And his relentless voice followed her out the door: "I am a man who always collects his debts."

14

Roseanna tried to hide the fact that she had been crying when she reached her rooms, but Kate was difficult to deceive. "What's the matter?"

"Nothing!" Roseanna sniffed. "I won every hand. Five hundred pounds, his ruby earring, and the unborn colt that his stallion sired."

"Didn't he win even one game?" asked Kate skeptically.

"When I saw that he was about to win the last game, I upset the board. Losing to Ravenspur would be too awful to conjure!"

"In other words, you had another brawl," stated Kate.

"How you exaggerate! We parted on the best of terms," she said, tossing her head and going through to her own chamber. Before she closed her door she added, "However, if he comes calling, I will not receive him under any circumstances!"

Alice was already apprehensive. "Kate, you got rid of him last night, but what will we do if he comes again tonight?"

"You can get rid of him tonight—it's your turn," said Kate, laughing.

"Oh, I feel sick. You can't mean that Kate," whispered Alice.

"Go on with you. I'll speak to him if he comes. Mind, you'll have to back up whatever I say. Two are a stronger defense than one."

"But Kate, it's his castle. I don't see how we can prevent him from visiting his own wife in his own castle."

"Listen, my gal. Our first duty is to Roseanna. We are her servingwomen, and we take our orders from her. Stop worrying your guts to fiddlestrings! Perhaps he's had enough of her naughtyworks for one night."

Alice crossed her fingers and prepared for bed. Kate donned a warm nightcap and flannel robe and extinguished the lamps. No sooner did they get into their beds than a low knock came upon the outer door.

Kate mumbled, "No rest for the wicked," and lit a candle. Alice caught her breath, her worst fears realized. Kate held the candle high and peered out the door, which she had only opened a crack. She knew full well it was Ravenspur but asked, "Who is it?"

"Kate, for God's sake, open the door. Don't keep me standing in this corridor all night," he said irritably.

"But my lord, as ye can well see, we've all retired for the night."

"Goddamn it, woman, let me in!" he demanded with controlled fury.

She stepped aside, and he entered and said, "Light the lamp."

Alice flew from her bed and fumbled endlessly until she finally managed to illuminate the room.

Kate said as assertively as she dared, "My lady has

long ago retired. She bade me not disturb her, and she locked her door."

He looked at her evenly and said, "Roseanna knew I would come."

Kate shook her head, crossed her arms across her chest, and planted her feet firmly. "No sir, that is a lie, or why would she lock her chamber door?"

His eyes narrowed dangerously as he looked from one woman to the other. "By Christ, this is a conspiracy!" His words were deadly and quiet. His soft, ominous tone was far more deadly than if he'd raved. "Tomorrow you'll both return to Castlemaine. I'll not have two damned dragons barring me from my own wife's bed! Start packing." He kicked open the adjoining door to reveal Roseanna hastily donning a scarlet velvet bedgown.

He was so large he filled the doorway. "Madame, this game is finished. This is the last time I come to this damned chamber, for you will occupy it no more! You will come to me from now on, and you will come tonight!"

She knew she dared not deny him, but she temporized. "My lord, I will need time to get my things together."

"Madame, I will allow you five minutes!" He slammed from the room in such a high temper that Alice slipped to the carpet in a dead faint.

"Good God!" Kate exclaimed. "The girl hasn't the guts of a louse, although I must admit that those dark eyes can put the fear of the devil into you." She lifted Alice onto her bed and rubbed her hands and arms vigorously. "Come on, lambie, wake up. He's gone now."

"How dare he?" demanded Roseanna, venting her own temper now that he was safely gone. "This is beyond the

beyond! To think he can actually dismiss my own servingwomen! By God, I'll tell you one thing—if you leave,
we all leave!" She picked up a silver hairbrush and paced
around the room.

Kate tried to reason with her. "Roseanna, he'd dare do
anything. He's all man. I told you you wouldn't get far
throwing your imperious orders at him." Roseanna angrily brushed the tangled mass of her curls. Kate continued. "You'll have to go to him, lovey. Your five minutes
were up long ago."

"Ha!" flared Roseanna. "I may have to move to his
chamber, but I shall certainly take my own sweet time
about it. It'll give that devil of a temper of his time to
cool down." She got a great deal of pleasure imagining
him waiting impatiently for her.

"Roseanna, if you were a clever girl, you could have
him eating out of your hand," pointed out Kate. "Sugar,
not vinegar, my girl. That's what softens a man."

Roseanna realized that Kate had a point. If she were to
control her temper and use more subtle means to get her
own way with him, her life would be more pleasant. After
all, she only had to go near the man, and he couldn't
resist touching her. She smiled a secret smile—she would
control him through his desires.

An hour had long passed before Roseanna obeyed her
husband's summons. She took no light to guide her. She
needed none, for she walked a direct path unerringly to
his chamber door. She opened it with a little flourish and
boldly entered.

Ravenspur stood naked to the waist; his body was
sleek, the muscles taut. He was handing a goblet of wine
to the young servingwoman who was with him.

The woman gasped, and her hand flew to her mouth.

Roseanna was stunned. The firelight turned her scarlet-clad figure to flame. His faithlessness hit her with such a blow, she was as still as death. After a full minute of frozen horror, Roseanna approached the young woman, snatched the goblet from her hand, and dashed it into the fire. "Get out!" She uttered the command like an empress. A detached part of her brain decided to send the woman to Castlemaine in the morning. A word to Joanna would teach the servingwoman her place. The young woman fled, eager to be gone from this highly charged atmosphere. When they were alone, she demanded, "How dare you forget your vows so quickly?"

"Your five minutes were up an hour ago! How dare you forget your vow?" he countered.

She ignored his words. "You faithless bastard! Know this, Ravenspur. There will be only one woman to hold the place of honor here, and that woman will be me. You will not put me in a position where I am laughed at or pitied."

His eyes raked over her assessingly. She was magnificent and wildly beautiful in her towering rage. "Then honor your vows and take your rightful place as my wife. I pledge never to be unfaithful! Otherwise, I will sleep with who I damned well please."

"I do not love you," she said with regal dignity.

He countered, "I am not asking for your love. I am asking for my marital rights."

She said slowly, "You mean that if I share your bed on occasion, you swear never to commit adultery?"

"A lot depends on how you behave in bed," he said slowly. But not wanting to push her too far, he added, "I suppose I could live with that. Is it a bargain?"

She didn't answer him. She went over her alternatives mentally and found they were intolerable.

"Yes," she said softly.

For a blank moment he couldn't remember the question and stared at her. Then realization of what she had promised hit him. "Roseanna!" he said with fervor and moved to take her in his arms.

"My God, not now! Not after you've touched her!" she cried, aghast. She put up her hand to fend him off; it came into contact with the crisp black mat of curls that covered his chest. Her touch branded him as if he'd been seared with a hot iron. He clenched his fists at his side to stop himself from snatching her into his arms and lifting her into his bed. "Tomorrow night!" he demanded.

She nodded.

"Swear it!" he insisted, remembering her deception at backgammon. "If you don't give yourself to me, I shall take you by force, Roseanna. Never doubt it of me!"

"Tomorrow," she promised, and turned to leave. Letting her go was the hardest thing he'd ever had to do. Before she left, she turned and spoke to him. Her delicate brows were marred by a frown. "She isn't even beautiful," she said.

His rich, deep laughter rang out. By God, she was jealous! He was halfway home!

Kate and Alice were avid for news when Roseanna returned, but she was disappointingly uncommunicative. Kate had already dragged out a large trunk ready for packing. Roseanna said quietly, "Go to bed; we're staying. Get me up early. I've many things to see to."

The next morning, Roseanna went down to the dining hall to join her husband for breakfast. His eyes lit up with pleasure at the sight of her. She wasted no time in stating her purpose. "I'll need one of your men to act as escort. I'm sending one of the servingwomen to my mother at Castlemaine."

Roger kept a straight face. He had no intention of interfering with her decision to be rid of the wench. God help any servant who crossed Lady Ravenspur! "Certainly, Roseanna. I'll send Dirk to you after breakfast. He can wait and take letters for you, if you care to write them."

"Thank you, my lord." She took a breath and asserted, "Naturally I shall be keeping Alice and Kate. I cannot manage without them."

"Naturally," he conceded smoothly. He smiled inwardly. Splendor of God, today she could ask for the earth, and he'd give it to her.

After writing a graphic letter to Joanna, she let Kate in on some of what had happened. "Ravenspur is sending one of his men to escort the bitch to Castlemaine. Dirk, I think, is his name. See to it for me, Kate. Watch her off the place. See that the man takes this letter to my mother."

Kate watched her and knew she was nervous.

Roseanna exclaimed, "The day is melting away like snow in summer. It can't possibly be time for the midday meal! Alice, I'll need water for my bath early tonight. I shall have it before I go down to dinner rather than after. Also, I want you to gather my brushes and toilet articles together for me."

Twice Roseanna went through everything that hung in her wardrobe. She had never had difficulty deciding what to wear; what was the matter with her today? She turned

to her women. "For God's sake, stop acting like I'm going to a funeral! Help me choose a gown for dinner and a
modest bedgown for later. That scarlet one won't do. I
made rather a spectacle of myself in it last night."

Alice brought out a white quilted bedgown. It was ap-
propriately virginal. "Alice, will you be brave enough to
attend me in Ravenspur's chamber tonight?"

"Oh, I don't think so, Lady Roseanna," gasped the
girl.

"Please?" cajoled Roseanna. "I'm afraid he thinks of
Kate as rather a dragon. I'll only need you for a moment
or two to unfasten my gown and brush my hair."

Kate said briskly, "Think of what she has to face.
Don't be such a coward!"

Roseanna went white around the mouth, and her knees
caved in under her. "Oh, Kate, is it so very bad?"

Kate pursed her lips and shook her head. " 'Tis different for everyone, but from what I've heard, a woman
fares better at the hands of a man with experience. Un-
tried youths make the worst bridegrooms in the world.
'Tis all fumbling and pain and over with before 'tis properly begun. Alice, don't you dare faint again!" Kate admonished.

There was a knock upon the chamber door. "That
must be Ravenspur's man, Kate. Give him this, and go
with him to see that they're away from here before the
midday meal."

The day lasted a thousand hours for Ravenspur. Each
one crawled past at a snail's pace. His eyes never left the
sky as he watched for dusk to descend.

Roseanna's afternoon sped past, hastened by a lively
altercation between Kate Kendall and Mr. Burke. It

seemed that in his efficient way, he had transferred Lady Ravenspur's belongings to the master's bedchamber. He got a mouthful of venom for his effort.

"Mr. Burke," pointed out Kate with the stubbornness of a terrier, "I and I alone see to Lady Ravenspur's belongings."

"Mrs. Kendall," he pointed out with the sweetness only an Irishman could muster, "I've been steward of the Ravenspur castles for twenty years. The baron likes the way I do things. Kindly stand aside."

"Put one foot across this threshold, and I'll shove you on your Irish arse," she threatened.

" 'Tis easy to see how the master mistook you for a dragon," he retorted.

"Mr. Burke, I've been insulted by experts. Don't delude yourself that your pathetic little barbs will find their mark."

"Because your hide, no doubt, like your skull, is as thick as that of a rhinoceros." He smiled.

Kate Kendall snorted like a gored bull. "Manners—pigs have none!" Then she addressed the world at large. "Every nation has its vermin, and I suppose the Irish are ours! Well, Mr. Burke, you may smile, but we shall have the last laugh. For you and your exalted baron are laboring under the idea that Lady Ravenspur is moving to the master bedchamber permanently. Such is a misapprehension," she said sweetly. "One night only, Mr. Burke, and since you insist on running errands, you may take this bedgown and these toilet articles. The rest stays here!"

Roseanna choked back her laughter. The two of them went at it like herself and Ravenspur. Her conscience smote her, however, when she glimpsed the look of despair on Alice's face. The poor girl hated noisy scenes between people who were stubbornly arrogant and flamboyant, but it seemed the young girl was surrounded by nothing but such people. "Come, Alice, let's visit Rebecca's chambers. You need a dose of peace and quiet, and that's probably the only place we'll find it around here."

Before the evening meal, Roseanna bathed and dressed in the most demure gown she owned. Then she bravely held her head high and joined her husband in the dining hall. His eyes caressed her, causing her heart to race at a frantic pace. She forced herself to breathe slowly so that she appeared cool and serene. She wore a silk apricot underdress with a high frilled neck and long, flowing sleeves. Over it she wore a deep amber tunic with a beaten gold girdle around her hips. Her hair was held back by a circlet of beaten gold.

Ravenspur's fingers ached to touch her; he let them have their way. He brushed them across her girdle and said, "You have so many pretty things, Roseanna. I am at a loss what to give you for a present."

"My mother designs jewelry, so I have a coffer filled with it." She gave him a sideways glance and said, "You don't need to give me presents. I will be satisfied if you pay me what you owe me." Her shafts and barbs had begun.

His eyes crinkled with laughter, and he teased, "And I will be satisfied if you pay me what you owe me."

She didn't challenge his words but let them slip past as if they were unheard. She let her eyes roam around the hall; it was safer than looking at her husband. "Your captain—Kelly is his name? Is he related to you in any way? For a moment I thought he was Tristan."

He grinned at her. "Not that I know of, unless he's one of my father's by-blows."

For one brief moment she thought he was deliberately insulting her and she stiffened. Then she let out her breath as she realized he could not know she was the King's by-blow. He was simply trying to shock her, so the last reaction she should give was shock. She pierced him with a glance. "Lechery runs in the family, then?"

The corner of his mouth twitched. What could he say when she had almost caught him in the act? "Tristan has a bit of a reputation," he conceded.

She gasped at his audacity. "I've been giving his poor wife advice. Perhaps between Rebecca and me we can cure him of his philandering."

"He should return from Ravenscar tomorrow," he said.

"Good," replied Roseanna.

An eyebrow cocked quizzically. "You've missed the young devil?"

She smiled serenely. "No. It's just that the sooner he returns, the sooner you will leave for Ravenglass." She looked pleased with that barbed arrow and hoped it found its mark.

His eyes lingered on her mouth. He didn't need to tell her that he intended to kiss the insolence from it. In her agitation she dropped her knife. It fell to her plate with a clatter. "Would you care for more venison, my love?" he asked smoothly.

She looked at him blankly. She couldn't remember one thing she had eaten during the meal. Her heartbeat thundered so loudly inside her ears that she saw his lips move and then curve into a sensual smile, but she had not heard him. She was about to nod, then thought better of it and shook her head. "No, my lord," she said, feeling

secure with the negative answer. She had missed his
words, "Do you wish to cry off?"

Her negative reply had sent his blood throbbing along
his veins, and he felt the familiar tightening and swelling
in his groin. He signaled to a page to refill her wine cup.

She lifted it to her lips and shot another barb. "Is this
to give me courage?"

He shook his head and murmured, "To give you fire!"

Her cheeks flamed. He was enjoying this game of wits
between them, and he had to remember when he finally
got her in his bedchamber to go slowly and not let the
demands of his body run riot and spoil this night. It was
Roseanna's night, and he vowed to pleasure her and savor the hours of arousal that it would take.

As the remains of the meal were cleared away and the
last dregs drained from the wine cups, Roseanna's insides
fluttered as if they were filled with a million butterfly
wings. Frantically her mind searched for a delaying tactic
but found none that was plausible.

As the dining hall emptied, she thought she glimpsed
Sir Bryan leaving, and her heart lurched in her breast. If
only they had been allowed to marry! Sweet Bryan, her
perfect knight. If it were his bed that she was going to
tonight, this sick fear that gripped her would be absent.
He was so gentle and good, and she suspected that he was
as innocent and pure as she was. Why, why hadn't they
allowed her to marry the boy her own age? The golden
fair boy who was almost beautiful to look upon? Her eyes
flew to Ravenspur's dark face as he murmured, "Whenever you are ready, Roseanna."

She shot him a look of hatred. "I'll never be ready,"
she assured him.

He pulled back the heavily carved chair to assist her.

His face made him look part hawk; his sharp eyes missed nothing. She felt his hand at the small of her back and quickened her pace to draw ahead of him, but his long strides easily kept up with her and the hand remained. Then they were outside his chamber, and she closed her eyes at the sight of the thick, heavy door. The next thing she knew, they were shut in the chamber to spend the first whole night together since they had been married.

She let out a great sigh as he moved away from her and went across the room. The furniture was made from heavy black walnut, and his large bed dominated the room. Its curtains were dark red velvet, and the deep carpet that covered the floor was patterned in red and black. Her quilted white bedgown lay starkly against the dominant colors of the bed.

Ravenspur came back to her with two goblets. "I want you to try this wine spiced with myrrh. I think you'll like it."

She had not moved from just inside the door. She asked, "Is it drugged?"

He masked the hurt he felt and answered her honestly, "No, Roseanna. I would not do such a thing."

A low knock sounded behind them, and Ravenspur moved to open the door. Alice stood there, pale but resolute. "I've come to help my lady undress," she whispered.

Roger said, laughing, "Nay, you'll not deprive me of that pleasure. I'll undress her myself."

"You will not!" gasped Roseanna, coming out of her trance. "You may go to bed, Alice. I'll tend to myself."

When the door closed, he slipped his arms around her and said, "Again I must overrule you. I will undress you, Roseanna. You have made me wait an eternity for this night, but now that it is here, I intend to have everything

I desire. We are going to do things my way tonight, my love, even if you scream your head off," he taunted.

"What things?" she asked, suddenly feeling very fragile.

"Ah, you shouldn't have left me alone so many nights. I feel like a stallion that hasn't had a mare in months," he teased, deftly removing her golden girdle. He slipped the amber tunic from her shoulders, and she stood before him in the thin silk underdress.

One hand encircled her waist, while the other caressed her deliciously round breasts that swelled up impudently. "These past nights I've had nothing to do but lie in bed and think up ways for you to pleasure me," he taunted. "You're not afraid, are you, sweetheart? What have you got for me under that apricot silk?" As he began to lift off her underdress, she eluded him and fled across the room in her transparent shift. He was after her in a flash and scooped her up squealing; her bare legs thrashed the air.

"Do you think you are woman enough to satisfy me, Roseanna?" He rubbed her body against his thick, hard shaft.

"Have you no shame? I am unused to men's coarse talk," she panted.

He bit back a retort about his coarseness. That would be playing directly into her hands. She wanted a knockdown, drag-out confrontation that would set them at each other's throats, but he had very different ideas about how their night together would be spent.

He had never believed her lies about not being a virgin, and he had no intention of being too rough with her once he began to make love to her. But he was enjoying taunting her now, drawing out the minutes to savor every second of this mating dance.

He tore the gauzy garment from her beautiful body and tossed her onto the bed. Her magnificent hair spread all about her like sable fire, and he drank in her nakedness for long minutes. He towered above her and slowly began to strip.

She would never get used to his nakedness; his size shocked her above all things. Again he taunted, "Surely you're not afraid of me?"

Her nervous laughter rang out. "Afraid? That's one weakness you'll not lay at my door!" He watched her bemused as she straightened her arms and legs and lay very still upon the bed.

"I'm ready!" she said in a shaky but determined voice.

15

Roger drew back the bed curtains all the way to let in the warmth and light of the fire. Roseanna lay rigid. She kept her eyes scrupulously averted from her husband's nakedness. He was transfixed by her sacrificial position; she looked for all the world like a vestal virgin.

She repeated, "I'm ready. Hurry up!"

Her innocence touched him, and in that moment he vowed never to hurt her. He slipped into the wide bed and pulled the covers over them. The firelight reflecting against the deep red curtains covered her with a rosy glow; he longed to see the bared flesh of her breasts and thighs bathed in its flickering light.

"Can't you just get it over with?" she asked.

"No, my love," he said softly. "You don't understand how your body works. If I penetrated you now, there would be only pain and blood and tears. Let me initiate you into the mysteries of lovemaking. Kissing and caressing begin the arousal. Then with my fingers and my lips I stimulate your body so that you will open to receive me. I don't want you to submit to my needs. I want you to have needs of your own that I can fulfill. My pleasure is heightened by yours. It is an allowable intimacy between husband and wife," he assured her.

He slipped his arm around her tiny waist and drew her into his embrace. He kissed her for an hour—gentle kisses, soft kisses, short quick kisses, and long, slow, melting kisses. Yet never once did he try to part her lips with his tongue and intrude it into her soft, exciting mouth. She did not respond with kisses of her own, yet she did not pull away from him or resist the warm persuasiveness of his mouth.

Roseanna was lulled by his magnetic closeness and by the delicious warmth of his body. His gentle lovemaking had not threatened her in any way, and the wine she had consumed and the heat from the fire made her relax against him as his kisses went on and on. *A hundred, a thousand,* she thought dreamily, floating on the edge of slumber.

He took his arm away, and she murmured a low protest. Very gently he slipped the covers down from her body so he could see her; then he took her in his arms again and drew her silken flesh against his body's hardness. She stiffened and tried to pull back, but he stroked her back. With his lips against her temple he murmured, "Don't be afraid, Roseanna." He kept it up until he had lulled her into security again. He resumed his kissing. When she sighed with pleasure, he took another risk.

He allowed the tip of his tongue to touch her lips. When she parted them slightly, he went deeper to play with her tongue and taste the honey of her mouth. Roseanna was stunned. Her body had curved into his as if it belonged there. She had to use all her willpower to stem the urge to lie in his arms and let him go on kissing her forever. Her hands came up to push him away but came in contact with the rigid muscles of his unyielding chest. The strength she felt beneath her hands made her go weak. As her fingers touched the crisp dark hair, she thrilled with the knowledge that he had the widest chest of any man alive.

With infinite tenderness his hands curved around her breasts to caress and stroke them. His touch clearly showed that her breasts were precious to him. Her hair brushed his cheek, and he buried his face in it, breathing deeply of its delicious fragrance until his very senses reeled. Holding Roseanna in his arms wildly assaulted all of his senses; he groaned with the sheer, deep, unbelievable pleasure she brought him. He had waited all his life for this woman. At thirty-two he had grown cynical, especially where women were concerned; then suddenly, unexpectedly, between one heartbeat and the next, he had fallen madly in love.

Her hair affected him so sensually, he promised himself that before many nights were over, he would wrap himself in it so they would be bound together by the silken bonds. His hands on her body were awakening new sensations for Roseanna—all new and strange yet deeply pleasurable.

She knew that what they were doing was wicked. He had stirred her wicked juices, and they flowed hot along all her limbs, sending tingling sensations across her body, weakening her resolve, sapping every ounce of her strength so that she could not resist him.

His hands went lower to her thighs, stroking the swelling curves of her buttocks. Then he gradually moved his hands until his fingers caressed the insides of her silky thighs. The intimacy brought her up from the bed.

"No, Ravenspur, you must not!" she cried huskily.

His powerful arms pressed her down upon her back. "Call me Roger," he demanded, his lips hot against her throat.

Her mouth went dry. She could feel his hard shaft throbbing against her thigh. Its size terrified her as it probed, seeking the center of her womanhood. She expected him to pounce on her and was flooded with warm, weakening relief when instead he began to kiss her again. His lovemaking was leisurely and his kisses long, slow, and melting, so there was no sense of urgency.

She drew in her breath on a quick sob as his fingers touched between her legs. Lightly he played with her triangle of curls, and a deep tingling ache spread upward from between her legs, through her belly, and up toward her breasts. She touched her own breasts and found her nipples standing erect like pointed little spears.

She must be different from other women, she thought. She enjoyed these wicked, shameful things he was doing to her! She knew she should fight him, but she would also have to fight herself, and the effort was too overwhelming to contemplate. She wanted to lie in the magic circle of his arms and let him evoke one sensation after another until every inch of her skin was sensitive to his touch.

Now the palm of his hand was massaging the high mount above her pubic bone, and she could hear herself making little moaning noises as the swirling sensations reached ever higher in intensity. Roger slipped one finger inside her warm womanliness. His heart wanted to burst with the joy of what he felt. He had been certain that Roseanna had known no man before him, but now he felt the little barrier that gave him proof. He slipped his fin-

ger from her; his mouth moved over her swelling breasts
and closed possessively upon the nipple.

Roseanna was panting and breathless, expecting, wanting, needing, she knew not what. Roger's long-starved
passion was unleashed now. He had crossed the high
point of no return.

He was aflame and lusting as he opened her thighs and
lowered his weight onto her. He thrust hard and deep,
and she cried out from the unfamiliar pleasure-pain, wondering wildly if she would be able to bear it. His mouth
took complete possession of hers, demanding it open to
his tongue as her body had opened to his hard, manly
boldness. She stopped thinking. She only wanted to feel
the fullness of him inside her. As he began to thrust,
there came a budding, a blooming as if some rare exotic
blossom inside her had opened its petals wider to receive
him. Unfurling, uncurling, she arched against him wantonly until suddenly the blossom inside her exploded and
splintered into a million fragments. Slowly her senses returned to the point where she again realized where she
was.

Roger lay pressed against her as if they were fused
together; his face was buried in her hair. Something cataclysmic had happened. Were they dead? she wondered
briefly. After what seemed an eternity, Roger raised his
head to look deep into her eyes. "My love," he whispered
raggedly. She could feel the thundering of his heartbeat
against her naked breasts.

When he rolled to her side, strange feelings enveloped
her. She was relieved, yet she felt bereft that they were
not still joined. He watched her warmly; her scent filled
his nostrils, that elusive fragrance that had haunted him
every night since he had met her.

She raised shameful eyes to his. "You made me behave wickedly, Ravenspur! Are you satisfied?"

His dark face was intense. "I'll never be satisfied, Roseanna; I'll never have enough of you."

She was covered with guilt and felt the blush would never leave her cheeks again. She moved away from him as if to flee the bed, but his arms forced her to stay. She knew he would keep her all night; the possessiveness of his touch told her he would keep her there against him. Ravenspur was the devil, and the devil was Ravenspur! She was tormented and frightened by her own feelings. She knew the barrier she had set up between them had challenged his manhood, and she knew he would not rest until he had smashed that barrier. But then she had made it so easy for him! Once engulfed in that warm bed, his nearness had overpowered her. Her senses were filled with the smell of him, and she could still taste him upon her tongue.

She turned from him and buried her burning face in the pillows. He slipped a possessive arm around the curve of her waist and moved close against her back. She tried to make her small body rigid with rejection, but he ignored it. He'd lain awake too many nights and suffered great torment because he knew she was close by, but he had not been able to touch her. Now he could touch her —and would!

Roseanna was consumed with guilt because she found him too darkly attractive and because the things he had done to her were wickedly exciting. She was shamed to her very soul.

Roger longed to possess her again within a very few minutes, but his good sense told him that her first time was better short and sweet. Her body would respond to

him swiftly next time because he had been gentle with her
initiation. With his arm around her waist, he began to
stroke her softly in a spot that would be soothing rather
than arousing, and after a while Roger slept, relaxed and
content, as he had not been in many months.

Roseanna lay a long time with her thoughts swirling in
chaos; then, exhausted, she finally succumbed to sleep's
irresistible beckoning.

Roger awoke early, as was his custom, and lay content
simply to look upon his beloved. First she stirred, then
turned over, then slowly opened her eyes. She was spell-
bound for a moment; then as memory came flooding back
to her, she began to tremble. Her soft lips quivered, and
the tears spilled over.

"My darling," he said with concern, and moved to take
her in his arms.

"Don't touch me!" she said with such venom that he
was stunned. Her words mauled his pride. He had taken
time to awaken her desire, and he knew she had received
deep pleasure from his lovemaking. Yet now she wanted
to deny it. She dashed the tears from her eyes with stubborn fists.

"So," he said with narrowed eyes, "with daylight the
barriers are again erected between us, and we are again at
daggers drawn."

"Nothing has changed." She tossed her head angrily.

"Roseanna, you are deluding yourself. You gave me
greater pleasure than any woman has ever managed to
give me, and your rich, womanly response told me that
you also took joy in it."

"No more than with any other man," she hurled at
him cruelly. He swept aside the bedclothes to reveal the
spots of blood on the snowy sheets. "You beast! You de-

flower and shame me, and now you are gloating over it!
'Tis all a game of dominance and submission to you,
Ravenspur. Hoist your bloodied sheets up the flagpole
and fly them from the castle's highest tower to shout
your virility to your men!" For a moment she was almost
overcome by her hatred of the man—or was it herself she
loathed?

He would not let her make him lose his temper. His
eyes suddenly glittered with amusement. "Lovemaking
has given you a fit of hysterics."

"Oh," she gasped, searching for cruel words of dispar-
agement that would exacerbate his temper.

He grinned wickedly. "Let's hope you recover by bedtime."

She drew herself up regally. "Ravenspur, be sure of
one thing. Tonight I sleep alone!" She swept from the
room and crashed the door with such force that the tail
end of her quilted bedgown was trapped in it. No matter
how she pulled, she could not release it. She almost
slipped out of it and ran naked to her own chamber, but
the thought of coming face to face with Mr. Burke prevented her. In exasperation she reopened the chamber
door to free herself and seethed as she saw Ravenspur
doubled over with laughter on the bed at her sore plight.

He knew a way to tease her that would make her livid.
He felt as carefree and exuberant as a youth after his first
conquest. He rang for Burke to fetch him hot water to
wash and shave, and he whistled a merry tune while
Burke selected his clothes from the wardrobe. Roger
shook his head. "Not black. Not today." He grinned like
a lunatic. "Give me the purple—I feel like a king!"

Mr. Burke kept his features totally impassive, but inside he was happy for Roger. The lad had known none

but bitches, beginning with his mother. It was time for him to seize a little happiness. By the looks of things it wouldn't be long before he'd breed some fine sons for the house of Ravenspur.

As a finishing touch, Roger fastened a diamond stud in his ear and cast an admiring glance into a mirror. Then he took out a key and unlocked his cash box. He removed a leather pouch, counted five hundred pounds into it, and slipped it into his doublet. He turned to his servant. "If Tristan returns today, we'll leave for Ravenglass tomorrow. Pack my saddlebags with enough clean garments for two weeks."

After he had gone, Mr. Burke shook his head. Ravenspur was never a man to shirk his duty, no matter what temptation was dangled before him, but Mr. Burke was willing to bet that it would be the hardest leavetaking he'd ever faced.

Roger walked briskly down the corridor that led to Roseanna's chambers and tapped lightly on the door. A startled Kate stood openmouthed as he dropped the heavy leather pouch into her hand. He winked suggestively and said, "For Roseanna. She was worth every penny!"

Kate closed the door and turned to Roseanna. "It was Ravenspur. He brought you money." Kate actually blushed—a thing Roseanna had never believed possible. She was so angry, she was incoherent and could only manage, "That damned devil, oh, that damned devil!" She could still see him laughing, and suddenly she didn't know if she wanted to cry or tear his face to ribbons. "The wretched man!" she cried helplessly. "Now I really feel like a harlot!"

Roseanna preferred her own company for the rest of

the day. She went for a long ride over to the town of Richmond, where the castle dated from the eleventh century. The town was once a great center of Norman power, and the castle was its dominant feature. Her groom, Kenneth, was happy to provide escort and fill her in on all the history of the place.

By the time they returned, Tristan and his men were back from Ravenscar and were preparing for their departure on the morrow for Ravenglass, on the opposite coast. Roseanna decided that Ravenspur would be well occupied in the dining hall and would not miss her sorely if she dined with her women in her own chamber this evening. If she could just avoid him tonight, she would be free of him for perhaps as long as a fortnight. Winter was fast approaching, and the brisk cold air she had encountered on her ride now took its toll and made her very sleepy. She retired early, relieved that she had not glimpsed Ravenspur that whole day.

The castle was steeped in silence as the hour passed three and headed toward four o'clock. Kate Kendall sat bolt upright in her bed when something awoke her. She was just in time to glimpse Ravenspur entering Roseanna's chamber. She blinked, knowing she could not again keep him from his wife. Then she shrugged and pulled the eiderdown up over her head.

Roseanna, suddenly awakened, had no idea what hour it was. Her words, "How dare—" were rudely cut off by Ravenspur, whose voice brooked no foolishness. "Be silent, Roseanna." He shrugged off his robe and got into bed. "I want nothing except to hold you. I had a nightmare that I returned from Ravenglass to find you gone. I must be up in about two hours, but I want to spend this short time with you." As he reached for her, she went

rigid and turned stiffly away from him. He ignored her
rejection, pulled her against him, and tucked her head
beneath his chin. Their bodies curved together like two
spoons, and with a possessive arm thrown over her, he
was soon breathing the deep even breaths of sleep.

Her rigid rejection was lost upon him, so gradually in
the warmth of his body she began to relax. But something
was stirring inside her that she refused to acknowledge.
An ache, almost a longing began deep within her body.
My God, this couldn't be happening to her! The ache
began between her legs and spread its fiery fingers up into
her belly and inched its way up toward her round, full
breasts like liquid fire. The ache grew unbearable until
she had to bite her tongue to prevent her low moans from
escaping. He was a devil of darkness who had played
with her body, leaving sensuous memory in every pore,
and now her weak flesh lay against the muscled length of
him craving his lovemaking.

Ravenspur turned over in his sleep, and momentarily
relieved, she sighed as he presented his back to her. Furiously she told herself that she must detach her thoughts
from him and let them drift off so that sleep could claim
her. Roger lay on his side with his back toward her. The
firelight made the room glow. She was suddenly admiring
his shape, his wide, strong shoulders. His breathing came
smoothly, slow and rhythmic. Slowly, as if compelled by
a force greater than herself, she inched closer until she
could again feel the heat from his body.

Suddenly she was desperately fighting the urge to
touch him. In her imagination she wanted to rub her
breasts across his back, to let her belly rub against his
buttocks. She wanted to glide her tongue over his skin
and taste the salty, manly taste of him. Her body had

become all nerve endings so that every inch of her skin tingled, and as the tightness of her lower body became unbearable, she let her imagination have its way. She fantasized that he released a breath that was half a sigh, half a moan. She dreamed that he turned to her and pulled her hips to his mouth; then his tongue began to dance over the delicate folds, teasing between her legs until the sensual ripples snaked upward into her belly. She moaned, and her hand reached out to caress him. Roger awoke instantly. As in her imagining a few moments before, he turned and lifted her hips to his mouth. "I dreamed that you let me love you this way," he breathed huskily.

Wildly, she thought it impossible that they had shared the same dream.

"Let me love you, Roseanna!"

She was shocked beyond anything she'd ever known as his tongue began its devilish dance in and out of her hot, throbbing womanliness. She tried to stop him, but an inner voice told her it was the most wickedly thrilling sensation she would ever experience, and she let him go on for long minutes. Finally she begged him to stop, but he was not ready to give up her sweetness. The throbbing pulse where his tongue thrust became heavier, threatening to erupt, yet he went on and on until she cried out and arched up from the bed. Finally, when the explosion came, it brought with it the most blissful feeling she'd ever known. Everything was totally new and exciting. The spark of sensuality had ignited into an explosion of erotic sex. He had her primed and willing now, and he wasn't about to let her retreat behind her cold, rigid barrier yet.

His hot mouth moved up her throat, and he murmured

into her ear, "Whisper to me your secret fantasies. What wicked reveries delight you?" She could not answer him, for she was beyond words. So he whispered his wicked desires to her and finished, "I would like to do that with you! Let me love you again, Roseanna, before daylight comes and makes you circumspect!"

She reached out, and her fingers closed around his swollen shaft. He groaned his pleasure, and they were shamelessly hungry for each other again. Her breath was ragged, and he knew her desires were as great as his. Her sighs of delight as his pulsing shaft thrust deep told him that she received almost as much pleasure as did he. She caught his rhythm and moved with him until they were both lost in the throes of passion. His seed thundered into her; her enjoyment was so intense, she almost fainted. His body shook with a great shudder of intense pleasure as he filled her with his love.

At dawn he slipped from her bed, taking infinite care not to disturb her. He caught his breath at her loveliness. Her hair was disheveled, and it suited her. She was wildly beautiful. He silently cursed his state of erection as he yearned for a time when they could awaken together. Then he would reach for her, and she would open to him and welcome his advances. The nightmare had shaken him, although he kept the lurid details to himself. In the dream when she'd been missing, he had searched for Roseanna and had found her dead, exactly as he had found Janet. His face grim, he silently put on his robe and went softly from the chamber.

16

Roseanna spent the morning visiting Rebecca. She wasn't surprised to learn that Tristan had spent the night with her. Their relationship was much improved; Rebecca was eager for Tristan's return from Ravenglass, for if the political situation seemed quiet, they would all be traveling back to Ravenspur.

"Did Roger tell you how long they would be away?" asked Rebecca hopefully.

Roseanna shook her head. "We didn't speak of it. I assume they'll be gone about two weeks, but I suppose it could be much less. Ravenglass is about sixty miles from here. If they ride hard, they could get there in a day."

Rebecca sighed. "The thought of moving the entire household again fatigues me, but I'll be glad to go home. I've had enough of the frozen North."

"I'm looking forward to going to Ravenspur Castle. I haven't seen my real home yet," said Roseanna.

"Oh, you'll love it. It's so much prettier than this place. It doesn't seem like a castle at all. In the spring and summer the gardens are like a picture, and the parkland between Ravenspur and the house where Tristan and I live is ideal for riding. It's nothing like the wild moors up here."

"I rather like these hills and dales, although they seem like mountains to me. I suppose I'd better get Kate Kendall started on the packing if we are about to move households. I'll consult with Mr. Burke; he knows everything that's going on, and he usually has everything under control."

Her mind was already busy with the horses. They'd take them all back to Ravenspur, taking special care with the three mares that were in foal. She'd have to speak again with Thomas about the white horses that those monks were known to breed. Now that she had money, she intended to buy a mare or two to breed with the Arabian.

That evening, she again dined in her chamber rather than go down to the dining hall, which would be empty except for servants and the castle women. Afterward, she took a notion to explore Ravenspur's chamber. What a great opportunity to satisfy her curiosity about the chamber—aye, and about the man! His possessions would give her insight into his personality and perhaps his weaknesses.

In his room she blushed at the sight of the bed, yet she spent a pleasant hour touching his belongings, looking into coffers and cabinets, and admiring his rich clothes, which were hung in two large wardrobes. One, she noticed, smelled of exotic sandalwood, while the other held the scent of newly mown hay from the herb woodruff.

Already she had known him for a fastidious man; now she realized how neat and organized he was. The room was furnished richly, and she could tell he loved luxury;

yet she knew he was Spartan enough to survive any hardship. She caught a glimpse of herself in the mirror and tossed her head in disdain. A mirror, indeed! To admire himself, no doubt. He was an arrogant and prideful devil, too.

She was aghast when the ache inside her began. In a panic she fled the room to dispel his influence. She closed the door with a soft thud to return to her own chamber, but as she passed the doorway that led up to the barbican tower, she came face to face with Sir Bryan. He was carrying a shuttered lantern, which he quickly set down, and he drew her into his arms. "Oh, Roseanna, my heart bleeds for lack of you."

She reached up to caress his face tenderly. "My sweet Bryan, don't pine for me. It breaks my heart."

He pulled her into the shadow of the doorway lest anyone see them. She glanced up the stairs to the barbican tower. "What were you doing up there?" she whispered.

"I go up there to be alone—to compose verses to you." She felt his breath upon her cheek; he sounded so young and sincere that she almost melted. "It must be freezing up there. What manner of lantern is that?" she puzzled.

"The shutters are for closing so the drafty winds cannot blow out the light."

Roseanna accepted his explanation, yet in the recesses of her mind she knew shuttered lanterns served a dual purpose.

When he whispered, "May I kiss you?" her heart nearly burst with pity. He demanded nothing but the crumbs that were left over from Ravenspur's table. She lifted her mouth to his and found his lips cold. They remained fused together until her warmth entered him.

She wanted to take him to her cozy chamber where they could be warm and private and share their precious thoughts, but she knew she must not. "Go down to the kitchens for something warm to eat and drink. I'll meet you there as if by accident. We can talk before the fire. None can deny us such a small pleasure."

They shared a high-backed settle before the enormous kitchen fireplace, sipping slowly on warmed ale and gazing into the flames.

"Does Ravenspur hurt you?" he asked.

She was startled at his question but answered truthfully, "No. Why do you ask?"

"He murdered his last wife, and I've learned the unspeakable way he did it. She was raped with his dagger!"

Roseanna recoiled, horrified at his accusation. "Nay, Bryan, I'll not believe it. Where did you hear such foul slander?"

"One of his own men told me. Ravenspur was arrested for the murder, and only the fact that the King intervened on his behalf saved his neck."

"If the King believed him innocent, then so do I," she said firmly because the alternative was unthinkable.

"Roseanna, the King didn't give a damn if his best friend was innocent or guilty. The woman was unfaithful and got what she deserved, or so most men would think."

Roseanna shuddered. She had given herself up totally to Ravenspur in the night, to do with as he willed! She blocked the dark memories and looked around to see if they were observed. What she was doing now with Sir Bryan could be construed as faithlessness by tale-carriers.

Bryan touched her hand tenderly. "Best go now, Roseanna. I won't approach you again unless we are chaperoned."

Bless him, she thought. *He knows exactly what danger he puts me in and would protect me.*

That night as she lay in bed, she worried that her dreams would be filled with unspeakable horrors because of what Sir Bryan had told her. But as she hovered on the brink of sleep, a deep longing began, a need to be enfolded and held by a pair of incredibly strong arms. Then as she slipped into sleep, she felt her husband's big body cover hers. He filled her with his long, thick manroot and covered her with kisses until she almost drowned in his overpowering love.

When Roseanna awoke, she lay in her lonely bed, and Sir Bryan's accusations washed over her. Damn it, she'd not let her mind go over and over it, filling her with sick dread.

She threw back the covers, dressed quickly, and sought out Mr. Burke. Although the hour was early, he had been about his duties since dawn. She found him in the small room he called the steward's office. She closed the door quietly and sat facing him across his desk.

"Mr. Burke, I beg you to answer my questions. No one else can help me."

Instinctively he knew what was coming, and knew he would not resist her appeal.

"Ravenspur's wife Janet was murdered. Is it true she had been raped with a knife?"

He nodded slowly. "She was mutilated. The knife was found beside her body."

"Ravenspur's knife?" she pressed.

He nodded again.

"He was arrested for the murder?" she asked.

Mr. Burke said quickly, "The verdict was not guilty!"

She looked deeply into his eyes and asked softly, "Mr.

Burke, was he guilty? I need the truth. Tell me what you know."

He took a deep breath. "I've told no one this—you are the first and the last. I caught a glimpse of a man leaving her chamber late that night, before I went in and found her. I do not know who it was. It could have been Roger, or it could have been Tristan. If it was Tristan, what could have been his motive? I've asked myself a thousand times." He shook his head and said low, "And if it was Roger, I prefer to think he found her like that and delivered a merciful coup de grâce."

"You truly cannot be sure of the identity?"

He shook his head. "He was tall and dark and coming from her private chamber."

She shuddered. "Thank you, Mr. Burke. I appreciate your confidence, especially since I know that your loyalty to Ravenspur rules your life."

Suddenly she had to get outside into the cool fresh air or faint. She went blindly down the main staircase, past the great dining hall, out into the courtyard. Pigeons and dogs scattered before her as she sought a place where she could be alone to sort out her thoughts. One voice inside her head screamed that the man they had bonded her to for a lifetime could not be a vicious murderer. *Why not? Why not?* another voice mocked. *You know nothing of him!*

She had not noticed that it had begun to snow. All at once she looked down at her hand and saw very clearly one perfect snowflake. Then as surely and as clearly as she saw its perfection, it came to her that she knew everything there was to know of this man Roger Montford, Baron of Ravenspur. His touch had told her that her body was precious to him. He had truly honored her with his body, as he had pledged in his marriage vows. His body was strong and powerful, but there was no cruelty in him, no evil. For the first time in the clear light of day, she allowed herself to relive their nights of love together, and she knew beyond a shadow of a doubt that those loving hands could be trusted with a woman's body. Not with just her body but with any woman's body; she would stake her life on it.

A weight was suddenly lifted from her heart. She was no longer afraid of him, and it was a wonderful feeling. They could fight and argue, have totally conflicting views, and drive each other to madness with their willful pride, but she knew she had nothing to fear from him— except that he might be able to make her love him. She pushed the thought away, regained her composure, and returned to the castle.

Two hours later, Roseanna was surprised to see a small troop of half a dozen men ride in. But when she saw that their leader was her brother Jeffrey, she was overjoyed. His arrival would dispel her somber thoughts. As he greeted her with a hug and a kiss, she marveled, "Jeffrey, you must have a crystal ball. Ravenspur left for the coast only yesterday, and today you turn up as if by magic!"

"Wonderful!" He grinned. "Now you will be able to be with Bryan openly while I am here to chaperone you."

She blushed and felt a pang of guilt. It was almost as if the whole thing had been planned. "I hope your men have been well taken care of."

"You have a most worthy steward who has extended the famous Ravenspur hospitality."

"Come, we will find you a comfortable chamber," she urged.

"That shouldn't prove too difficult. By the looks of the

place Ravenspur lives quite splendidly, doesn't he? I wonder if his other castles are as richly appointed as this."

"I'm led to believe that this is a barren pile of rocks compared with Ravenspur Castle." She grinned as she threw open the door to a very masculine room with black oak furnishings and mulberry velvet hangings. Jeffrey couldn't conceal his envy; for a fleeting moment she wondered if it was Ravenspur he envied or her, because it had all been bestowed upon her.

He said bitterly, "Things come so easily to some!"

"Easily?" she echoed. "The price I paid was high indeed. Need I remind you that I was forced into marriage against my will instead of being allowed to follow my heart?"

"Ah, brat, don't take offense. As soon as I get rid of my travel stains, you can show me your stables."

She felt that he was deliberately placating her by changing the subject to horses. She shrugged. What did it matter? The three of them would be able to spend a few happy days together.

The week sped past quickly. Jeffrey almost took on the role of the baron. He enjoyed sitting in the dining hall in Ravenspur's great carved chair, ordering the servants around to fulfill his every whim. Kate Kendall fussed over him, spoiling him as she always had at home, and he was the cause of half a dozen brawling matches between herself and Mr. Burke, who did not take kindly to the petulant young lout who treated the servants like dirt— but not, he noticed with cynicism, in front of Roseanna.

Bryan and Jeffrey became inseparable to the point that Roseanna began to notice sudden silences in their intense conversations whenever she came upon the scene. She

put it down to the fact that the two friends had been
separated and were making the best of the reunion while
it lasted.

Roger had only to close his eyes for a moment on that
long ride to the coast and Roseanna would be with him.
His spirits were high, for he could not remember a time
when he had been as happy and contented with his lot.
He still couldn't believe his luck in securing Roseanna for
his bride, for he knew without doubt that she was the
most beautiful woman he'd ever beheld. She literally took
men's breath away. He enjoyed nothing more than ob-
serving men who were meeting her for the first time. He
saw their eyes widen and their jaws slacken. He'd hide his
amusement as their tongues tripped over their words,
turning them from polished courtiers or fierce men-at-
arms into clumsy youths with their first infatuation. He
enjoyed the envious looks other men cast his way. He
knew exactly how the beautiful creature affected them,
for many were the times he glanced at her and felt his
heart lurch!

He closed his eyes, and her beautiful face was before
him. Her hair fell to her knees in a dark cloud; her marvelous violet gray eyes changed color as she looked at
him; her mouth was as soft and inviting as a pink velvet
rose. His body became aroused just thinking of her. He
had to crush down his desire, knowing that he would not
be able to slake it until he returned to her. His men and
Tristan would indulge themselves when they reached
Ravenglass, but he would not. He desired no other
woman, and he had given her his word that he would be
faithful if she yielded herself to him. And yield she had!
Her body was fashioned for love, and he exulted that she

showed promise of a rich sensuality. His happiness needed only one thing to make it perfect: He needed Roseanna to love him, and he was determined that she would.

They arrived at Ravenglass tired from the fast pace their lord had set. He had observed no movement of troops, nor anything untoward to cause suspicion. As soon as he had inspected the cargoes that his merchant ships had brought, he would ride full speed back to Roseanna and make the arrangements to move his household and people back to Ravenspur, his main castle, the place he thought of as home. He couldn't wait to take Roseanna home.

Ravenspur had a total of nine merchant vessels; he kept three at each of the ports where his castles were built. All three of the Ravenglass ships had recently returned from long voyages, and their captains were in residence at Ravenglass. Roger arose at dawn and led his men through a day of arduous labor, unloading, inspecting, and tallying the cargoes. He was driving, tireless, overpowering, and exploding with energy. At one point, Tristan argued with him that it was unreasonable to drive men until they dropped. They exchanged curses and expletives and foul language to no avail, for Roger merely grinned and said, "I guess we understand each other. Let's get to work!"

One vessel had taken the northern passage to Norway, taking grain there and fetching back a cargo of amber and magnificent furs that were worth their weight in gold. There were rich dark sable, mink, delicate ermine, and gloriously thick silver and red fox. The prettiest by far was the snowy arctic fox. Roger set a bundle of these furs aside for a cloak for Roseanna.

The other two vessels had gone south. One had taken casks of English October ale and smoky Irish whiskey to be traded for wines in France, Spain, and Portugal. The third vessel, its holds filled with wool, sailed all the way to Gibraltar and Tangiers and came back with hides of soft Cordoban and Morrocan leather and an almost priceless amount of ivory. Roger came across a sandal-wood chest filled with pure silk caftans in heavenly shades and a small ivory casket of perfume vials, each one more exotic than the last. He sniffed them apprecia-tively, and these also he marked for Roseanna. Then when all three cargoes had been unloaded, he gave his men orders to reload one vessel with the most luxurious of the items to take to the London docks for the King's Court at Westminster.

Tristan fell into his bed in utter exhaustion. He was dumbfounded when Roger awakened him to go convey to his men that they would be returning to Ravensworth at first light.

Although it was early in the day, back at Ravensworth Jeffrey lounged in a chair with a filled wine cup. "I've a mind to see Middleham Castle. How about a ride over that way?" He spoke casually, as if it mattered little whether she came or not.

"Oh, Jeff, the Abbey of Jervaulx is close by Mid-dleham. The Cistercian monks there breed white horses, and I want to see if I can buy a couple of mares. I'll get ready at once."

Jeffrey frowned slightly. Then his brow cleared, and he nodded and told her he would meet her in the stables. He drained his wine cup quickly and sought out Sir Bryan. "A slight hitch in our plan has developed, but I think it

will serve our purpose even better. Roseanna wants to go
to the Abbey of Jervaulx to buy mares. All we need do is
keep her there overnight until the prisoner is secured,
instead of keeping her at Middleham. This way, if she
isn't needed, we can return her here without ever arousing her suspicions."

Sir Bryan considered for a moment, then he agreed
completely.

Jeffrey said, "So that we are not seen together by
Ravenspur's stablemen, you go now and meet us south
on the road to Richmond. You will be such a sweet surprise for my dearest sister!"

"Do you never tire of playing cupid?" drawled Bryan
with a leer.

Roseanna quickly changed into a warm riding skirt
and covered her silk shirt with a warm quilted jacket.
Then she donned her warmest cloak overall. She took the
leather pouch containing the five hundred pounds she'd
won from Ravenspur and went in search of her women.

She met Alice coming upstairs with freshly laundered
bed linen. "I'm going out with Jeffrey. We should be back
for dinner, but if I'm late, don't worry. And don't let
Kate have any more tiffs with Mr. Burke about packing
the household furnishings to take south!"

"Tiff? That's English understatement if ever I heard it.
And what, pray, can I do? They'll be at it the minute
your back is turned."

"Yes. Well, on second thought, stay out of their way,"
advised Roseanna, laughing as she skipped down the
main staircase and headed for the stables.

Roseanna was enjoying herself. En route, Zeus was
soon given his head, and with ears pricked and tail flow-

ing, horse and rider almost flew down the Great South Road. Her hood flew off, and the wind caught her hair and sent it streaming out across the horse's flanks. Her heart was high. She would buy Ravenspur the mares as a present to surprise him. She didn't know why she had a sudden desire to please him, but it filled her with elation.

She was slightly shocked when she saw Sir Bryan awaiting them at a fork in the road. She turned to her brother sharply and asked, "Did you arrange this?"

"Of course, brat. You're still lovebirds, are you not?"

She blushed and wished Jeffrey would stop trying to push her into Sir Bryan's arms. She felt a twinge of guilt that she was keeping Bryan tied to herself. How selfish she was! He should forget her and find another to give his heart to. She determined to find a way to gently discourage him.

When they reached the land that belonged to the abbey, Jeffrey suggested he handle the business with the monks since they might not wish to deal with a woman.

Roseanna was incensed at his suggestion. "I am capable of handling any situation that arises, Jeffrey. I don't need you or any other man for my mouthpiece," she assured him.

Sir Bryan cut in smoothly, "Middleham Castle is only three miles off. Why don't we go over there and return for Roseanna when she has completed her business?"

She gave him a dazzling smile of thanks and relief. Her brother and his men took off in the direction of Middleham, leaving her at the abbey gates. Visitors to Jervaulx were not rare, but seldom were those visitors women. She explained the reason for her visit to the young monk who attended the gate, and he took her along to his superior. Only the head of the order would have the authority to sell any of the strange white horses whose ancestors had been imported from the Continent and had made the first hoofprints on the moor. But until he was free to speak with her, Brother Ben would be happy to give her a tour of the abbey and show her how they used sheep's milk to make their famous flaky cheese.

The shadows were starting to gather before the head of the order made time to see her. She was ushered into a tower room of the abbey that, though sparsely furnished, was immaculately clean.

"Thank you for your patience, my dear," said the white-robed man with a lean face and large teeth, like a wolf's.

"I'm Lady Ravenspur, and I've come to see if I can persuade you to sell me a pair of your famous white horses." She smiled at him and clearly saw that he admired her in spite of the fact that he was a man of religion.

"Why did Baron Ravenspur not come himself?" he puzzled.

"I want to surprise him with a gift of two mares. We have a white Arabian that we wish to breed."

The tall monk was not embarrassed to discuss such matters with a female, as one might have expected. For he had sized up Roseanna shrewdly and realized she was a rare woman. "We don't usually sell our horses, but in your case I am willing to make an exception."

"Thank you. I'm willing to pay a good price," she assured him.

His eyes twinkled. "Good. I won't let them go cheaply."

She smiled at his candor. "May I see some of them?"

He nodded. "Tomorrow you may choose two from what we have."

"Oh, I had hoped to return home tonight," she exclaimed.

He spread his hands. "The horses are scattered on Middleham High Moor. They are allowed to wander freely."

"Oh, I see. Then I shall have to ask you to extend your hospitality and put me up for the night. Also, my brother and his friend are returning for me. They are probably here now."

He arose and smiled down at her. "We can feed you and put you up for the night, and then in the morning you can choose your mares." His eyes twinkled again. "If we had concluded our business today, the abbey wouldn't have benefited from three paying guests, would it?" He opened the door and turned her over once more to Brother Ben.

Ravenspur's cavalcade clattered into the castleyard. The horses were well lathered from the long, hard ride. Roger felt an impatience to be with Roseanna that he'd never before experienced. He turned his horse over to his head stableman, unloaded a leather trunk from a packhorse, and hoisted it to his shoulder. He took the stairs to his chamber three at a time, set the trunk down by the great bed, and lifted its lid. He carefully moved the furs to his wardrobe and lifted a pale turquoise silk caftan with one finger, closed his eyes in appreciation of the exotic scent that lingered in its folds, and called loudly for Mr. Burke. His steward had sent the servants for hot water for the master's bath the moment he had heard them clatter into the courtyard.

When the bath was filled, Roger stripped and stepped into the hot water, vigorously lathering himself with clove-scented soap. "Mr. Burke, summon my wife."

Mr. Burke's eyebrow went up slightly, and Roger grinned. "On second thought, issue her no summons, Mr. Burke. Ask her if I may have the pleasure of her company." He quickly stepped from the tub and was vigorously toweling himself dry before Mr. Burke got to the door.

Roger reached for his clean garments that had been laid ready for him and was dressed before Mr. Burke returned.

"Apparently, my lord, Lady Roseanna is not here. Her foolish women don't know where she went off to."

Roger frowned. "I'll speak to them." He moved swiftly along the corridor that led to Roseanna's chambers. Kate and Alice curtseyed as he came upon them. "Where is she?" he demanded.

Kate Kendall explained, "She told Alice she was going out with Jeffrey and would return in time for dinner." Alice visibly trembled as Ravenspur's dark eyes swept over her.

"Her brother was here?" he asked.

"Yes, my lord. He's been here all week."

"Do you actually mean to tell me you don't know her whereabouts?" he demanded angrily.

Alice drew in her breath on a sob, but Kate Kendall straightened her backbone and stood up to Ravenspur. "My lord, Roseanna is not one to keep in leading strings. She is her own woman, as you more than any other should know."

He cursed under his breath. Had he not dreamed that she would be gone when he returned? He looked at Mr.

Burke. "Find out if Sir Bryan is with her," he ordered. Roger looked at the two women coldly. "What's been going on while I've been away?" he asked silkily.

"Nothing, my lord. Lady Roseanna spent the time entertaining her brother."

"And entertaining her brother's intimate friend. How very cozy for the three of them! How strange and convenient that he should show up the moment my back is turned!"

Kate pressed her lips together. She was not going to dignify the unspeakable things he was insinuating with a response.

Actually, Roger was concerned for Roseanna's safety more than her virtue. If it were known she was the daughter of the King, she could and probably would be used as a pawn in the deadly game of power. He strode from the chamber and made his way to the ground floor of the castle, where his knights were housed. Mr. Burke confirmed that Sir Bryan was missing.

"Send Tristan to me," said Roger shortly. He began to search the small chamber. He saw the signaling lantern and surmised that Sir Bryan had signaled to Roseanna's brother the moment they had left for the coast. He carefully searched his belongings, then went through the pockets of his clothing. When Tristan came in looking weary, Roger handed him a scrap of paper that said, "The prisoner is to be taken to Middleham."

"Roseanna's missing. This is all I have to go on," he said shortly.

Tristan read the note. "No name, no date." He knew Roger would not wait for morning, so he covered his weariness and asked simply, "How many men do you want?"

"Twenty, for now. Tell them to take fresh horses."

Ravenspur was slightly astonished that the drawbridge at Middleham Castle was lowered as soon as the small troop of horses came in sight of the castle. Did they expect him? Was this a trap? Then, just as swiftly, he realized that they could not be recognized in the dark and had been mistaken for others. He gave signals to Tristan and Kelly, and the moment they were inside the walls, they dismounted and had their knives at the guards' throats.

"Who were you expecting?" demanded Ravenspur, letting the point of his knife slip in quarter of an inch.

"Only the night patrol," gasped the terrified guard.

Ravenspur eased the knife away from the man's throat and asked himself why Middleham needed a night patrol. The guard sighed his relief too soon, for Roger pressed the blade close again and demanded, "Was a woman brought in here today?"

"No. There's been no women brought here. I swear it!"

It was apparent that the guard knew nothing; Roger decided to change his tactics. He sheathed his dagger and signaled to Tristan to follow suit. "Sorry for the rude greeting. It was merely a test."

"Warwick's idea, no doubt," the guard said grimly, wiping the trickle of blood from his neck.

"Just so," agreed Roger with a wolf's grin. "We will take advantage of Middleham's hospitality tonight and be gone at dawn," he announced as if this had been his plan from the beginning. He would scour this building from dungeon to turret and learn for himself if Roseanna was a prisoner here.

As the men stabled their horses, Roger noted that the stables had been freshly cleaned. But the huge piles of horse dung outside the buildings indicated that the castle had been full to overflowing—and recently, by the looks of things. Roger was fully alerted. He had been scurrying from coast to coast while the plotters had been holed up at Middleham under his very nose.

A thorough inspection of the stronghold revealed only a normal number of soldiers garrisoning the place and the usual number of servingmen and women necessary to run a castle. The castellan, as he was assigning them beds for the night, shook his head and remarked, "Never expected you to throw in with Warwick again, my lord."

Roger tried to fish for information. He shrugged. "There's safety in numbers. So many earls of the realm are involved—why not a mere Baron?"

The castellan grinned but named no names. He didn't have to; Roger could smell treason when it was this close. After his men had settled for the night, Roger slipped away to search the castle again. He was relieved to find no trace of Roseanna, yet he was baffled by her disappearance. God willing she was home safe by now. She was a willful woman who did and went as she pleased. He realized he had better learn to put up with her whims if he loved her.

Tomorrow he would effectively remove any who threatened her safety, and that included her own brother, whether she liked it or not.

Brother Ben brought Roseanna to a cell-like room that was austerely furnished with a bed and a washstand with jug and bowl. It was immaculately clean, with hand-loomed linen on the bed. The whitewashed walls were adorned with only a crucifix. One window, too high for Roseanna to look from, let in what was left of the fading light.

When the bell rang to call the monks to vespers, Brother Ben brought her a tray with freshly baked bread, a generous supply of churned butter, and the flaky cheese of Jervaulx. Then he brought Sir Bryan to her small chamber. An earthenware jug of October ale completed the meal. "Your brother's room is next door," Brother Ben said quietly as he withdrew.

Roseanna said, "I'm sorry we have to stay overnight, but the horses are grazing on Middleham High Moor, and I couldn't very well demand they go and round them up instantly. I hope Jeffrey doesn't make a fuss."

Sir Bryan walked over to her and said quietly, "Roseanna, Jeffrey did not return with me."

She looked at him blankly. "Where is he?" she demanded.

"At Middleham he met up with Northumberland, and I think they rode south together," he said evasively.

"The wretched boy! He took offense because I wanted to do my own horse trading rather than let him do it for me!" she said hotly.

"Nay, love. I think rather he did it for us, so we could be alone." He took her hand and raised it to his lips. Very gently, he slipped his arm around her waist and drew her to him; then he slowly lowered his head and kissed her. She returned his kiss.

When it ended and they drew slightly apart, she gazed up at him in wonder. Where were her pink blushes? Her fluttering heartbeat? She felt no response to this golden

boy who had once held her in such thrall that she had
dreamed away whole days sighing over his verses. Then
she realized she had put her finger on it exactly. He was a
boy! She had known a man since her infatuation, and she
was no longer a girl. She was a full-blooded woman who
had a deep need for a man, not a boy. She realized that if
Bryan had loved her well enough, he would never have
allowed her to go to another man. All efforts to escape
Ravenspur had come from her, not from Sir Bryan.

A secret smile touched her mouth as she thought of
Ravenspur. Bryan, thinking that look of love was for
him, pulled her to the bed. His hot mouth pressed into
the valley of her breasts in the deep V of her shirt; his
hands, too, came up to caress the heavy round globes.
Once, not long before, she would have been out of her
depth in a situation like this, but now the boy before her
presented no great problem. She wished to be gentle and
not hurt him, so she took his hands from her breasts and
stood up. "Bryan, this is a holy place." Her eyes raised
pointedly to the crucifix on the wall, and she saw him
flush with discomfort for his actions. She squeezed his
hand in a gesture of comfort and promised low, "We'll
speak tomorrow. Good night, Bryan." He left without
protest, effectively banished from her chamber.

At first light she found herself on horseback between
two similarly mounted monks, flying across Middleham
High Moor, a huge sloping oval of green. Its turf was
reputed to be the springiest in all of England. The moor
was a world of its own, filled with lark song and lapwing
cries. As she lifted her eyes, she saw the high walls of the
round tower of Middleham Castle and beyond the Penine
chain of mountains, the backbone of England that linked
all the moors, valleys, and rivers. It was easy to imagine

herself the first rider to leave hoofprints on this wild, deserted expanse.

She watched, enthralled, as the monks rounded up the white mares. They slipped a rope bridle onto each until they had a string of half a dozen. Then they returned to the abbey, where Roseanna was hard pressed to choose the best. They were all beautiful, so she examined their teeth to determine their age and finally picked two that were of an age to be bred.

She had expected to pay two hundred fifty pounds apiece for them, but when she was given a price of one hundred fifty, she quickly picked out a third mare and counted out four hundred fifty pounds from her saddle-bag. To her delight she had fifty pounds left over.

Sir Bryan was in the abbey stables saddling his horse when she found him. She greeted him gaily, "I've acquired three of the loveliest creatures you have ever laid eyes on. Come and see!"

Roger and his men had left Middleham at dawn. He and Tristan had discussed nothing inside the walls of Middleham, but when they departed, Roger said, "There has clearly been a great gathering of men back there recently. It stinks to high heaven of treason. I want you to ride to Edward at York and warn him. If he's gone back to Westminster, he'll escape their plotting and will be safe. But if he's still in the North, you must warn him to leave immediately. He has too many enemies up here. There's Northumberland, Stanley, and Percy—all thick as thieves with Warwick—and then there are neutrals like Somerset and even our own overlord, the Earl of Lincoln. If it comes to the crunch, the devil only knows on which side they'll jump. We'll ride east to the Great North

Road; then you can turn south. Take half a dozen men with you in case you are ambushed." Roger rode back to Ravensworth praying to God that Roseanna was safe at home.

17

Two hours later Roseanna rode into the courtyard at Ravensworth. Zeus was in the lead, the mares were strung out behind him, and Sir Bryan was in the rear. To her surprise she was met by Ravenspur in a towering temper.

"Where in hell have you been?" he demanded.

Stung to be so addressed in front of his men, she immediately took the offensive. "How dare you question my whereabouts?"

"I dare, madame, because I am your husband, a thing you seem to have conveniently forgotten!" he said pointedly as his dark eyes raked over Sir Bryan.

She said quickly, "My brother Jeffrey took me to buy mares from the Abbey of Jervaulx."

"Your brother, madame, is conspicuous by his absence —and a good thing, too. I'd give him a damned good thrashing if he were here! I forbid you here and now to go off with your brother ever again!"

"Forbid?" she asked icily. "I think not, my lord." She prodded Zeus with her heel; he sprang forward, past Ravenspur, and into the stables.

Roger glared at Sir Bryan and gave the order between clenched teeth: "Seize him! Lock him up!"

Inside the stables the new white mares created a sensation. Old Dobbin untied their ropes and chuckled, "The Arabian will think it's his birthday." Tom and Kenneth ran their hands along the mares' flanks in appreciation. "You picked real beauties, my lady."

"Well, I'm glad someone appreciates the presents I've bought for my husband." She unsaddled Zeus herself and gave him a brisk rubdown and a generous feeding of oats.

Only then did she go to the castle to face the music. As she mounted the staircase that led to her chambers, Roger's tall figure loomed above her. "I wish to speak with you," he said firmly.

"I need a bath, my lord," she said coolly.

"Damn it, the bath can wait! I want you in here now, Roseanna."

He flung her into his chamber but she turned to face him with her hands on her hips. His dark eyes roamed assessingly over her. She was wildly beautiful in her windblown disarray. "Go on, vent your spleen on me— let's get it over with!" she demanded.

He leaned back against the doorjamb, his arms folded across his chest. "Roseanna, I never want to return home again and find you missing!"

"How was I to know you would return so quickly?" she flared.

He spoke patiently. "Is it not reasonable to let your women or Mr. Burke know where you are going?"

She ignored the question. "When we wed, you told me I would be free to come and go as I pleased!"

"And you are, but I ask again: Is it not reasonable to let someone know where you are going?"

"I suppose so," she conceded. Then she added quickly, "But I don't appreciate being shouted at in front of your men. After all, the mares were meant as a surprise present for you. You could at least be grateful!"

He grinned and closed the distance between them in two strides. His fingers threaded through her hair, and he brought her face up for his kiss. "Let me show you how grateful," he murmured against her mouth.

She felt the kiss all the way down to her knees. He slipped her breast from her shirt, and she cried out as he dipped his head to put his hot mouth onto her sensitive nipple. She pulled away from him. "My bath, Ravenspur."

"Do you mean to deny me?" he asked softly.

"Without a moment's hesitation." Her words were cut off as his mouth descended onto hers to take the kisses he lusted for. "Have I not taught you that I will take whatever I want from you, whenever I want it? I think another lesson is in order."

"Ravenspur, my bath!"

"To hell with your bath!" he swore. He had an overwhelming need to assert his authority over her, to brand her flesh as his. He almost tore the silken shirt off her; pushing her back onto the bed, he pulled off her riding skirt. The soft suede riding boots came up almost to her thighs, and she presented such an erotic picture, lying nude save the boots, that he went on his knees to her, burying his head between her legs. He tongued her, seeking her honey, which sent pulsating waves of heat up inside of her.

"Please . . . no!" she cried, thinking she couldn't

bear the intensity a moment longer. But his tongue was like wildfire stroking her secret place, arousing pleasures that were before unknown. At last she cried out her pleasure; he did not withdraw his tongue until she lay quiet and panting to catch her breath. He stood up and grinned down at her. "I have other presents, brought all the way from Tangiers on one of my ships," he added persuasively. "Come back after your bath and see if the things please you."

"If this is your way of apologizing, I'll think on it," she said grandly.

The corners of his mouth twitched. Even naked, her manner showed her royal blood as clearly as if she had proclaimed from the rooftops that she was the King's daughter.

Late in the afternoon, when she thought perhaps he would not be in his chamber, she slipped along to satisfy her curiosity about what was in the leather trunk. She cautiously opened his door but gasped when he grinned at her.

"Oh, I didn't think you'd be here," she said artlessly.

His eyes crinkled at the corners. "Roseanna, you are a damned little cheat!"

She laughed. "Ravenspur, I have to be as wily as a fox to deal with you. Now, my lord, what did you bring me?"

"You are all woman! In spite of yourself you adore presents." He indicated the trunk. "Help yourself."

She knelt down and lifted the trunk lid. She gasped with pleasure at the sight of the brilliant silks. She pulled out a silken caftan of scarlet, and another of bright turquoise, and yet another of pale orchid. Beneath these was a robe of pure white with a white turban encrusted with small topaz jewels and golden beads. She opened the

ivory casket and sniffed each bottle with appreciation.
She was so absorbed in what she was doing that Roger
removed his doublet and shirt without her noticing.

"Try them on," he said huskily, and when she turned
to look at him, she was stunned by his naked chest, pow-
erfully muscled and covered with black hair. His powerful thighs showed clearly in his skin-tight breeches; his
half-naked body disturbed her deeply. He exuded mas-
tery over himself and, she imagined, over any situation in
which he found himself. "Put one on," he urged, "and I'll
have Mr. Burke fetch our supper up here."

She could not resist the pure white robe with the
matching turban and lifted it reverently from the trunk.
Her mother's words drifted back to her—*"Enslave him"*
—and she wondered if it would be possible to enslave this
man.

A low knock came upon the chamber door, and Roger
uttered a fertile oath. He opened the door to admit Dirk.
The young man handed Ravenspur a ring of keys. "The
prisoner is secure for the night, my lord. His horse has
been locked away as an added precaution."

Roger nodded curtly and closed the door after him.

"What prisoner is that?" asked Roseanna with interest.

Roger's face was closed and forbidding, and suddenly
an ugly suspicion raised itself.

"Who is your prisoner, my lord?" she asked again.

"Leave it, Roseanna," he warned.

Her mouth went dry. "It's Sir Bryan, isn't it?" she
demanded.

"I suspect him of being involved in a plot of treason,
Roseanna. I want him secure under my hand for the next
few days."

"Treason? You must be mad! You're doing this because of jealousy—admit it!" she cried.

He grabbed her by the shoulders and looked into her eyes. "Have I reason to be jealous?"

"No, damn you! No, no! This is utterly ridiculous. You will release him at once!"

"No, Roseanna, I will not release him. Leave it be. You know nothing of the matter," he said in forbidding tones.

"I know that he went with me and my brother to buy horses. Why, you might as well accuse my brother of treason!"

"I do," he said quietly.

Her eyes widened at his words. "You are mad, or lying, or both!"

He went over to his discarded doublet and drew a scrap of paper from the pocket. He handed her the note that read, "The prisoner is to be taken to Middleham." She read it, then looked at him uncomprehendingly.

"When I found you missing, I searched Sir Bryan's belongings and discovered this message along with a signaling lantern. As soon as I was safely out of the way, Sir Bryan signaled for your brother to come; then together they held you overnight in case they had to use you."

"But they didn't take me to Middleham," she protested.

"I know, for I went to rescue you. They didn't need to take you to Middleham. Jervaulx Abbey served them just as well without arousing your suspicions."

"Ravenspur, I have no idea what you are talking about. Why would I be of any use to them in this deep plot?"

"Because you are the King's daughter," he said quietly.

She was stunned. "You know?" she whispered. "You know Edward is my father?"

"Of course, Roseanna. Ned is my dearest friend."

"That's why you married me at all costs! 'Twas ambition masqueraded as love!" She flew at him with doubled-up fists and battered against his bare chest. "Damn you, damn you, Ravenspur!"

"Stop it, Roseanna. You are working yourself up to hysterics." He set the paper down onto the bedside table and placed his ring of keys atop it. "If Sir Bryan is innocent of wrongdoing, he has nothing to fear."

"Release him; I will vouch for him," she pressed.

"Nay, Roseanna, I will not!"

She was panting now with anger. "I will never speak to you again!" she spat as she slammed out of his chamber.

Her frustration was so great that she couldn't help telling Kate that Ravenspur had locked up Sir Bryan. Roseanna wrung her hands as she sat in Kate's chamber. "I cannot bear to think of him in the dungeons. Ravenspur is heartless!"

Kate Kendall shook her head. "Such a nice North-country laddie. But ye've driven your husband to this with your own willfulness. Running off, not telling where you were going. He thinks Sir Bryan's your lover, and he means to put a stop to it!"

Roseanna clenched her fists. "He'll not best me in this, you know. If it's the last thing I do, I'll free Sir Bryan."

"You'll not get around Ravenspur with that high temper. There's more flies caught with honey than vinegar."

"Say me no sayings, Kate—you'll drive me mad!" She went into her own chamber and shut the door with a bang. She paced the room like a caged cat; her mind

raced over the recent events. It was true that Bryan had
been in the barbican tower with a signaling lantern and
that the following morning Jeffrey had shown up. But
whatever they were up to was probably some boyish
prank. How was it that Tristan could get up to any mischief and Ravenspur would dismiss it with an indulgent
chuckle, but her brother was guilty of treason? Treason!
She'd never heard such a preposterous notion.

But Kate was right—she could never bully him into
releasing Bryan. She'd have to get around him by subtle
means. She picked up her brush and began to brush out
her hair vigorously. When it began to crackle, she
brushed more slowly; the soothing strokes aided her
thinking.

That was it; she'd seduce him! Then she shook her
head impatiently. She could never gull Ravenspur; he
was too wise and experienced in women's ways. Her
wicked juices bubbled as she went over her dilemma from
every angle. She wanted this from him, but in order to get
it she would have to exchange something he wanted from
her. He made no secret of what he wanted from her, she
thought, her pulse quickening. If she offered to strike a
bargain—one night in which she would do anything he
desired in exchange for Bryan's release—would he agree?

Here was her chance to use every womanly weapon she
possessed to see if she could enslave him. Her color high
and a frantic pulse beating in her throat, she emerged
from her chamber and walked on a direct path to his. She
took a deep breath and turned the handle of the heavy
door. It swung smoothly open to reveal Ravenspur; one
hand was already withdrawing his knife from its sheath
against the intruder who entered without knocking. He
quickly sheathed his knife and cocked an eyebrow at her.

"I have something to say to you, Ravenspur," she said in a rush.

The corners of his mouth lifted in amusement. "Are you not the lady who vowed never to speak to me again?" he teased.

She stamped her foot in annoyance. "Be serious, can you not?"

He schooled his face with great care and said solemnly, "I'll try."

His dark eyes upon her, she was suddenly shy about what she had come to say. The touch of his glance was almost physical as it moved over her, as if he wanted to commit to memory the length of her lashes, the exact shade of her eyes, the contour of her mouth, and the size of her swelling breasts. As his gaze moved lower and lingered on the curves of her body, she knew he was undressing her with his eyes. Then she clearly saw his physical response to her: his manhood swelled and hardened, stretching the material across his groin to the bursting point.

Instinctively, she had picked her moment perfectly. "I've come to bargain with you," she said softly, allowing her eyes to linger on the bulge between his legs before she lowered her lashes demurely.

A slight frown creased his brow as he realized what she was about to propose. "Sir Bryan's release in return for what?" he asked low.

"Anything you desire," she said with a seductive, sideways glance that drew him irresistibly until he was close enough to touch her.

What he desired was that she love him, but he knew she would not give him that. So he'd settle for the next best thing. "A sample first, Roseanna."

She stood upon her toes and, lifting her arms behind his head, kissed him softly. Her breasts pressed against the curly mat of his naked chest; he could feel their heat through the material of her gown. His eyes lingered on her mouth for long, tension-filled moments.

"Well?" she asked at last.

"You know the answer is yes. I'll let the young devil go free in the morning." He moved toward a side table to pour himself a drink, then stretched his long length upon the bed.

She watched him uncertainly, wondering what he would demand of her. Then with a wicked grin he made all plain: "Seduce me, Roseanna."

For a moment she was shocked; then the corners of her mouth lifted as she realized she was certainly woman enough to do that. Her laughter rippled out and sent a delicious shiver of anticipation down his spine.

She picked up a stool and set it down at a distance from the bed, which allowed him an unobstructed view. She sat down gracefully, and as she bent low to remove her slippers, her full breasts swelled temptingly from the neck of her gown. She heard him draw in a swift breath as she pulled her skirts up above her waist, exposing her thighs. Then she elevated one slim leg and removed the stocking and garter. Her fingers moved with such tantalizing slowness, he felt impatience building within his demanding body. She treated him to the slowest, most seductive undressing imaginable, and he schooled himself to lie back and enjoy it to the full. She removed her gown and folded it and placed it upon the stool; then she slipped off her panties and stood before him clad only in her shift. Its material was so fine that when she passed before the fire, he was transfixed. Every movement was

intended for seduction, and as she reached her arms high
to pull off the shift, she bared her body for him an inch at
a time. She stood proudly naked before him for long minutes, then she lifted her hair with both arms and let it
cascade over her nudity like a silken waterfall.

His eyes feasted hungrily on her impudent nipples that
thrust upward; then they fastened onto her creamy
thighs, which were topped by a deliciously swelling Ve-
nus mound that he needed to taste.

Roseanna threw her husband a bold smile, then went
on her knees before the leather chest. Slowly she opened
the lid and drew out the ivory scent casket. She selected a
perfume made from attar of rose and proceeded to drive
him to distraction as she perfumed all the most intimate
and secret places on her body. Then she selected the
flame-colored silk caftan and lifted her arms high once
more; it floated over her head and down her body. The
performance was complete.

Roger could no longer bear the distance between them.
He came up from the bed and lifted her high in his strong
arms, then let her slide slowly down his body.

She felt his shaft hot and throbbing against her thighs,
then her belly, and when her toes touched the carpet
again, he bent his head to capture her mouth and make it
his prisoner. His kiss was demanding, and she opened to
his plundering tongue as a flame seared upward through
her body, setting her afire with the need for him. The silk
robe shivered against her breasts as he slowly pulled it
from her body; moving backward, he took both her
hands and drew her to his bed. He lay back and pulled
her on top of him; then he whispered, "Love me, Roseanna."

She smiled her secret smile and kissed his eyelids. Then

she traced his lips with the tip of her tongue before moving to the thick, corded column of his throat. She nuzzled his neck, while her fingers played teasingly with his small male nipples. When they hardened, she dropped her hot mouth first to one, then to the other, sucking until a throbbing began between her legs, deep in her woman's core.

With a cry, she pulled down his tight black breeches, and his manroot sprang free, long and hard. She caught her breath at his size. With one swift movement he freed himself of his breeches, then took her hands and drew them down to his fully aroused manhood. She stroked and explored until he was groaning with the pure pleasure her touch gave him. Then, inspired by the delicious feel of him, she took his manhood and guided it to her breasts, where she encircled her nipples with its tip. "Lord God, how you make me quiver!" he gasped.

Roseanna was stunned by the intense desire aroused in herself the moment she fondled his thick shaft. She had intended to enslave him, but at this moment he was her master, and she wanted him to fill her. And she almost fainted with rapture as he took over then, kissing her wildly, filling her mouth with his deep thrusting tongue, then moving on to tease her nipples and suck them until the throbbing between her legs heightened. Then he was lifting her hips to his demanding mouth and darting his fiery tongue across her little coral bud.

She gasped for more; he lay back against the pillows and gently lifted her onto his upthrusting shaft. With a moan of pleasure he thrust himself as deep inside her as he could go, then stopped and lay still. He knew she was too far gone to remain passive, and the climax he had begun to build in her with his tongue would scream for

release. Then she did exactly as he desired her to do: She
began to thrust up and down on him, writhing and grind-
ing her hips into his. Each time, she withdrew her sheath
the full length of him; then she drove back onto him
again and again until she cried out his name and gained
her release.

Roger was not yet ready to finish, so he swiftly turned
over with her until she was beneath him and lay quietly
so she could enjoy the pulsations of her climax. Slowly
she became aware again. "You are still big inside me!"
she cried, trembling with spent passion. Roger lifted one
round breast to his mouth, licked the nipple, then sucked
hard. Slowly the throbbing began once more deep within
her, and as his sensitive tip felt her contracting muscles,
he swelled and hardened to his full length. He waited for
her tight sheath to accept all of him; then he began to
thrust deeper and deeper until her head thrashed wildly
from side to side on the pillow. "I want to bind you to me
forever, Roseanna," he cried raggedly. "I love you." He
held her in firm control until it pleased him to give her
release; then when he wanted her to come, he slipped his
tongue into her delicious mouth and thrust in the same
rhythm as his hardness thrust between her legs. They
exploded together and lay spent in each other's arms.

Always before after their passion, Roseanna had with-
drawn behind her barrier; yet tonight she knew she could
not do so. She had promised things, and she was gener-
ously determined to give to the full like a real woman. He
lay on his side looking down at her, cradling her tenderly
in the curve of his strong arm. She slipped her arms
around his waist; then her hands slipped lower to his
buttocks, and her fingers touched curiously two hard
spots.

"What are these?" she whispered.

He chuckled low. "Calluses, my darling. Welts from the saddle. When I was in training with Warwick, I had to stand in the stirrups for weeks. He kept us so long in the saddle, my arse was raw. Now of course, they are well calloused and hurt no more. Your father shared my misery. Somehow it made it easier knowing the King also had a sore arse."

She asked softly, "You knew he was my mother's lover?"

"Yes. They should have wed, Roseanna. It would have prevented the realm from becoming divided over the cursed Woodvilles."

"You, like everyone else, hate the Queen? Tell me why my father loves her."

"I'm not sure I'd call it love, but she has an unbelievable hold on him."

Roseanna said boldly, "I've heard she holds him by his prick. She must be very practiced in bed."

"No, Roseanna. In my opinion she is one of those cold women who hates sex, so she has become an expert at holding him off. She plays him on a line like a damned salmon. He's like an eager boy panting after her, while she lures then rebuffs, forever denying him; therefore his desire for her grows. She closes her eyes when he takes other women, then extracts money and favors for her ambitious family from the guilty Edward. She is an expert at manipulation. I thank God you are not like that," he murmured against her temple.

She felt a pang of guilt, for she was trying to manipulate and enslave him to the point where he would eat out of her hand. "What do you mean?" she asked defensively.

"I thank God you are not cold. Your body receives almost as much pleasure as mine."

"How do you know?" she breathed.

"When I first hold your breasts, they are warm and very soft; but when I caress them and stimulate them, they grow very round and firm. Then your nipples thrust up, tempting my tongue. I love to feel your breasts change in my hands. Let me show you."

The bed was gloriously warm. The feeling of splendor between them made their bodies sing. Hot it was, and thrilling. Their desire rose up in towering waves, then smashed down into showers of sparkles. It towered again and toppled. It mounted and shook in a rhythm as if set to music. They wanted to fling their bodies to it as a sacrifice. Each longed to become a part of the other. It was a wonder and a glory and a terror that made them so alive, they felt immortal. After what seemed an aeon, they were exulting and shivering in every inch, and the stardust whirled about them in an extravagant frenzy that almost pulled them into unconsciousness.

Roger hadn't felt so fulfilled and relaxed in years. He was hovering deliciously on the brink of exhausted slumber when he heard her say, "You will let Bryan go free in the morning?"

He murmured, "If this whole night has been for him instead of for me, you have sealed his death warrant, my beloved."

Icy fingers gripped her heart. Was he serious? She knew he was. She must get Bryan away, or Ravenspur would hang him for treason and jealousy.

She lay without moving for an hour and listened to her husband's deep, even breathing. Then she put out a tentative hand to the bedside table and slowly felt around until her fingers felt the keys. Cautiously she picked them up with the paper they lay upon and clasped them tightly to her breasts to muffle any clink of metal. Her heart beating wildly in her chest, she slowly moved away from the sleeping man until she had a foot on the floor. She stayed like that for long minutes without breathing until she was certain she had not disturbed him; then she softly stole naked from the chamber.

Kate Kendall stirred, then sat up and gasped as Roseanna's naked figure stole into the room. "Put the blanket over your head, Kate. You have seen nothing of me this night. For what I am about to do, I may never be forgiven."

Roseanna dressed in her warmest velvet riding clothes, woolen stockings, and high riding boots; then she pulled a long warm cloak overall. She put what money she had in a leather purse and belted it at her waist. Taking the keys and the paper, she bade Kate farewell. Ordinarily she would have been nervous about going below the castle in the dead of night, but her own danger was nothing compared with Bryan's.

The dungeons smelled of damp and decay; she shuddered to think of the golden-haired youth in such a dreaded place. Dim candlelight came from the only cell that was occupied. As she crept toward it stealthily, a tall, dark form loomed out of the shadows. She almost jumped out of her skin—she knew she had been discovered. "Roger!" she cried in alarm; then she saw that it was Captain Kelly. "Oh, I thought you were my husband —you are so alike."

His eyes gleamed at the prize he had caught doing what she shouldn't. Suddenly a thought hit her in the pit of her stomach: This could have been the man Mr. Burke

had seen the night Janet was murdered! Her mouth was
so dry, she could barely swallow. Kelly reached out a
bold hand to touch her breast; in her misery she did not
stop him. Emboldened by her acceptance, he said low,
"I'll look the other way while you free your lover if you'll
spread yourself for me."

Numb with fear and loathing, she nodded her head
and fumbled the key in the cell lock.

"Roseanna, thank God," breathed Bryan, slipping
from the cell.

She could not get out fast enough. If she didn't get the
stench of the place out of her nostrils soon, she would
faint. They crept to the stables, and in the dim light she
handed him the paper. "Ravenspur took you prisoner
because he found this paper among your things. Tell me
truly, Bryan. Did you mean to imprison me at Middleham?"

He laughed shakily. "Nay, Roseanna. The paper refers
to the King," he swore fervently.

She was stunned. Ravenspur was right! Bryan was involved in treason—and what of her brother?

"Goddamn it, he's locked up my horse," swore Bryan.

"Take Zeus. Leave him at Castlemaine." She knew
that she was doing an insane thing in letting him go, but
she had loved him once, and she would never be happy if
his blood were on her hands. He went to take her in his
arms, but she recoiled in horror. "Go quickly before
someone cries the alarm."

He needed no second urging but threw a saddle onto
Zeus and secured the belly strap. Only seconds after he
rode off, old Dobbin ambled up with a lantern. "What do
you want, my lady?" he croaked.

"The Arabian. What have you done with Mecca?" she asked.

He cackled. "As soon as ye brought them mares in, he began screaming until I give them to 'im. I've put them in the small stable behind this one. Come on, I'll show you."

"Go back to bed, Dobbin. I'll see for myself," she said with regal authority. He knew the tone and shrugged. When Lady Roseanna was up to intrigue, it was best to look the other way. He touched his forelock and ambled off.

She found the Arabian in a roomy, loose box stall with the three mares. One of them had a bite on her neck from when he had forced her to his will. Roseanna washed the wound and disinfected it as the young mare stood trembling beneath her ministrations. She muttered a low oath at the stallion as she saddled him: "By God, if you've got so much energy, I'll run it out of you."

He snorted and tossed his head, but she made him take the bit with determined hands. She had no plan yet except to go to her father. But as she rode toward Middleham, she knew the Abbey of Jervaulx would be close enough to shelter her until she found a way to see him.

Roger opened his eyes; the emptiness of the chamber was tangible. His eyes flew to the table where the keys had lain, and he knew. He sprang from the bed and pulled on his clothes. He ran down four flights until he was beneath the castle, and he saw for himself that she had freed his prisoner. Fear was a stranger to Roger Montford, but it snaked through his belly as he ran to the stables. Fitzhugh's horse was still locked in its stall, but a quick search confirmed that his fear was justified. Zeus and Mecca were missing; they had gone together! He turned on young Dirk, his temper in shreds. "Who guarded Fitzhugh?" he demanded.

"I gave the only keys to you, my lord. No guard was posted," he said, shamefaced. He was saved from a tongue-lashing by Tristan and his men clattering into the yard at full tilt. Roger could see Tristan's agitation. Roger's heart sank as his brother shouted, "They've taken the King!"

"Come upstairs where we can be private," Roger bade him. "Kelly! Ready a hundred men and horses." Grim-faced, Roger led the way to his chamber and slammed the door. The sight of the tumbled bed was like a knife turning in his breast. Quickly, he poured two goblets of wine and handed one to his brother.

"Two weeks ago, Ned left York. But instead of going straight to London, he decided to visit Nottingham Castle to see the extensive building renovations that are being done there. He got word that Warwick was going to move against him, and he was caught with his feet up on the table. He had only his Court with him.

"He foolishly delayed at Nottingham over a week trying to raise an army. He got Pembroke and Devonshire with their armies of Welsh archers, but Warwick's forces were too great. Warwick has Ned at Warwick Castle, and he has had the gall to summon a Parliament for York. He has called on all subjects to join him in arms against the King. His war cry is 'Death to the Woodvilles.' Warwick says if the King won't take action against them himself, he must be made to do so by others!" recounted Tristan.

"You're certain they took Edward to Warwick Castle?" asked Roger.

"As certain as I can be. He's more a guest than a

prisoner, according to Warwick. They have made Warwick Castle their headquarters."

Roger paced the bedchamber like a caged animal. He
was wracked with indecision. The scrap of paper had said
the prisoner was to be held at Middleham, yet Warwick
Castle made more sense. It was close to Coventry, where
the Queen's father, Lord Rivers, held sway. Edward had
made his father-in-law his chief military officer, and he
held the exalted rank of Constable of England. It was
Lord Rivers whom Warwick intended to bring low.

Roger made his decision. They would go to Coventry
and swell Edward's army. There was strength in numbers, and they would join Hastings, Herbert, Stafford,
Pembroke, and Devonshire. He would try to influence
Norfolk and as many others along the way as he could. If
it meant bloody war again, then so be it! He ground his
teeth over the little creeping louse who had escaped from
his own dungeon; he should have gutted him while he
had the chance.

18

Roseanna used every excuse she could think of to stay at the abbey. She told them she had come to look at more horses; she also wanted to buy some sheep; and she had decided that Jervaulx should provide Ravensworth with their famous flakey white cheese year round. She hoped God would forgive her for lying to men of the church but wasted no more thoughts on the matter.

She needed to figure out how she could get close to Edward if she saw him around Middleham Castle or on Middleham High Moor. She concluded that a monk's white robe would be her best camouflage. Holy men came and went everywhere almost unnoticed. She hadn't been inside the Abbey of Jervaulx two hours when she stole a robe from a clothesline outside the laundry.

She rode out onto the moor and put the large white robe over her other clothing as soon as she was away from the abbey. The Arabian blended in with the other white horses grazing on the moor. Roseanna decided she would ride in close proximity to the high walls of Middleham every single day until she saw her father. She hung around all afternoon; then just at dusk she couldn't believe her luck. A large troop of men-at-arms came riding over the ridge with King Edward at their head. She rode slowly toward them, hoping and praying that her father would recognize the Arabian.

He did! Edward held up his hand for the troop to rein in. He felt inside his purse for gold. The King was famous for his generosity, so when he asked if he could approach the monk to give him alms, it raised no suspicions. Edward spurred his horse the few yards toward Roseanna. His own gentlemen who had been allowed to attend him while he was a "guest" at Middleham rode up close behind him to partly screen him from his captors' vision.

Roseanna whispered hoarsely, "How can I aid you?"

He shook his head quickly. "I am in no danger. But oh, my Rosebud, I beg you to ride swiftly and get the Queen into sanctuary. Warwick means to destroy them all!"

She nodded quickly and took the money he proffered. Then she slid from her horse and knelt with bowed head until the cavalcade had passed on its way into Middleham Castle. As the enormity of the task ahead of her dawned, she began to panic. London lay hundreds of miles to the south. She didn't know how far exactly or in which direction exactly, and she was a woman alone. Should she go to her husband, beg his forgiveness, and lay the matter onto his strong, capable shoulders? He'd raze Middleham to the ground to free Edward, but what of Elizabeth Woodville? She knew he would never allow her to ride to London, and her father was counting on her. The Arabian certainly had enough heart for the journey; the question was, had she? Should she spend the night at the abbey and start out at dawn? No, she would set out now; even if she only rode twenty miles or so, she would be that much closer to London, and the Queen's life depended upon her.

She kept the monk's robe on for safety's sake and was glad of the extra warmth it lent her. Though she was cold and hungry, she kept going until she saw lights from a town in the distance. As she got closer, she realized with joy that it was York. She was elated that she had done so well and on impulse sought out The Fighting Cocks, where Ravenspur had caught her.

No skulking about this time! She removed the white robe in the inn yard and brushed off her traveling cloak. She turned Mecca over to a stableman with a haughty warning: "This horse is a priceless Arabian. See that he is well fed and watered, and I want a warm stall for him with a blanket." She fished a coin from her belt and walked regally into the inn. It was hot and smoky as before and was filled with drinkers who seemed noisier than last time.

"I am Lady Roseanna Montford, Baroness of Ravenspur. I'll need your best room and a good hot meal." She looked the innkeeper straight in the eyes, daring him to offer her insult or even excuse because she was a woman alone. But he remembered her from when she was there with Ravenspur; no other woman in England had hair like that!

No sooner was she safely in her room than a loud fight broke out in the taproom below. When a chambermaid brought her half a capon and some hot apple pie, she questioned her: "What's amiss tonight?"

"Oh lawdy, feelin's is runnin' high. There's rumors thicker than whores in York on a Friday night! They say as Warwick has taken the King prisoner an' is goin' to set up George, but England wants none of the likes of 'im. I tell you, they'll be riotin' in the streets if these rumors have any truth to 'um."

"I must be away at first light. Knock very loudly until I answer; no later than five, please," instructed Roseanna.

The long, cold day and the hot food made her very drowsy. She felt buoyed by the report of the public opinion, but the sooner she got to London, the better. She crawled into bed in her shift and was asleep between one thought and the next.

The next day at Doncaster and Newark, the streets were filled with milling crowds that looked and sounded angry. She was very close to Castlemaine but decided that she could not afford to take the time for a visit home. Joanna would be distraught at the news of Edward's capture, and she might also not be in favor of her daughter riding pell-mell for London to save her hated rival, the Woodville woman.

The next day she hoped to get as far as Cambridge, for the weather held good and Mecca was a strong steed. But in the late afternoon she noticed the Arabian had a loose shoe. As she bent to look closer, it seemed to Roseanna that the stallion's shoes were wearing thin. She picked up a hoof to inspect it and blinked in disbelief. The horse-shoes were made of silver! How extravagant of the King to gift her with a horse with silver horseshoes!

She stopped at a blacksmith's shop and had him remove all the shoes and replace them with iron. Enough silver had worn away that this sprint to London had already cost a fortune. She put the silver shoes into her saddlebags. She'd probably need the silver in London before she was finished. Darkness was falling fast on that

winter's night by the time the job was done, so Roseanna
decided to stop at an inn at Buckden.

In the morning, when she lifted her head from her
pillow, a wave of such nausea hit her that she had to
reach for the chamber pot beneath the bed. She vomited
twice, cursing fate that she had perhaps caught something and wouldn't be able to continue. But miraculously, after the second time she was sick, the nausea
passed off as quickly as it had come. She nibbled dry
biscuits and sipped a little wine, for she knew she had to
keep up her strength if she were to reach London this
day.

She was within sight of the great city of London when
her luck with the weather ran out. The heavens opened,
and great sheets of freezing rain were flung from the sky.
All light had vanished from the day by four in the afternoon. She rode into the stables attached to Westminster
Palace and paid a royal groom handsomely to rub down
and feed her horse; then she ran into the palace and asked
a palace guard to direct her to the Queen.

Roseanna looked like the sole survivor of a shipwreck,
as if the sea had spewed her up from its depths. She stood
streaming water onto the magnificent red carpet. The palace guard was insulted by her very presence: "Get out
before I have you arrested."

"You don't understand. I have a message for Her
Grace the Queen. I have been sent by the King!" She said
it with all the regality she could muster, but the guard
poked his halberd at her until she retreated. In frustration she sat on the floor, refused to budge another inch,
and began to scream. A covey of palace guards arrived,
along with the chancellor.

"This beggar woman wants to see the Queen," said the guard indignantly.

"The Queen is at Greenwich. Put her out," ordered the chancellor.

"You pompous ass, why didn't you tell me the queen wasn't here?" cried Roseanna. Drooping with fatigue, she went back to the stables. No one noticed her. She finally found Mecca in a stall, so she crawled in with him and huddled in the hay. So close, and yet so far. She had to get to the Queen. It was her last thought before she sank down into dreamless exhaustion.

She awoke with a start and jumped up to find Mecca nuzzling her feet. She wished she had not moved so quickly, for she then found herself on her hands and knees vomiting into the straw. The morning sickness was repeating itself. "Morning sickness!" she cried aloud. She groaned. "Oh, Ravenspur, what have you done to me?" She pushed the thought away. She had no time to waste in foolish speculation about whether she was or wasn't with child. She had to get to the Queen before her enemies or she would be dead, and from what she had heard, enemies were all that Elizabeth Woodville had.

She wiped her mouth and staggered to her feet. Bits of straw clung to her as she emerged into a London street. It was crowded with citizens and hawkers selling every imaginable need. Milkmaids with cans and ladles cried, "Sweet milk"; fishwives outdid each other offering "oysters, cockles, mussels, winkles, and 'errings." Old women hawked bunches of lavender, and old men offered "dead men's boots." Carts and barrows held fruit, coal from Newcastle, hens, and hares. She bought a spiced custard, then wondered if she could keep it down. She went into a

silversmith's and exchanged the horseshoes for coin of
the realm.

On the next street she found a ladies' dress shop. They
bought and sold used clothing. Roseanna swallowed her
distaste and chose a presentable crimson velvet gown.
She would never gain audience with the Queen unless she
made some show of wealth. The shop owner assured her
that the clothes came from the royal ladies-in-waiting;
when Roseanna departed, she left behind her own clothes
and considerable coin in exchange for a rather gaudy
cloak of what could only be described as blue cloth of
silver upon satin. But more important, she departed with
directions to Greenwich.

The fastest route was by Thames barge. The oarsmen
called out the waterstops along the way. The river,
though wide, deep, and fast flowing, stank. It stank of
Billingsgate Fish Market and of public latrines. Roseanna
shuddered and wondered what it was like in the hot
months of the summer.

On the barge, a group of gaudily dressed young men
were returning to the Court after a night of carousing on
the town. They tried to be familiar with her, first by leers,
then by suggestive remarks tossed her way. Finally one
swaggered over, doffed his jeweled cap, and said with
double meaning, "May I serve you, mistress?" They were
absurdly young to be so dissolute, and she suspected that
they had not quite sobered from the previous evening.
Though they were of an age with her, she felt like a ma-
ture woman among boys. She smiled tolerantly and
quipped, "I don't believe you're up to it!"

His fellows were helpless with laughter, and she
brought a blush to his young cheek. The barge pulled up
at the waterstop; she allowed the young men to leave first

and then followed them up the incline to Greenwich Palace.

Lord Hastings was the chamberlain of the Royal Household, but he was in the North, supposedly with the King. His deputy, Montague, served in his place. It took Roseanna the rest of the day to gain an audience with him, let alone the Queen. He was a small, officious man, and he informed her in a lordly manner that when the Queen dined, she was welcome to observe. Apparently, every evening Elizabeth Woodville and her Court dined "on display." Foreigners and visitors were invited to watch the magnificence of the meal as if it were a play— and in very truth it was a theatrical event.

The Queen was fast becoming one of the sights of Europe, like a shrine. Foreigners could gawp at her while she gave them neither a look nor a word.

Roseanna was awed by her first sight of the Queen. She was slim and beautiful and shone luminously like the inside pearl of a shell. Her hair was silvery-gilt, and she wore shimmering cloth of silver sewn with crystal drops. She looked to be as hard as a diamond. Roseanna was surprised to discover that she was great with child, although the cut of the gown was designed to hide the pregnancy. Toward the end of the meal, Roseanna approached Lady Margery, one of the Queen's ladies-in-waiting, and asked if she could speak to the Queen. She was a rather plain-faced woman, as all the Queen's ladies were. It was evident that Elizabeth Woodville wanted no competition.

Lady Margery looked doubtfully at Roseanna, so she pressed her case more urgently and said, "It is a matter of life and death! I have a secret message from the King!"

In the face of such urgency, Lady Margery quickly

drew Roseanna over to the Queen's table and repeated her message to Elizabeth.

The Queen's gaze dropped to Roseanna, and her eyes narrowed. She assessed every inch of her with glittering eyes. Who was this woman the King had sent with a message? She was far too beautiful for her own good, Elizabeth decided. She was also young, and that was unusual, for Ned usually preferred his women older and more experienced. Although he thought that having many bed partners was his natural prerogative, he was no ravisher of innocent virgins. Still, in spite of her tender years, this one before her stood out as a woman among girls. Yes, she was all woman, Elizabeth decided with her shrewd gaze.

It seemed to Roseanna that the Queen was not going to speak with her, so she did an unheard-of thing and spoke first. She dropped one knee in a curtsey and said, "Your Grace, I beg you to allow me to speak."

Elizabeth drew in her breath in shock. "Who are you?" she demanded coldly.

"I am Lady Roseanna Montford, Ravenspur's wife."

The Queen's eyebrows went up, and she was visibly relieved. So she was not one of the King's whores, after all. Ravenspur's new bride would be out of bounds to the King. After all, hadn't Ravenspur mutilated his last wife for faithlessness? "Follow me," commanded Elizabeth. Roseanna fell in with her ladies-in-waiting, and the procession moved gracefully from the public dining hall to one of the Queen's sitting rooms. "Speak!" commanded Elizabeth, settling herself onto a thronelike padded chair with a footstool.

"Your Grace, the message is bad news, and I hate to upset you. But the King has been taken prisoner and is being held at Middleham Castle. I speak the truth, Your Majesty—I saw him with my own eyes."

"Warwick! That whoreson Warwick is my sworn enemy!"

"Your Grace, I have ridden without rest from Middleham to bring you the King's urgent warning. He said he was in no immediate danger, but that I was to get you to sanctuary because they mean to kill you."

"God wither Warwick's hand if he dares raise it against me, the insufferable bastard!"

"Madame, from what my husband told me of Warwick, he dares!" answered Roseanna.

When her women began babbling with fear, the Queen held up her hand for silence. "As a precaution you will ready my household, and tomorrow we will take temporary sanctuary at Westminster."

The doors burst open, and the deputy chamberlain hurried in. He bowed low. "Your Grace, there is rioting in the streets of London because it is rumored that the King has been taken prisoner."

Fear showed on Elizabeth's face. "What is being said in the streets?"

"It is rumored that Warwick will set up George as King, but the people will have none of it!"

"I told Edward to put those damned brothers of his in the Tower! They are so jealous of my family, they will stop at nothing to ensure our downfall."

Roseanna urged, "Your Grace, you must go into sanctuary tonight. Tomorrow may be too late!"

The Queen's face, pale as a rare pearl, went white. "My little girls," she whispered, then said to Roseanna, "I have three little girls by Edward, three royal princesses I must get to safety."

My half sisters, realized Roseanna with a jolt.

"My sons, Montague! Holy Mother of God, get word to my sons Thomas and Richard Grey." Then she had an afterthought. "My mother. Send for my mother, and I will take her with me into sanctuary. Hurry, hurry! Return with her within the hour," instructed Elizabeth.

Her women scattered, some to the nurseries to ready the children, others to the Queen's bedchamber to pack the clothing and linen needed for a stay in sanctuary. If it were of any duration, she would have her lying-in there, and that meant moving a great deal of baggage from Greenwich.

"Someone stay with me," cried Elizabeth. Roseanna said quietly, "I will stay, Your Grace."

Roseanna had been prepared to detest Elizabeth Woodville, and her first few moments with the brittle woman confirmed all her preconceived ideas about her. Yet there was something about the woman that Roseanna admired. Her towering ambition was not for herself alone but for her family. She had to be in her middle thirties, yet she kept an immaculate, youthful appearance that would attract a man of any age. At her age she had been willing to bear the King three daughters and apparently would go on bearing him children until she produced the desired male heir to the throne.

Roseanna's thoughts strayed to the child that was more than likely already in her own womb. Would she fight as bravely for her child's position in life as Elizabeth was doing for her children? The answer was a resounding yes.

The three little princesses were brought down by their nursemaids, and their baggage was piled by the door. The Queen's women added her boxes; the stack of luggage

reached toward the ceiling. A message was sent to the
Royal Bargemaster at the Lambeth Sheds to ready the
King's barge and anchor it in readiness at Greenwich
Palace.

When it arrived, Elizabeth was urged to go aboard, but
she insisted on waiting for her mother. Myriad servants
began to transfer the Queen's baggage to the barge, and
the little girls were taken aboard. Lady Margery brought
the Queen's white furs and wrapped her in their splendor.
Just as Roseanna was thinking she had never seen anything so exquisite in her life, Montague burst in and announced baldly, "Your Grace, your mother has been arrested for witchcraft!"

Elizabeth clutched her belly with both hands as if to
protect the unborn child. She cried, *"Mon dieu, mon
dieu!* If she comes to harm, I'll tear Warwick to pieces
with my own hands."

Roseanna, annoyed that Montague had shouted the
news to a woman in her condition, said to Lady Margery,
"I think the physician should be sent for. We cannot wait
longer. Send a message that the Queen goes into sanctuary at Westminster and that his services will be needed
very shortly."

With Roseanna on one side and Lady Margery on the
other, Elizabeth Woodville, refusing their aid, walked regally from the palace. The servants were assembled with
torches to light the quay where the Royal Barge stood
waiting. It was painted gaily in the York colors of murrey
and blue and was heavily gilded. On both sides was
painted the device of a White Rose upon the Sun in
Splendour; it had ten strong rowers. Roseanna shivered
as the barge's torches streamed their tails of sparks into
the darkness and the oars splashed in the fetid water. As

the barge passed Dowgate Hill, where Warwick's townhouse, the Erba, stood, Elizabeth Woodville spat into the water, and she put a curse upon the kingmaker. They went under London Bridge and the other bridges before the barge slowed in its approach to the Palace Stairs of Westminster.

It was a miracle that the Queen and her little girls reached sanctuary, for before midnight that same night Westminster was swarming with Warwick's men-at-arms in their scarlet livery emblazoned with the Golden Bear and Ragged Staff. Guards were at every entrance and exit to the Queen's apartments; none were allowed in, and none were allowed out.

Roseanna discovered that information could be gleaned from the guards on the door; they could not resist taunting the vile Woodville bitch and her women. She learned that Elizabeth's mother, Jacquette, was in the Tower, but that Elizabeth's sons from her first marriage, Thomas and Richard Grey, had gone into hiding and could not be found.

One week melted into the next. The Queen spent her time bathing, dressing, having her hair styled, adorning herself with jewels, playing with her children, and listening to her ladies' endless gossip. Roseanna had never seen such magnificent gowns in her life. The styles at the Queen's Court were entirely different from what they were in the North. The sleeves of gowns were very important here and were slashed to show the brilliant color of the material underneath. The bodices were cut so low, they were considered indecent outside the Court; bosoms were bared almost to the nipple.

One fashion that Roseanna did not care for was that of plucking a lady's hair. When the Queen and her ladies bathed, she saw that the hair between their legs had been denuded. When it started to grow back, hours were spent plucking it out. They all laughed at Roseanna for her quaint, old-fashioned notions; Roseanna, having such black hair, had a triangle of glossy curls between her legs.

The weeks in sanctuary passed in an odd way for Roseanna. The days sped past, filled to overflowing by the large household of women, their needs, their talk, their gossip. Yet the nights were endless for her, long, lonely nights in which she clung to her memories of her husband. How she missed him! Not just his lovemaking, although her body ached for the release only he could give her. She also missed his strength, she missed his companionship, she missed their fights, and yes, most of all she missed his love. She knew now that she loved him in return. What a fool she had been to throw away the splendor that was theirs for scum like Sir Bryan! Would Roger ever forgive her? She was unsure and trembled at the thought of his terrible wrath.

It was almost a month before anyone from the outside was allowed into sanctuary, and then it was the Queen's priest. Elizabeth looked at him coldly and said without demur, "I would have preferred a doctor over a damned priest!"

Roseanna suggested that the priest bring a nun who was skilled in midwifery on his next visit. He went off assuring them that he would try his best.

The next day's events were unforgettable. The guards outside the door reported with gloating satisfaction that Warwick had taken the Queen's father and her brother John in Coventry and beheaded them. He had done this because Rivers was the King's chief military officer and held the title of Constable of England.

Elizabeth screamed until she shook, and suddenly she clutched her belly in agony. She went into a false labor and was bleeding. Her women got her to bed, but still she screamed and poured venomous curses upon Warwick's head. The more she screamed, the more she bled.

Roseanna was very worried. She had never attended a woman's birthing before, though she had helped many mares to foal. Firmly she took the Queen's hands in hers and commanded, "Talk to me! Elizabeth, stop this screaming and talk to me!"

Elizabeth's breath caught in her throat as she tried to stifle her screams; then she began to talk. "There were twelve of us. My mother is a silly Frenchwoman who let her heart rule her head. To everyone's horror she married a lowly squire. We were impoverished. I had six sisters and five brothers. They married me to Sir John Grey of Lancaster while I was still a child. Before I knew it, I had two little sons. When my husband died, his family took everything and left me a poor widow with two children and no prospects whatsoever. The only thing the Woodvilles had were good looks and ambition.

"Oh, I know I have a reputation for being a scheming bitch, a whore of Babylon, but those years taught me a lesson. I became as hard as a mason's block. I was beautiful, so my mother and sisters scraped together enough money to make me a fine gown, and I threw myself at the King. The country said I bewitched him, that I was different from his other mistresses. Well, they were right there. I had enough brains to know that if I became his mistress he'd never marry me. I was determined that if he wanted to get between my legs, he'd pay for the privilege.

"Warwick forbade the marriage, and though Edward was King of England, he was afraid of Warwick in those days. So afraid that he married me in secret because of that bastard, that creeping louse, that devil's spawn!" She rocked back and forth. "My poor little brother John. Only twenty years old! So filled with ambition, he willingly married that eighty-year-old harridan, the Duchess of Norfolk. My God, My God, that he should die before her is unbearable!"

Roseanna sponged Elizabeth's drawn face and suffered her contractions along with her. She had never known that giving birth could be so horrific. A knot of fear was growing inside her, for she knew that in a few months she would face the same ordeal. Elizabeth was in her midthirties, and in labor without her makeup and finery she looked every minute of it. Roseanna knew she had the reputation of the whore of Babylon, but here, now, in this place she was just a woman having a difficult birth. Her heart was wrung with compassion. The labor dragged into a second day and then a third, and then the slow bleeding suddenly burst into a hemorrhage. The linen was so bloodsoaked that the bed looked as if it were surrounded by bowls of liver. Then Elizabeth began to vomit into her beautiful silver-gilt hair.

Whether the vomiting propelled the child forth or whether the arrival of a midwife-nun brought the heir to the realm into the world was never quite clear. But Roseanna's relief was so great that she almost lost consciousness when the holy woman took over and stanched the bleeding. Elizabeth Woodville might look delicate, but she was as strong as an ox. Roseanna felt a chill for Elizabeth's enemies, for she was a survivor. If King Edward regained his throne, Elizabeth would smite down those who had harmed her and hers.

Elizabeth's powers of recuperation were almost miraculous. In two weeks she was up out of bed having fittings for all her gowns to be altered to show off her new slimness. The midwife-nun had brought the longed-for news that Warwick had flown too high and would have to restore King Edward. He had summoned a Parliament to meet at York to put the King's brother George upon the throne, but the people would have none of him. They rioted all over the country and on the London Streets to show that the imprisonment of the King would not be tolerated.

Warwick was wise enough to realize that there would be another outbreak of savage war unless he restored Edward. He postponed the Parliament, then sent the nobles a writ of supersedeas canceling it on the excuse that England was being threatened by invasion from France and Scotland.

The King's brother Richard, along with Hastings and Ravenspur, had rescued Edward from Middleham and taken him in triumph to York. Edward immediately stripped Warwick of his high military office and gave it to his loyal brother Richard; he also made him the new constable of England—a heavy responsibility for a boy who had just had his eighteenth birthday.

19

The King and his loyal nobles were coming to Westminster to free the Queen from sanctuary and to see the newborn heir to the throne.

Elizabeth was frantic. Her hair had been without the special paste that changed its color from gray to silver-gilt. Roseanna knew how important it was to Elizabeth that she retain her youthful appearance in the King's eyes. She had been through so much, and though the fine lines left by her suffering could not be erased, there was something that could be done about her gray hair.

Roseanna persuaded the nun to loan her the nun's habit and slipped quietly from the imprisoning rooms of their sanctuary to the bustling London streets, where throngs were gathering to welcome the King. She found an apothecary shop, bought the necessary ingredients for the Queen's hair dye, and hurried back to Westminster.

When she returned she found that the guards at the doors had been replaced by loyal King's men and that there had been no real need for the disguise. She rushed her purchases into the skilled hands of Lady Margery,

who had already washed the Queen's hair to ready it for
the paste. Before Roseanna had time to change her garb,
the King strode into the apartments and boomed in his
large voice to bid them bring forth his son. His little
daughters recognized him immediately and shrieked their
delight to see their soft-hearted father again. Edward
raised his eyebrows at what Roseanna was wearing, but
he made no comment. Instead he grasped her hands.
"What a pleasure to see all my children together! Rosebud, how can I ever repay you for saving Elizabeth?"

"I did it because it was my duty, but in doing so I saw
the woman beneath the surface. All my preconceived
ideas flew out the window, and I know what it is that
made you choose her for your wife."

His laughter boomed out. "God's feet, then you're the
only woman in England who does!"

Roseanna's mouth turned up at the corners. "She's
having her hair washed. She won't have you see her looking anything less than perfect."

The King turned around and bellowed, "Ravenspur!
Where the devil is the plaguey fellow? Come and claim
your bride!"

Roseanna began to panic. Her husband was here! As
his tall, dark figure came into view, her heart skipped its
regular beat, and she found herself breathless. Her last
act had been one of deceit and defiance of him. The
shadow of the young knight she had risked all to free
stood between them like an impassable barrier.

Roger moved closer, the expression on his face inscru-
table. "Explain yourself," he demanded.

She raised her eyes to his, and her lip trembled slightly.
Then she remembered the intimate moment when she
had felt the calluses on his backside, and she gave him a

wicked grin. "The explanation depends on whether you intend to punish me or kiss me!"

In one swift movement he swept her into his arms and his mouth came down possessively on hers. It was like a hot brand, telling her and the world that she belonged to him now and forever. Roseanna could not help but respond. She felt the kiss all the way down to her knees. Then the melting sensation was replaced by fierce desire for this man, and she returned the kiss passionately, moving her body against his in a way that was most pleasurable. He held her at arm's length to fill his eyes with the sight of her and grinned. "I've never made love to a nun before."

The King, overhearing the remark, made the bawdy rejoinder, "Oh? I thought a nun's habit was a specialty of Cassandra's."

Roseanna's eyes kindled. "I happen to know who Cassandra is! You're a pair of damned lechers, sharing your whores as casually as you do a bottle of wine."

The King said, "For a well-bred young woman, you have a very salty vocabulary."

She shot back indignantly, " 'Tis my parentage; I learned the words from my mother and father!"

The King chuckled. "Get you upstairs into Westminster Palace, and choose yourselves a comfortable suite with a big bed."

Roseanna tossed her head regally. "The first thing Ravenspur can do is take me to the most expensive shop in London., If I'm to be at Court, I'm going to be the best-dressed woman there!" She gave Roger a sideways glance. "You can spend some of that fortune I married you for."

Roger looked at Edward. "She's incorrigible."

The King nodded. "You'll have to beat it out of her."

Roger grinned. "I don't know if I've a big enough weapon."

Roseanna leaned into his broad chest and turned up her face to him. "You have, my lord, for I've felt it."

That night at dinner in the medieval Palace of Westminster, the lights blazed, and they dined from plates of gold. The Queen reigned on a small throne at the head table. She wore a magnificent diadem crown and a virginal white gown encrusted with precious jewels. She gave no hint of her recent ordeal in childbirth, nor of her state of mourning. While she surrounded herself with her brothers, sisters, and sons, the King mingled with his nobles, moving easily from group to group, standing out from the crowd because of his great height rather than the magnificence of his apparel.

Ravenspur wore black velvet and stood out as a raven among peacocks. The men of the Court were almost gaudy in the latest styles, with particolored hose, exaggerated shoulders, and beribboned codpieces.

Roseanna knew she looked beautiful. Her gown had cost a small fortune, and it gave her an air of supreme confidence. It was of the palest shell pink silk with puffed sleeves slashed to show deep rose pink underneath. The bodice and skirt were embroidered with tiny glass beads in a delicate pattern of mauve butterflies on rose pink flowers. Her beautiful round breasts were all but bared. Her magnificent hair fell down her back to the hem of her gown and was held back from each temple by jeweled butterflies.

The women of the Court had spent a collective fortune for their clothes and jewels. Roseanna, sharing a goblet of

wine with Ravenspur, told him, "If we are to be long at
Court, I will need a complete new wardrobe."

His dark eyes clearly showed how lovely he found her,
and how desirable. "You may have anything you want,
but we will not be long at Court. We'll stay only for the
christening of the heir. Then I want a week or so at
home, at Ravenspur, before . . ." He hesitated.

"Before what?" she asked.

"The state of the realm is anything but secure. Richard
goes north to defend it against Scotland; Hastings goes to
secure the Midlands; and I'm being sent to Wales again.
It's so wild, but Edward places great trust in me, thinking
I can control it."

Fear touched her with its sharp finger when she
thought of the babe she would bear him in about seven
months. He smiled into her eyes and took her hand in
his. "That's why I want you at Ravenspur, where it's
safe. If you find yourself too lonely, you are close enough
to Castlemaine to spend time with your mother."

She gave him a taunting, sideways glance. "You don't
want me at Court because the game of seduction is so
rampant."

"Tonight, every man's eyes have lingered on you with
speculation. If I were not here, they would move in like
wolves devouring a doe."

"You exaggerate," she said lightly.

"Nay, you are beautiful enough to tempt a saint, let
alone a sinner—and at Westminster I'm afraid all are
sinners. Be careful whom you dance with, lest they take
you to an alcove and have your breasts from your gown.
It wouldn't be difficult to do. Shall I show you?" he
teased. She felt her cheeks grow warm, and he laughed.
"Thank God you still blush; a month at Court, and you

would never blush again." He watched indulgently as she was partnered by Hastings, Herbert, and Stafford, and then twice by the King's young brother Richard, who now held the highest office in the land. But when Thomas Grey, the Queen's eldest son, slipped a possessive arm around Roseanna to partner her in a dance, Roger frowned his displeasure. Before the dance was over, he was on his feet and heading for his wife. The reputation of the Queen's young sons stank to high heaven. They were lechers of the first order, and no attractive woman was remotely safe with them. Roger took her from Thomas Grey before the last notes of the dance sounded. "Madame, you have eluded me long enough."

Thomas Grey sneered, "Keep your knife sharp." It was a common enough saying from one noble to another, but Grey meant it as a reminder of the gossip that had touched Ravenspur when his wife was found murdered.

Roseanna gasped. "That was cruel. Are you going to allow the insult to pass?"

"The Queen's sons can do no wrong. Besides, I don't care what the young swine says to me, just as long as he keeps his hands from you." The music struck up again, and they danced a few measures. He gazed down at her, then let his dark eyes sweep over her. Christ's bones, she was beautiful!

Her breasts began to swell with longing as he towered over her, making her feel very small and feminine.

"I want to make love to you," he said huskily.

"I know," she said breathlessly, wanting it every bit as much as he did.

The thought of her in his bed sent shivers down his spine. He spied a balcony and guided her out onto it. His big hands caught and held her face, and he kissed her almost brutally, seeking her silken tongue and caressing it with his. Her reaction was instantaneous—hot and passionate and filled with lusty, unconcealed desire. Dear God, how she responded to his kisses, and he knew it! No words were needed. He took her hand and led her back through the ballroom, and they slipped upstairs, even though protocol demanded they stay until the King and Queen retired.

Inside their chamber she quickly removed the expensive gown before his impatient fingers could damage the delicate material. In the frantic race to disrobe, Roger was naked before she; he finished undressing her by pushing her back onto the bed and peeling off her stockings. His hot lips left a trail from her ankle all the way up to her soft thigh; she moaned as his lips approached the throbbing center of her womanhood. His desire was so great, he had to crush down the need to mount her instantly; that would be a waste. She was not to be used quickly but savored and cherished. Besides, he wanted more from her than a sexual response. This time he wanted a commitment—and he'd get it, he decided ruthlessly.

She threaded her fingers through his crisp dark hair and tried to pull his mouth up to hers, but he wouldn't leave the flower between her legs until the bud burst into full bloom. His tongue found the bud, and he pleasured her furiously with his mouth until she came.

"Please, Ravenspur," she begged him, not nearly satisfied with what he was doing to her. She closed her eyes and thrashed her head against the pillows crying, "Please, please."

"Look at me, Roseanna," he demanded. "I know what

you want, but I'll not take you like a whore. Admit that you have fallen in love with me!"

"No!" she cried, denying him.

He rubbed his big organ between her legs. "This is what you want, isn't it?"

Passion devoured her. His hard, swollen, shaft throbbed against her, and she sobbed her desire for him.

"No," he denied her when she reached out with teasing fingers to tempt him. "If you do not love me, yet give me your body, you are no better than a common whore. You lock your heart away from me while greedily satisfying the lusts of your body! Do you want me to use you like a whore?" He grabbed her breast roughly and jammed his knee between her thighs.

"No, no, Ravenspur," she sobbed.

"My name is Roger," he said softly.

"Ravenspur!" she repeated stubbornly.

"Damn you, you heartless bitch! I only want you to love me a little." His voice cracked with emotion, and suddenly she broke down. Tears flooded her eyes and streamed down her face. "Oh, Roger, I do love you! I love you more than I ever knew it was possible to love a man. I love you beyond my wildest dreams!"

A surge of joy such as he had never felt before swelled his heart. He parted her thighs and plunged into the sweet, hot sheath that drew him deeper and deeper inside her with every thrust. In a time that is never, ever long enough for lovers, they reached their peak, and she felt the contractions of an orgasm so great, she thought she would faint. Over and over again her body shuddered with the force of her climax; it was heightened and pro-longed by Roger's climax as he joined in her ecstasy.

He cradled her against his heart. "Oh, my sweet, sweet

Roseanna, how I love you." As she lay against him, utterly safe, utterly protected, all was right with her world. In that moment it felt so right that she thought that this was what she had been born for, to love this man and bear his children. He hugged her close and whispered, "I nearly went mad when I found you had released Fitzhugh and when I found both your horses missing. I assumed you'd gone off with him."

"Forgive me, Roger. I should never have released him, for your suspicions were correct. He was somehow involved in the plot to imprison the King. But I truly believed you would take his life, not for any treasonous plot but because you thought I loved him."

He nuzzled the soft spot on her neck beneath her ear. "I was jealous of the young lout, but I was convinced you were in love with his chivalrous idealism. The dashing young knight, pure in purpose, ardent in romance, steadfast in allegiance."

"I must have seemed very young and foolish to you."

He chuckled. "I was so madly in love for the first time in my life, I must have seemed old and foolish to you."

"Let's go home soon," she breathed.

"Tomorrow, if I can manage our escape. Try to sleep, my love."

"I cannot sleep with the chamber so brightly lit." As she slipped from the bed to blow out all the candles, he watched her in awe. No other woman in the world could possibly present the beautiful picture Roseanna's nude body made, cloaked in her dark hair that fell to the carpet.

The pleasure of awakening in each other's arms was short lived.

"Shall I kiss you awake?" Roger asked, smiling deeply into her eyes.

She confessed, "When you found me in the sanctuary, I feared you might beat me."

He teased, "Would I beat a nun?"

"A very pregnant nun," she added.

His face changed instantly. "No! Tell me you are joking, Roseanna."

She couldn't believe the change in him. It was obvious that he was displeased by the news; she was deeply wounded. Tears sprang to her eyes, and she jumped from the bed and wrapped her nakedness in the fur cover.

"Damn you, Ravenspur! I let down all my defenses, and when I am totally vulnerable, you deliberately hurt me."

"Roseanna—" he began.

"Don't speak to me! Don't dare speak to me!" she choked.

He knew he had made a dreadful blunder and wondered what he could say to make amends. Although he searched frantically for words, nothing occurred to him that would wipe away the suggestion that he did not want a child.

Her mind whirled around, looking for a reason that would explain his displeasure. Then she hit on it. By God's bones, perhaps he thought it was Sir Bryan's child that she carried! "How can you think me faithless?" she demanded.

He stiffened. "I did not until you suggested it, madame!"

Eyes blazing, he walked out into the small dressing room.

* * *

Many ceremonies were planned at Westminster for the week to come, but Roger closeted himself with Edward and begged to be excused from the christening. The King waved his hand. "It's not important to me; it's just a formality. But Elizabeth won't forgive."

"I think it best to remove Roseanna while she is in Elizabeth's good graces. If Elizabeth ever found out she was your lovechild, all hell might break loose."

Ned sighed. "At the moment other things occupy her mind. She is bent on revenge and urges me to it every waking moment. I'd like your advice, Roger. Northumberland, Warwick's brother, stayed loyal to me through all this. I think I should honor that loyalty. Divide and conquer makes good sense in my book, although Elizabeth is in a rage that I should honor Warwick's brother."

"Honor his son instead. Give him a dukedom. It will bind Northumberland and his son yet will not offend Elizabeth so greatly."

The King nodded. "I am going to give Elizabeth's brother Anthony his father's title of Lord Rivers."

Roger asked bluntly, "Will you arrest George?"

Edward shook his head regretfully. "Behind bars someone would find a way to dispose of him. I'll not be party to it. Though I doubt my brother's loyalty to me, I shall remain loyal to him."

Baron Ravenspur and his wife headed the cavalcade of their knights and men-at-arms traveling from Westminster to Ravenspur, which was located halfway up the east coast of Lincolnshire on that beautifully sheltered bay known as The Wash. The men knew they were going home only for a couple of weeks before riding off to wild

Wales on the opposite coast. Although their lord and lady rode abreast, she held herself aloof and only spoke to Ravenspur when it was necessary. They broke their hundred-mile journey at Cambridge, where Ravenspur spent the night with his men.

Next day, all about them lay signs that spring would be early this year. The stark silhouettes of the winter trees were softened by new buds, and birds were busily building their nests.

When they reached Ravenspur land, Roseanna was pleasantly surprised by its beauty. She was amazed when she saw Ravenspur Castle. She turned to her husband, momentarily setting aside her hostility. "Why, 'tis not a castle at all, really. 'Tis more a palace!"

Ravenspur Castle was built in the shape of the letter H, with magnificent outdoor terraces surrounded by what would be breathtaking gardens once everything began to bloom. It was a lovely, soft, rose-colored brick edifice, half covered by ivy. It sat in its own parkland where deer roamed about beneath the trees.

Tristan rode out to meet them with his little daughter before him in the saddle. Roseanna's face softened with love as she saw the three-year-old child. "Oh, Tris, this must be Becky," she said happily.

Tristan shrugged. "Her mother's under the weather again. I'm glad you're here, Roseanna. You're just what Rebecca needs."

"I'll come and see her tomorrow. But couldn't I take Becky? Just for tonight?"

Tristan looked questioningly at Roger, who nodded slightly.

"You're welcome to her if you don't think she'll be too much trouble." Tristan grinned.

"Thank you," she said, reaching up her arms for the child. "I'll bring her home safely." She trotted her horse into the stables, holding the child with great care. The first to come forward to help her was old Dobbin. Roseanna gave a little cry of delight, for it was a sign that all their people were at Ravenspur. "Look after Mecca for me, Dobbin. He's worth his weight in gold."

The old man's eyes twinkled. "There's summat in that stall over there will take yer fancy."

She took Becky by the hand, and they went to investigate. A soft-eyed spaniel had a litter of puppies about six weeks old. The child was delighted at their antics. "May I have one?" she implored.

"I think they're old enough to be weaned. Pick one out, and we'll take it to the house with us."

At the front door she was greeted by Alice and Kate Kendall. At the sight of their dear, familiar faces, she realized how much she had missed them. The sight of Kate's capable face also eased some of her fears of childbirth. She wouldn't have to face the ordeal alone; Kate would be there. Roseanna said, "I have so much to tell you, I don't know where to begin. First you can show me all of Ravenspur. I'd no idea it was so lovely."

Kate looked doubtfully at Becky and the pup. "You'll not be taking that wee imp of Satan to be peeing in every room!"

"I don't pee my pants!" said Becky indignantly.

"No, sweetheart, Kate meant the pup. Alice, take Becky and the puppy and find them something good to eat. Kate, there are four beautiful floors here to stretch my legs over. Come on."

"When you're my age, a house with four stories is more of a curse than a blessing," grumbled Kate.

The first floor east housed kitchens and laundry rooms and in the west was the men's barracks. In between was a vast complex of armor, gun, and map rooms. The second floor east comprised living quarters for the married knights and their wives, while the vast number of servants who ran Ravenspur were housed on the second floor west. The third floor held a ballroom, large and small dining rooms, magnificently appointed receiving rooms, a dozen guest bedrooms, and a nursery. Lord Ravenspur occupied the west wing of the top floor. He had a comfortable living room, library, bathroom, dressing room, and large bedchamber. The four-poster in its center was massive, but it was raised so high up from the floor that three small steps were mounted on its right side to assist anyone under six feet tall in climbing up onto it.

The wall at the foot of the bed boasted a white marble fireplace with a black bearskin rug in front of it. The color scheme of black, red, and white was repeated in the oriental lacquered cabinets and wardrobe against the opposite wall. The chamber was filled with costly *objets d'art* that his ships had brought from exotic lands. A magnificent screen stood in one corner inlaid with mother-of-pearl and lapis lazuli, and behind it sat a bright red enameled hip bath. A discreet cough behind her told Roseanna that Mr. Burke was also here.

"Welcome to your home, Lady Roseanna. May you know happiness here."

"Thank you, Mr. Burke."

"And just to be on the safe side, I chose a room for you in the east wing"—he coughed discreetly again—"for when you wish to be alone."

Kate Kendall sniffed loudly. Roseanna, ignoring her disapproval, winked broadly at Mr. Burke and said,

"Becky and I will sleep there tonight. You may show me the room, Mr. Burke."

It was lovely, indeed. It was done in white, pink, and burgundy; she silently marveled at Ravenspur's taste. Was there no end to the surprises he always managed to give her?

She sent a cool note to her husband that stated that she realized he would be occupied on his first night home and that she would take a tray in her chamber and retire early.

Roger was annoyed when he read it. He hated it when she threw up barriers between them. He'd rather by far have a knock-down, drag-out fight in which they hurled vile insults at each other, got things off their chests, and cleared the air. He was torn both ways and hesitated. He knew he'd made a tactical error in letting her sleep alone when they were first married, and he didn't want a repeat performance. Yet she'd had a hard two days' journey on horseback, and in her condition he wanted her to have a good rest.

His heart always won where Roseanna was concerned. He'd leave her in peace tonight, but tomorrow he'd lay down the law and move her into his bed, where she belonged. Damn, thinking of her always produced an immediate physical response, and though he could control it to a degree, he was left with a taut ache in his loins for hours.

If he had seen the wild romping Roseanna was doing with Becky when he left her to rest, he would have been more than annoyed. They were playing a game of tag, and the puppy was dashing around like a mad furry ball. When they were exhausted, she took the greatest pleasure in bathing Becky and putting her in the big bed. Kate brought Roseanna a tray that groaned beneath the number of dishes upon it. She shared her meal with the child, both of them eating with their fingers and giggling with every mouthful. At last Roseanna was ready to retire, so Alice brushed all the tangles from her hair and helped her to bed. Then they sat for hours talking about the Queen and the Court and the things Roseanna had seen in London.

When daylight arrived, Roger had not yet closed his eyes. He had passed one of the worst nights of his life. Two days in the saddle usually guaranteed a good night's rest, but apart from Roseanna he was like a dog separated from its meat. The entire night, desire had ridden him with cruel spurs. He was more than ready for a confrontation.

He pulled on dark hose and boots and a white linen shirt and walked a direct path to Roseanna's room. What he saw arrested his attention immediately. His wife, clad in a silk nightrail, romped around the bed with Becky and the puppy until it was in shambles.

His face softened as he watched his beautiful wife playing with the child. He thought he'd never seen a lovelier picture. Roseanna lay on her back and was lifting Becky above her at arm's length. She said, laughing, "I want a little girl just like you."

"I want a son," Roger interjected. They both became aware of his tall, dark figure leaning against the doorjamb.

"Come and play with us, Uncle Roger," begged Becky. Roseanna was never more surprised in her life when he dove onto the bed and teased, "How's my old ticklebones this morning?"

The child squealed with delight, and the little dog barked excitedly. Becky was almost helpless with laughter and giggled, "Don't tickle the puppy. It'll pee on the bed!"

"What?" he cried in mock outrage. "Haven't you taken the little beast outside to pee yet?" He lifted Becky from the bed and set her on her feet. "Hurry, take it out," he urged.

"Ask Alice to take you," called Roseanna after the disappearing child. She was kneeling on the bed, flushed a delicate pink from her exertions. Roger lay back across the bed and looked up at her.

"I thought you disliked children—or is it only my children you are averse to?" she asked, her mouth pouting with the hurt she felt.

Roger's blood began to pound and surge. His senses were filled with her. The fragrance of her warm woman's body assaulted his nostrils; his eyes devoured her breasts, which swelled from the silken nightgown. Her pouting mouth filled his mind with wildly erotic images of the uses to which he could put it.

He gripped her shoulders and pulled her above him. "Every single time I've made love to you, I've had to seduce you. Must it always be so?" he demanded hoarsely. His lust was so hot for her, it blotted out all thoughts. Swiftly he tumbled her to the bed and held her beneath him. Her soft breasts pressed into his hard chest, and her nightgown was twisted around her waist exposing her long, slim legs.

She struggled frantically to free herself, but his strength was unyielding. His eyes gleamed triumphantly before his mouth swooped to hers. His senses reeled with

the feel of her soft, exciting, provocative mouth, and he
explored it thoroughly.

Roseanna's struggles increased. But her body wanted
to cling to him and let him have his way with her. Damn
him, not only did she have to fight him, but now she had
to fight herself.

Suddenly Becky was on the bed again, wanting to join
in the game and climbing onto Roger's back. Alice stood
watching as if struck dumb. Slowly, he came to his senses
and released his iron grip on Roseanna. He sat back,
panting from the intimate encounter. Roseanna arose
shakily and said, "Excuse me, my lord. I'm going for my
bath." She retreated into the adjoining bathroom with all
possible speed. Alice scurried after her.

The child looked at Roger with wide eyes. "Why are
you angry, Uncle Roger?"

"I'm not angry, sweetheart. 'Tis just a game we are
playing. Roseanna runs from me so that I will chase her."

In the bathroom Roseanna handed her nightgown to
Alice. She was about to step into the bath when Becky's
voice cried excitedly to her, "Run quick, Roseanna! Uncle Roger is coming to catch you! Run, run!"

Roseanna heard and obeyed. She fled from the room
and ran naked along the hallway. Roger shot after her in
full pursuit. She came to the stairway and descended
quickly, knowing it was her only escape. He didn't catch
her until she reached the second floor, where he picked
her up. Half a dozen servants looked on openmouthed.

She struggled like a wildcat. Her soft body rubbed
against his as she twisted and turned. Like a man intoxi-
cated, he took her mouth and drank from it. Slowly he
mounted the stairs; his mouth was fused to hers, and he
reveled in the feel of her body as her breasts brushed

warmly against his naked chest where his shirt hung open. From the second floor up to the third and then to the fourth, he held her thrashing thighs with one strong arm. Her buttocks rubbing against his hard groin made him dizzy with pure sensual pleasure.

In spite of herself, Roseanna found it exciting to be carried in his strong arms, his hard body holding her captive. His kisses had a drugging effect on her at first; then, as he continued kissing her hungrily, taking her inexorably up to his bed, his mouth never leaving hers, her coldness toward him melted forever. Her fingers curled possessively into his dark hair, and she pressed his head closer to hers as her mouth accepted his with a soft moan. Then he was lifting her onto the high bed.

His blood sang joyfully that she was responding to him. They both gave themselves up to the dark magic world they created whenever they came together. He eased his big body between her thighs and slipped his hands beneath her hips to lift her to him; then with stunning intensity her hot body opened to him, stretching to take the full, hard length of him. His hands held her prisoner while he drove deeply into her silken softness; his mouth filled hers in the same relentless rhythm as his body filled hers. She responded wildly, wantonly, and arched her body to meet his every thrust, finally reaching her peak and sobbing softly with the release it brought. Roger tightened his hold, and his movements became almost violent as he too took his shuddering release.

Time stood still. She knew irrevocably that she had fallen in love with her husband and that it was the greatest love she would ever know.

He whispered, "Roseanna, I love you more than life. I

must explain my reaction to you about the baby. My own darling, childbirth terrifies me."

With sudden clarity she saw that he had lost his first wife in childbirth and that he feared the same thing might happen again.

He continued low, "I long for a son, but I'd give up the hope of having one forever rather than risk your life."

"Roger, women have children every day. There's nothing to it." She laughed shakily. My God, was this herself speaking these comforting lies? Hadn't she just watched the Queen go through hell to produce a son? All that blood splurging from her! Towels had been stuffed between her legs, and she'd vomited into her hair. Childbirth had turned the pretty, fastidious woman into a revolting creature.

She pulled his head down to her breast and said calmly, "I think I'm woman enough to give you a son."

The next two weeks were the happiest Roger had ever known. Roseanna had fallen in love with the house as well as its owner. Roger experienced a deep contentment as his wife lavished her love upon Ravenspur. It was a sweet time for Roseanna, too, although she dreaded the time when Roger would leave for Wales. She would have to keep herself busy while he was gone to make the time pass more quickly. She would again be able to devote time to the horses, she would furbish the nursery, and if she got too lonely, she would visit Castlemaine.

"I will leave you half a dozen men-at-arms. I wish you would give me your promise not to travel any distance without them, Roseanna."

She smiled her secret smile for him. "No orders, my lord?"

He grinned. "I know better than to give you orders, my beauty. Shall I leave Kelly with you?"

Roseanna recoiled. "No, no! I detest the man!"

Roger was concerned, "Why, sweetheart?"

She did not tell him of the captain's advances to her but said honestly, "My love, because of his resemblance to you, I suspect he was involved in your wife's murder."

Roger frowned. "I'm sure you're wrong, Roseanna."

She reached up and kissed him quickly. "Just promise me that you will watch your back. Never trust him."

Roger had had the magnificent arctic fox furs made into a cloak for Roseanna. He gave it to her early on the morning they rode out together to familiarize her with the countryside. He wrapped her in the fur, pulled the soft hood up around her face, and kissed her with lingering expertise.

"Oh, Roger, it's beautiful!" she cried, rushing to the mirror and admiring her appearance with the greatest delight. She was thrilled with the gift and, womanlike, buried her face in the luxurious softness. She lightly blew on the fur to admire its depth and thickness. "They are nicer than the Queen's! The white fur flatters me outrageously—I'll never stop admiring myself."

"It's to keep you warm when you ride out like a mad thing in inclement weather." From behind, he slipped his arms around her, and his seeking fingers slipped under the fur. As long as he held her thus, every sensitive part of her body was open to his hands; against her buttocks rose the insistent demand of his body.

She glanced up at him provocatively. "If you don't stop this moment, we shall find ourselves back in bed, our ride forgotten."

"We could have a different sort of ride," he said wickedly.

"Tonight," she promised him as she removed his hands from her breasts.

They had ridden over the park and lands of Ravenspur before, but today he was taking her farther afield. They rode to the seacoast, and he showed her the part of his fleet that was anchored on the east coast. She was deeply touched when she saw one ship riding at anchor with the name *Roseanna* emblazoned on it. Then they rode down the coast toward the The Wash, which was also known as The Fens.

"Never ride into The Fens. It looks innocent enough today, but it is treacherous in the extreme. Anyone who ventures in there needs an experienced Fenman for guide, one who has been born and bred on these bogs and marshes."

Roseanna shuddered as if she were experiencing a premonition. She was glad when they rode back toward Ravenspur and left the eerie, waterlogged salt lands behind.

Before Roger and his men left for Wales, he organized a large hunt. It served a twofold purpose: it provided Ravenspur with enough game and venison for the next couple of months, and it made for a large celebration so that the leave-taking would not be too solemn. Before the party Mr. Burke and Kate Kendall had another set-to that resulted in Kate's grumbling to Roseanna and Mr. Burke's bending the master's ear with his complaints.

Roger grinned at his faithful servant. "My God, man, the way you two carry on, I suspect you have designs on the woman."

Mr. Burke swore, "I wouldn't swive her with another man's prick! I just want it made plain to the woman that my authority exceeds hers at Ravenspur once you are gone, milord."

"For God's sake, man, that goes without saying. Women and horses are alike. You have to gentle them, but use a damned firm hand."

Roseanna looked more splendid than ever. She wore a scarlet gown that was slashed at the sleeves to reveal cloth of silver and that was fastened at the neckline with silver ribbons. Her hair was decorated with a silver moon and stars, and she wore cosmetics on lips and eyes, as they did at Court. She had bullied Rebecca from her bed and now watched with satisfaction as Tristan danced often with his pretty young wife. She was determined that the evening would be gay and leave the men with happy thoughts of home until they could return. She had ordered a lavish spread of food, and Roger saw to it that the ale and wine flowed freely.

The party ended at midnight, for the men would be off at first light. As Roger and Roseanna sought their bedchamber, they knew their first celebration at Ravenspur had been a resounding success. As she undressed, he looked as if he would devour her, a wolf bringing down a white doe. He had a power over her that set her to shivering. Tonight she would unleash the devil in him! She licked her lips, her appetite whetted.

Roseanna joined in Roger's foreplay until he took her fiercely. When he was inside her, they both ached to delay the inevitable end. She moaned and bit at him and drew him deeper and deeper into herself. He brought her to climax after climax, and during them he lay absolutely still to feel the heart of her inner trembling. He kissed her softening breasts and caressed the satin swell of her stomach. "Take care of our child. I promise to be home long before you are due."

"Oh, my love, I'm not due until July. Surely there's no possibility you'll be gone six months?"

"Hush now. Haven't I promised to be here?" He crushed her in his arms to quell his fear and tucked her head beneath his chin. As they lay touching, all three heartbeats intermingled.

20

Roger had been gone a month when Roseanna received
an urgent message from her mother that read:

> Roseanna, I have held off sending you distressing
> news, but I dare not wait longer. Neville has fallen
> ill, and his condition worsens each day. He is ask-
> ing for you, and I hope a visit from you will im-
> prove him.
>
> All my dearest love, Joanna.

Roseanna handed the letter to Kate and Alice and told
them to ready everything immediately for a prolonged
visit to Castlemaine. She chose two men-at-arms for their
escort and told them to come straight back to Ravenspur.

Roseanna made the journey of twenty miles that same
day. When Joanna took her up to her father's bedchamber, she was shocked to see his deteriorated condition.

Kate took over his nursing, and Joanna took her
daughter into her workshop, where they could talk in
private. "My God, Mother, how long has he been like
this?"

"For some time now. I've nearly gone mad trying to discover what ails him. I've had a terrible dispute with his physician because all the fool did was bleed him, and he's feeble enough."

"His color is alarming, and so is the sweating and shaking," said Roseanna in a frightened voice.

"I've tried everything. He can keep nothing in his stomach. We nurse him day and night—he is never left alone. I stay with him all day and Jeffrey stays with him at night."

Roseanna was surprised. "Is Jeffrey here?"

Joanna nodded. "He stepped right into your father's shoes. He's taken full responsibility for your father's men, and he sits up half the night. I don't know how I'd manage without him."

Roseanna was disturbed. She suspected that Jeffrey had been involved in the treason against the King. His service had been with George, and he was therefore a Warwick man; but Neville and his men-at-arms had always fought in the King's service. She said nothing about her suspicions to Joanna, for her mother was clearly distressed enough. "I will sit with Father tonight. It will give Jeffrey a respite."

When her brother came up to his father's sickroom after the evening meal, he greeted Roseanna sweetly. But when she arose from the bedside chair and revealed her condition, he said in an accusing voice, "You are breeding!"

She observed his face carefully and said quietly, "Yes, Jeffrey. You will soon be an uncle."

He bit his lip and said, "You cannot sit up all night in your condition. I will stay with Father."

"No," she said with quiet firmness. "I shall stay with him tonight."

"We've managed without you so far," he pointed out.

As she watched him, she realized that he hated her. She cast about in her memories of the past for a reason; it was clearly deeper than mere sibling rivalry. "Father has been asking for me, so I'll stay with him tonight," she repeated firmly.

"Suit yourself, princess," he said with venom, and left the room quickly as if he could no longer stand the sight of her.

So that's it! He knows I'm the King's child, and he hates me for it, she thought sadly.

In the middle of the night Neville roused and whispered, "Roseanna, sweet Roseanna." In the morning, though he was no better, he was at least no worse. Joanna took over from her, and Roseanna went to the stables to stretch her legs.

On entering, she was greeted by the familiar whicker of Zeus. "Oh, my beauty, how I have missed you!" crooned Roseanna, and the black stallion almost danced in his excitement. *So,* she thought, *Sir Bryan kept his word and brought Zeus to Castlemaine. I wonder if he is still here.* The thought was disquieting.

Sir Bryan was indeed at Castlemaine. He was watching her from a concealed vantage point, but he avoided her. In the afternoon Kate again took over the sickroom, and Joanna and her daughter went for a walk to get some fresh air. Roseanna hesitated, then plunged in. "Mother, is Sir Bryan here?"

Joanna looked guilty. "Roseanna, he has been a great comfort to me while your father has been ill. I can see now what your attraction to him was all about."

Roseanna was alarmed. "Mother! He's not your lover?"

"No, no—at least, not quite, not yet. Oh, Roseanna, I've had no one to turn to."

Roseanna took her mother's hand. "Don't put your trust in him. Ravenspur is convinced that he was involved in the plot to imprison the King. My husband had him locked in a cell, and I freed him because I feared Ravenspur was jealous of him. I feared for his life. But I, too, am now convinced that he is guilty of treason."

"If I thought he had planned to harm Ned, I wouldn't have him here! Roseanna, he is your brother's dearest friend!"

"Mother, I know. I suspect Jeffrey was involved in it, too."

"How dare you make such an accusation about my son!" she flared.

"Mother, only think for a moment. They took their service with George."

Joanna was adamant. "George is Edward's brother. I don't believe he'd be disloyal to the King. 'Tis that devil Warwick! There is nothing to implicate poor George in this. My own son could not be disloyal to the King. Ned is and always will be my dearest love!"

Over the next two weeks a pattern was formed. On the nights when Roseanna sat with Neville, his condition remained steady; but on the nights when Jeffrey attended him, his vomiting increased, and he was on the verge of slipping into a coma.

Kate Kendall called Joanna and Roseanna together and said in her forthright manner, "Lord Castlemaine is being poisoned, in my opinion."

"That is impossible, Kate. Only you and I and his children attend him."

Roseanna said quietly, "I agree with Kate, Mother. There is ever the smell of almonds about him."

"Dear God, do you know what you are saying?" cried Joanna.

"Has the suspicion of poison never crossed your mind, Mother?"

"God help me, yes! 'Tis the only thing that seems to fit." Joanna straightened to her full height as if her spine needed strengthening for what she was about to do. "Kate, go and watch over him. Roseanna, come. We will go to the west wing and search your brother's apartments."

The two women began a methodical search of Jeffrey's chambers. He had two large rooms with an archway between. One was his bedchamber; the other was his private living room—dressing room, where he kept his armor and his weapons. The walls were decorated with the heads of animals that he had taken in the hunt, proudly displaying his accuracy with the crossbow.

In the drawer of the bedside table Roseanna found a bundle of love letters and poems written by Sir Bryan. She blushed as she read them and puzzled as to why her brother had not given them to her, especially since her every waking thought had been centered on the young knight last summer. How mean Jeffrey had been to keep them from her! Then as she read one of the poems, she realized that they were not intended for her. They were from Bryan to Jeffrey!

Suddenly, Joanna gave a little cry: "No!" It came from the dressing room. The letters clutched in her hand, Roseanna moved through the archway. Her mother stood staring in disbelief at a box she had just opened. The white crystal powder inside it was the same poison the head groundsman used to destroy rats and vermin.

"There must be a reasonable explanation for Jeffrey having this poison," whispered Joanna, turning imploring eyes to Roseanna. Yet they were already filled with hopelessness.

Roseanna was still in shock from her own discovery. "Mother, Jeffrey and Bryan are lovers," she whispered, and held out the letters.

Joanna recoiled at the suggestion. How could that be, when the young knight had almost made love to her on several occasions? The two women looked wordlessly into each other's eyes as the implications of what they were discovering became clear.

Suddenly they heard voices and were horrified to realize that Jeffrey and Bryan had just entered the other room. They held their breath and remained motionless behind the curtained archway.

"If that interfering little bitch had stayed at home, he'd be dead by now!" stated Jeffrey flatly.

"You are too impatient, my love. The longer he lingers on, the less suspicion there will be. The men will be yours to command very soon now."

"That royal bastard has tainted my life ever since her very conception!" spat Jeffrey.

"Come to bed, love; let me soothe you. Sometimes I think you are in love with your hatred for your family. You love your hatred more than you love me," said Bryan petulantly.

"Nay, nay. Come here to me. Let me undress you. The girl means nothing to me." He paused to disrobe, then pulled Bryan down onto the bed and fondled him. "The only one I truly hate is my mother, the King's whore! Have you been able to bed her yet?"

"Patience. You are like a bull ready to charge," said Bryan, laughing.

"You like me to be a bull, don't you?" asked Jeffrey silkily as he rammed his hard member into Bryan's body.

Bryan gasped, then moaned with pleasure. "I love it! You know that."

Jeffrey began to thrust so brutally that Bryan grasped the coverlet with tight fists to prevent himself from screaming from excitement.

"If she was determined to give the King a child, why wasn't it me? Why is that nobody, Castlemaine, my father? That's why the bitch must die in the special way I've devised. You will do it for me, won't you, my love?"

"Yes, yes!" gasped Bryan, far gone in the throes of passion. "Now, now!" he begged.

"First repeat to me what you must do to her," demanded Jeffrey.

Bryan had trouble making a coherent speech, but he knew his lover would withhold his release until he obeyed him. "It must be in bed. . . . She must die—as she reaches her climax."

"Yes, yes, you must plunge in the knife exactly when she comes!" gasped Jeffrey, excited by his own words and by the deed he pictured in his head. They cried out as they spent together.

With swift action Joanna took up her son's crossbow and fired an arrow at the bodies on the bed, which joined them forever throughout eternity. The arrow impaled both naked bodies, piercing Bryan's heart and killing him instantly. Not so Jeffrey; he lay writhing and screaming, attached to the body of his dead lover.

Roseanna had been rooted to the floor as the nightmare scene unfolded before her eyes. The evil in the room
had had to be destroyed, and she knew that if her mother
hadn't taken action, she would have.

The two women approached the bed without hesitation, joined solidly in their purpose. Roseanna took a
small knife from the belt at her waist, but Joanna held
out her hand steadily. Roseanna placed the knife in her
mother's hand and watched with horrified fascination as
she gave her son the coup de grâce by slitting his throat.

"I could forgive him everything but the slow poison.
Poison is a coward's weapon."

Roseanna gathered her mother into her arms and
rocked her until her body turned limp. Then Roseanna
urged her from the room. She took the chatelaine's ring
of keys from her mother's waist and locked the chamber
doors behind them.

In Joanna's workroom, Kate Kendall, Roseanna, and
Joanna spoke in hurried, low tones. "I must nurse him
back to health. If he dies, I will never forgive myself,"
sobbed Joanna.

Roseanna said firmly, "Go to my father now. Keep
Alice with you, but say nothing to her. This must be a
conspiracy of three. Kate and I will do what is necessary.
We will say they died in a hunting accident."

"I will never hurt Neville by telling him that his son
tried to poison him," said Joanna firmly.

"Of course not," agreed Roseanna. "He too must be
told that it was a tragic hunting accident. But keep the
news of his son's death from him until he is stronger.
Once we are sure he will recover, we can tell him. I will
stay at Castlemaine to comfort him until he is strong
enough to command his own men again."

They all agreed to the plan, and Kate and Roseanna set about the unpleasant task of separating the bodies and preparing them for burial. They burned the bloody sheets and dressed the young men in their finest doublets. When news of the hunting accident reached the Castlemaine men-at-arms, they did not ask many questions, for they had little love for their lord's arrogant son who ordered them around as if they were dogs.

The following day brought news of a terrible feud between the Welleses and the Dymokes, two prominent families in Lincolnshire. Over the next weeks, the feud rapidly spread into a rebellion against the King. Since both Castlemaine and Ravenspur were in Lincolnshire, it touched all their lives closely. On March seventeenth— St. Patrick's Day—Roseanna decided she had better return to Ravenspur, for she knew that if there were trouble, her husband would be returning immediately.

Joanna bade her daughter farewell. "Your father is still too weak to lead his men into a fight, although he argues otherwise. Tell Ravenspur that if he wants to add the fighting men of Castlemaine to his own, he is welcome."

That night Roseanna prepared for bed, happy to be home at Ravenspur. She warmed her hands at the fire, then pressed them to her abdomen where the child nestled. She hoped that the ugly ordeal she had undergone would not mark the child in any way. She drew back the curtains of the great bed to let in the warmth from the fire and smiled at Kate as she climbed the three steps up into the bed. "I feel guilty about taking you away from my mother, Kate. She probably needs your strong shoulders to lean on more than I do."

Kate shook her head. "Joanna is very strong, and so are you for that matter. But as long as you are with child, my place is with you."

Somewhere on the far side of midnight, in the long hours before dawn, Roseanna came up slowly from a deep slumber. Her heart leaped as she realized Roger had tumbled into the bed beside her. At the time when Ravenspur had received the urgent messages from the King, he had been over a hundred miles away, behind the impassable mountains of Wales. He and his men had ridden nonstop through snow, day and night back to Lincolnshire—no easy task in winter. Once they had crossed the Welsh border, they rode north across flat Cheshire Plain; then they had climbed through the Penine Hills, where the cold rain came down in bucketfuls. There he met up with Lord Stanley, the greatest lord in Lancashire and Cheshire; Stanley had ten times as many men as Ravenspur. He was Warwick's brother-in-law, so Roger knew he was on his way to aid Warwick and not the King. Roger recognized the blue and white banners instantly with their golden Eagle's Foot and Three Stags' Heads.

Ravenspur dismissed the herald sent to him. "Go back and tell Lord Stanley I'll have a word with him. Tell him I act on the King's behalf."

Soon Stanley rode up flanked by two men-at-arms; Ravenspur did not hesitate. "I wish to use this road unmolested. If you do not move your army aside within the count of ten, I shall ride straight through it." He held up both hands and began to clench one finger at a time. Lord Stanley stared, aghast. Ravenspur had the nerve of all the devils in hell; he hadn't even bothered to use the forms of address proper for an earl of the realm. When Stanley saw this determination, he changed his mind about aiding Warwick.

This night, when Roger fell exhausted into the bed, he mumbled, "I didn't mean to awaken you, darling."

She drew his roughened hand to her belly, where the child kicked vigorously. "I don't mind, but he does."

He was asleep between one breath and the next. Roseanna scanned his dark features where the firelight illumined them. He looked much younger in sleep and disturbingly vulnerable, she thought with a catch in her throat. She had longed for him to return so that she could pour out the horror of the ordeal she and her mother had gone through and receive his absolution. But as she watched him sleep, she knew she wouldn't burden him with her own conscience. He was burdened enough with leading his men to protect the King and the realm.

When Roger awoke, her breast was hot against his cheek. He gently played with the nipple to rouse her so they could make love before he had to leave again. This precious time at home was time stolen from the King.

Everynight since he'd been separated from her, his body had screamed aloud its need to be enclosed within hers. Slowly he drew down the covers, kicking them to the foot of the bed so that he could enjoy the full beauty of her nakedness and later observe their two bodies fuse together in their mating. An urgency in the very air told them that they would soon be parted again; their loveplay was rough and frenzied in its intensity.

His lips kissed and sucked and licked her entire body; her hair was wrapped around him, and he gloried in the delicious scent of her, filling his senses with the taste and touch of her.

Roseanna's emotions were so intense, her kisses turned

to bites. Her hot mouth moved down from his throat and across his wide, muscled chest. She stroked his maleness with hot hands, feeling his crisp black hair against her palms. Suddenly she wanted to kiss him there, and she moved down his body with her burning mouth. No experience had ever been as sumptuous as this one for them both. Roger was so wild for her that with one swift, smooth movement, she was beneath him and he straddled her. He sat back on his haunches to catch his breath, and his great lance thrust forward.

Suddenly he lifted her up from the bed, cradling her in his massive arms, and lowered her onto his weapon. They rocked back and forth until Roseanna shuddered with her fulfillment. Then he pressed her back down to the bed and, towering above her, impaled her deeply until it brought his own shuddering climax.

When their breathing slowed, he looked down at her, his dark eyes slumbrous with love.

"Oh, Roger, you are the strongest man I've ever known. I feel so safe with you. What am I going to do when you are gone?" she whispered on a half-sob.

After having tasted her richness, he felt like a god—invincible. He tried to calm her whispered fears.

"Roseanna, my love, it took me so many years to find you, I'll treasure you forever. Our souls are entwined; you make me feel whole, complete. Do you think I'd let anything destroy our togetherness?"

"Oh, darling, I love you too much. I cannot help being afraid for you," she whispered.

He wanted to make her laugh. "There are only two ways I'll die—on the upstroke or on the downstroke!"

"Darling, be serious." She clung to him. "There's no danger that the King will lose?"

"It all depends on who joins Warwick against the King," he answered truthfully. "For instance, my own overlord, the Earl of Lincoln, has so far been neutral. His father was a staunch Lancaster supporter against the King, but he died last year. His son, the new earl, has never lifted his hand against the King. Edward always says, 'Those who are not against me are with me.'"

"I have Zeus back. You will need more than one horse if you are riding into battle. Take Zeus or Mecca."

"I thank you, my love. I'll take Mecca, for I know how deep your love runs for Zeus." He kissed her roughly with the depths of passion he felt for her, then swung his long legs from the bed. "Love, I must go."

She was bereft, but she loved him too much to burden him with hysterics. "I know it," she whispered. "God-speed!"

21

King Edward and his brother Richard, the constable of England, rode from York with their army. The first skirmish was at Stamford. Warwick's brother John, the Earl of Northumberland, failed to support Warwick, and his other supporters in Lincolnshire deserted. As the rebels ran away, they cast off the livery that showed they belonged to the King's brother George, the Duke of Clarence. The body of George's servant was found with letters and written evidence that, aided by Warwick, the Duke of Clarence was trying to seize the throne.

Warwick and his supporters fled to the south of England, to Dartmouth, to his fleet of warships, for Warwick was still captain of Calais and master of the Channel. Edward, Richard, and Ravenspur were about four days behind them.

When Warwick arrived at the coast for his ships, he had a nasty surprise. Anthony Woodville, the newly appointed Lord Rivers, had seized half his ships. The King's proclamation not to give Warwick aid had already reached Calais, and the French port was full of Edward's men. Warwick and George had to sail to Honfleur, in France, before they could set foot on land.

Roger returned to Ravenspur in May. He devoted the following two months to spoiling Roseanna outrageously. At the end of July, right on schedule, her labor began. Roger stayed dutifully at her side, rubbing her back, bolstering her confidence, and helping her bear the endless hours of wracking labor pains. Finally in desperation she said to him, "For God's sake, Roger, please leave me! Go to the farthest turret of Ravenspur where you cannot hear my screams, for scream I must. Since I cannot bear to distress you, I've bitten my lips raw to stifle my cries, but I can hold on no longer. Go!"

He retreated with a bottle to blot out his deep anxiety. After two hours Tristan joined him; then after four Mr. Burke, too, sought their company and had the good sense to bring another bottle.

Roseanna's labor was normal for a first child. Fourteen hours after she felt the first twinges, she bore a son and heir for Ravenspur. By the time the news of Roseanna's safe delivery was brought to them, the three men were nervous wrecks. They came down from their high turret on shaky legs, vowing never to go through a similar ordeal again.

"Don't forget Roseanna's gift," prompted Tristan, "not after all the time and trouble you took to have it made."

Roger unlocked a coffer and took out a velvet box. Then the three of them entered the room where Roseanna was lying in. They were all grinning like lunatics as she held up her beautiful son for inspection; then before

any of them could actually touch him, she tucked him
back protectively at her side.

Kate Kendall ushered Tristan and Mr. Burke out of
the chamber. "We'll leave them alone for a minute, shall
we?"

Mr. Burke turned to her and said, "You did real good,
Katie," and Kate actually bridled.

Roger looked at his wife, pale but triumphant, and
said, "Roseanna, my heart overflows with love for you."
He gently caressed her and held her to his heart. Then he
pulled down the blanket to have a good look at his beautiful son.

"I'd like to name him after both my fathers—Edward
Neville," she said.

He nodded. "We'll call him Ned."

She lifted her face to receive his kiss; then as his mouth
went lower, she threw her head back, and his lips devoured her throat. Her hands slipped inside his shirt, and
her fingers came into contact with the velvet box.
"What's this?"

She gasped as she opened the box. It was a magnificent
necklace of diamonds and rubies with a large teardrop
pearl to nestle in the cleft of her breasts. There were
matching pearl drops for her ears. "Such precious jewels!" she exclaimed.

"Roseanna, you are my precious jewel," he whispered.

"Hand me my mirror," she urged him after he had
fastened the necklace for her. As she gazed at the reflection of her creamy skin, her jet black hair, and her throat
encrusted with the glittering diamond and ruby stones,
she thought breathlessly, *I am beautiful.*

The christening was held in August, and a very lavish

affair it turned out to be. The King and his Court arrived, as well as his brother Richard, Duke of Gloucester.

In actuality, the North was in an uproar, ready to flare like a bonfire. From Yorkshire to the northernmost border of England had always been Warwick country; Edward and Richard were on their way to York to shake their mailed fists at Warwick's supporters.

At the banquet following the christening, the King presented Roseanna with the Queen's gift. Elizabeth had stayed behind in London, but she had sent a lavish gift of gold plate for Roseanna's new son.

"She is too generous, Your Grace," said Roseanna with the utmost delight.

The King grinned. " 'Tis my money she is generous with, my Rosebud. Ravenspur, now that you are starting your own dynasty, why don't you let me raise you to the peerage?"

Roger shook his head. "Nay, baron is high enough for me, as I've often told you before."

"Roger!" scolded Roseanna. Turning to the King, she said, "If you are in a generous mood, Your Grace, you may give my son a title in his own right."

Roger looked abashed. "My God, the woman is insatiable where her new son is concerned. Are not my wealth and titles enough for him, madame?"

Edward bent to whisper to his friend Roger, "She cannot help her ambition; 'tis in her Plantagenet blood." He considered for a moment, then said, "From henceforth he shall be Viscount Gainsborough. There is a small town that goes with the title. 'Tis on the River Trent, just north of Lincoln."

She swept into a deep curtsey. "I thank you from the bottom of my heart, Your Grace."

The King spoke up. "Richard, I hereby make you Warden of the West Marches against Scotland." A hush fell on the room, for the title had been Warwick's since he was seventeen years old. Richard knew the people of the North would resent him bitterly and that it was no easy task the King had set him.

"Henry Percy," the King called in his booming voice, "to you I give the titles previously held by Warwick's brother John. The Wardenship of the East Marches and the Earldom of Northumberland are yours."

Everyone in the room gasped. At last Edward was stripping Warwick and his family of their land and titles. Such was the price of treason; yet none in that room sat easy, least of all Ravenspur. He was glad he'd refused the title Ned offered him. He wanted no title that had been stripped from Warwick, for he knew the mettle of such an adversary.

In France, Warwick had wasted little time. For generations, the sons of the noble families of Scotland had done service with the Kings of France. At the present time King Louis XI even had a hundred archers known as the Scotsguard. Warwick easily persuaded King Louis to lend him ships and troops to return to England and seize the throne.

In September, Warwick sailed for England with an escort of French ships. Two great landholders who had been visiting France, Jasper Tudor and the Earl of Oxford, joined forces and sailed with him, as well as, of course, the King's brother George, Duke of Clarence.

King Edward's spies reported that Warwick set sail on September ninth. As soon as he received the messages, he sent for Percy and Ravenspur to join him in York. They expected Warwick to land in Yorkshire, where his following was strongest, but news soon came to York that Warwick had landed in Devon and had been welcomed in Exeter like a returning hero.

King Edward sent to Warwick's brother John to bring his soldiers from Pontefract, but John had been stripped of his titles and had decided to join Warwick, who was marching toward Warwickshire and Coventry with a vast army. A few men deserted in the dead of night and joined the King.

The news for Edward was all bad. Everywhere Warwick went, he raised troops easily, he met no opposition whatsoever. Edward, Richard, Percy, Ravenspur, and the other Yorkist nobles rode from York into Nottingham to rally men.

Roseanna was thrown into total confusion when the King and most of his army landed at Ravenspur without notice. Every room was filled to overflowing with his knights and lieutenants, and the park was a sea of tents. Though it was barely October, winter had arrived with a vengeance, bringing with it high gales. She saw little of Roger, as he spent hours with the King and his nobles making plans, arguing, and listening while each man had his say.

His voice was almost gone from shouting. He wanted the King to stay and fight, and he argued day and night that they should take the offensive and march out to meet Warwick. But the King received much conflicting advice. The thing he wished to avoid at all costs was becoming Warwick's prisoner again. Edward realized that if it happened again, he would not escape with his life. His and Warwick's fight was now a fight to the death; whoever fell into the other's hands would die.

The Duke of Burgundy was Edward's brother-in-law. He decided to flee England to gather a force greater than Warwick's.

Roger was also kept on the run planning provisions for the great number of mouths to feed. He would fall into bed at night exhausted, with only enough strength to pull Roseanna against him for the rich succor she offered. In the privacy of the great high bed, he held her fiercely.

"God's balls, it is not in my nature to back down from a fight!"

Roseanna was filled with a nameless fear. She went hot one moment and ice cold the next. She bit her tongue to prevent herself from begging him to stay; then a moment later she pressed her fist to her mouth to stop herself from begging him to flee. In a calm voice that surprised even her, she asked, "What will you do?"

The question amazed him. "My duty, of course. My loyalty is pledged to Edward. He has decided on Burgundy, and that is where we go." His arms tightened around her. "Warwick is close on our heels. We leave at dawn. I have to lead the King and his men through The Fens to the coast."

"No!" she cried, unable to hide her fear any longer.

Their voices disturbed the sleeping child, and he cried lustily in protest. She was out of bed in a trice, crooning to the child as she rocked his cradle. Roger could not bear the emptiness beside him.

"Bring him into bed with us. We may not be together again for a long time. I wish to God you were safe in sanctuary again with the Queen."

The baby nuzzled her breast, seeking the nipple, so she undid the ribbons and removed her nightgown. Her breasts swelled so beautifully, Roger was transfixed. "I'll guard him with my life," she promised softly.

Silently he thought, *That is what I am afraid of.* Aloud he said, "I have only three of my ships anchored on this coast; the other six are sailing out of Liverpool on the west coast. But they bring in great wealth, Roseanna. I've signed the papers necessary for you to administer everything in our son's name. Should anything happen to me, he will come into the wealth and title immediately."

She put her fingers to his lips to silence him, and he veiled his eyes because he did not want her to see that her most casual touch had exploded desire in him like gunpowder. Her throat ached with unshed tears as she clung to him for these last precious hours. Finally, when the child slept, she took him back to his cradle and stood over him a long time, tears staining her cheeks.

Roger knew of only one way to make her fears recede, if only for a little while. He slipped from the bed and enfolded her in his strong embrace. When their bodies touched, desire exploded between them, making them unable to think, only feel. He lifted her high above his heart, then let her body slowly slide down his until he was sheathed to the hilt inside of her. She cried out with the pleasure-pain and wrapped her legs tightly around him. Then slowly he carried her back to bed, keeping his hardness deep inside her body. He began a rhythmic thrusting, drawing his length almost fully out, then driving back into her again and again until they both exploded and cried out together from the intensity of their passion.

He knew she would sleep deeply now. When her relaxed body drifted into slumber, he arose and went down to break camp and lead the men through The Fens.

During the next two days, Roseanna tried to curb a

fierce restlessness. She felt as if the walls of Ravenspur were closing in on her; she could not dispel a feeling of impending catastrophe. On the third day she could stand being cooped up no longer, so in spite of the gale-force wind that was blowing, she saddled Zeus and rode hard and fast away from the park, which was still littered from the army that had been encamped there such a short time before.

She rode for two hours and was beginning to feel her spirits lift. But as she galloped back into the courtyard of Ravenspur, her heart caught in her throat at the sight of a troop of horses awaiting her.

George, Duke of Clarence, watched avidly as the ravishing woman rode up on the wild black stallion. She was wrapped in white furs, and her black hair, disheveled from the wind, swirled around her like a second cloak of sable. He felt his jaw sag as the full impact of her beauty hit him. So this was one of his brother's women! No wonder he lavished gifts on her. Well, now she would be his to enjoy, along with the crown!

Roseanna recognized him instantly, though she had never before seen him. His extraordinary height and resemblance to the King were impossible to mistake. He strode forward and took her horse's bridle as she dismounted. She did not curtsey to him but offered him his correct title. "Your Grace, what do you want here?"

He leered down at her. "You, now that I have seen you!"

Her eyes snapped, and she lifted her chin in defiance, but she kept a rein on her tongue. "If you are passing through, allow me to offer you refreshment before you leave."

The smile left his face. "You know damned well why

I'm here, you arrogant little bitch! My tight-arsed brother has escaped, thanks to Ravenspur—fled like the coward he is. Don't try to deny it—the evidence of his army is everywhere. When did they leave?" he demanded.

"A week ago," she lied.

He was secretly relieved that they were too long gone to pursue further. When he rejoined Warwick, he would keep his mouth shut about finding evidence. He'd keep the treasures of Ravenspur for himself! He licked his lips in anticipation as he looked his fill at Roseanna. His brother wouldn't keep a whore who wasn't well versed in the arts of the flesh. Her lush mouth and breasts spoke volumes.

Roseanna's color was high as she stood amid the gaping mounted men. The Duke of Clarence remounted and leered down at her. "One day soon I shall return, madame." His eyes narrowed, and he added, "I mean to have you."

Roseanna was incensed. The man was vile! How could two brothers be so different? Now she realized why Roger had urged the King to put his brother in the Tower, and she understood fully Elizabeth Woodville's venomous hatred of the man. *Just wait until Roger returns,* she thought heatedly. Then with hollow despair she realized what Roger's exile meant.

22

The next morning, two half-drowned men-at-arms emerged from The Fens; one dragged the other, who suffered two broken legs. They insisted on speaking with Lady Roseanna before their injuries were tended. Her heart in her throat, she whispered, "You have news?"

"My lady, our news is terrible! The army took the Fen Road that leads along the shores of The Wash to the Port of Lynn. The wind was strong enough to blow the clothes off your back and cold enough to freeze the bones of the dead in their graves. The worst of the storm came up as we crossed the River Nene. It was a nightmare, flipping small boats over and drowning men and horses. The King and young Tristan were away safe on the first ship and the King's brother Richard and Henry Percy on the second; but the hardest task was getting the horses aboard. Lord Ravenspur stayed to the last, doing the impossible as usual. But my lady, he went down 'neath that great white stallion. He didn't stand a chance. Both of 'em are drowned, my lady. Saw it with our own eyes, we did."

"No!" Her wail was heard in the farthest corners of Ravenspur; the servants came running in time to see her crumple to the floor. Kate Kendall immediately took charge and put her to bed. As she came up out of the blackness, she fought it to return to oblivion, for she knew full consciousness held something she could not face. She cried nonstop for three days, until her milk upset her baby son. Then she got a tight grip on herself for his sake.

Rebecca came to stay with her and found their roles were now reversed. Roseanna walked around like someone in a trance. Quietly she sought out Mr. Burke. "There's no one else I can ask, Mr. Burke. Would you go into The Fens and try to find him?"

James Burke picked two stout stablehands and set out immediately. It took them two days to locate the scene of the disaster. In the end, it was the stench and the cry of the scavenging sea birds that led them to the bodies. It was easy to identify the body of the white Arabian stallion, but the bloated bodies of the drowned men were so decomposed that one could hardly be told from another. With superhuman effort, they half lifted the body of the horse. There, crushed beneath it, was what was left of the dark head of Ravenspur.

James Burke took the decision upon himself. They would take back no remains. He would not let her see or smell what had once been her well-beloved husband. When he returned, he took her into Roger's library, where they could be private. His grave demeanor confirmed her worst fears.

"I found him," he said quietly. "We buried him where he lay. It was impossible to bring him back through the waterlogged sedge and endless salt lands."

A solitary tear rolled down Roseanna's pale cheek. "How did you find him?" she choked.

"He lay beneath Mecca."

Her eyes glazed over, and he could tell she had drifted into the past, where she spent most of her waking hours these days. He quietly left her to her ghosts.

Finally, Kate Kendall had had enough. She put pen to paper and wrote out a message to Joanna, Lady Castlemaine:

> You will be relieved to know that the King and most of his nobles and army have safely sailed for Burgundy, but by now perhaps you have learned that Baron Ravenspur lost his life while aiding the King's escape. I beg you to come to Roseanna. She is like the living dead, and I fear for her sanity. I pray that your arrival will snap her back to life, as she is numb with her grief.
>
> > Your obedient servant,
> > Kate Kendall.

In her chamber Roseanna stood listlessly as Kate helped her don a black silk mourning gown. Alice took up the brush to tend her mistress's hair. Roseanna spoke plaintively as her son lay crying in his cradle: "Why does the baby cry so much lately?"

Kate compressed her lips in annoyance, then spoke up in her most caustic tone. "He cries because you neglect him! You're not the first woman to lose her man, nor will you be the last. All this belongs to that child now, and he needs someone strong to administer it for him, not some pathetic shadow that feels sorry for itself!"

The words stabbed into her heart like the talons of a bird of prey. "Kate, how could you?" she whispered.

Kate sniffed and gave Alice a sign to follow her from the room. She would leave her alone to think about the accusations she had just hurled at her.

Roseanna went to the cradle, picked up the baby, and, holding him against her heart, crooned a soothing lullaby. She had fed him earlier, but she had not picked him up to cuddle him the last few days. She smiled down at him through her tears, seeing a small replica of Roger, and she whispered to him what was in her heart. "I'm sorry, my darling. I love you more than life itself. I promise I will be the best mother the world has ever known."

She talked to him and hummed and became so absorbed in what she was doing that the world receded. The baby slept contentedly. As she put him into the cradle, she gradually became aware of someone screaming and crying far below. The commotion was muted, yet Roseanna was vaguely annoyed at the racket. How dared they disturb her? Didn't they know this household was in mourning? She hurried down two flights to the main reception hall, and her heart sank as she recognized George, Duke of Clarence. He was having a furious altercation with Mr. Burke, whose cheek, Roseanna was horrified to see, had been slashed by the riding crop that the King's brother carried. She could hear Alice's voice begging, and Kate Kendall was shouting profanities in an adjoining room.

Roseanna strode past the duke and flung open the door. Two of George's gentlemen had stripped Alice naked, and a third was holding Kate Kendall immobile from behind.

Roseanna spun around furiously to face George. "Stop them instantly! That girl is a virgin!"

George drawled, "Where would be the sport if she were not virgin?" but he held up his hand for his men to leave off their game. Kate led a sobbing Alice from the room.

Furiously, Roseanna ordered, "You will leave my home at once! We are in mourning here."

"And you have no man to protect you," George finished smoothly. "Therefore I am taking you under my royal protection."

"You are not King yet," she pointed out bluntly.

"I am King in name; it lacks only the crowning. Therefore, little girl, it would be in your best interest to please me, for with a mere lift of my hand I can do anything I desire."

"Piffle!" she disdained, her own royal blood boiling over.

His eyes narrowed. "All titles conferred by Edward are null and void. Therefore your little Viscount Gainsborough is viscount no more."

She gasped. "You cannot do that!"

He smiled and said silkily, "It is done." He knew by her reaction that he had chosen the perfect means to gain his desires, namely her son.

"What do you want here?" she cried.

He spread his hands. "We only ask a little hospitality—guest rooms for the night, a meal, a little wine, somewhere where you and I can converse in private."

Quietly she gave orders to the servants to prepare the rooms and a special dinner. In the meantime they were to be given the best that Ravenspur's wine cellars could provide. "If you would follow me, Your Grace," she said coolly, and led the way to Ravenspur's library.

Slowly he took a turn around the room, picking up art objects and setting them down again. "I am beginning to realize the extent of Ravenspur's wealth. I had to go into debt for my needs over the years."

She made no comment. He was adorned in white satin and diamonds, and she knew in that instant that he would indulge himself no matter what the cost to others.

"Your son is the new Baron of Ravenspur. I am considering making him a ward of the crown so that I can administer his estates."

"No!" she cried, her hand going to her throat.

"Everything rests in your hands, my sweet Roseanna. Please me, and I will increase your son's lands and titles tenfold. Spurn me, and I will have him removed from this household!"

The blackmail threat enveloped her; no matter which way her mind turned to escape him, she was caught securely in his web. Suddenly she heard the voice of Rebecca cry out in anguish.

"Do not let them harm my sister-in-law," she begged.

"She's not a virgin, I believe?" he drawled.

"Stop them!" she implored him.

"I have already told you—it is in your hands, little girl. Only say that you will come to me tonight, and everyone in your household, including your son, will be safe from harm."

"I will come to you," she promised softly.

Roseanna bade Kate mix a sleeping draught for Rebecca and told her to put an abortifacient in it to be on the safe side; Rebecca was hysterical and refused to say what the men had done to her. Then Roseanna sought out Mr. Burke and examined his facial laceration. "Do not provoke them, Mr. Burke. I will take care of the duke's needs. Pray God they will be gone tomorrow."

He looked at her with anguished eyes. "If only there were something I could do to aid you, my lady."

"There is. I want you to bury the gold plate the Queen sent for my son's christening. Then get Roger's coffers to a safe place where they will not be found. I must hide my good jewels, for mark my words, Mr. Burke, he will have everything from me before he is satisfied."

She did not dine with her guests but bathed in the privacy of her room. Then she put on a simple warm white velvet robe with wide sleeves, poured a goblet full of pale golden Chablis, and sipped it slowly to calm her nerves. She told herself bravely, *I am more of a woman than he is a man! I shall emerge victorious from this encounter!*

When the dregs of the wine cup were drained, she took a deep breath and went to George's bedchamber. He had been drinking most of the afternoon, and his face was flushed from the wine. It had loosened his tongue, and she noted with disgust that his conversation was coarse.

"Welcome, little girl. You'll not regret it, for I have the biggest cock in England."

She lowered her lashes to her cheeks, lest he see the fear in her eyes. He reached out long fingers to toy with her nipples beneath the robe. "Your breasts are magnificent," he said thickly. Where he rubbed her nipples, two tiny wet spots became visible on the bodice of the velvet robe. His eyes dilated and his organ swelled and hardened.

He took her hand and placed it on his groin to give her an idea of his unusual size. He whispered, "I won't be satisfied until I've put my yard up you more times than my brother."

She knew he was obsessed with his brother the King. She wanted to cry out that Edward was her father, not her lover, but she dared not. If he knew her child was Edward's grandson, he would take not only his lands but his life.

George pulled her to the bed. He quickly disrobed and lay back awaiting her. She had expected him to fall upon her and ravage her, so this behavior surprised and alarmed her. It would be worse than she had imagined if he expected her to service him. She stood quietly by the bed, gathering her courage for what had to be faced.

"I'm waiting, little girl," he said in a menacing tone, narrowing his eyes.

Slowly she removed her robe and knelt upon the bed. She looked at his sex organ with alarm. It was enormous. Using the coarsest language, he told her in shocking detail what he wanted her to do to him.

As she knelt down to him, her silken hair swept forward like a curtain to cover her shame. Suddenly his hand shot out to grab her hair in a cruel grip. "You intended to bite me, didn't you?"

She offered no denial but quickly veiled the triumph in her eyes lest it incense him further. He got off the bed and ordered her to kneel at its edge. He came up from behind her and tried to enter her. Roseanna had had no experience of what it was that he attempted.

"Christ Almighty, you've never been initiated—you're too small!" he ground out. Frustrated in everything he desired, he flipped her flat onto her back and ordered thickly, "Spread yourself!" He thrust inside her cruelly until she thought she would burst. "Respond to me!" he ordered. Then his avid mouth fastened onto her breast and he sucked her milk from her. Once he'd satisfied his cruel desires, he fell into a stupor.

Later that night, Roseanna sat in the window embrasure. She was too numb to feel or think. George roused in the great bed.

"What are you doing over there?" he demanded.

"I couldn't sleep," she murmured.

"If you cannot sleep, I haven't used you enough. Come back to bed."

In the morning she escorted the duke and his gentlemen to the stables. She wanted to see with her own eyes that he had quit the place. His greedy eyes fell upon the white mares. "Are these Arabians?" he asked.

"No, sire. They are bred by the Cistercian monks at the Abbey of Jervaulx."

"I have a fancy for them," he said smoothly.

"These are only mares. I'm sure if you visited the abbey, you would find the stallions more to your taste."

"Perhaps," he temporized. "Next time I visit you, little girl, perhaps you will be generous enough to gift me with the mares."

The mares meant a great deal to her, especially since they had all been bred to Mecca, but she heard only the words *next time I visit you.*

She reached her bedchamber on shaky legs. As Kate came toward her with the baby, she cried, "Don't bring me the child while I've the stink of that pig on me. Get me a bath, Kate!" She scrubbed herself until her skin was raw, and she would not come out of the water until Kate said, "The shame is his, not yours, Roseanna."

"You are right, of course, Kate. I have no time to waste in this fashion. I must be up and about, making plans to protect my son. I'm going to have to wean him, Kate. I must place him where he will be safe, and that may not be at my side." She donned a black mourning gown and went briskly around, giving her household orders. In the midst of all this, her mother arrived.

"Kate, what lies have you been telling me that Roseanna was half dead, walking around in a trance?" asked Joanna.

"I've had a rude awakening," said Roseanna caustically. She took her mother up to a bedchamber close to her own and told her everything that had happened, leaving out no detail. "I want you to take my son to Castlemaine. That isn't out of George's reach, but Ned won't be nearly as vulnerable. Take Alice back with you, and I would appreciate it if you also took Rebecca and her little girl. Tristan will never forgive me if I don't keep them out of harm's way."

"What about Kate?" asked Joanna.

"Kate is my strength. Without her, I'd go mad," Roseanna said simply. "I'm going to arrange for old Dobbin to take all the best horses home to my father."

"Isn't that going a bit far, darling?" asked Joanna.

"I'll not let that whoreson swine have even the smoke off their horseshit! Everything belongs to my son, and I'll die saving it for him!" she vowed.

"It's a man's world, Roseanna. Haven't you just had that lesson driven home to you?"

"Then I'll get a stronger man! I'll go to Warwick if I have to," she threatened.

"He's above temptation—I tried years ago. His God is ambition, and he will sacrifice everything to it. Women mean nothing to him."

"Then I'll appeal to Ravenspur's overlord. Surely the

Earl of Lincoln will at least listen to me if I swear him allegiance for my son's land and title."

Joanna looked at her daughter with admiration. " 'Tis said he is a young man. If he has a young man's appetites, he will not be immune to your beauty."

Kate brought a heaping tray for Joanna, for she knew what a lusty eater she had always been. Roseanna said, "Kate, find Mr. Burke and come back. I want to speak with you both." When they returned and stood waiting for her decisions, she was very grateful to have such loyal people who really cared about what happened to her. "Mother is taking my son to Castlemaine. Alice and Rebecca will accompany them. I must leave tomorrow on an important mission, and I want you both with me. Ravenspur's fleet of merchant ships is anchored at Liverpool. I must speak with the captains and get the ships safely out of the country. They are responsible for much of Ravenspur's wealth, and I cannot let them fall into the hands of the Duke of Clarence. Mr. Burke, do you think it would be feasible for them to sail out of Drogheda?"

He nodded. "Aye. The Boyne empties into the sea close by Drogheda."

"Good. You'll both come with me to Liverpool? Tell no one," she cautioned. "We travel in secret."

James Burke spoke up. "The most direct route is through Derby. There is a Roman road from that town that leads directly to the coast."

Roseanna spent the next twenty-four hours patiently trying to feed her son bread and milk. He ate it hungrily, yet still cried for his mother's breast as if that were the only thing that would satisfy him. Kate fashioned him a dummy teat that he sucked willingly enough, but he screamed furiously when no milk was forthcoming. Finally Roseanna came to a hard decision. "Mother, my time is running out. I want you to leave for Castlemaine today. Little Ned won't starve; his appetite is too voracious for that. He'll adjust much more quickly when I'm not available."

Once the child was not there to occupy every waking moment, she found herself longing for Roger. She busied herself with preparations for the journey to Liverpool throughout the day, but that night she found she couldn't sleep because her body ached for him. Thinking back, she found it incredible that she had ever rejected him, and she regretted all the time she had wasted defying him. Yet it had been a sort of mating dance they had performed; irresistibly, male and female had been drawn together, becoming one. But how cruel it was to be wrenched apart! She felt mutilated.

It was late when the closed carriage drew up at the innyard in Derby. James Burke went into the hostelry while the women waited inside the coach. He secured two bedrooms and a private dining parlor and asked for extra logs for its fire.

Roseanna pulled her hood closely around her face as she quit the coach and entered the inn. She did not remove it until they were safely ensconced inside the private parlor. A door that joined the room to another private parlor opened and a servant brought an armful of logs. Briefly, before the door was closed, Roseanna saw a man staring at her with open admiration in his eyes. She was used to men staring boldly at her and thought nothing more of it.

The young man in the next room immediately inquired about the lady's identity. The innkeeper could tell him

nothing. He sent wine around to her; it was politely refused, and he felt thoroughly frustrated.

He was a young nobleman returning from Coventry,
where he and the other earls of the realm had been closeted with Warwick, deciding England's future—if they
could ever come to an agreement. He did not know what
intrigued him more, her outrageous beauty or the air of
mystery surrounding her, but in that one brief glimpse he
had been snared.

Roseanna would not have been indifferent if she had
known the man occupying the other private parlor was
the Earl of Lincoln.

She met with the captains of Ravenspur's merchant
fleet. At least two of them were familiar with the Drogheda estate in Ireland. She appointed one of them captain over the others and authorized him to take care of
her son's shipping enterprise. She told them they must
never drop anchor in an English port unless King Edward was returned to the throne. She arranged to travel
to Ireland the following summer, when most of them
would be returning from trading ventures in far-off lands.

It would be easy to sail to Ireland with them and
thereby escape the Duke of Clarence. She had the deed to
the estate in Drogheda, which Ravenspur had given her.
It was separate from the other landholdings and could
not be taken from her, but if she abandoned Ravenspur,
it and the other castles would be snatched from her son
forever. Resolutely, she prepared to return home.

The closer she got to Ravenspur, the more she dreaded
another encounter with the Duke of Clarence. She shuddered. The memory of him clung to her like scum on a
pond! She calmed herself by making plans to visit the

Earl of Lincoln and beg him for his aid. Upon her return, she rested for one day only, for she found herself at the upper windows anxiously scanning the countryside so often that she knew she could not let another day pass without taking action.

The ancient town of Lincoln was pre-Roman in origin; it was dominated by a cathedral built by William the Conqueror four centuries before. The castle seemed ugly to Roseanna after the elegance of Ravenspur, but it was a formidible stronghold. She took Kate with her to attend to her toilette, for Roseanna was a woman who knew the true value of appearance. She was a woman appealing to a man, and she intended to use every feminine device she possessed.

There was nothing she could do about the color of her gown: she was in mourning, and it had to be black. But she chose the finest black silk gown, which rustled provocatively; its neckline, which seemed modest, was deceptive in that it molded her breasts and exposed them when she dipped into a deep curtsey. She had swept her hair back to show off her heart-shaped face. It was held in place by a gold filigree clasp, then fell straight down her back in a silken waterfall. With her hair pulled back, her cheekbones stood out, and her eyes were slightly slanted. Her mouth was painted the same deep luscious red as the rubies in the diamond necklace Roger had gifted her with. Its huge pearl nestled in the deep valley between her breasts.

The castle chamberlain led her into the reception room, where the earl received the people of Lincolnshire who requested audiences with him. A calmness came over her. The Earl of Lincoln was seated at an ornate refectory table doing paperwork, when he glanced up and saw her approach. His eyes widened, and he was on his feet instantly, coming forward to meet her.

She was surprised by his youth. He could be no more than twenty-five. He was of medium build but so good-looking, she couldn't help but stare. He had silver gilt hair and silver eyes.

"Who are you?" he asked, forgetting his manners completely. His voice was deep and rich as if it belonged to a much older man.

She sank into a graceful curtsey that displayed her magnificent breasts. "I am Lady Roseanna, Baroness of Ravenspur."

"I've seen you before," he told her.

Her eyebrows went up in a question, and he supplied, "At the inn in Derby a fortnight past."

The corners of her mouth went up deliciously. "You were the gentleman who stared so boldly?"

"I confess I was, madame. You were right to treat me with disdain."

Her lashes swept to her cheeks. "I—I am recently widowed, unprotected. I am easy prey, my lord."

He stiffened. "Some man is forcing his attentions on you," he said with perception.

She sighed deeply and sadly and nodded. "I came to you for advice, my lord. Though you and my husband were on different sides, you are technically my overlord."

"Who is this man who dares offer you insult?" he asked.

Her eyelashes sparkled with unshed tears. "I am frightened to tell you his name," she murmured.

He took her hand between both of his and pressed it reassuringly. "Come through to the inner room, where we can be less formal, Lady Roseanna. It grieves me to see your evident distress."

Obediently she allowed him to take her into a small drawing room with comfortable sofas and a cozy fire. He poured wine into two small crystal glasses and handed her one. As her fingers brushed his, she heard his sharp intake of breath. She sipped her wine in silence; the sexual tension between them almost crackled in the air.

He said low, "Please trust me. Whatever you tell me will be in strictest confidence, and I pledge to do anything that is within my power."

She smiled tremulously, and his heart turned over. "My lord—"

"My friends call me Linc," he invited.

"I'm being blackmailed."

His eyes widened, but he held his silence, hoping she would continue.

"By a man of high rank," she finished.

"So high, you are frightened to give me his name?" asked Linc, incredulously.

Roseanna nodded. "Two months before my husband was killed, I had a son. He is now Baron Ravenspur—except . . . except the Duke of Clarence threatens to become his guardian and take his lands away unless—unless I give him access to my bed." She sat facing him; the firelight turned her jewels to flame.

He whistled at the royal name. "He's married to Warwick's daughter! The kingmaker will take a dim view when it becomes known to him."

"My lord—"

"Linc," he insisted.

"Linc, tell me if it is within his power to do this to my son."

Linc nodded slowly. "He could either take your son's wealth in wardship until he comes of age, or he could issue a warrant of attainder and have everything revert to the Crown—but only if he becomes King, Lady Roseanna."

She drooped visibly at this news, so he hastened to explain, "It is by no means a certainty that George will be crowned. I tell you this in strictest confidence. The nobility does not want him. Most of the Lancastrian lords want old King Henry restored."

"But he's mad! He resides in the Tower of London."

"Mad, yes. Yet still they prefer him to the Duke of Clarence."

"You have given me hope, at least. When will this be decided?"

"Soon. We all want this matter settled. Continual war drains the lifeblood of a realm."

"Will you add your voice to those who oppose the crowning of the Duke of Clarence?" she begged.

"Mine will be the loudest," he assured her.

She rose to bid him good-bye, and suddenly he did not want her to leave. "You cannot go without taking dinner with me, Lady Roseanna."

She hesitated. She knew the value of leaving a man when he desired more of your company. "I'm sorry, I must go. It is starting to snow, and I don't want to get caught in a storm."

He wanted to ask her to stay the night, but this would place him in the same light as the seducer she was running from. "May I visit you?" he asked eagerly.

"Please do. It is very kind of you to want to check on my welfare, my lord."

"Linc," he begged.

23

A week passed, a week in which Roseanna scanned the horizon and prayed to God that the Duke of Clarence had enough trouble on his hands that he had no time to spare her a thought. It was agony for her to live without Roger, and she missed her baby so much, she wanted to scream.

She looked out from her bedchamber window; her heart caught in her throat as she saw riders approach. When she recognized the Earl of Lincoln's silvery hair, she went weak with relief. With shaking fingers she brushed her hair and went down to greet him. "Linc!" she cried joyfully; his heart lifted that she welcomed him so warmly. She wore a simple white linen dress, and with her dark hair loose and falling to the hem of the gown, she looked heartbreakingly young. She was the loveliest, most desirable creature he'd ever known, and he wanted her.

"Roseanna," he breathed. "Lord God, the days have dragged since I saw you." He took her hands between his, then raised them to his lips.

"The days drag for me, too. I miss my son so much."

"Where is he?" he asked.

She hesitated.

"Trust me!" he begged.

"He is with my mother at Castlemaine."

"I shall take you to visit him," he declared.

"Oh, no! Really?" she asked breathlessly.

"What is there to stop us?" he asked.

"Nothing!" she cried joyfully. "Oh, Linc, thank you for coming."

"Tell them to ready your carriage." He grinned.

"Let's ride!" she suggested, suddenly bursting with energy.

Kate served them a light repast, then helped Roseanna into a fetching black velvet riding dress and frilled white silk shirt. Linc was concerned when he saw Zeus, but his fears were put to rest as he watched her mount and ride from the stables. "Wait until you see the horses at Castlemaine! My father breeds the finest horses in England."

Joanna was at her best when entertaining. She had a knack for creating intimacy without sacrificing formal traditions. Linc marveled at Neville's stable and listened attentively while the older man went into detail about Roseanna's natural ability when it came to horse breeding. He watched Roseanna with her child and knew these two should not be parted.

They decided to stay overnight. When it was time to retire, Roseanna showed him to a guest chamber. He pulled her inside and took her into his arms. His lips came down on hers, leaving her in no doubt that he hotly desired her.

"Roseanna, I'm in love with you," he murmured against her hair.

She put her fingers to his lips to stop his words, then slipped quietly from the room.

Joanna was in her bedchamber before Roseanna was, admiration gleaming in her eyes. "By God, you wasted no time! Are you prepared to give him what he is after?"

"Yes! I'll become his mistress if that's what it takes to protect my son from that pig Clarence."

"I'd better leave before he seeks your chamber," teased Joanna. "Sleep well, darling."

Linc did not come, although Roseanna had half expected that he would. In the morning she said her goodbyes reluctantly, not relinquishing her son until the last possible moment.

Linc was unusually silent on the return ride to Ravenspur. Roseanna knew that when they got back and were private, he would make his move. As they neared home, the snowflakes turned to rain; then a sudden downpour forced them to dash from the stables to the house before they became drenched. They ran inside laughing; then as she shook the raindrops from her fur cape, he enfolded her in his arms and said, "Marry me, Roseanna."

She was stunned. This wasn't what she had intended at all! "Oh, Linc, whatever have I done?" she whispered.

"What do you mean?"

"I can't marry you; I can't marry anyone. I've only just lost my husband. I loved him so deeply, I don't think I'll ever be able to love anyone else." She knew with certainty that Roger had been the grand passion of her life and that none would ever take his place. She was perfectly willing to become Linc's mistress, but to become his wife was out of the question.

His eyes were like silver ice. "Then tell me, why did

you come to me? What was all this about?" he demanded
quietly.

"I needed your help, your protection, and in exchange
I thought I would—" She stopped, embarrassed.

"Give me your body?" he shouted. "Roseanna, I don't
want just your body, I want you. God's feet, since I became Earl of Lincoln, women lie down for me before I've
even glanced in their direction. I don't want you for a
casual tumble! I want you for my wife."

"Why?" she asked, trying to follow his reasoning.

"For a hundred reasons. You have an air of fine breeding about you that tells me you would make a magnificent countess. I enjoy being with you; I enjoy your vitality, your intelligence. I want you to give me a son like the
one you gave Ravenspur. And yes, I want every other
man to be sea green with envy because you belong to me!
Roseanna, marriage is the only honorable estate."

He is so young, he is still idealistic, she thought sadly.
"Forgive me, Linc. I didn't mean to hurt you," she said
softly. "I care for you a great deal, but my heart is en-
cased in ice at the moment."

He smiled into her eyes and brushed his lips across her
troubled brow, "Perhaps if I give you time, it will thaw a
little."

She watched him walk away; she didn't call him back.

Christmas was almost upon them. To cheer herself one
December afternoon, she thought she might ride out to
gather holly to festoon Ravenspur, but a lethargy crept
upon her. She had begun to live in the past. If only she
could turn back the clock! If only her little family could
celebrate Christmas together again! If only Roger . . .

Linc's visits had stopped. Though Kate did not reprove her for sending him away, Roseanna knew the practical North-country woman thought her God's own fool.

She was almost afraid of her mother's reaction when she learned that her daughter had turned down a marriage proposal from the Earl of Lincoln.

This day, though it was only midafternoon, the light was already waning. As Roseanna lit candles, her nostrils pinched distastefully at the smell of the hot candle wax. She would go to bed early. *What else is there to do?* she thought listlessly as she slowly ascended the staircase. Suddenly, the door was thrown open below, and the Duke of Clarence and his gentlemen crowded into the hall. Her lethargy vanished instantly. It was replaced by hot, seething anger.

"Christ, little girl, the place is like a tomb! Throw open the wine cellars. Henry, get some young girls from the village, and we'll have a party." They were drunk, and the men laughed helplessly whenever George spoke.

"Get out!" she cried.

"What? Is that a fitting welcome for your lover?" He leered. "I've come to give you your Christmas present."

"You conceited pig!"

"Bitch!" he snarled, and took the stairs two at a time.

She threw a heavy silver candelabrum at his head and ran along the second-floor landing. Then she ran into a bedroom and fastened the door tightly against him. He kicked the door in rage until the frame splintered and it gave way.

She backed away from him. "If you touch me again, I'll make sure Warwick learns of it. If scandal is to your taste, I'll give you a feast!"

" 'Tis no scandal to bed a whore," he sneered.

"I am the King's daughter. You are my uncle. What you do is incest!"

"Lying bitch!" He drew back his arm and knocked her halfway across the room. "Where is your son?"

"With my sister-in-law," she half lied.

His hands dipped into the neck of her gown, and he tore it from her body. She cowered like a cornered animal, and he became aroused. "You are very like your brother; he was a particular favorite of mine."

"He's dead, thank God," she spat.

His eyes narrowed cruelly. "Your brother dead—your husband dead. Isn't it strange that death always comes in threes? Where did you say the child was? With your mother at Castlemaine?"

"No, no!" cried Roseanna, paralyzed with fear.

He smiled slowly as he removed his clothes. "If it is true that you are Edward's misbegotten lovechild, I shall enjoy your total submission."

And submit I did, she thought later, brokenly, as her sobs were turning to dry heaves. Clarence was long gone, and the house was so still, one could hear the ghosts walk. When Kate helped bathe her, she saw a large blue bruise across her breast and said, "Be a sensible lass; go to Lincoln."

Roseanna nodded, unable to speak.

She put aside her mourning garb and donned her crimson gown slashed with silver in honor of the festive season. When she arrived, with Kate and Mr. Burke in tow, she found Lincoln Castle in the midst of Christmas celebrations. The courtyard was filled with villagers, and the stables were bulging with mounts belonging to Lincoln's guests. The earl had his whole family there, including his mother, his three sisters, their husbands, and his two young brothers. When he saw her, his face lit up. He went forward to take her hands in his. "Roseanna!" he exclaimed.

"Can we talk in private, Linc?" she asked.

He took her into a small anteroom off the ballroom. Kate Kendall and James Burke stood outside the door, trying to ignore the stares they were receiving.

Roseanna was suddenly tongue-tied. She stammered, "I—missed you."

"Oh, love, if you will only marry me, it will put an end to all your fears. I'll become your son's legal guardian and your devoted protector."

"Your family—will they not object to me?"

"Roseanna, I am the paymaster. Every one of them depends on me for their living—and a damned good living it is, too. They have no say in anything."

"Send for the priest," she whispered.

"Now?" he asked incredulously.

She nodded. The priest was sent for, and Kate and Mr. Burke were brought into the chamber to act as witnesses. When Linc and Roseanna emerged from the anteroom, he led her to the top of the ballroom and held up his hands for everyone's attention. Grinning like a lunatic, he said in his deep rich voice, "Ladies and gentlemen, I wish to present the Countess of Lincoln."

There was a stunned silence that lasted for minutes; then a whisper grew into a rumble and finally a tumultuous roar as everyone realized the handsome earl had just taken a bride. He hugged her to him; her cheek felt the brown velvet of his doublet, and her eyes saw clearly the rich sheen on his sable collar, and she was giddy with relief.

"What would you like for a wedding present, my love?
I will give you anything you desire."

"I want you to take me to get my son," she said simply.

"Now?" he asked incredulously.

She nodded. He threw back his head and laughed.
"Then so be it! We'll do it up right—we will take an
escort of fifty."

It was past midnight when the cavalcade rode into
Castlemaine, but because of the Christmas revels, they
hadn't yet retired for the night. When Joanna and Neville
heard the news, they were beside themselves with happiness at their daughter's great good fortune. The celebrations took on new life and would last until morning.

Roseanna hardly waited until a toast was drunk to
their health before she headed upstairs to see her son.
When she saw him lying in the cradle, safe and peaceful
in his slumber, she began to sob with relief. Linc came up
behind her. She turned her face into his chest, and the
floodgates opened.

"Hush, my love, hush," he soothed. But she could not
stop. Looking apologetically at Joanna, he lifted Roseanna into his arms and carried her to the bedchamber
Joanna indicated.

Roseanna cried herself into a state of exhaustion. Very
gently he undressed her and put her to bed. He saw the
bruise and began to understand what she had been
through. He undressed quickly, got into bed, and gently
drew her against him. He brushed back her long hair and
placed his lips against her temple.

"I'm sorry, Linc," she whispered.

"It will do you good to cry; cry it all out. If it is inside, it has got to come out." Silently, he thought, *I'll see to it that that bastard never becomes King!*

As she lay in his arms, her fears vanished one by one until she finally slept. After about two hours something wakened her, and she was disoriented for a few moments. Then she remembered her new husband and sat up on one elbow to look at him. How lucky she was that he was so kind and understanding! Poor Linc—to spend his wedding night with an hysterical bride! Her heart overflowed with gratitude; she bent over and gently kissed him. He awoke instantly. "Roseanna!" he whispered huskily.

He was young and extremely virile. He was quick to desire and quick to take his release. He was madly in love with her and went over the moon at her generous response to him. She realized that she had complete power over him; she would have to be very careful never to hurt him.

Roseanna's marriage to the Earl of Lincoln effectively removed her and her son from any contact with or even threats from the Duke of Clarence. Although there was much discord among the nobility, Warwick decided to restore mad King Henry to the throne. George, Duke of Clarence, was bitterly resentful that the crown he had coveted for so long was being handed to another. He now hated Warwick's authority, and he rained curses on Elizabeth Woodville, who was the author of all his misfortunes, he thought. It dawned on him that he had been better off under Edward's rule than he was under Warwick's. He would gladly return to Edward if his brother could be restored to the Crown.

The Earl of Lincoln knew he must go to London for the recrowning of King Henry. The nobility were flock-

ing to London, where a great procession through the
streets was being planned. Warwick's brother, the Archbishop of York, was the first to reach the capital and pay
homage. London was soon filled with Warwick's men in
smart red livery, speaking in their barbaric northern ac-
cents.

Roseanna begged Linc to let her stay at home. He accepted her excuse that she was still unused to her position
as Countess of Lincoln; but he also knew she wanted to
spend some quiet time with her son. It was decided that
she would stay at Ravenspur while Linc was away. Old
Dobbin once again brought all Roseanna's mares up from
Castlemaine, and her time was almost totally taken up
with their foaling.

During the month that Linc was away, the mare that
had been covered by Zeus produced a fine black colt, and
Roger's stallion sired twins on one mare and a sturdy,
sable-colored colt on another. She couldn't wait to see the
results of the three white mares that Mecca had covered.
The Arabian was no more, but she had high hopes for his
progeny.

The first mare had a difficult time; Roseanna spent two
days in the stables soothing the restless animal and helping it with the delivery. She fed it warm gruel, then warm
ale, and finally black treacle before she could rid it of the
afterbirth. The results of the matings were well worth the
money and time she invested. Within a couple of years
Ravenspur's stables would equal those of Castlemaine.

When Linc returned he hesitated to tell her the latest
rumors that were thick as flies in London. Word had it
that Edward had not been idle during the months he'd
been in exile. He had applied everywhere he could for
loans of ships and money and fighting men to help him

retake England. He asked for weapons and horses but no supplies that would take up valuable ship space. The Hanse merchants, it was rumored, had pledged a great fleet of ships and fifteen hundred soldiers. He had apparently signed bonds for loans with the French, Germans, and Dutch. Warwick was alarmed. If Edward landed in Norfolk, the most likely port, the Duke of Norfolk, a great landowner who was Edward's kinsman would undoubtedly give him support.

Warwick took the Duke of Norfolk into custody and was about to arrest Lord Howard as another Yorkist supporter, but Howard eluded him by going into sanctuary at Colchester. Warwick ordered all his nobles to take a firm grip on their own territory and defend it against a landing and invasion.

The Earl of Oxford had control of the east of England, so Warwick felt secure that if Edward landed there he would quickly be defeated. He ordered George to go into Somerset and raise an army and at the same time patrol the borders along the Bristol Channel to prevent a landing.

Roseanna listened quietly as Linc repeated the news to her. She was torn emotionally, for if the news were true it would mean a war in which Linc would be involved. In her heart she wanted King Edward to regain his crown, but her husband would be fighting against him; he had pledged himself to Warwick on his guarantee that George, Duke of Clarence, would not be crowned. Although her son's castles, land, and titles had come through Edward, it was Linc who had secured them for him.

She tried to push all thoughts of war away from her. She would remain neutral—it was the only way she could retain her sanity. She wished she had Kate to talk with, but Kate and James Burke were keeping Ravenspur working smoothly while she was in Lincoln.

She busied herself with her child and spent a lot of time in the stables at Lincoln Castle trying desperately to ignore Linc's fighting men and archers as they sharpened their war skills.

24

Roseanna awoke with a headache. She winced and put her hand to her forehead. Linc chuckled. "Serves you right for taking too much wine last night." Then his face became serious as he asked anxiously, "Roseanna, do you need wine before you can give yourself to me?"

She stared at him aghast. Their intimate relationship had always left something to be desired as far as she was concerned, but she had no idea that he was aware of it. He was always so quick to passion that it left her feeling vaguely unsatisfied and empty. She felt guilty at this moment, for she knew that if she had taken the time, she could have schooled him to be leisurely in his lovemaking. Then he could explore his own sensuality to its limits, too. She was far more skilled in every aspect of making love than he, and she knew how to make a man feel virile. In fairness to him, she realized it was time to put quality into their bed play. She touched his face tenderly. "Linc, how would you like me to make love to you for a change tonight?"

He grinned delightedly. "I would love it more than anything!"

She smiled quietly when she heard him singing in his dressing room. She realized that she had never fully committed herself to him. She had given him her gratitude but not her love.

Part of Edward's fleet which Richard was commanding stood off the coast of Norfolk for days before they discovered that the Duke of Norfolk was in custody. They learned of Oxford's patrols along the southeast coast and finally decided to sail up past Yorkshire to Northumberland, where the strong Percys would aid them.

Three of the ships were grounded in a storm off Lincolnshire. One of them capsized and sank, and it took all night to get everyone ashore. They were wet and cold in the March night, but Richard headed the men south toward The Wash to a predestined meeting place with Edward and the rest of the Hanse fleet.

James Burke couldn't believe his eyes when Roger Montford strode into the hall at Ravenspur. Putting a silencing finger to his lips, he said, "Hush, man. I want to surprise Roseanna."

Mr. Burke crossed himself and muttered, "Mary and Joseph, you'll do more than surprise her!"

"We are back! Did you ever doubt it? You look like you've seen a ghost, James."

"My lord, we thought you dead! Lady Roseanna near went mad with grief when two of the men who almost drowned crawled back and gave us the news. She sent me into The Fens to find your body, and I thought I had found it—beneath the body of the white Arabian stallion. I buried the remains," argued Mr. Burke.

"That was Kelly," said Roger grimly. "The storm had inflamed our tempers, and I accused him of Janet's murder. He knifed me and tried to flee on Mecca, but they went down together and were drowned."

"God's balls!" exclaimed Mr. Burke at the appalling mess in which everyone's lives were now tangled.

"Where is Roseanna? Fetch her, man, so that she can see with her own eyes that I am alive!"

"She is not here, my lord," said Mr. Burke cautiously.

"Damn, don't tell me she's at Castlemaine! I've not much time. Edward has landed with an army to retake England. We are heading into Nottingham to raise more men."

Kate Kendall had heard Ravenspur's unmistakable voice and came into the hall on quaking limbs.

"Kate, I'm returned from the dead!" He laughed. "When is Roseanna expected back from Castlemaine?"

Kate Kendall and James Burke exchanged significant glances; each dreaded the task of revealing to their lord what had to be told.

"What is it?" he demanded. "My God, she's not ill, is she? Is my son all right?"

Kate took a deep breath. "You'd better come and sit down, my lord. James, get him a drink—something stronger than wine."

White-lipped with apprehension, Roger seated himself beside the warmth of the fire. James Burke handed him a potent goblet and took himself off so that Kate and Roger could have privacy.

"Try to be patient, my lord, while I tell you my incredible tale. George, Duke of Clarence, rode in here hot after

Edward's fleeing army. It would have been useless to deny to him that the army had been encamped here, for the evidence lay everywhere. When that swine Clarence saw Roseanna, thoughts of pursuing you and the King went out of his head. He had only one goal from the minute he laid eyes on her. He made no bones about it but told her baldly he meant to have her."

Roger swallowed the contents of the goblet and shuddered slightly.

"Well, you know Roseanna, sir. She bade him begone in very salty terms. The day after that, news of your drowning came, and Roseanna didn't care if she lived or died. She fell into a trancelike stupor. Even the baby knew something was wrong with his mother, and he cried all day. Then, God help her, something happened to snap her out of it in a hurry."

"Thank God," whispered Ravenspur.

"Nay, my lord. It was not God's work, it was the devil's. The Duke of Clarence returned. His men were drunk. They stripped Alice and raped Rebecca. He threatened Roseanna with the only weapon that would make her submit to him: He threatened to take your son's lands and titles. He even threatened to take the child away from her."

Ravenspur was on his feet, cursing the soul of the man who had abused his wife. "He's dead meat! I'll search him out on the battlefield and disembowel the swine!"

"My lord, there's more to my tale," said Kate quietly.

"More?" he roared. "I've heard enough, woman! What more could there possibly be?"

"Lord Ravenspur, I warned you that you would have to be patient, but you have to get a grip on your temper, aye, and on your sanity for what I have to tell you."

Cold fingers clutched his heart. He feared his beloved was dead.

Kate's voice quivered as she continued. "She was vulnerable, easy prey without a strong man's protection. So she sought out the Earl of Lincoln, who is your son's overlord."

"Did he help her?" Roger demanded.

"He did more. He fell in love with her and married her."

"What?" The word exploded from him as if he spat fire. "The faithless bitch! I'll kill her!"

"She refused to marry him, but that degenerate pig Clarence returned and forced his abominations on her. Her mother and I urged her to accept Lincoln. My lord, she had no alternative!"

Roger sank down and buried his head in his hands. His precious Roseanna! He felt as if his heart were bleeding. Kate left him alone.

After a while James Burke got up enough courage to go in to him and offer him another drink. Roger threw off his inertia and strode from the hall. Edward's battles would have to wait. He had one of his own to win first!

Lincoln received a message from Warwick that Edward had landed and was approaching Nottingham. Warwick asked that Lincoln join him in Coventry. He had also sent urgent messages to George, Duke of Clarence, to bring the four thousand soldiers he had recruited.

When Ravenspur strode into the hall at Lincoln Castle, Linc thought he was another messenger. Roseanna turned from her husband to the messenger and gave a joyous cry from her heart: "Roger!" Her hands flew out to steady herself, but her legs and head swam with unreality, and she fell into a dead faint.

Ravenspur strode up to Lincoln and dared him with his eyes to touch Roseanna. He bent swiftly and lifted her into his arms. "This lady is my wife," he said implacably. "Show me to a couch where she may recover."

"You're not dead?" asked Linc with deep dismay.

"Not yet!" replied Roger shortly.

Although Linc was devastated by Ravenspur's arrival, he led the way to Roseanna's chamber and with great effort allowed Ravenspur to go in alone with her.

Roger laid her down and shook her gently. "Roseanna! Open your eyes and look at me!" As her eyelashes fluttered open, what he needed to know was written there pure and clear. There was no fear or dismay, only love for him. Her mouth was like a pink velvet rose, and he was starving for the taste of her. Their lips touched, then clung fiercely. He caressed her lovingly and held her to his heart. He loved this woman beyond his wildest dreams, and he was about to prove it by providing safety for her future. "Rest for a few minutes. I have to talk to Lincoln."

"Roger!" she cried, alarmed at what he might do.

He gave her a reassuring smile and said, "I'll be back in a few minutes. Trust me."

Ravenspur approached the Earl of Lincoln calmly. "We have things to settle."

"We do." Linc nodded stiffly. The two men were such a contrast to each other. Lincoln's silver-gilt hair made him seem younger than his years, while Ravenspur's darkness made him seem years older.

"The law is on your side, Ravenspur. Technically,

Roseanna is still your wife," Linc conceded. "But I think she should be allowed to choose between us."

Roger said, "Let us approach the matter with our heads rather than our hearts. We are at war. We will fight a battle, perhaps many battles, before it is done. If I die, I would like your oath that you will be a good husband to Roseanna and work for my son's best interests."

Lincoln's eyes widened. "You have my oath."

Roger continued, "If you die, I will give you the same pledge. If I live, Roseanna remains my wife unless she chooses otherwise. Is it agreed?"

"Agreed," nodded Lincoln, feeling admiration for Ravenspur in spite of himself.

Roger hesitated. "Roseanna is too much woman to be long without a man. I am not unmindful of the service you have done me by protecting my family. I'll just say my farewell to Roseanna."

He went back to her chamber and found her with his son. "Look, he can take a few steps, and he can even say words," she said with great pride. She pointed to Roger; "Dada," she coached.

"Mama," said the baby. He had the darkest eyes and the blackest curls Roger had ever seen, and they evoked the strangest emotions in Roger. Suddenly he wanted to cry.

"I'll pack and go home immediately," said Roseanna, looking sorry for all the trouble she had caused.

"Roseanna, do nothing," he cautioned. "There will be terrible fighting when Edward and Warwick meet. Your husbands are pledged to opposite sides in this conflict. If one of us dies, you will still have the other."

"You won't die!" she cried.

"No, I won't die," he promised. "Sorry, little one, but

you may have to wait awhile before you become the
Baron of Ravenspur."

He kissed the child good-bye but did not trust himself
to touch Roseanna. He turned so swiftly, his cloak swept
a vase of early snowdrops to the carpet. As Roseanna
knelt to pick up the fragile white flowers, tears stole
down her cheeks. She cried for joy that Roger lived; she
wept for sadness that she had caused Linc pain; she
sobbed with fear for them both in the bloody battles that
were inevitable.

When Roger joined Edward and Richard in Nottingham, he was relieved that Percy's men from Northumberland had arrived. They all realized that by reaching
Nottingham without being challenged, both Lord Stanley
and the Earl of Shrewsbury had held their hands and had
done nothing to stop them. Edward's mood was high,
and he grinned and repeated one of his favorite axioms:
"He who is not against me, is with me!"

Warwick's brother John had an army at Pontefract
fifty miles north, yet he hadn't challenged Edward yet. So
Edward cautiously moved his army southward from Nottingham to Leicester, which was only twenty miles from
Warwick's army at Coventry. Edward's spies told him
that Warwick's brother was not at Pontefract but had
joined Warwick at Coventry. Exeter and Oxford were
also with Warwick.

Then an amazing thing happened. Edward received a
message from his brother George, Duke of Clarence. He
offered to join Edward instead of taking his four thousand men to aid Warwick. Richard mistrusted his brother
and reminded Edward of their brother's past treachery.
Ravenspur was also against it. He desperately wanted
Clarence on the enemy's side so he could kill him with

impunity. Edward, however, saw the wisdom of accepting George's offer; it immediately doubled the size of his army.

After accepting George's offer, Edward moved his new combined army of eight thousand men outside Coventry, ready for the fight. Suddenly George suggested that Edward send a conciliatory message to Warwick to settle everything peacefully. Ravenspur wanted to run his sword between his eyes, but he could not, for Edward needed him. Roger felt a great relief when Edward refused to parley. "If Warwick comes out of Coventry and surrenders, I will give him his life."

When it became clear that Warwick would not surrender yet would not come out of Coventry to fight, Edward headed to London to seize mad King Henry. The mayor threw open the gates, and suddenly everyone in London was Edward's friend. He marched straight to the bishop's palace and put Warwick's brother, the Archbishop of York, in the Tower. Mad King Henry followed him there. Edward's next stop was Westminster Sanctuary, where he brought out his Queen and the princesses and prince she had borne him. Now that he had secured London, he was ready to march upon Warwick and settle things once and for all. Warwick had now marched his army to St. Albans, only twenty miles away. This time one of them would be finished forever!

Edward selected three thousand men as a vanguard to lead the attack. He placed Richard in charge of them; Ravenspur was his second-in-command. It was a colossal responsibility but a coveted honor. It went without saying that Edward would ride in the front row of the vanguard.

Roger bade his men make camp; in the darkness they

could hear the noises of the enemy encamped nearby. His mood swung from desolation to elation as he sat beside his campfire. He realized the irony of the situation: Edward, Richard, and himself had all been trained by Warwick, and he remembered his lessons to the letter.

He got up and moved among the men, urging them not to get drunk the night before the battle. He cursed the noisy, restless stallions and thought, *By God, Roseanna is right. Geldings would be better-behaved mounts for the knights.* Suddenly his senses were filled with Roseanna. He longed for her so much that he vowed no power on earth would keep him from her.

The night turned damp and cold, and though he was freezing, he sweated inside his armor. He moved among the men and warned them against having doubts. They must be convinced that they would win the day; to think otherwise was to invite death. He advised them to conserve their strength and energy when the battle was joined. It would be a long day, in which endurance and persistence would count for more than wild acts of bravado. "Stand solid, and parry everything that comes at you," he repeated over and over. He thanked God for the experienced faces he picked out of the crowd, for a lot of these young men would go into battle for the first time. The horror they would experience would be beyond belief.

He avoided telling them about the red mud of battlefields—mud made from the blood of men fallen and crushed underfoot. He did not tell them of the numbing exhaustion that came after a battle yet banished sleep for days because of its horrors.

When dawn arrived, a thick fog blanketed the whole area so he could not see his hand before his face. It changed nothing! They would still attack first, going by sound and feel rather than sight.

Roger came up against his first enemy with such force, their breastplates crashed, and it knocked the wind from him. His sword dripped blood; he kept his sword arm high, and soon his leather gauntlets were soggy with sweat and blood. His arm ached, his lungs were afire, and his eyes stung from his own salty sweat. His brain dimly told him that if his feet encountered something hard, it was armor; if something soft, it was flesh.

His strength was ebbing. Then miraculously a trumpet rally told him the enemy had faltered. He was filled with a second wind and renewed vigor. Gradually, inch by inch, yard by yard, he gained ground until the enemy was on the run, and then he saw the enemy's retreat with his own eyes as the fog lifted. He saw Edward's yellow hair when he removed his helmet and ran over to him. He stood above Warwick's body, and he was weeping. Roger stripped off his own helmet. His face was wet from blood and sweat and tears. It was over! Praise God, it was over once and for all!

The King looked at him and said, "You are wounded, Roger. Get you to a surgeon." Until that moment he had been unaware that his left arm hung useless and bloody, but now he began to feel the burning agony of a deep sword thrust through his shoulder. Common sense told him to obey Edward, for he knew from experience that a wound tended immediately healed quicker; yet a stronger force within him compelled him to go to Roseanna.

He mounted his horse and headed away from the army. He was driven by a madness to reach home. Ravenspur lay eighty miles to the north. The pain came and went, washing over him in waves. Sometimes he was barely conscious, yet relentlessly he pressed on. He was within sight of home before he allowed himself to fall unconscious from his horse.

Roseanna was at Ravenspur. She had been scanning the horizon hourly for signs of her husband. She saw the black stallion and saw Roger pitch from the saddle, and she was out of the hall, running immediately, crying for the stablemen to aid her.

Roger was filthy and stank to high heaven. He was covered with dried sweat and caked blood. His black hair was encrusted with filth and was plastered to his head. They carried him in unconscious, and with the help of Kate Kendall and James Burke she stripped and bathed him. He gained consciousness fast enough when she began to tend his wounded shoulder but he lay without flinching as she trimmed the gangrene with her sharp knife. She signed to Kate to pass her the goblet of wine; she held it to his lips and dared him to protest against the sleeping draught.

He took only one mouthful, then his hand came up to push it away. His fingers brushed her hand and suddenly she couldn't bear to share him with anyone else. She lifted her eyes to the others in the room and said, "Thank you for your help; I would like to be alone with my husband now."

Reluctantly they left their newly returned lord and Roseanna began to sponge his good shoulder and wide chest.

"You called me your husband."

"Yes, of course, that's who you are," she said, as if she were stating the most obvious truth to a simpleton.

"But what about Lincoln?" he asked, gritting the words through his teeth.

"Oh, my God!" She stopped sponging his chest. "I didn't even think of him! Is he all right?"

"I can't be certain, but I thought I saw him retreating from the battle with Warwick's men." He watched her face closely. When he saw relief there and nothing more, his heart began to lighten.

"I do hope he's safe. He's such a good man. Roger," she said slowly as she met his gaze, "you must understand I needed protection desperately. That's why I married him. I don't want to hurt him, because he's shown me only kindness, but I am not his wife. I'm *yours.* You are my heart's deepest desire." She bent down and kissed him with all the emotion she was feeling.

Roger groaned with happiness and put his good arm around Roseanna's waist. *Roseanna still loved him. She had chosen him.*

Ravenspur's dark eyes burned into hers.

"By God woman, your kiss makes me want to jump from this water and ravish you," Roger said.

She laughed softly. "One thing is sure, my husband, I am safe from you this night."

"Safe from me?" he demanded. "By God, you'll never be safe from me. Get me from this damned water and bind the wound so I can take you to bed and drive Lincoln out of your system!"

"Roger!" she scolded as she blushed. She didn't think for one moment that he would carry out his threat, but she was suddenly as shy as a bride before him. She helped him from the water and dried him thoroughly. As her hands touched him intimately his shaft rose up rigid to show her that he was indeed capable. With tender hands she padded and bandaged the wound, binding his arm securely to his chest so that it would remain immobile until it healed.

Her heart was lighter than it had been in a year. Spring was here and summer would follow, when every garden and stone wall in England would be riotous with roses. It promised to be the happiest season she had ever known. Suddenly she was overwhelmed with how much this man meant to her. He was the only man who had awakened her sensuality and taught her how to love. She could never love another as she loved this man; all others, even Linc, an earl of the realm, who had been so good to her, paled in comparison. Her heart sang with her great good fortune in having Ravenspur returned to her. Dear God, never take him away again, she prayed.

Suddenly she felt his dark eyes on her. "How do you feel?"

He leered at her. "I'll show you if you take me to bed."

"You're incorrigible," she scolded, but she undressed and joined him in the vast bed. He was so strong-willed, so challenging and damned exasperating, but she didn't want him any other way.

He gripped her strongly with his good arm, his hand cupping her breast possessively, and she felt him hard and swollen against her thigh. Suddenly she realized with clarity that he was about to reclaim her and brand her as his woman. She was alarmed at his roughness, not for herself, but for fear he would reopen his wound.

"My love," she whispered, "do you remember how you loved me that first time? How you conquered me with kisses until I was helpless with love?"

He smiled into the darkness. Roseanna needed a little time to get used to him in bed again. He kissed her slowly, gently, softly; short quick kisses and long, slow, melting kisses which showed her he remembered every detail of their first delicious mating. At first she moaned with pleasure but soon sighed in frustration. She wanted him more than anything in the world, wanted to feel again the fullness of him inside her, but she knew that with his wound he should not make love to her. His mouth scorched her temples, her closed eyelids, and the corners of her trembling mouth, then he plunged his tongue inside to taste her to the full.

"Roger, you are wicked to arouse me so; you know we mustn't do this."

With his lips against her throat, he chuckled. "My wound isn't a mortal one, so prepare to defend yourself!"

"By God, I've had to defend myself against your wicked lust from the first day I woke up in your bed and you tried to ravish me!"

His hot mouth found her breast and he licked it hungrily and sucked on the nipple. His hand slipped between her legs, and she began to writhe and moan with desire.

"*My* lust?" he whispered, covering her mouth with his so that she could not deny his accusations. "What about yours?"

"Mmm," she managed to reply as she arched high against his hand.

"Admit it to me, Roseanna. Admit it to me and shame the devil!" he demanded playfully.

She groaned. She knew he would not be denied, and thanked God for it. She touched his ear with the tip of her tongue and whispered very, very low, "I'm as hot as you are, my darling Ravenspur."

Her words inflamed him with passion. He swept her beneath him with such towering strength she was breathless and not a little afraid. He mounted her and drove himself into her. For one small moment he hurt her and she cried out in pain. Then she opened herself to him totally and felt exquisite pleasure at the way he filled her so deeply.

Rapture pulsed through their bodies as they clung to each other in an embrace they hoped would never end. Each touch was fire, each word was bliss, each movement brought them closer to the consuming cataclysm that left her weak in his arms, and him totally exhausted. He buried his face in her hair to savor its fragrance and then they were lost to the world, bound by their bodies, their hearts, and their souls. Bound by an everlasting love.

WIN A FREE BOOK
AND SEND ONE TO A FRIEND!

You can win a brand new, top quality, passion-filled historical romance from Dell for yourself and a friend just by telling us how you felt about *this* one. If you are among the first 500 respondents*, you will receive the exciting and unforgettable novel **TO LOVE AN EAGLE** by bestselling author Joanne Redd and you'll have the opportunity to have the book sent to a friend ABSOLUTELY FREE! Send your answers to the following questions along with the attached coupon with your name and address and the name and address of a friend and YOU MAY BE A WINNER!

Look for these future titles from Dell:

DESIRE'S MASQUERADE by Kathryn Kramer
AVENGING ANGEL by Lori Copeland
CLOUDCASTLE by Nancy Henderson Ryan
and the new historical romance by Meagan McKinney

Mail your responses postmarked no later than July 15, 1987 to:
Dell Publishing Co., HISTORICAL ROMANCE OFFER, 6 Regent St., Livingston, NJ 07039

Please enter my name to win **TO LOVE AN EAGLE** by bestselling author Joanne Redd.

Name_____

Address_____

City_____ State_____ Zip_____

And send a copy to my friend:

Name_____

Address_____

City_____ State_____ Zip_____

*In the event of tying entries, winners will be chosen at random. Completion of survey not necessary to win.

1. Try to remember back to when you were picking out this book at the store. What ONE thing attracted you most to this book? (Please read the full list before you make your ONE selection.)

☐ the artwork on the cover
☐ the title
☐ the author
☐ the price
☐ the recommendation of someone working in the store.
☐ the recommendation of a friend
☐ an advertisement in a newspaper
☐ comments in a newspaper or newsletter
☐ the historical time period and setting
☐ the description of heroine
☐ the description of hero
☐ the description of the plot on cover
☐ the excerpt from the book on first page
☐ other:_____

2. Would you buy another book by this author?

☐ definitely yes   ☐ probably   ☐ definitely no

3. Would you like to see more humor in historical romances?

☐ yes   ☐ no

4. In your opinion, what makes a historical romance a really good one?

_____
_____
_____
_____

Rebels and outcasts, they fled halfway across the earth to settle the harsh Australian wastelands. Decades later—ennobled by love and strengthened by tragedy—they had transformed a wilderness into fertile land. And themselves into

The Australians

WILLIAM STUART LONG

_____ THE EXILES, #1	12374-7	$3.95
_____ THE SETTLERS, #2	17929-7	3.95
_____ THE TRAITORS, #3	18131-3	3.95
_____ THE EXPLORERS, #4	12391-7	3.95
_____ THE ADVENTURERS, #5	10330-4	3.95
_____ THE COLONISTS, #6	11342-3	3.95
_____ THE GOLD SEEKERS, #7	13169-3	3.95
_____ THE GALLANT, #8	12785-8	3.95
_____ THE EMPIRE BUILDERS, #9	12304-6	3.95

At your local bookstore or use this handy coupon for ordering:

DELL READERS SERVICE—DEPT. B1553A
6 REGENT ST., LIVINGSTON, N.J. 07039

Please send me the above title(s). I am enclosing $ _____ (please add 75¢ per copy to cover postage and handling). Send check or money order—no cash or CODs. Please allow 3-4 weeks for shipment.

Ms./Mrs./Mr _____

Address _____

City/State _____ Zip _____